WHEN THE SKY GOES DARK

To Alex,
   Watch out! There are crazy people in this book!

OLIVER C. SENECA

HELLBENDER BOOKS

Hellbender Books

Mechanicsburg, Pennsylvania

HELLBENDER BOOKS

an imprint of Sunbury Press, Inc.
Mechanicsburg, PA USA

For information about special discounts for bulk purchases, please contact Sunbury Press Orders Dept. at (855) 338-8359 or orders@sunburypress.com.

To request one of our authors for speaking engagements or book signings, please contact Sunbury Press Publicity Dept. at publicity@sunburypress.com.

ISBN: 978-1-62006-224-1 (Trade paperback)

Library of Congress Control Number: 2019952278

FIRST HELLBENDER BOOKS EDITION: October 2019

Product of the United States of America
0 1 1 2 3 5 8 13 21 34 55

Set in Garamond
Designed by Chris Fenwick
Cover by Chris Fenwick
Edited by Chris Fenwick

Continue the Enlightenment!

For my family.

You've always been there for me.

ONE

A Scream

Piercing shrieks shook the second floor of Lecture Hall. They echoed down the tiled floors and bounced off the white brick walls. A girl's scream. Terrifying and as ear-shattering as an explosion.

Jon had just been leaving his Psych 310: The Study of Sleep and Psychology class with his friend Trevor when the sound blew through them like a train. Some of the other exiting classmates put their hands over their ears to shield themselves from the noise coming down the hall.

"What the hell was that?" a red-headed, freckle-faced girl asked through clenched teeth. Her painted nails cupped her lobes.

Another student began quick stepping in the opposite direction. "Fuck that," he said, and a few others followed as if they were convinced it was a school shooting. The thought of being in a college massacre made Jon's heart pound even harder than it already was.

The sight of two EMTs leading a stretcher from around the corner of the hallway, near where the bathrooms were located, relaxed his heart rate down a few beats. A girl, who Jon didn't recognize, was lying with her eyes closed. She was strapped on a yellow stretcher with collapsible wheels, blonde hair going every which way. Beneath the harsh, fluorescent lights on the ceiling, she looked dead. Jon's stomach tightened.

"Damn," Trevor said. His eyes were as wide as flying saucers. "What do you think happened?" he asked, turning toward Jon for a moment.

Jon only shrugged. "You think she passed out from screaming so loud?"

Trevor shook his head as his eyes traveled beyond the blonde-haired patient. "I don't think she was the one who screamed."

"AHHHHHHHHHHHHHHHHHH NOOOOO! JESSIE! NOOOOO! WAKE UP, SWEETIE!" a girl's voice shouted.

The red-haired girl squinted. Now she put her fingers in her ears, nails and all.

Behind the EMTs, the girl's screaming reached a higher volume as her unconscious friend approached. The medical volunteers were trying to shoo her back and away from the scene, one of which spoke with the authority of a cop. "Miss, please step back. We are going get her taken care of, okay? She's going to be ok. We're taking her downstairs to the ambulance. We just need to you calm down for us, okay?"

There were groups of lingering college students, standing and filling the hallway to get a glimpse at the cause of the horrific screams. Their bags and backpacks were blocking the way.

"Please, make a path! We need to get her to a hospital. Please, move!" one of the EMTs said, waving his blue-gloved hand at the students. His voice was transitioning into a yell, clearing a pathway for the stretcher.

The girl, whose voice filled the hall earlier, now had tears streaming down her cheeks and swollen eyes. Her black hair was coming undone from the back of her tied bun. Her skin was thin and pale. She had stopped her screaming but followed her friend around another corner, toward the elevators.

Professor Hill stepped out from the classroom doorway. "What in God's name happened down there?" She was adjusting her wired glasses and stepping on her tippy toes behind Jon and Trevor to see above the heads of the crowded corridor.

Before either Jon or Trevor could respond, a girl named Samantha with a sleeve tattoo of vines and flowers up her left arm said, "Overdose. Gotta be an overdose."

"Really? You think so, Sam?" Professor Hill asked with an almost angered tone. Angered at drugs or Sam, no one knew.

Yeah, really? Jon thought to himself. *How would you know?* Trevor had the same expression. Their eyebrows were both raised in morbid questioning.

"I've heard Jess was a user. I mean, I've never seen her myself doing it, but word in the halls is that she's on the H." Sam's hands were up as if she was making an educated guess.

"My God, I hope she's ok. That's just unbelievable." Professor Hill held her black binder up to her chest and shook her head both in sorrow and disappointment as if Sam's overdose diagnosis was what had happened. "That's just not right."

The *ding* of the elevator sounded. The metal doors *slid* open. Students were making their way towards Jessie as she was being loaded on.

"Away, away!" the EMT blared.

"I just hope they shoot her with the Narcan stuff to bring her back," Sam said in monotone. She seemed unaffected by the whole thing.

Heroin. Is it heroin? Jon didn't know Jessie and thought perhaps Samantha was right. *Maybe Samantha's more familiar with the junkies. She does have tattoos. Tattoos and drugs go hand in hand, don't they?*

Jon, although judgmental in the confines of his mind, is an innocent guy. No tattoos. He wouldn't even know what to get. He was never one to try smoking or drugs. Never one to drink alcohol before he turned 21. Even now he rarely drank. The bite and bitterness of alcohol kept Jon away from indulging in the poison. Sacrilegious some would say. College was the time to try out different vices, to have experiences of sex, drugs, and rock n roll. From the looks of it, maybe Jessie did all three.

Another *ding*. The elevator descended.

"Shit, man. That's some twisted stuff. You think that chick really OD'd?" Trevor asked as he rubbed the top of his nappy hair. He and Jon began to head down the hall where all the lingering groups merged into one before the elevators. Sam and Professor Hill were talking about heroin and the opioid epidemic in America. Their voices faded away as Jon and Trevor approached the anxious students.

"Beats me," Jon said.

"Ay, Jordan!" Trevor shouted. Another Black student turned from the back of the group of the crowd. He squeezed through two girls' backpacks and approached Trevor. He was tall and wearing a blue WHITE HAVEN ATHLETICS T-shirt. In his hand, he clutched an iPhone with a gold back.

"Yo, this shit's crazy," Jordan said, punching his fist into his other palm. He was almost smiling.

"What she do?" Trevor asked.

"That girl was on the floor of the bathroom, in one of the stalls. My girl was in there, washing up."

"Natasha?"

Jon wasn't familiar with Jordan nor Natasha, so he just stood there awkwardly as he tried to listen through the sounds of the chattering witnesses.

Heroin. Heroin. Heroin.

"Yeah, she was in there when all a sudden that girl came in, starts screamin' all loud after she bends down and looks under the stall. That girl, Jessie, was out and wasn't talkin', wasn't breathin'."

"Damn, were there needles? A girl from our class says that Jessie's on dope."

"Shit, man. I don't know about all that." Jordan turned back around. He was bouncing his phone back and forth between his hands. "I don't know where Natasha went off to. She mighta went with Jessie." He looked down at his phone, tapped the screen with his finger and then brought it up to his ear. "Tasha? Tasha, where you at?" Jordan turned back toward the group and began pushing people aside.

Jon looked back at his friend. "Well, I guess we won't find out what happened until all this dies down."

"Guess so," Trevor replied. "Least she'll get out of finals."

An untimely joke to make, Jon thought. But after he had seen the empty chairs in both in Professor Weiss' and Professor Hill's classes, something told Jon that a lot of students will be getting out of finals.

T W O

The End is Near

It was that time of the year.

The spring season was coming to an end as the warm summer air began to creep in, turning jeans and jackets into shorts and short-sleeved shirts. Excitement and anxiousness filled the campus as students walked to their last classes for the semester, eager to find out what their final projects and exams would be for the following weeks that would unlock their freedom into summer vacation. Some will return for the fall semester while others will graduate and be thrown into the frightening and mysterious "real world."

If you weren't paying attention while driving down College Hill Avenue, you might just miss it as the lush green trees that line the sides of the asphalt almost swallow the entrance sign that reads WHITE HAVEN COLLEGE. You'd have more luck getting into campus at night when the tall, black light poles with orange bulbs shined over the sign and pathway onto the school grounds.

White Haven College was a comfortably sized school located in White Haven, Pennsylvania. With its size, you'd think it wouldn't have dorms, a cafeteria, and sporting areas. But you'd be wrong. You'd also think that since this college is so hidden that no one would even know to apply here. You'd be wrong again. In fact, students come from all over Central Pennsylvania and beyond to go here because of the low tuition and easy access to the local bars. College students love to drink.

The town itself, however, was out in plain sight. Restaurants and dive bars sprinkled the area with some mom and pop stores in the mix. If you traveled just a bit more down the road you'd find houses. Townhouses to be exact. Not the nice, newer built style, but the older and run-down kind that looked like they've been around since the college first came into existence. The paint chipped on the buildings. The roofs were torn up. This is where all the White Haven locals lived. With how much nicer the college looked, you'd think aliens brought it down and dropped over an unsuspecting, backwoodsy town. But it was a nice little town. A town that didn't start and didn't want any trouble.

***

Jonathan Barnes looked like any other run of the mill college student, at least that's what he thought of himself. But then again, Jon never really thought much of himself at all. *Painfully average* is how he felt. He had brown, messy hair. Hair that he often needed to swipe away so it wouldn't go into his hazel eyes which sat behind his black, square-framed glasses. His skinny physique didn't make him feel any better about himself either. The lack of any muscle tone or six-pack helped reinforce his mediocre self-esteem.

The only thing he thought he had going for him was that he was smart and tall. At just 6'0, Jon would tell a woman that he was 6'1. They never questioned it, but they never had to since it was rare for Jon to have more than a five-minute conversation with a person of the opposite sex. Even if he did, it was most likely about homework. To Jon, it seemed that the only reason anyone would ever talk to him was to get help on an assignment or to proofread a paper. That was ok though. It gave Jon opportunities with girls over the years that, without his book smarts and ability to listen, probably would have never occurred. The girlfriends he had back in high school were all products of his patience and intellect.

Perhaps it was his wardrobe filled with T-shirts of various pop culture references that was holding him back a bit. The girls he was into didn't understand much of the designs and references on his shirts that displayed imagery from various movies, TV shows, and video games that Jon enjoyed. He'd sometimes wear a button-down shirt or polo, but he was usually decked out in his signature style of Vans sneakers, jeans, and a shirt with some character on it from God knows what. But it wasn't Jon's fault, it was hard to have a full, lavish set of outfits when you're living in a tiny dorm room with a cabinet-sized closet squeezed into it.

Jon didn't want to go away to college, but his parents lived almost an hour away and they thought it would be a good idea for Jon to get out of the house and experience what life outside his room had to offer. He fought with his parents about it and, being the only child, he almost got his way until his father decided he was either living at college or not going college at all. Jon needed to learn what it was like to be off on his own. Alone. Get a taste of the real world. To be a man and find a nice girl to call his own.

Lucky for Jon, there were many fish in the sea as his major, psychology was a popular major for girls at White Haven College. Girls of all shapes, sizes, and personalities filled the seats in each of his classes. Jon had choices. However, Jon had to act quick because time was running out. Not for Jon, but for a certain special someone. This wasn't Jon's last semester at White Haven College, but it was for Skylar Doyle. The apple of Jon's eye. At least for now. Jon has had many apples in his eye, Skylar was just the current one.

A beautiful curled, blonde-haired girl that always dressed nicely for class even though she didn't have to. She could outshine anyone, anywhere. In the fall she would wear grey sweaters with blue jeans and nice brown boots. During the spring semesters, she would show a little more skin with flowing shirts and, if Jon was lucky, thigh-hugging short-shorts. But the truth was she would've looked good in anything, even in sneakers, raggedy jeans, and a Star Wars T-shirt like Jon wore.

She was like an actress playing the lead role in the movie *PSYCH 343: Control and Analysis of Human Behavior*. A fascinating piece of cinema that captures the beauty of young love. Two classmates who find one another through the studies of their own behavior. Two strangers whose morning studies blossom into a passionate romance.

In reality, it was just his morning class he had with Skylar. Three days a week. Mondays, Wednesdays, and Fridays. 10:00 A.M. to 10:50 A.M. with Professor Weiss. This was the only time he got to see her unless you count the awkward times they've passed one another in the hallway where Jon doesn't know if he should wave or say hello. He always ended up doing neither. Sometimes it made him feel better to think she at least recognized him from class.

Skylar was a commuter student who drove almost thirty minutes from Evergreen Hills, a place Jon has never heard of, every day to go to her classes. She's always well prepared and attentive in class even though she sat by her talkative best friend, Melissa Ricci. Melissa was another psychology major who was only as good looking as she was because she sat beside Skylar. Any chick within Skylar's radius automatically made them a little hotter. Her long, black hair was always put together, and she seemed to have a modern sense of style. It was her attitude that kept her from being on Skylar's level.

Melissa always seemed to be stuck in the middle of the drama, whether it be with some guy she was with or another girl talking trash behind her back.

Jon knew this because he would sometimes try to listen in on their conversations.

He didn't know all of the details for sure, but from what he could make out from eavesdropping this semester, it sounded like Skylar had a good job lined up after she graduates at a hospital near her town or something like that. He couldn't remember and was too afraid to ask. How could he?

"Hey Skylar, I was listening to you and Melissa talking the other day and I know we never met before but where are you going to be working again? I forgot. I'm Jon. I sit in the back of the class. I'm not a stalker or anything!"

Jon still had one year left. He hoped to become a therapist spending his time listening to people, helping people. Jon liked to help people and not just with their assignments. Jon had spent a lot of his free time in high school listening to his classmates go on about their issues. Texts and phone calls from friends would light up his phone every night with tales of school stress and issues at home. Jon liked to listen to people. Jon also liked Skylar.

Graduation was only three weeks away with one more week of classes, one week for studying, and one week for final exams. Skylar was about to be moving on from White Haven College. Jon had wasted the entire semester coming up with "what if" scenarios instead of trying to talk to her.

What if we get assigned together for a group project?
What if I asked for her number?
What if she likes the movies and shows I like?
What if we got married?
What if she owns a cat?

The scenarios went on and on. Jon daydreamed so much about how they could get to know each other that he failed to realize that all he had to do was say hello.

"Hello, Skylar"

"Hey, Skylar"

"How's it goin', Skylar?"

"Will you marry me, Skylar?"

Jon is 21 years old and behaving like this.

THREE

PSYCH343: Control and Analysis of Human Behavior

Professor Weiss came into class five minutes late as usual. The reason behind his constant tardiness could only be on thing: his weight. Weiss was a short, balding and gray-haired man whose stomach spilled over his belt as the poor leather clung on for dear life. He always shuffled into class huffing and puffing while gripping a plastic jumbo-sized cup of diet soda, which clearly wasn't doing anything for him.

Everybody in the class enjoyed having Weiss as their professor as he was a kind man who always had time to help his students. He'd often wait after class until he answered all the questions the students had for him. Most of the time, he would have some type of story to tell about when he was a college student. The typical "when I was your age" and "back in the dinosaur ages when I was in school" spiel.

"Alright everyone," Professor Weiss said as he entered the room, placing his bucket of diet soda on the computer podium that sat in the front-left of the class. A projector screen pulled down over the whiteboard behind him. He took a breath as he was tired from his walk up the steps. "How are we all doing this morning?"

A sweaty eyebrow raised as he scanned the classroom, noticing the holes in the crowd. Students were absent. On the last day of class before the final, it surprised him to see so many people skipping.

"Good, how are you doing professor?" one of the students sitting in the front replied.

"Oh, I'm doing just fine, thank you. Does anyone know where half the class is?" Professor Weiss said with a red-faced smile of concern.

"Michelle has been sleeping all day," a red-haired girl named Jamie Patton said from the back corner behind an empty desk. "She's been really sick. She hasn't gone to any of her classes this week."

"I think something is going around campus professor, all the guys from the radio club are out as well," a bearded student named Damien Fulton chimed in.

"Well hopefully, it's not the flu going around. I saw on the news there are some cases sprouting up. I'm sure you all will inform your absent friends about today, right? Quite a touch of bad luck to have so many people out during our last time together as a class."

The students nodded as Professor Weiss pulled out a remote from the computer podium and pointed it at the projector that was installed snugly on the ceiling in the back of the room.

Jon sat in the last seat in the first row of desks. His back was against the white bricked wall, the same type that was found in his dorm. He sat in the back of classes because he never had to pay all that much attention in school. The concepts weren't all that hard for him to figure out and he thought the seats closer up should be used by the students who needed to listen to the lectures. Not to brag or anything.

The projector lit up and displayed a PowerPoint presentation entitled PSYCH343 FINAL EXAM PAPER.

"I'm sure you are all excited to hear about your final paper that's due next Friday," Professor Weiss said while clicking the mouse on the computer which brought up the next slides. Big bullet points appeared on the screen. "What I'd like you all to do is pick your favorite psychologist that we've studied this semester and write fifteen-hundred words on why you believe their theories and works are important and how they have shaped the field of psychology."

The students all looked and made faces at one another. "Fifteen-hundred words?" whispered throughout the room.

Melissa gave Skylar a look of disapproval. Skylar gave one back.

Professor Weiss took a sip of diet soda through the fat straw of his cup. "Now I understand there may be a few of you doing the same psychologist. That's fine, I just don't want everyone jumping on Sigmund Freud or B.F. Skinner. Keep in mind there are many different people we've covered in our textbook." The PowerPoint jumped to a large list of names of dead psychologists.

A hand rose.

"Yes, Mike. Go ahead," Professor Weiss said, pointing at the student.

"Does it have to be *exactly* fifteen-hundred words? Is it ok if we're close to it?"

The rest of the class nodded their heads in support of Mike's question as if to say *hey yeah, does it really have to be that long?*

Professor Weiss chuckled and said, "Yes. If you get around the fifteen-hundred mark you will be ok."

There was a sigh of relief from the class. Melissa grabbed Skylar's arm in relief and they both giggled.

"Thank God, cuz you know I ain't gettin' all those words in," a girl said, laughing to herself from the back corner near Jon. Others laughed with her.

Professor Weiss took another sip from his soda. His hands extended out. "Here's what I'm gonna do. I am gonna take the rest of class today to answer all questions about the final. Is that okay? Then if we're done early you guys can get the word out and get started on your papers so they can be turned in on time next Friday. Do we have a deal? I'll also send out an email to the class just in case."

A unanimous "yes" came from the students.

Jon zoned out for the remainder of the class as the students each asked questions. What's the format of the paper? How many sources are necessary? When's it due again? He was thinking *what if I asked Skylar who she was writing about for her paper? What if I could somehow help her write it?* Then another voice in his head added, *Just say hello you idiot.*

Before he knew it, class ended. The class would usually go until 10:50. It was only 10:30. Everyone jumped up from their seats and funneled to the door making the exiting process slow. There was still heavy chatter about all of the requirements for the paper. Fifteen-hundred words? That was the biggest problem for most of them it seemed. At this point in their college careers, you'd think they'd be accustomed to writing that many words, but it seemed a surprise every time.

Jon got up from his seat in the back, grabbed his backpack from underneath, and placed it on the chair, throwing in his pen and notebook off the desk. He slung the backpack over his shoulder and attempted to pace his steps out of the door with Skylar's in the hope of getting stuck in the funnel with her. Looking at his phone would slow his steps. Before he knew it, he was beside Skylar and Melissa in the small but clogged crowd by the door. They were standing beside him, still talking about the paper. Jon figured this was his moment to get himself involved in the conversation.

But the nerves got to Jon and he froze up as they were still funneling out of the door. Jon's phone was still in his hand. He looked down at it, not actually texting anyone or looking at any apps. Jon was just looking down at the home screen.

He had to say something, anything. He couldn't leave the last PSYCH 343 class without even saying hello. HELLO! That's all he ever had to say to her for Christ's sake. Say something Jon, say *something!*

"After you," Jon said with a shaky voice as he put his phone down and gestured his arm out to show them to go out the door before him. He tried to present himself as a real gentleman. Yuck.

"Oh, uh, thank you," Skylar said. Melissa just smiled. They both walked out of the class. Jon walked out directly behind them. His lips began to move as he went to chime in about the paper. Perhaps agree with how crazy the fifteen-hundred-word count is. Maybe ask who they were going to write about. *You're doing B.F. Skinner?? No way! So am I! Skylar wants to hang out at my dorm tonight? We can work on it together!* Jon's thoughts ran wild and yet nothing happened.

"Hey ar-" Jon couldn't even finish his question as Skylar and Melissa made a left and turned the corner down the hall to go into the lady's room. Not that it mattered, he said it too quietly for anyone to hear. It didn't help that everyone walking behind him was being loud. It was like he wasn't even trying. He had issues asserting himself in these kinds of situations but was sort of proud of himself for at least saying a word to Skylar. Well, it was two. After. You.

Great job Jon, you really put yourself out there, he thought to himself as he walked down the rest of the hall alone with his thoughts and the rest of the class still walking behind him in deep discussion about the paper. He pulled out his phone again and looked at it as he did in the classroom.

We'll get it right next semester, just not with Skylar.

Next semester. That's what it always seemed to be for Jon. *Next* semester. At some point, Jon won't have any semesters left. He had to shape up. Or, in the words of his father, man up.

How could he expect to be a therapist? Hearing tales of childhood traumas and adulthood anxieties from desperate people and Jon couldn't even say hello to a cute girl. Well, he *could* and he *had,* but there was something about Skylar that was nothing like he had seen before. Perhaps it was perfected beauty. Or, it was just his obsessive thoughts keeping him from acting as they did. The swirling, never-ending questions he constantly asked to himself. The who, what, why, when, where, and how were relentless. Any idea planted in his mind would grow and grow until it came into full bloom, giving Jon a mental breakdown.

He wanted out of his head.

He wanted to get in with Skylar.

F O U R

Dancing in the Dark

Just when Jon thought he had seen the first and last emergency during his time at White Haven with the girl named Jessie, something else came out of left field.

He was walking out of Lecture Hall after his sociology course that ran three hours. Six to nine. A brutally long and somewhat boring class. He hadn't eaten since lunchtime and his stomach was groaning at him, begging him to put something, anything inside to fill it up. Luckily, the cafeteria across from Lecture Hall was open until ten.

There were plenty of options for food during the day like pizza, subs, salads, and various fried things. All served by the students who worked there to get money off of their tuition payments. Seemed practical, although many of them would have preferred the cold, hard cash. Who wanted to worry about loans? It's not like their little minimum wage positions put a dent in them. Might as well fork over the money so they can buy what they really want: alcohol. That's what Jon thought all college kids wanted anyway.

Jon pushed in the silver door to the eating area where a few students lingered. Some were in groups talking underneath the televisions while others were alone at the tables with their laptops open, lighting their faces in the darker corners. Things were winding down for the night. So much so that an Asian student was sound asleep on a couch that sat outside the lounge rooms at the end of the eating area.

With his backpack slung over his shoulder, Jon walked down the wall of what remained of today's food. Coming into the cafeteria during the last hour of it being open meant that you were more limited in freshness and selection. Even the students that prepared the food weren't interested. If you came in with an order for a pepperoni pizza or a big sub sandwich, they'd roll their eyes and slap the dough with disinterest or slap down some lettuce on a six-inch bun. Anything else, sir?

Jon went with the chicken tenders and fries that sat bathing beneath a hot, yellow bulb that kept everything in its rays warm throughout the day. Over twelve bucks it was. Are you kidding? Between the prices of tuition, room and board, and textbooks, where did White Haven get off charging ridiculous prices for only three fried tenders and a side of fries? Who knows and who cares? Everyone here was broke and in debt. Might as well go all in, right?

He paid for his late-night dinner and brought the tray over toward an empty, circular table that looked out through glass to the light pole lit campus. It looked pretty at night with the orange lights shining over the concrete pathways. Except, when Jon sat down and looked out the window while shoving a ketchup-covered tender in his mouth, he saw that there was a group of people outside that appeared to not be enjoying the lights and sights of White Haven after-dark.

For a moment, Jon thought the people outside were dancing. He hadn't noticed them when he walked over. Their arms were being thrown in the air and feet were kicking and whipping around. A dance-off in the grass it looked to be. But soon Jon realized that they were fighting one another when he saw one of the guy's fist connect with another's face. A girl with a pigtail was trying to hold the punching man back, but she was failing. Then, as a total shock to Jon, the punching man turned and struck the girl square in the head, sending her down. Jon's stomach twisted and he stood up from his chair.

A Black student that stood by the group took off his backpack and started to swing it around like a lasso until it connected with another guy's face. The punching man and the pigtailed girl were rolling around on the grass. Jon could only stand in silence in the cafeteria, frozen with his uncertainty of what to do. His appetite diminished and his mouth hung open at the scene.

An acne-faced girl that worked behind the fried-food bar came rushing out. Her grey apron flailed as she flung the door open and went out into the night toward the fight. Jon could hear her screaming at the group, but no one seemed to notice her. At first. She pulled out her cell phone and started to dial what Jon assumed was 911 until the Black student with the rodeo backpack went toward her and knocked the phone to the ground with the light from the screen flying until it landed face down. Jon didn't know what to do. His mind was saying *help her, help her, help her* but his body was saying *stand still and keep watching. Don't look away.*

"Dude, you gotta call the police!" a curly-haired, blonde guy said as he sprinted with a shorter guy in a grey tank top behind Jon and toward the door. The short guy was clutching a pool cue from one of the lounge rooms. Together, they ran into the fight and started pushing back the attackers. It was getting crowded out there and it looked to Jon like everyone was swinging punches and launching kicks at one another. The pool cue was smacking around, the wood jutting in and out between the faces.

"Hello?" a female voice said near Jon. He turned and saw a pretty, tall, brown-haired girl with her phone up to her ear. "My name is Ashley Tolsen and I'm a student at White Haven College…" She told the operator that there was a fight that broke out on campus and gave the address. "Yes, I'll stay on the line."

Jon was still frozen in his place. If Ashley hadn't been there to call 911, would he have done it? Probably, but it wouldn't have been as fast. He could barely take his eyes away from the fight. He had seen all kinds of videos on the internet. Street fights, videos of war, and even beheadings on some of the sketchier sites on the web that he's afraid to admit. But to see something like this play out at his own college was a first. Not even in high school did he ever encounter a fight. He had heard about them, sure, but never was a spectator.

What on earth are they fighting about? Why punch a girl?

Jon was still stunned. His body couldn't move, and his eyes couldn't look away. He was in a trance watching the fight outside.

Jon could see the blues and reds flashing off the side of the buildings. It seemed like a lifetime, really it was only a couple minutes, but the police finally showed up. In the darkness, Jon could see an officer's bald head. A second one stood behind him. He thought that the presence of the police would be enough to get the students to calm down, but it did the opposite. Several of the students went after the officer.

"Holy shit!" Ashley shouted. "Are you seeing this?" She was recording everything with the camera on her phone.

Jon nodded without looking at her.

There were shouts beyond the glass. Silhouettes of the bodies beneath the orange-colored lamps danced. Jon's heart rate was rising. *They're gonna have to shoot them* he thought. *This is getting too out of control.*

I don't know if I can see this. But the shots never came, at least in the sense of using bullets. Electricity, however, appeared to be more appropriate for this kind of situation.

Jon couldn't tell which one it was, maybe the Black student with the backpack, but one of the bodies screeched and squirmed under the light as one of the officer's used his taser on him. A quick flash of blue lit up the electrode string that stuck into the chest of the student. His arms and legs shook like he was having a seizure. Another guy tried to stop the tasing officer, but more police were on the scene, holding the psychotic students down now. None of them appeared to be giving up their struggle.

Heroin? No. Heroin doesn't make you do this, Jon thought. *Does it?*

Like a wrestling match, the police officers dove on the flailing students, whipping them around like they were ragdolls. They had no choice. They couldn't straight up shoot the students, but they were doomed if they didn't use force to keep them down. There were more shouts and commands coming through the window that Jon couldn't decipher as the officers hauled the fighters away, including the grey-aproned girl who was only trying to break it up.

Jon turned to Ashley, who was already looking back at him. They looked at each other with pale, frightened faces unsure of what to do or say. Then Jon broke the staring contest and looked back into the night and saw blood splattered on the concrete pathway under the light. The dark blood contrasted the white concrete beneath the light. He could tell it was wet. Fresh.

"I'm afraid to go out there now. I'm afraid to go back to my dorm," Ashley said, almost in a whisper. Her eyes darted around at the rest of the cafeteria where the remaining students all stood in equal shock, recording video and taking pictures.

"So am I," Jon replied. "What do we do?"

"Would you walk with me?" she asked. "When it all dies down out there, would you mind going with me?"

Jon couldn't have thought of a better idea.

FIVE

Not Like Father, Not Like Son

The only thing that Jon and his father had in common were their first names. Jonathon Albert Barnes: the father. Jonathon Edward Barnes: the son. To avoid confusion, Jon's mother, Catherine Marie Barnes, would often refer to them as Jon and Jon Jr., or Big Jon and Little Jon.

The dark-brown hair was now greyed atop a balding head, but the bushy mustache remained in full color. He used to tower over Little Jon but nowadays what Big Jon doesn't have in height, is made up for in weight. Big Jon had a stomach. Years of drinking with his old high school and college buddies helped with that.

Big Jon was a popular guy back in his school days. Not only was he named homecoming king and senior class president during his high school career, but Big Jon was also a star player on the Highland Hawks. Quarterback. His athletic ability on the field helped bring Highland to the state finals and gained him a full ride to Union University where an unfortunate knee injury caused him to sit out his first season and the rest of his football career. The scholarship still stood though. He studied business, which included a course on accounting. That's where he met the beautiful Mrs. Barnes.

Originally Catherine Marie Regan from Pittsburgh, the two of them married after graduation and found a nice little home in Springsdale, Pennsylvania. It wasn't long after settling down that Little Jon was born. Big Jon made enough money selling health insurance that Jon's mother was able to stay home and take care of him during the day. And she sure took care of him. Little Jon was pampered. Babied. Even until high school.

"He's gotta learn to do some things himself ya know," Big Jon would say to her. "Someday he won't have his mommy to take care of him."

"I know, I know," Catherine would reply. But being one of four children, she always thought her mother never gave her much attention growing up. She wanted Little Jon to feel different toward his mother than she felt toward her mother. She wanted him to know she cared. That's why he always had fresh, washed clothes and packed school lunches. Everything Little Jon needed, he had. Courtesy of Mrs. Barnes.

S I X

A Night to Remember

Late. At least late for Jon.

Having spent the entire week studying for his other finals and getting lost in the art of cinema, Jon focused on Professor Weiss' paper that was due tomorrow morning, right at ten.

He sat at the tiny wooden desk across from his bed that was pinned against the corner of his dorm room. The white bricked walls were lined with posters of his favorite films. There was a picture of him and his parents that they gave him when he first left for college taped on the wall, too. The only light in his room was a little black desk lamp on the corner of the desk.

Jon typed away on his laptop. He still had about five hundred words to go and that upset him. Most of the time, Jon could crank out these papers and get to watching movies. Tonight, it seemed he had already spent too much time already doing so.

There were also distractions. Whether it be checking his phone, looking for emails, or watching pointless videos on the internet, his essay had hit a brick wall on the last page.

"Alright. I gotta finish this, no more fulling around," Jon said to himself as he leaned back in his chair and stretched his arms in the air. He yawned.

Jon heard the dorm door outside his room swing open. The brass knob hit the side of the wall with a *thump*.

"Anybody home?" a deep voice asked.

It was Jon's roommate, Brandon Ford. He entered the little living area/kitchen of the dorm and into Jon's room with a big smile on his face.

"Hey man, what are you working on right now?" Brandon asked, clicking on the overhead lights to Jon's room. He ran his hand through his sweaty, short brown hair. It looked like he had been sprinting. He placed the keys that hung on a black and white lanyard around his neck atop an unwashed pit-stained gym shirt.

Brandon and Jon were good friends and got along fine as roommates, but it was clear that they couldn't be more opposite from one another. Jon was quieter and more reserved while Brandon was loud and extroverted. Brandon also had an athletic background while Jon was never encouraged to play sports after he was discovered to be a klutz. He always found a way to fall or trip himself which made his parents shy him away from any form of sports.

"Oh, I'm just working on this final paper for Weiss' class tomorrow. I'm almost done, just a page to go," Jon said with his arms still extended.

"Listen man," Brandon said with his grin still gigantic and beaming, "you think you can take a break from that paper for a little while?"

Jon checked the time on the top corner of his laptop. 10:25.

"Maybe for a little bit, why?" Jon didn't like to work long into the night. It always put him in a bad mood the next morning.

"You might not believe this, but you know Melissa right? Isn't she in your class?" Brandon asked.

Jon nodded.

"She wanted me to see if you'd want to come with me over to her dorm tonight to hangout. I think her roommate is lonely and looking for a smart young man to keep her company."

Jon laughed by blowing air from his nose and shook his head. He thought back to when he let her and Skylar out the door from class.

"I'm serious, man. Hey, you never know what could happen. Didn't I show you what she looks like?"

"No, I don't even know her name."

Brandon dug into the pocket of his basketball shorts and pulled out his phone.

"Let me show you. I think she's just your type."

After typing and swiping around on his phone, Brandon turned it over to Jon to show a picture of three girls standing together in a dorm room. All of them were pretty, except the one in the middle didn't look as much. Not ugly, but not hot either. Definitely not his type.

"I'm guessing she's the middle one?" Jon said in an unenthusiastic tone, continuing to look at the short, chubby girl with curly black hair. She almost looked hot standing next to two better-looking girls.

"You got it. Her name's Kat and she-"

"Cat? Like the animal?" Jon was allergic to cats and even the mention of it made him upset. How he hated those grumpy creatures.

Brandon grabbed his stomach and gave a genuine laugh in response to Jon's almost disgust in the name.

"No, no! Not like the animal. It's Kat with a K. It's short for Katie. She's always talking about how she can't find a good guy around here. You might be the one to change all that if you come with me."

Brandon now stood as if he was about to run back out the door. He was ready to go.

"Are you coming or what?" Brandon asked.

"I really gotta finish this last page, it's due tomorrow morning."

"Oh, c'mon dude, don't do this now. We will have plenty of time to finish your paper. Just think about how much fun you could be having right now. I promise we won't stay long. If we stay longer than an hour, I will write your paper myself!"

Brandon was a business major and was always trying to negotiate some deal that led Jon out of his comfort zone.

Jon checked the time again. It was now 10:30.

"I bet Melissa and Skylar are probably there telling her all about you," Brandon said, still looking like he was ready to run out at any moment.

Jon's eyebrows raised. His heart sunk. Skylar was there? *Could she really be there? Doesn't she have the same paper to write? Maybe she was done.* Maybe Jon could ask her about it and strike up a conversation. *Forget Kat.*

"At least come for me, you know I'm trying to get it in with Melissa," Brandon said.

They both shared a laugh.

Jon let out a deep breath. The deep breath he always had right before deciding like this. A social decision. This wasn't the first time Brandon did this to him, but this was different. Jon's last chance with Skylar was on the line.

"Alright let's do it. But no more than an hour, you have to promise me ok? I can't afford to bomb this final. My dad will have my ass," Jon said.

Brandon's smile somehow grew bigger than it already was. "Thank you! You got it, man, I promise we won't be long, I mean unless you and Kat hit it off!"

Jon laughed out of his nose again. He turned to his laptop to save his work, even though he hadn't typed any new sentences. Brandon ran over to his room, which was across the hall. He fumbled around in the dark until he came back out with a stick of deodorant. "I almost forgot this. Can't be stinking up Melissa's place."

Between Jon and Brandon's dorm rooms was the bathroom which had the space equivalent to a closet. It had a shower, toilet, and a sink with an oval-shaped mirror all shoved in a tight space.

Brandon painted the deodorant onto his armpits. He adjusted his hair and moved his fingers all around his face checking for any pimples or marks that had to be taken care of.

"You need anything? Any cologne? Perhaps a corsage?" Brandon said to Jon while still checking himself in the mirror. He laughed but kept checking his face.

Jon looked down at his shirt. He was wearing a T-shirt from one of his favorite bands. *Twenty-One Pilots.* He thought about changing it, but then he convinced himself that it could be a conversation starter. Perhaps Skylar liked them, too. They were a popular group.

The reality was he didn't have any other clean shirts and the fact that Brandon was wearing a sweaty gym top made him feel more comfortable.

"Nah, I'm good," Jon replied. He was feeling nervous about seeing Skylar. His heart began to race.

"On second thought, let me just check my hair right quick," Jon said, almost pushing Brandon into the shower.

Another smile came over Brandon's face and he said, "I knew you'd be a little interested in Kat. It's ok to admit you want to impress her."

Jon didn't want to explain how he was more interested in Skylar, so he just laughed and said, "Hey man, we will see what happens. I don't like to go out looking disheveled is all."

He moved his messy hair around and cleaned off his glasses in the sink, drying them on a towel that looked like it hadn't been washed all semester. It probably wasn't.

"How about mints or gum?" Jon asked Brandon.

Brandon fumbled back into his dark dorm room. There were bags being zipped and unzipped until he came back out with a little green packet of gum.

"Here you go," Brandon said, taking a handful of the sticks out of the pack and giving them to Jon. "You might want to save a few in case things get hot and heavy." He winked.

"Right," Jon said as he shoved all but one into his pocket.

They both popped in a stick of gum. He clicked off the overhead lights, leaving the desk lamp as the only light. Brandon turned off the bathroom light. They both headed out into the living/kitchen area and headed out of their dorm.

***

Jon and Brandon walked down the outside steps of the dorm building, out into the big circle that had walkways leading to the surrounding dorm buildings. The quad. A large section of grass sat in the middle of the walkways where students were sitting crisscross applesauce and talking. There were other students hanging around smoking cigarettes under the orange streetlights that followed the trails. A few guys were kicking a soccer ball around on the other side of the circle under one of the streetlights. Two of them looked like they were having a wrestling match. Sounds of sirens were playing in the distance.

It was a warm night as the semester was ending and summer was getting closer, making the students rowdy. A couple of loud screams and yells came from the dorms, followed by laughter. Loud music came from another dorm on the opposite side of the quad.

"People are already partying before the semester is even over it seems," Brandon said.

"Guess they got all their papers done early," Jon replied.

"Hey, did you hear anything else about that girl? Jessie?"

The thoughts of *heroin, heroin, heroin,* found their way back into Jon's mind. Except, Trevor found out from Jordan, who found out from his girlfriend Natasha, there weren't any needles, or any evidence of heroin discovered on the bathroom floor. Jessie was probably still in the hospital. Her health status still a mystery.

"Guess it wasn't dope after all, at least not what they could tell. Trevor told me the bathroom was clean. Could've still been heroin. Sometimes they want to keep that under wraps. That other girl who was screaming behind her could've quick stashed it, but who knows. I don't want to assume anything I know nothing about," Jon said.

"Maybe she was anorexic? I knew a girl once that had that, she would go for days and days without eating anything but a single frosted flake. Sometimes she would pass out, just collapse on the floor. She came around though. I think she's working to be a counselor or something for other anorexics," Brandon said.

"Yeah, in high school we had an anorexic and a few bulimic girls."

"What's bulimic mean?"

"That's when you throw up everything you eat to stay skinny. You know, how they say models do it."

"Jesus. I don't think that's even worth it."

"Yeah, crazy stuff. Rots your teeth. It's amazing the mental disorders people can get that turn physical like that. Those girls would run into the bathroom after lunch and start heaving. You could hear it in the hallway sometimes." Jon chuckled. "Sometimes I'd hear it and start gagging myself."

"Speaking of crazy," Brandon said. "How about that brawl you saw the other night? Any word on that? I know they arrested those guys. Steve Wilkins was a dude I had statistics with."

"Not that I'm aware of." Jon was trying to forget that night. The thought of what happened still made his stomach crawl. He wondered if Ashley was ok. He hadn't seen her again since that night. Part of him was pissed he never asked for her number or anything. Not even a Facebook request. She seemed sweet, but perhaps the night shook her up too much.

"I couldn't believe it. I knew Steve, too. That guy was a big clown. Never would have thought he would punch someone in the face, let alone a chick. Damn," Brandon said after nodding at some guys passing by. "And what about the library? You see what those guys did at the library today?"

"No, what happened?"

"These dudes were fooling around on the second floor of the library. I guess they were pushing each other, fighting or some shit. One of them slammed into the window and somehow knocked it loose. The whole pane of glass popped out and nearly fell off the side."

"Jesus. I didn't hear about that," Jon said. He thought the students were getting *too* rowdy for the end of the semester.

"Yep. Pretty nuts. They pulled it back inside though. Could you imagine if that fell off outside the building? It could've destroyed somebody. Forget heroin and starving yourself. If that glass falls on you, you're fucking toast. Would take your head clean off!"

"Yeah… Holy shit…" Jon uttered.

"The librarian was pissed, and they had to call a guy to put some plastic covering over it. I bet if you go to the library tomorrow, you'll still see that giant piece of glass up there leaning against the wall. It's so big they can't get it down yet."

"Did they catch who did it?"

"No. I guess they ran off before anyone could see what they did. No one has fessed up, but it's pretty dumb to do it so close to the end of the semester. Especially if they're going to be graduating. Could you imagine having to tell your parents after spending thousands to come here that you can't graduate because you were being a fucking moron?"

"If that was me and I got caught, you'd never see me again," Jon joked, but there was truth behind it.

"Same, man. My dad would beat my ass six ways til Sunday. I wonder what the hell has gotten into these guys. Everyone's getting fucking crazy all of a sudden."

Jon wondered if Brandon's dad could rage as much as his father. A few times while growing up, Jon felt the wrath of Big Jon. Those moments would stay with him, being a constant reminder not to screw up around his old man. It was a flip of a switch. One moment Big Jon was happy-go-lucky, your best pal. Then, once he caught wind of trouble or disobedience, he became someone else entirely. Screaming and ranting with a shout that did more damage than a slapped bottom could ever hope to. A real Dr. Jekyll and Mr. Hyde situation.

One time, Jon had forgotten about an English project that was due. Seventh grade it was. Mrs. Roberts' English class. Jon had the assignment to create a poster board for the book *To Kill a Mockingbird*. Unfortunately, Jon had spent the entire weekend playing video games without a thought to break out some poster board or scissors. It was out of his mind as virtual blasters and aliens were more interesting.

The poster was due on a Monday and Jon showed up to class after the weekend dumbfounded. Surprised to see his classmates bringing in large, colored pieces of poster board plastered with pictures of Atticus Finch and Boo Radley from the film adaption.

Oh, shit Jon had thought to himself as his stomach sunk deep down inside of him. His grade was surely going to suffer, but that wasn't what upset him. He could get a day's extension if he pleaded with Mrs. Roberts to prevent a big fat F, but it was the fear that if his father found out about this on the next progress report, he was fucked. Royally fucked.

Progress reports were like report cards but weren't the final grades. They were little updates to show parents what their child had been doing in the past month and how they performed on tests and assignments. Even though Jon would get his poster board in, the report had a bold **LATE** written next to the assignment. It would come out to a D. *A goddamn D?*

He pleaded with the teacher, but she was adamant that not only did Jon turn in the poster late, but he misread the assignment guidelines, failed to cite references, and, for whatever reason it mattered, the size of the poster board was too small.

His father seeing the progress report was inevitable and it was only a matter of time until Little Jon would feel the pain.

The time for pain fell on a Friday afternoon after school. Early April. The reports were mailed out at the beginning of the month. Big Jon had it almost crumpled in his hand as Jon came through the front door.

"What the hell is this?" Big Jon said with the tone of *trouble's coming.*

"What's that?" Little Jon asked, acting as if being oblivious would get him anywhere.

"Your progress report. I got it today in the mail. What's this D all about in English?"

"Umm, well. . . " Little Jon's mouth went dry.

"Hmmm? It says **LATE** next to this assignment here, Mockingbird Poster Board. Why the hell does it say late?"

"Dad, I just forgot. I-"

"You were playing games, weren't you?" Big Jon had a way of asking questions when he was angry and then not allowing the other person to answer. Even if they did, no matter how they answered, it wouldn't calm the beast. This is how the rage builds up to a tipping point. Little Jon knew there was nothing that could save him now. "Jesus Christ!" Big Jon slammed the paper down on the kitchen island, creating a loud *SLAP.*

Little Jon shuttered.

"Dad-"

"Do I have to take away your Xbox to make sure you're getting your GODDAMN homework done, huh? Do I have to go upstairs and sit in your room until I've seen that every one of your FUCK-ING assignments is completed? Do I? Am I going to have to waste MY TIME to make sure MY SON isn't being a FUCKING, PISS POOR STUDENT? Getting Ds in English. NOT IN MY HOUSE, not while you're under MY ROOF!"

The sound of his father's yells were so pure. So rage-filled. They came from the depths of his soul, blasting from his mouth like cannonballs. One after the other. Striking and knocking down Little Jon internally. They hurt. Every word was another hole through Little Jon's chest. He wanted to cry but couldn't now. It would only make matters worse for him. Crying came later tonight when Little Jon was alone.

"And you couldn't tell me, right? YOU just had to wait until I got it in the mail. Making me feel like an absolute FUCKING MORON thinking MY SON is taking care of business at school and getting the grades I EXPECT HIM TO GET IN THIS HOUSE AND TO REMEMBER HIS GODDAMNED ASSIGNMENTS." Big Jon picked up the crumpled progress report and *slammed* it down again. Little Jon remained standing with his backpack slung over one shoulder. Glasses foggy from the sweat of fear. He couldn't move. There was nothing that could be done. It was an impenetrable anger.

"UnFUCKINGbelievable, Jon. Get the HELL out of here! Go to your room! Get the HELL out of here! Get the FUCK out of here!" Big Jon was pointing to the stairs. His other hand gripped to his hip. "Your room and I don't want to hear any of those FUCK-ING games playing, FUCKING movies or anything! And if I hear ONE of those FUCKING things, even a peep, you can bet your ASS I'm coming in there and ripping them out of the FUCKING wall, do you hear me? Out of the FUCKING WALL and into the GOD. DAMN. TRASH!"

Little Jon began to shuffle toward the stairs without looking into his father's eyes. No way could he meet them.

"Do you hear me, you little bastard?" Big Jon asked.

Little Jon nodded. His body trembled. "I. . . I hear you, dad. I'm sorry."

"Go on! And don't say sorry to me, sorry means SHIT! I don't want to see you for the rest of the night. You get in your room and do all the assignments you have RIGHT NOW! And if you don't have any assignments, MAKE SOME UP OR I'LL GIVE YOU SOME PAPERS TO WRITE! All I want is a son to remember his GODDAMN assignments and not put things off until the last minute. Jesus Christ! What a DOPE of a father I must be, letting my son FUCK AROUND and not do his WORK!"

Little Jon retreated to his room. The battle had been lost. A brutal defeat. The words would leave a scar just as the ones that had proceeded it. More scars would come. But it was alright. Little Jon understood there were times for punishment and discipline. You could at least give points to Mr. Barnes for not getting physical with his son. That would have left literal scars you could see. Those would lead to therapy and Jon was more interested in providing therapy than being a client to it.

Still, Little Jon knew that his father recovered quite quickly from an outburst like that. It would be awkward the next time Jon would see his dad when he had calmed down and acted almost as if he was unaware of the amount of volume and cursing capacity he provided. It was as if his dad would have to become a character of an angered and disappointed parent to put on a fiery, theatrical performance for all to hear. This would include Mrs. Barnes who heard everything, even though she had sat in her bed with the TV on the entire time Jon was being bombarded with shouts. They couldn't make a TV to go up loud enough to drown out that sound.

The next morning, Big Jon would apologize to his son over Frosted Flakes for what he had said and the two of them would discuss the matter in a more civilized manner as Jon choked down the sugary flakes that cut his throat. Little Jon said he would promise to be more organized and less focused on entertainment. Made sure he completed his work and ask the teacher for help if he was confused.

Big Jon would explain how his dad yelled at him, even worse so, how his dad used a leather belt to whip his ass when he stepped out of line. Thankfully, that tradition stopped. After enough years had passed, Big Jon and Grandpa would even laugh about it. Jon figured that time healed all wounds and made them funny.

"Alright, son," Big Jon said at the dining table the following morning. "Are we ok?"

"Yeah, we're ok."

Big Jon would then kiss the top of Little Jon's messy, brown hair. All was well and back to normal. They would get back on to good terms, until the next time when the same progression of yelling, tears, and awkward makeup would play out just as it had before.

Just as Grandpa did it to Big Jon and Big Jon did it to Little Jon, Little Jon would one day do it to his son. Hopefully, not with the same amount of anger. And if he did, he would at least try to remember what he had said.

The Arrival

They walked right through the grass as Melissa's dorm was in the building across from theirs. As they strolled toward the building, Brandon swung his lanyard keys around his fingers.

The group of students sitting in the grassy circle all talked to one another. Jon couldn't quite make out what they were saying as his nerves ran wild. The closer they approached Melissa's dorm, the closer Jon was to having a heart attack.

"You ready for this?" Brandon asked Jon as they approached the stairs leading up to the place.

"Ready as I'll ever be," Jon said, sounding like he was out of breath. He put his fingers in his hair to fix it up, forgetting he had just done it a moment ago in the mirror. In fact, he messed it up again by doing it.

Walking up the stairs to Melissa's place, they heard yelling coming from one of the other dorms above them. It wasn't clear what was being shouted, but it startled Jon.

"What the hell is going on up there?" Jon asked as he paused for a minute on the stairs, looking up.

"Probably a couple of kids getting wasted is all," Brandon replied. "Don't worry about it. We won't be going up there anyway. Melissa and Kat are right here."

Kat. Ugh.

After one flight of steps, Jon and Brandon arrived at the cemented hallway outside of the dorm rooms. The smell of a warm breeze and cigarette smoke blew through it. The outside walls were made from regular red brick that looked gritty and dirty from the shine of the harsh, florescent rods above. A small lamp hung in front of each of the doors, casting light on each of the numbers.

"Room 203, right here," Brandon said, approaching the door while fixing up his shirt.

Knock. Knock. Knock. Knock. Knock. KNOCK. KNOCK.

"Coming!" a female voice uttered behind the door. Jon could hear her footsteps approaching the door to answer it from the other side. His heart was beating in his ears at this point. *Was Skylar going to open the door? Would it be Melissa? Kat?*

The yelling was still going on in a dorm above them. Loud music. Yells.

Melissa greeted Jon and Brandon at the door to her and Kat's dorm. She was dolled up with heavy eye makeup, more so than she usually does. She was wearing a black, flowing shirt that cut off right above her stomach. There was an exotic looking silver piercing in her belly button. Jon never saw that outfit before. He pondered if Skylar was into that look and was wearing that same outfit tonight. He'd like to see that.

She looked tired, but her eyes lit up at the sight of Brandon in front of her. Jon stood behind him trying to play it cool as his now messy hair peeked over Brandon's shoulder. Brandon was about six inches taller than him.

"Hey, guys!" Melissa said and reached up to give a hug to Brandon.

"Thanks for having us over Lis." Brandon bent down to hug Melissa as he was almost double her height. "This is my roommate Jon."

Jon stuck his hand out to shake Melissa's.

"Of course! Jon! We have Weiss' class together! It's nice to meet a familiar face!" Melissa said, seeming tipsy. Brandon's always said that once you get a little alcohol in a girl she will be friendlier than ever before. Jon never saw Melissa be this personable. Brandon must be on to something.

"You too Melissa, Brandon has told me all about you," Jon said, trying to appear normal and not anxious at all.

Melissa laughed and ran her fingers down her hair. She shook Jon's hand and said, "Oh is that right? I hope it was good things!" She gave Brandon a flirtful nudge on his arm as he walked in.

"Absolutely!" Jon said and smirked.

"Well, it's very nice to meet you, Jon. Please come into our lovely dorm and make yourself at home!"

He and Brandon entered the living/kitchen area of the dorm. It was identical to theirs, as they all were, with a cozy living area including a blue fabric couch, two matching chairs facing each other on either side of a circular brown and worn-down coffee table. One chair had a pile of books stacked on top. The other had napkins on it. There were multiple water bottles thrown down on it with some glasses of what looked like wine. Jon couldn't tell as he wasn't much of a drinker. It could've just been cranberry juice for all he knew. A TV set sat on a wooden shelf across from the couch playing some show on mute. A poster of the Eiffel Tower was taped above the couch with fancy cursive lettering plastered around it. LIVE. LAUGH. LOVE. EXPLORE. It was typical college chick dorm decor.

On the opposite side of the room was the kitchen, which appeared not too well maintained. Dishes were piled in the sink. There were old cereal bowls with remnants of sugary flakes still stuck on the sides sitting on the bar by the fridge. The trash can was filled to the brim with cardboard boxes from microwavable meals, empty soda cans and water bottles crunched up on top.

You'd think Melissa would tidy up since she was having company. That's what Jon thought to himself anyway. He wondered what their bedrooms must look like.

With the mess that was the living and kitchen area of Melissa's dorm, Jon didn't realize that there was another person in the room. Sitting in the middle of the blue couch was a tall, dark, buzzed-hair guy with a scruffy beard whom Jon didn't recognize. He held his phone in his hand as he was laying back into the couch cushion, causing his navy-blue shirt to ruffle. It wasn't sweaty like Brandon's shirt but looked similar. He was another athletic guy.

For a second, he was confused and thought it was Melissa's boyfriend. What were they doing alone in this dorm together before Brandon and he showed up? Then he wondered where Skylar was. How about Kat?

"Yo man," Brandon said. He reached out and slapped the guy on his hand. "This is my roommate Jon."

"How's it going man, I'm Hunter, I'm Brandon's buddy from basketball. We go way back," he said, nodding his head back with a smile. He looked high, or drunk. Perhaps he was a mixture of both. He and Melissa would make a great couple.

"Nice to meet you," Jon said, returning the nod.

"Yeah man," Hunter continued, "Brandon was the shit back in high school. The ladies loved him. If you stuck with this guy, you could get any girl you wanted just by standing next to him. Even in that sweaty ass shirt, he could score. Did he ever tell you about that one chick, what was her name? Stephanie something."

Brandon laughed and said, "I don't think we gotta get into all that now dude."

"Oh man, there was this chick named Stephanie. You gotta tell Jon about it. After that one game, we had with Cedar Heights, man. . ."

THUD. It sounded like someone fell down on the dorm from upstairs. Everyone looked up for a moment.

"I honestly can't even remember," Brandon said in an effort to get off the subject.

Hunter then turned his head over to Melissa, who was clearing off the cluttered chairs. "Hey Lis, you still think Brandon's cute with his stinky clothes? Would you let him smash? I bet you would huh?"

Melissa looked up from her cleaning and blushed. "Oh my God, Hunter! Shut up! You're such a fuckin' creep!" She picked up one of the small textbooks on the chair and chucked it at him.

"Woah, chill!" Hunter said as the book just missed hitting his big drunken head. Or stoned head. Either would be an appropriate description of his head. Jon still didn't know what his gig was.

All three of them laughed. Brandon's faced turned red.

"I can't believe you'd even say that," Melissa said, looking pissed off. She turned back to cleaning off the chair. "Please don't mind him, Jon."

Then Brandon asked Hunter the million-dollar question, "Where's Skylar?"

HEY YEAH, WHERE IS SKYLAR? Jon was screaming in his head.

"She's here. She's usin' the bathroom," Hunter replied as he pointed his thumb toward the small, dark hallway that separated the living area from the kitchen. It led back to the girls' two rooms and the bath.

Jon heard a door *creak* open. Then, as if Hunter had summoned her, the woman of Jon's dreams came walking out of that dark hallway and into the living area. She stood underneath the fluorescent light.

Skylar Doyle.

There she was, wearing a yellow and white striped shirt with tight white shorts. Her legs were smooth and tan. Jon didn't know what to do. He froze as if he just saw Medusa. His mouth could've been hanging open, there was no way he could know at this point. Time stood still.

"Sky, this is Jon. He has Weiss' class with us," Melissa said, jumping up from cleaning off the coffee table. She introduced the two with a smile.

"Of course! I'm Skylar." Skylar extended her hand out. She had what looked like flowers painted on her nails. "It's nice to meet you, Jon. How did you like Weiss' class this semester?"

"Nice to meet you, Skylar. Yeah, I, uh. . . " For a second, Jon didn't know what words were.

Another loud *THUD* came from upstairs.

"I've actually had him for class before and I think he's a really nice guy," Jon said with his heart beating a thousand times per second. "His philosophy course was really interesting. Have you ever taken it?" The words got out, but in Jon's mind, they sounded like mush. *Hah, you evvr ttoo et?*

"Yeah was that a freshman course? Intro to philosophy?" she inquired.

Jon smiled and nodded, afraid to speak anymore as the speed of his heart was now making him lightheaded.

"That class was cool and he's a real sweetheart. Have you finished your paper?" Skylar asked.

Before Jon could answer and pass out, Hunter piped in and said, "Yeah she did, Skylar is a good little student."

Skylar leaned over the side of the couch and slapped Hunter on his arm. Not in a flirty way. She seemed annoyed. Hunter snickered in response.

"I'm sorry Jon, don't mind him. I don't even know why I put up with him," Skylar said half smiling.

Melissa chimed in, "Yeah I don't know why you don't BREAK UP with him. All he does is drink and start SHIT." She threw an empty water bottle at Hunter.

Break up? Wait, wait, wait. Does that mean Skylar is dating this guy? Hunter? This slob? A girl of Skylar's stature couldn't be with a guy like that, right?

"Yeah maybe you're right," Skylar said and then slapped Hunter's arm again, but this time it was harder. Hunter laughed and pulled her in to give her a hug. She fell into the couch beside him.

"Hunter you smell like whiskey, ew! Let go!" Skylar said in disgust. She ripped herself out of his hug but remained on the couch next to him. "I'm sorry Jon," she said with a disappointed look on her face. Jon's face also had a look of disappointment and that's probably why she appeared to feel so bad.

Jon tried to laugh it off. "That's alright, he's ok."

"Jon, Brandon, please have a seat," Melissa said. "I've cleaned these chairs for you. I don't know where Kat's been. She should've been here earlier to tidy the place up."

Jon took a seat on the big blue, square-cushioned chair. "Thank you," Jon said. Brandon sat on the other one.

Who cares where Kat is? Jon forgot all about her, especially after feeling the giant bomb drop on his heart upon seeing Skylar with her boyfriend.

THUD.

Melissa took the rest of the bottles off of the coffee table and stuffed them into the trash can that was already filled to the brim. She crushed them all down into the white trash bag. *Crunch. Snap. Pop.*

She turned and came back into the living area and sat to the right of Hunter on the couch, closer to where Brandon was sitting. Jon was sitting by Skylar's end of the couch. He felt so out of place. The door was right by Brandon's chair and he wanted nothing more than to stand up and run right out. But he couldn't. It would be too embarrassing. He just had to sit there and soak in the misery and discomfort.

"Where is Kat? Did you text her?" Skylar asked, thumbing on her phone.

"Yep. I texted her, I called her. She didn't respond," Melissa said. "The last I heard from her was yesterday when she was at the library studying for her biology final. I'm not even sure she slept here last night."

THUD.

"For real, is anyone else hearing this shit?" Hunter asked. He looked at the ceiling, annoyed.

"Yeah, it's been going on for the past hour. I'm thinking about going up there and telling them to knock it off or I'm calling the fucking cops," Melissa said, equally as annoyed.

"If it happens again, I'm gonna go tell them myself. Brandon's goin' too," Hunter proclaimed.

Brandon just smiled over at Melissa and said, "Well hopefull–"

THUD. CRASH.

It sounded like dishes were being dropped now.

"That's it, c'mon B-man we're going up there now," Hunter said, popping up from the couch and pulling on Brandon's leg. "Let's go."

Brandon shot up from his chair.

Skylar got up and grabbed both of Hunter's arms from behind. "No, no. Hunter, you can't do this. You're not getting in another stupid fight."

"Babe it's alright. I won't hurt anybody," Hunter said. He was wiggling his arms out of Skylar's grip.

"Seriously," Skylar continued, "if you go up there, I'm going home. I'm not putting up with this tonight." It was as if this wasn't Skylar's first rodeo with Hunter.

"C'mon Brandon." Hunter motioned over and they both started toward the door. Brandon told Jon to come along with them. Jon couldn't refuse, so he just nodded and followed the two guys out from the dorm room and away from Skylar and Melissa.

EIGHT

Room 303

The familiar scent of cigarette smoke and warm air helped put Jon at ease as the three of them exited Melissa's dorm, back onto the cemented outdoor hallway of the second floor. He still wasn't happy as Hunter was still there. However, the fact that he didn't have to see him tugging and pulling on Skylar made it better.

Skylar and Melissa were talking to each other back in the room, but Jon couldn't make out what they were saying through the door. Jon hoped it was Melissa explaining to Skylar how Hunter was talking while she was in the bathroom. He hoped this would be the final straw for the two and maybe Skylar could try things out with good ole' Jon.

"Alright guys let's check these fools," Hunter said, punching his fist into his palm. He was ready to give a pounding.

"Let's just see what they're up to. We don't have to get physical," Brandon said.

The three of them started up the steps to the third floor. Brandon and Hunter were chatting back and forth as Jon stayed at a reasonable pace behind them, trying to get his mind straight.

"Sorry, what I said to Melissa, man. You know I didn't mean that," Hunter said to Brandon as he was still giving punches to his palm.

"Shut up! Of course, you meant it, asshole," Brandon said. "You were trying to blow my cover!"

Jon looked out into the giant grass circle as he climbed up the steps of the building. There was no longer anyone sitting crisscross-applesauce on the grass and talking. Only a girl walking on the asphalt path on the other end of the grass by herself. The loud music played. Another yell. Screaming. Laughter. More screaming. *Where are the campus cops?* Tires *skidded* beyond the campus trees. Horns *blared* into the night. It made Jon jerk around for a moment.

Something was going on, and it wasn't only on campus.

The guys made it to the third floor. The smell of smoke still lingered, but not as strong as it had below. As they approached the door to room 303, they could hear two people arguing inside. It sounded like a man and woman in the middle of a heated debate.

CRASH. It sounded like a plate shattered against the wall inside.

Hunter was in front. Brandon was standing over Hunter's right shoulder. Jon stood further back behind Brandon on the other side of the hall in case a plate came hurling out. With his luck, Hunter and Brandon would duck and it would still have enough momentum to smash him in his face. Jon didn't want that. He already had enough problems.

KNOCK. KNOCK. KNOCK. Hunter mashed the side of his fist on the door. The arguing continued inside. *KNOCK. KNOCK. KNOCK. KNOCK.* Still, no one answered as the shouting match went on.

"HEY! WE CAN HEAR YOU IN THERE! OPEN THE DOOR! YOU GUYS ARE AWFULLY LOUD!" Hunter said in a loud, commanding voice. He seemed serious and not as drunk or high as before. Sobered up. Now he was banging with both of his fists, so much so that the little lamp on the wall beside the door flickered with each pound. He pounded out each syllable. "O-PEN THE DOOR!"

The yelling inside stopped for a moment and Hunter looked back at Brandon with his eyebrows raised as if he had just performed a magic trick. Brandon looked back at Jon, who was waiting for the plate to launch out.

Footsteps marched to the door. They weren't the same excited footsteps of Melissa who was happy to see Brandon and Jon just a moment ago but pissed off and unwelcoming. *It sounds like a goddamn elephant in there,* Jon thought to himself as his nervous fingers were now running along the rough, white lines between the bricks.

The door yanked open and there stood a short, black-haired guy with sweat on his beat-red forehead. His height surprised all three of them considering the sound of his stomps. You'd think it would have been a great big, burly man. The opposite was true. Even Jon was taller than him.

"What the FUCK are you guys doing banging at my door?" the short man yelled up at Hunter and Brandon. Jon moved up closer because he almost couldn't see him with those two towering over him. The short man didn't look familiar to Jon. The same went for Hunter and Brandon as they didn't say his name or appear to have recognized him.

"Hey man, we were in the room below and heard a ruckus coming from up here. You mind knocking it off? If you d-"

Suddenly a girl came up from behind the short man and *SMASHED* a plate over the back of his head. Hunter and Brandon jumped back and covered their faces. Shards of white porcelain flew and bounced off their arms. Jon was behind them with both of his hands covering his eyes. The short man hit the floor face-up while the girl stood above him kicking the side of his chest.

"How do YOU like it you piece of SHIT. HUH?" The woman screamed as she kicked and kicked.

"Kat?" Brandon said, brushing off his arms.

"Kat, what the hell is going on here? What are you doing? Who is this guy?" Hunter asked after.

That's Kat? Jon thought to himself as he checked himself for any cuts.

Kat stood bloodied and battered in the doorway to room 303. She was short, just like the man whom she just blasted with the plate. She had a chubby look to her. Not fat, but not skinny. Full figured you could say. Her curly, black hair looked like it had been tugged on as strands shot out in every direction. Her eyes looked red from crying. There was dried blood under her nose and red scratch marks on her neck and arms. The yellow shirt she wore had been torn almost completely in half and her plump stomach was out. Her large, purple bra was exposed. Her black yoga pants were also ripped. She looked better in the photo that Brandon showed Jon on his phone earlier.

"Get the FUCK out of here you guys, RIGHT NOW!" Kat screeched at them.

The short man on the ground jolted his head up and grabbed Kat's legs, causing her to fall to the ground, hitting her head on the side of the coffee table on the way down. She was knocked right out. Her body fumbled and slumped down next to the table with the guy's hands still wrapped around her legs.

Hunter and Brandon jumped onto the guy, pulling his hands away from Kat's legs. They pinned his arms down on the carpet of the living area. They had to be careful as shards of plate stuck out from the floor. It wasn't easy to restrain him. His body squirmed and his legs kicked up in the air, trying to get his body free. Hunter gave him a *slap* across his face that didn't seem to settle him down in the slightest.

"Did YOU just FUCKING slap ME!?" the short man shouted.

Jon stood in the doorway, frozen in time again. Instead of being trapped in the beauty of Skylar Doyle, he was trapped in the ugliness of what had happened to Kat. She remained on the floor, appearing lifeless. The kitchen area looked like a tornado blew through it. The furniture was shoved around. The cushions were strewn. Dishes were shattered everywhere, making little white paths of jagged edges in the carpet. Forks. Spoons. Knives. All were ripped from their drawers and scattered across the room. Glass cups were shattered by the hall. The fridge door hung open. *What on earth led to this?*

With the scene overwhelming him, Jon didn't realize Brandon was calling out to him.

"Jon. JON! Close the door! See if Kat's alright. JON!" Brandon said as he crouched and pressed down on the short man's right arm. He threw in a *slap* or two to his face, making him shout.

Jon snapped out of his funk. He turned and closed the door, not locking it. Then, he stepped over the guy's leg when it wasn't kicking up. Watching himself, he got down to the ground and grabbed Kat's wrist to check her pulse.

"She's alive," Jon said.

"What?" Brandon said as the short man was now trying to bite at Brandon's hands.

"She's OK! She's ALIVE. She has a PULSE!" Jon said speaking up, his voice almost cracking.

"That BITCH!" the short man said with spit flying off his lips.

"Thank God," Hunter said, still struggling with the guy. "Call 911! We need police and a fuckin' ambulance!"

"Shit! I don't have my phone on me," Jon said, patting all the pockets on his jeans. "I left it in my room. Shit!"

The door swung open.

"Oh my god!" a female voice screamed from the doorway. They all looked over to see a bald police officer was standing there with Melissa's head peeking around his chest. There was a look of absolute horror on her face. "What the fuck happened?" She scooted around the police officer before he could stop her and hopped over the guy's leg, almost tripping over one of his kicks. She crouched down with Jon, nudging him out of the way. "Kat? Kat are you alright? Katie? C'mon Katie. It's Lis, okay? It's me." She was too upset to hear Jon trying to explain that she had a pulse and was breathing. She turned her head to the short man on the ground who looked like he was having a seizure.

"Michael?" she asked in an angered whisper.

The site of the police officer appeared to make the short man angrier. His legs jolted up, trying to kick at him.

"What the HELL did you do to her?" Melissa shouted as her mascara was now running down her cheeks. She got up to go towards him, but Jon held her back.

The officer turned his head into the radio on his shoulder and clicked the button on the side. "10-47, we need an ambulance at the LeRone Dorm Building." He leaned back to see the room number. "Unit 303. White Haven College. We have an unconscious female student and a male student having a violent mental breakdown." There was a cut of static. A voice came back through the radio, but Jon couldn't hear what it said. It sounded like another number.

"What's going on here tonight, folks? We've been getting calls all over," Officer Cherry, one of the local White Haven cops, said in an almost too calm and friendly manner. He pulled out some blue, latex gloves from his back pocket and snapped them on both of his hands.

Hunter and Brandon explained what had happened as best as they could and remained on the ground, pinning the flailing psycho. Officer Cherry got down with them, assessing the situation. Michael's eyes were bulging from their sockets. "If you don't get them off of me I'm gonna shoot you with your own FUCKING gun!" he shouted at Officer Cherry.

"Sir, I'm gonna have to ask you to you calm down for me okay? Stop kicking your legs for a minute," Officer Cherry said. He was reaching behind his back to get his handcuffs out from his other back pocket. No compliance from Michael, aka the short man. "This will be a whole lot easier if you'd relax. I'm not going to hurt you." Hunter and Brandon moved back slightly, still pinning him down so that Officer Cherry could get a grip on him himself.

Michael turned his neck and took a bite out of Hunter's left hand.

"Ah fuck!" Hunter pulled his hand back. Blood oozed out between his pinky and ring finger. "He just fuckin' bit me! Jesus Christ!"

Michael's top teeth were dipped in red. "That's what you get! I told you!" he shouted.

Officer Cherry threw his handcuffs beside him and hovered his hand over his taser. Michael, now with a free right hand, lunged his arm out, attempting to grab Officer Cherry's gun on his belt.

ZAP ZAP ZAP ZAP ZAP. Officer Cherry unleashed the lightening wire into Michael's upper chest. His body shook and contorted all around the carpet like a fish out of water. Both of his eyeballs rolled to the back of his head.

"Agh agh agh agh agh!" Michael squirmed. Officer Cherry released the trigger. Brandon let go of pinning his right arm as it went limp from the shock.

"Out of the way please, out of the way from him!" Officer Cherry shouted. Brandon popped up and moved from Michael's body toward the kitchen area where Hunter was wrapping paper towels around his hand that was still fresh from Michael's bite. Melissa and Jon were still sitting by Kat's body as it remained by the coffee table. Her breathing remained.

Officer Cherry put his taser back in its pouch on his belt, opposite side of his loaded Glock 22. He grabbed Michael's shoulders and flipped him over on his stomach. Michael made weak and angry groans. The groans you'd hear from someone not wanting to get out of bed in the morning. *Click. Snap. Lock.* Officer Cherry had Michael's wrists locked together with nickel cuffs. He clicked on the radio on his shoulder again. "10-23, we have the male suspect in custody."

"10-4" the voice replied from the speaker.

"Alright buddy, let's go. Come on, stand up. Can you stand up?" Officer Cherry asked, pulling Michael from the floor. He started to chuckle. "You were just using your feet a second ago, what happened tough guy?" Michael still made groaning noises as he tried to get up on his jelly-like feet. "C'mon, up. You can do it." Officer Cherry motioned over to Jon and Brandon. "You two mind helping me get him downstairs?"

Jon turned back to Brandon.

"Sure, come on Jon. Lis, you stay with Hunter and Kat until we get back alright?" Brandon said, walking back over.

"You guys will be fine, the ambulance should be here any second. We have extra units out tonight. For now, we just have to get this guy in the back of the car before he starts using those feet again. Keep that thing wrapped tight for me okay?" Officer Cherry said to Hunter. Melissa got up and went towards the kitchen to assist Hunter, whose hand was wrapped in a blood-soaked mitten of paper towels.

Jon and Brandon helped Officer Cherry take Michael down the steps to the building. Michael jolted a bit at them as they lowered him down the three sets of stairs, but his energy was still too low to rattle them around again.

"Too bad this had to happen on the top floor of all places," Officer Cherry said, chuckling again. "This could've been a whole lot easier. But we've been getting calls like this all night, so I guess you could say we're used it by now. Must be something in the water tonight with all the ruckus."

As they descended the steps, Jon glanced out at the giant grass circle. There was still no one sitting there but he noticed a group of people standing in the hallway of the dorm building across from them. They all stared at the scene of two students and a cop dragging a short man down the stairs. Jon could hear them trying to shout things out like "Hey! What happened?" along with "Ooooo what did he do?" and "Is he dead?" None got a response. There was an ambulance siren playing out into the night, making Jon feel calm and the people more curious. They began to shuffle down the steps toward Jon and them.

They got Michael down from the third floor and to the police cruiser on the crosswalk that connected the dorm area to the school buildings. The group of students grew larger as they all stood back, watching Michael getting placed into the back of the police vehicle with its blue and red lights beaming onto the walls of the surrounding buildings.

The ambulance siren got louder and louder until it appeared on the road. It pulled beside the police car, blocking the crosswalk. A man and woman EMT jumped out right as the ambulance came to a halt. They were both wearing grey polo shirts and navy pants. One was holding a black bag filled with equipment.

"Where to?" the woman EMT asked Officer Cherry.

"Follow these guys. The girl is right up there. She's breathing," Officer Cherry said, pointing to the LeRone Building and motioning over to Jon and Brandon to take the lead.

"This way," Brandon said to the EMTs. He was trying to break up the large crowd of students that were standing on the asphalt path. "Excuse us, please move. There's an emergency. Out of our way!" Brandon shoved someone out his way.

"Hey, don't shove me you ASSHOLE!" the shoved guy said.

"I'm sorry, I'm sorry, you have to get ou-"

Brandon got punched right in his jaw. The person he shoved was now attacking him, pushing him, punching him more until he fell back hard on his back. Then someone else joined in and began thrashing Brandon while he was still lying on the asphalt. The EMTs tried to stop the two guys but were met with fists to their faces instead.

"Officer!" Jon shouted back as he ran and knocked the two guys back as best as he could away from the EMTs and Brandon. They both tripped backward over Brandon's body and into the crowd, causing some to fall over each other like dominos.

A girl got pushed down. She screamed, then got slapped in the face from a guy standing above her.

"Get the FUCK off of me" a voice in the crowd cried.

"Get up, you BITCH," another girl's voice said.

Officer Cherry rushed over, having to push more people aside from the crowd. There was an all-out brawl starting to take place within the students. Punches. Slaps. Kicks. Grabs. Twists. Shoves. Pulls. Anyone was fair game.

Then, someone slipped Officer Cherry's Glock 22 from his pouch as he tried to control the crowd. *BANG.* A shot rang out over White Haven College. A gush of blood burst out of someone's head standing in the middle of the crowd, spraying down on the rest of them like rain. Jon's included. He squeezed his eyes shut to prevent the gore from blinding him. Officer Cherry went for his gun not realizing that it had been his own that had just gone off. His fingers glided over the pouch beside it, feeling for the taser. That was missing too.

ZAP ZAP ZAP ZAP ZAP ZAP ZAP. A girl screamed and flailed to the ground. *BANG.* Another gunshot, only this time no rain of blood. Students scattered and ran in different directions, some being chased by other students. *BANG.* A girl got shot in her back. She fumbled to the ground.

"10-81! 10-81! Requesting immediate backup at White Haven College. Rioting with armed suspects. Rioting with arm-"

BANG. BANG.

Officer Cherry got shot twice in his chest. One bullet blasted his radio, destroying it in an instant.

Jon screamed out to him, but it was short-lived as he got shoved by an Indian student wearing glasses and pajama pants.

"I don't want any trouble," Jon said to him, putting his hands up. He got shoved again.

"FUCK YOU!" the Indian man said with a crazed look in his eye and went at Jon again. Another person joined and tried to grab Jon's face, making his glasses crooked. Brandon was still on the ground with his arms over his face. Three men were kicking him with no signs of stopping.

Jon broke for it towards the dorm building that they pulled Michael from. The Indian man followed him and almost caught up until he got pummeled by a blonde-haired girl. She jumped on his back, wrestling him to the ground. Jon didn't have time to look back another second to see that the girl who pounced on the Indian man was Ashley Tolsen, the pretty girl he walked back to her dorm room after the fight outside the cafeteria.

The big, grassy circle had people running in and out of the surrounding dorm buildings. Some stopped to fight while others were trying to get the hell out of the way. Screaming and yelling came from every angle. Sirens came from the distance, but it didn't bring that sense of calmness to Jon like it did the first time. He was convinced it was going to lead to more trouble, considering how Officer Cherry ended up. *Keep running.*

Almost out of breath, Jon hustled up the steps to the third floor of the LeRone Building. There wasn't anyone coming up or down the steps now, however, Jon noticed many of the doors to the dorm rooms on each floor were wide open, including Melissa's room. 203. But first, he had to get to room 303. He clung onto the stair railing as he whipped himself around onto the next set of steps.

Room 303's door was wide open just like the rest of them and Jon was sure to get in as fast as he could and lock the door behind him. *Click.* The place was empty. Not even Kat's body remained. "Guys?" Jon said. "Hunter? Melissa? Where are you guys? Brandon's hurt!

Someone shot the cop and people are going at each other like lunatics!"

He walked back into the little hallway and checked the bathroom. Nothing. It was odd how eerily quiet it was in there with all of the mayhem going on outside. Had they run outside after they heard gunshots? *They must've,* Jon thought, *unless one of those psychos came in here.*

Jon walked back into the living/kitchen area that appeared to be unaltered since he was last there. The furniture was still moved all around. The kitchen was still in disarray and the shards of smashed plates still poked out of the carpet leading to a small blood stain by the door where Michael took a bite out of Hunter. Then a thought came barreling into Jon's mind: *Skylar. Skylar stayed downstairs during the whole ordeal, she might be down there with the rest of them.*

He rushed to the door and unlocked it. *Click.* The noises of hell returned as the door swung open. The chaos. The pandemonium. It all came whooshing through the open hall as Jon exited room 303 and toward the steps. Out on the grassy circle, people were tearing each other apart. Screaming and cursing. Shoving and slapping. Kicking and punching. One of them looked up at Jon and shouted, "What the FUCK you think YOU'RE looking at!?" and began running towards the stairs. Jon panicked and almost slipped down the steps, trying to get into room 203 before the psycho smashed his head in like they did to Brandon.

Jon fumbled into room 203. He closed the door. Locked it. *Click.* Then, just seconds later, banging came from the other side.

POUND. POUND. POUND.

"Open this FUCKING door NOW!" the psychotic man shouted. Jon fell to the floor and scooted backward like chicks do in the horror films he watches.

POUND. POUND. POUND.

"Skylar?" Jon said, trying to be louder than the pounding on the door. He looked around the room. No one was there. He got up and went back to the bedrooms, the door still being beaten like a drum behind him. "Is anyone back here? Skylar? Hunter? Melissa? Kat? Hello? Hello? It's Jon!"

He searched the bedrooms. Nothing. He looked in the bathroom, behind the shower curtain. Nothing. Jon was alone again. Just like he was upstairs, except this time he had a visitor that he sure as hell wasn't going to allow in. His heart began to race at top speed.

POUND. POUND. POUND.

"I'm NOT kidding, you BETTER OPEN THIS GODDAMN DOOR!" The psycho sounded like he was for sure *not kidding*. It was still loud even standing by the bathroom door down the hall.

He needed a weapon. Something. Anything. Hand to hand was not an option. Brandon was overrun, and he was fit and muscular. Jon wouldn't stand a chance even if it was one on one. He ran back to the kitchen side of the room. The first drawer got yanked open. Little spoons, forks, and butter knives with colored handles were inside. No good, but he took one of the butter knives just in case. *They gotta have something sharper around here.*

POUND. POUND. POUND.

He threw open the next drawer. Dish towels. The next drawer. Plastic baggies. The bottom drawer. Empty. *Goddammit!*

POUND. POUND. CRACK.

A screw on the top door hinge came off. Jon turned his head and saw it fall to the carpet. *Jesus Christ!* He turned back to the kitchen bar, hands starting to tremble. The cabinet doors flew open. Nothing but plates and cups inside. The cabinet doors slammed shut. Jon, with a green-colored handled butter knife in hand, ran back into a bedroom. Another screw flew out of the door hinges.

CRACK. POUND. POUND.

Jon was in Melissa's room. He knew it was her room because the walls were plastered with little collages of photos of her with family and friends. Better times. A big pink letter M was taped on the wall above her desk, which Jon was now rummaging through. He found a pair of scissors in the drawer. Real scissors. Not the childish kind similar to the likes of his butter knife, but real heavy-duty ones. *If he breaks down the door, go for the jugular.*

CRACK. POUND. CRACK.

It sounded like the hinges were breaking off altogether. Jon's heart beat hard in his chest as he went to close Melissa's bedroom door, locking it. *CLICK.* Now it was just a matter of time. The psycho was either going to break in and kill Jon, or Jon was going to kill him. *CRACK. CRACK. CRACK. THUD.* The door came off its hinges and slammed to the carpet with a loud *THUD*.

"Where are YOU? Come out NOW!" the psycho said. Jon positioned himself up against the wall by the door. That way if the psycho broke down the bedroom door, he could come from the side and surprise him with a pair of scissors to the neck. Easier said than done.

The psycho grunted and stomped around the dorm, looking for Jon as Jon's hands coated the scissors in sweat. His hands shook like leaves. Then, he heard the sounds of another person coming through the dorm. There was no speaking, only movements. It got quiet. Too quiet. There was no more stomping or grunting sounds. Jon waited thirty seconds. Silence. Another thirty seconds. *Did he leave?* Jon raised an eyebrow and slid his head slowly on the wall until he had one ear up against the wooden door. Silence still. Only the sound of Jon's unstoppable heart.

Did he give up? Did someone else walk by and he chased after them? Did somebody shoot him? Jon was mad with his thoughts. *No, I would've heard the gunshot. Should I peek out? No. Don't.*

NINE

Sports

Big Jon tried. Oh, how he tried. He did everything he could to get Little Jon into sports. Little Jon enjoyed throwing a ball back and forth outside with his father and going to the Hillcrest High School gym to play basketball after school. But when it came to the actual sporting events themselves, no matter which physical activity he got involved in, it always ended in some form of injury or annoyance. Baseball: bloody nose. Soccer: bruised knees. Football: didn't like wearing all the equipment. Basketball: hit in the face, broken glasses. Hockey: wouldn't even try.

"It's alright, Jon! Walk it off! Rub some dirt on it!" the coaches would shout across the field as if the dirt would miraculously heal Little Jon's aches.

Little Jon taking his high school to states was out of the question.

The two of them had plenty of fun times together, but Big Jon always felt there was yet to be an activity that the two of them could bond over. He'd try to play video games with his son a few times, but that was only mindless fun. A time killer. Same with movies, though Little Jon very much enjoyed those. Especially action and sci-fi. Little Jon liked those things because he couldn't get a black eye while holding a controller or having his face smacked with a puck while watching *The Fast and Furious* and *Alien* movies.

Then, Big Jon thought of his father, Jonathan William Barnes, aka Grandpa Jon. Growing up in rural Pennsylvania, a lot of his bonding with his father involved getting up early and tending to the farm. Milking cows. Feeding the chickens. Typical stuff like that for a rural family. He and his father didn't have many activities other than the usual work. Except for one thing. There was one activity that Big Jon and his dad did together that provided a proper father-son bonding experience.

If it was that certain time of year, Grandpa Jon would take his son deer hunting.

T E N

The Morning After

The pale ceiling light shined down on Jon like a morning sunrise. His eyes fluttered a moment before he rubbed them. For a brief second in time, he thought he was in his own bed, back at his dorm, thinking everything had been a nightmare. If only. As he became more aware and back to the waking world, he started to realize that he was in Melissa's bed on top of her light-blue comforter. Funny, Jon had never woken up in a girl's bed before.

How long was I out? He leaned up from the bed to see that the door was still locked. Untouched it seemed. The pair of heavy-duty scissors lay next to him along with his glasses. He wiped the glasses off with the bottom of his shirt, trying not to touch the bloodstains that had now dried to a crust. *What time is it?*

Jon rolled off the bed, hoping not to make any noise in case the maniac had returned. He knelt by the desk. Melissa's black and pink-trimmed backpack lay beside it, leaning against the wall. A small hand sanitizer bottle with an apple tree picture hung from the zipper. Jon squirted some out and rubbed it between his hands. The scent gave Jon a moment of ease and cleanliness.

Zip. Inside was a textbook and a laptop. Its charger underneath. He plugged it into the nearby wall socket. A virtual *ding* sound ringed from it. Jon tried to cover the noise. It didn't have much battery life left but Jon turned it on right away to the log in screen to see MAY 4, 7:05 A.M displayed in the bottom-left corner. MELISSA R it said on the center screen with a picture of the ocean in the background. There was no way Jon could log on, it was password protected. Jon searched more in the backpack, hoping to find a cell phone. No success. Melissa probably had it on her wherever she was. People these days always had their phones on them.

He got up, grabbed the scissors off the bed, and headed toward the door. It was still quiet. Jon put his ear up to the door again and listened for a minute but there was nothing to be heard. Then, his stomach growled. *I can't stay here forever.* His hand slowly raised up to turn the lock above the knob, ear still pressed up against the wood. *Cl-click.* Jon unlocked it and pulled on the knob. He got back up against the wall and peeked his head around, looking out of the slight crack of the door. The living area was clear. He could see the corner of the broken door on the carpet and some light from the morning sun coming through the wide-open doorway. He then swung his head around to look straight across the hall to see Kat's room how it was before. Nothing was out of place it seemed. He angled his head again, now looking at the bathroom door which was cracked. Again, as it was before. Jon couldn't notice any difference that he could remember from last night.

They could be around the corner, waiting to jump out from the kitchen or behind the bathroom door. Another growl came from his stomach. *When did I eat last?* He clenched the scissors and opened the door halfway. Jon paused, listening again, then opened the door all the way. He stepped out, almost tiptoeing like a cat burglar into Kat's bedroom. Still no success in finding a cell phone. The bathroom had pink and purple bottles of lotions and shampoos. Nothing of use there. Back up front in the living/kitchen area, Jon could hear the early morning birds outside and feel the cool air that poured into the entranceway. The door lay on the ground with its hinges and screws beside it.

He poked his head out into the cemented hall. First to the right, then to the left. It was clear. No sign of the maniac, yet. The adjoining dorm rooms were closed, wide open, or cracked but he didn't dare to check in any of them. His main concern was getting back to his own room if he even had one. He wasn't even sure if *that* was a good idea.

As he walked toward the steps, Jon covered his mouth with his hand. His eyes widened.

Bodies lay all throughout the quad. Bloodied and battered. Faces and limbs scratched and covered in red. Bodies were contorted. Some faced up, others faced down. Jon almost called out to see if any of them were alive, but he stopped himself. He felt sick and not so hungry anymore. Although he couldn't see him around the corner of the LeRone Building, Jon knew that Brandon's body was still there, lifeless. Same with Officer Cherry's and most likely the same for the EMTs. *All those bodies.* Jon felt sick. He couldn't stop staring at what looked like a twisted version of *I Spy* as his eyes jutted around, looking for anyone familiar in the heap.

The walk down the steps was slow as his eyes remained on the crowd of bodies. "Fuck!" Jon yelled out, then he slapped his mouth. A girl's body lay at the bottom of the last steps. Her head looked like it was recently bashed into the side of the railing. Blood stained her once blonde hair, black. *Skylar? No, she wasn't wearing that outfit. Oh, Jesus…* Jon stepped over her and walked around out onto the asphalt path in front of the grassy circle of death. He wasn't interested in cutting through the grass this time. The asphalt path seemed an easier route to take.

He didn't want to look but he had to. Coming around the bend toward his own dorm building, Washington Building, Jon looked to his right, down the path where all those people had formed the night before to watch Michael get put in the cop car. The lights of Officer Cherry's cruiser still beamed in the morning light. The ambulance's too. There were more bodies lying there, Brandon's included. He could see the two EMT bodies thrown down beside Brandon. Officer Cherry remained on the ground with bullet holes in his chest. Jon looked away, back towards the Washington Building until he realized he needed the keys to his dorm. He had left all of his stuff in his bedroom before going to Melissa's place and Brandon was the only one who had the keys for the night out. They were the ones connected to his lanyard. Jon had to walk down by the crosswalk and fetch them from Brandon's lifeless neck. He winced at the thought and almost started crying.

Brandon's head looked like a worn-out punching bag. His eyes had a blackness to them, one was bulging out, and his teeth had been painted red and jerked back into his mouth. He laid in the grass beside the asphalt walkway with his mouth slung open. The EMTs didn't look much better. The one looked choked-out with her own stethoscope.

Officer Cherry was in a pool of his own blood.

Jon knelt on the grass beside Brandon and pulled the lanyard keys up and over his big, lifeless head. It felt wrong. Jon gagged and put his hand over his mouth and closed his eyes. He placed the lanyard keys in his front-left pocket and stood up. The sound of the police cruiser's engine caught Jon's attention. It must've been running all night. The light bar still flickered red and blue. Jon glanced down at Officer Cherry as he walked by him toward the car. Officer Cherry's eyes were open, and his mouth looked like it had frozen right in the middle of a conversation. For a second, Jon thought he was alive. That idea ended when he nudged the body of the officer and found a deadly silence in reply.

As he came up to the cruiser, Jon noticed Michael was still laying in the back seat. His chest was rising up and down. It looked like he was fast asleep inside. *He's alive! Holy shit! What do I do?* Jon made a fist like he was about to knock on the window. There was some hesitation as he wasn't sure what to expect if Michael woke up. Suddenly, a voice called out for him from the other side of the blocked crosswalk, behind the ambulance.

"Hey, you! Hey, hey! Over here!" a man's voice called. Jon was so startled that his fist shook and hit the window, almost punching right through it. Michael didn't even move inside. His chest was still rising and falling. Jon perched his head up above the police car. He could see a brown-haired guy through the windows of the ambulance, standing on the edge of the opposing crosswalk end. He moved toward Jon.

"Hey! Are you ok?" the man asked as he appeared around the ambulance and saw the very disheveled Jon with bloodstains on his shirt and hands. The man was wearing a grey tank top and khaki cargo shorts with flip flops.

Jon began to back up, frightened. He almost tripped over Officer Cherry's body. For all he knew, this man was another maniac, ready to pounce.

"Are you alright, dude? I'm not going to hurt you, trust me," the man said with his eyes squinting from the sun. It sounded genuine and not rage-filled like the maniac who chased him last night. Jon stopped backing up and stood frozen for a second.

"Who are you?" Jon asked.

"My name's Mark. I promise I'm not going to hurt you. It's alright."

"What's going on? What happened last night?" Jon said, still frightened. "What the hell is all this?"

"I don't know exactly, but you need to come with me to the library. Are there any others with you?"

"No, I-I'm alone."

"Ok, follow me."

Jon reached down in his pocket and grabbed his lanyard keys. "I gotta get back to my dorm, my phone, and everything is in there. I gotta call my parents."

"No time for that. We have working phones and computers in the library. Look." Mark took his phone from his pocket and held it up. The sun reflected off its screen like a prized jewel. "You can call them from mine. Come on! There's a group of people back at the library. It's safer there than out here. It'd be best if you'd come along." He waved at Jon to cross the street.

Maybe Melissa, Hunter, Kat, and Skylar are in that group. He asked Mark if any of them were there.

"No, I'm sorry to say." He shook his head.

Jon looked back at Brandon's body and then to Officer Cherry's. He moved back up to the car to see Michael still asleep inside. "What do we do about him?" Jon said, pointing. Mark walked over to the opposite side of the cruiser and peered in with his hands on the window.

"Is he dead? The door's locked. Did you knock?" Mark asked, still peering in.

"I knocked, and he didn't move at all. He's alive, see? He's breathing."

"You're right, I can see his chest moving. Is he a friend of yours?"

"No, not mine. His name's Michael. He attacked my-well, it's a long story. The cop," Jon pointed back at Officer Cherry's body, "had to handcuff him. He was mental. My roommate got killed by a swarm of them." Jon became visually upset as he tried to explain the horrendous night.

"I'm sorry, man." Mark took a deep breath. "I was here last night in that crowd when all this shit went down." Mark nodded over to the pile of bodies past Officer Cherry's body behind Jon. "But we have to go. I can explain more once we're inside."

"I just don't want any trouble alright? Please…"

"Hey, I don't either. No trouble at all. We just gotta move. Are you with me or not?"

Jon took a breath and looked back at his dead roommate and then at Officer Cherry. "Yeah, let's go. We can leave Mike in there. I don't know what he'll do if he wakes up."

"Me either."

ELEVEN

The Library

Mark and Jon hustled through the vacant campus grounds of White Haven College. The morning was silent as they walked on the white concrete paths that connected all the buildings together.

It was like stepping into a different time as they walked further away from the scene of countless bodies piled and thrown around in the dorm area. Usually, at this time, students would be getting up and heading out all over campus, hanging out, studying. Not today. Maybe not ever again. There might as well had been a tumbleweed blowing across the ground. No one in sight.

If you were standing in the center of where they were and looked to the north, you'd see the main building: Lecture Hall. That's where most of the classes took place in a large, rectangular structure with windows wrapping around it. If not there, you'd have classes either at the Science and Technology Building which was east, across from the library, smaller in size. Or you might have classes in the Activities and Cultures Building, which was almost as large as Lecture Hall, behind you. All of the buildings surrounded the square which had nice patches of grass and shrubbery that trimmed the walkways. Green, metal benches sat in the grass along the paths.

One of the double doors to the library, which had a splatter of blood on it, opened upon their arrival. A tall, thin man with a scruffy dark-blonde beard and a John Deere hat held the door as Mark and Jon ran in. He shut the door, clicked the push bar in, and used a small, brass key in a hole on the bar. *CLANK CLICK.*

"We got another one!" the scruffy man yelled out with a slight country accent. He sounded the way he looked.

The library should have been filled with students at this time. Students taking up the square tables and computer desks, anxiously studying and writing papers. Comparing notes. Asking to proofread paragraphs. Someone would be in the bathroom throwing up from an all-night booze bender. But this morning it was just six people,

Jon included, lingering around the library help desk that was front and center guarding rows of bookshelves.

A girl with a nose ring and a blue streak in her black hair sat on top of the help desk with her legs dangling off the front. She was wearing a tie-dyed shirt and ripped jeans. Two guys were sitting behind the help desk on swivel chairs. One with glasses who kind of looked like Jon and the other a tall, Black guy wearing the same athletic attire Brandon would wear. *He knows Brandon,* Jon thought. They all looked like they hadn't slept a wink.

"This is Jon. He was over by that cop car," Mark said to the group. Jon waved to the group. They waved back.

"Is he. . .," the girl sitting on the front desk said, looking at the bloodstains on Jon's face and shirt, ". . . stable? Mentally stable I mean?"

"Yeah, I'm alright, I'm not looking to fight like everyone was last night," Jon said, answering for himself. "Are you guys alright? Do you know what's going on?" Jon asked the question with his arms out. Sort of how Professor Weiss would put his arms out when he asked the class a question.

"Come around here and take a look," the Jon look-a-like said from behind the desk.

Jon walked around the side of the help desk and leaned down at the computer monitor. They had CNN streaming on the internet. BREAKING NEWS was on the bottom banner of the screen in red text with MASSIVE RIOTING AND CASUALTIES ACROSS THE COUNTRY underneath. The blond-haired news anchorwoman was in the studio, speaking with a split-screen of images and video being played next to her depicting bodies lying throughout cities. New York. Los Angeles. Atlanta. Houston. All piled up and thrown about, just like at White Haven College. Some looked like they were breathing. Some dead. Their faces blurred out. Videos showed people running and being chased down streets at night. Neighborhoods were on fire. Cars were colliding on highways.

"Could you turn it up please?" Jon said. The look-a-like turned the dial up on the speaker.

". . . we are getting reports sent to us from all over the country of these incidents that took place last night," the anchorwoman said. "As you can see, we have unsettling footage coming from social media. Please keep in mind that viewer discretion is advised. If you have any children nearby, please make sure they are away from your screen as this is very graphic content. We're now going to David Bernard who is out in the Los Angeles area where some rioting is still taking place. He has more breaking news for us. Let's go there now."

"Oh man," the Black guy sitting beside Jon's look-a-like said. Mark and the country bumpkin came around the desk to watch.

The camera cut to a dark-skied Los Angeles. Being three hours behind, the time in the corner read 4:30 A.M.

A helicopter shot showed a highway of mayhem lit only by the orange light poles above and flames of a jumbo jet that crash-landed into the middle of it. Luggage bags and bodies sprawled out among the rubble and bits of the wings lay across every lane. Nearby cars were completely obliterated.

Surrounding the plane were more cars. Scattered, crashed and torn apart. Bodies lay lifeless half outside of the shattered windshields. Blood was painted on the concrete ground. An overturned car was on fire with smoke billowing out of it.

The screen split again to show the newsman, David Bernard, shaking and standing with the highway behind him in the distance. The helicopter footage remained rolling on the right side of the screen.

"Sandra, we're here just outside of Los Angeles where a major catastrophe has hit. As you can see from the helicopter camera, a United Airways jet has crash-landed onto the 405. We are not positive if this is an act of terrorism at this point. And, Sandra, it looks like there aren't any survivors."

The girl with a blue streak in her hair still sat on the help desk, head facing the entrance. She didn't seem interested.

David continued. "This occurred in the middle of what appears to be city-wide rioting. People were reported to be driving recklessly, starting fights with everyone and anyone. We also have a lot of reports of this going on all over California, this is not just affecting Los Angeles. And I'm sorry to say I've also been getting reports that children are being attacked. It appears the attacks aren't on any specific targets. It's a free for all. Now we have the tragedy of a plane crash on top of it all."

The helicopter shot zoomed in on a woman getting out of her car that had just been rear-ended a few feet before the scene of the plane crash. She hopped out of the driver seat and was running toward the vehicle that struck hers. Bullets began to fly out of the car's windows into her head and upper body. Blood spurted out of her. The whole split-screen cut to black. Then anchorwoman Sandra Smith was back on the screen.

"We apologize for that," Sandra said. Her mouth was agape until she made herself look more professional. "We had to cut David's feed because it was getting too graphic to show what was going on just then. We'd like to tell our viewers again that this is graphic material we are showing and since it's live, we can't always cutaway in time. We truly apologize. As David said, we are still uncertain of the origin of these attacks but will keep you updated with any information that we receive. We ask our viewers to continue to send us their information through social media with photos and videos as long as they are at a safe enough distance to do so. . . ."

"Jesus," Jon said. "So, they haven't mentioned what caused this? Other than the possibility of terrorism?"

Jon's look-a-like nodded his head and remained staring at the screen. "That's right. But this doesn't look like terrorism to me. Well, maybe the plane crash. I don't know. Those people on the streets and on the highway seem like regular everyday folks."

The country boy chimed in, "Yeah Kev, I didn't see any of the terrorist-kind on those videos. Y'know, people from the Middle East and such. I wouldn't be surprised if they at least crashed that plane though, just sayin'."

Jon's look-a-like, now revealed as Kev, nodded his head again. His eyes remained on the news. "Why would this happen all at once? Maybe a terrorist EMP? Although it seems New York is already finished."

Kev was right. The split-screen now showed New York City on the left and Los Angeles on the right. New York was covered in bodies, but the carnage seemed to have ended as the emergency responders tried to treat everyone that lie on the ground. Some were unconscious and breathing. Much like Michael, who was sound asleep in the back of Officer Cherry's cruiser.

Meanwhile, Los Angeles was still shrouded in darkness with the blood still flying and death raining down from the sky.

"Have you guys called 911?" Jon asked.

"We all have. Multiple times. All we get is an automatic message saying there is a massive intake of calls," Kevin replied.

Then, Mark spoke. "Yeah," he leaned closer to the screen, "just like last night. It all happened so quickly. One thing after another and now it seems to be over. For now, that is."

"You think anything's gonna happen again?" the country boy said.

"I hope not. I'm headed back to Philly. Fuck this shit," the Black guy said, looking like he was ready to get up from his swivel chair.

"I wouldn't go just yet," the blue-streaked girl said. Her head didn't move. It hung still, aimed at the entrance doors. The Black guy remained sitting. His eyes rolled.

"Emily's right, Shawn," Mark said to him. "None of us are leaving campus until we know what's going on out there. Honestly, I didn't even want to leave the library, but I figured Jon here seemed normal." He put his hand on Jon's shoulder. "I didn't want someone out there alone that seemed to have his shit together. Who knows what could've happened to him?"

"Whatever man," Shawn said, still sitting in his chair. "All I know is my cousin said the city is fucked up just like New York and LA and my mom's ain't pickin' up her phone. Man, I used to get my ass whooped if I didn't pick up the phone after like three calls. I tried like a hundred times by now. If she doesn't pick after another hundred, I'm headin' back to Philly I don't care what ya'll say, man. This is some twisted shit."

That reminded Jon about his own mom. His parents.

"Hey Mark, you said I could use your phone?" Jon asked, looking over to him with wide, watery eyes.

"Oh yes, of course. Sorry about that, it must have slipped my mind there," Mark said, digging the phone from his pocket and entering his passcode to unlock it. He handed it to Jon. Mark's hands trembled.

"Thanks, I'm gonna try to call my parents. Give me a minute, I'll be right over there." Jon motioned over to the rows of bookshelves.

Mark nodded and turned his eyes back to the computer screen with the rest of them. Emily remained where she had been on top of the desk.

Jon knew his parents' landline by heart. They had the number as long as he could remember. The dialing noise played after he tapped in the digits. *C'mon.*

Dialing. Dialing. Dialing.

Please pick up.

Dialing. Dialing. Dialing.

Then, Jon heard his mother's voice. His heart rolled over in his chest.

You've reached the Barnes' residence. We're unable to pick up the phone right now so please leave us a message after the beep, thank you!

Ugh.

BEEP.

"Hey, it's Jon. I hope you guys are alright. PLEASE call me as soon as you get this. I'm safe at the campus library with a few others. I'm using a guy named Mark's phone. I don't know if you've looked at the news at all but there's a lot of stuff happening here and all over the place. Brandon's dead." Jon now spoke sounding as if he was out of breath, trying to get everything out. "I will have to tell you more about it when I get to talk to you. I'm going to call both of your cell phones too, okay? PLEASE call this number. It's Mark's phone. I'm gonna try to get my cell phone back from my dorm, okay? I love you. Okay, call me as soon as you get this!"

Jon tapped the red button on the phone's screen to hang-up. He was about to dial both of his parents' cell phones until he realized that both of them recently changed carriers, which gave them new numbers. Jon didn't have them memorized yet, he only had them on his phone which was laying beside his laptop that had an unfinished paper on B.F. Skinner. He almost laughed to himself remembering the paper that would be due in just a few hours. *That paper isn't going to be turned in anytime soon. Professor Weiss will probably give us an extension.* He chuckled and then frowned as the horrid realization came rushing into his mind. *Professor Weiss is probably dead.*

Jon stood for a moment in the middle of the forest of books, looking at the ground in fear and uncertainty until Mark came over.

"You get a hold of anybody?" Mark asked.

"No. Just got their voice mail. They'll call your phone if they get my message," Jon said, handing the phone back over to Mark. Now his hands trembled too. "Thanks for letting me use it, man. I gotta get mine from my dorm. It has my mom and dad's cell phone numbers on it. I don't have them memorized."

"I'm not sure how safe it is out there yet. There's still all kinds of shit going down in Los Angeles." Mark pointed his thumb behind him.

Jon sighed.

Mark could see the disappointment in Jon's face and thought how scary and depressing the whole shit show was.

"Alright maybe you, me, and Dan can go," Mark said, hoping to raise Jon's spirits. "If we all decide it's safe that is…"

"Is he the dude in the John Deere hat?" Jon asked, whispering.

"Oh yeah, that's him. I'm sorry. I guess you weren't introduced to them during all this mess," Mark said and turned to point at each of them. "That chick that's been sitting on the desk with the colored hair is Emily. The Black guy from Philly in the shorts is Shawn. Kevin is the guy behind the computer. He actually got us into the library. I guess he's an assistant to the librarians or something like that. And Dan Snyder there is a friend of mine who I had a few classes with. He always wears that hat by the way." Mark laughed a little looking at it.

"And you were in that crowd last night you said?" Jon asked.

"Yep." Mark turned back to Jon and took a breath. "In fact, we all were. I wasn't standing by any of these guys though. We all sort of just ran this way. As soon as that first shot went off, we fled toward the library. If it wasn't for Kevin and his key to the door, we would've been fucked. No doubt. Did you notice that big bloodstain on the door when we came in?"

Jon nodded.

"There was some dude chasing us the whole time from that crowd and was about to grab Shawn until we got in and his head slammed right into the door. Headfirst. Then he started pounding the door, smearing it all around. He even tried the handle. I don't know if you saw that had blood on it too. Dan and I held that door bar as tight as we could. Then Kevin used that key again to lock it. Kevin's really the one who saved our lives."

"Wow." Jon didn't know what to say. His mind was still on his parents.

"It's a miracle. Then we stayed put here. We could still see the area you were standing at through the windows of the doors. It was horrible. But it was like a train wreck, we couldn't look away. I think it shook Emily up, that's why she's been sitting like that. She's been that way for a little while now."

Jon looked over at her and she was still, in fact, sitting that way.

Mark continued. "None of us have slept at all. We figured if someone was tired, they could go upstairs and sleep while someone was downstairs and watched the door. I think Emily gave that position to herself, although I'm not sure she'd move even *if* someone came through." Marked looked down at Jon's blood-stained shirt. "What's your story?"

Jon told the tale of his night. The little get together at Melissa's place. The noises coming from upstairs. Michael and Kat's tantrums. Officer Cherry coming in and handcuffing him. The big brawl outside. The death. Running from an Indian man in pajama pants. Then, running from an even more psychotic man. The scissors. Hiding in Melissa's dorm room. All of it. Jon could remember every little detail from last night as the mental wounds were still fresh.

"You're lucky to be alive," Mark said. "I'm not sure about your friends but if they're not out there in that giant heap of bodies, they might be alive somewhere. There's no way they could've outrun those people for too long. They might be in hiding. Maybe they even somehow got to their cars and left."

"Yeah," Jon said, looking down and nodding his head. He was so worried, so confused. Mark could pick up on that.

"C'mon. Let's go see what's going on in the news. Maybe we can do something soon about getting your phone from your dorm so you can try reaching your parents again," Mark said and patted Jon's shoulder.

The two of them walked back to the group. Kevin, Shawn, and Dan were still watching the news coverage while Emily stayed where she'd always been. Staring. The split-screen of the reporters and carnage remained on the broadcast.

"Any updates?" Mark asked.

"Not really," Kevin said. "More footage of Los Angeles. People crying on the phone, looking for their families."

"Scary shit," Shawn said, chiming in. "Like a horror movie."

"You get a hold of your folks, Jon?" Dan asked.

Jon shook his head as his eyes looked saddened. "No, I just got their voicemail."

"Kev, you think it's safe enough to go back outside?" Mark asked.

"Doesn't look like it. We are better off waiting it out until we can get an answer on what caused all this. Maybe wait for the police."

"I don't think the police are coming," Emily said.

"What makes you say that?" Shawn asked with his eyes bugging, shocked at the statement.

"I saw what they did to our campus officer last night. We all did. And if he couldn't defend himself around a bunch of college kids, imagine what the other cops had to deal with." Emily then turned her head back to the group with her pale, tired face. "Whatever the fuck is going on isn't a joke."

"That's a good point," Mark said with his hands on his hips. "But we can't stay here forever. At least not another night."

"Are we supposed to wait to be rescued by somebody?" Dan asked while he rubbed his scruff.

"I don't know if we can count on that," Kevin said while pulling his phone out and checking to see if anyone had called or texted. No one had.

"Well, we have to do something. What if we went out as a group? Do any of you wanna come with us? It'd be safer to have more people. Dan, what do you think?" Mark asked.

"Hey man, if ya'll are leaving then I'm leaving," Shawn said, standing up from his chair, phone in hand and ready to go.

"Hold on Shawn. We aren't leaving campus. We're just going to the dorms. I don't think it's a good time to go just yet. We should just go out and see exactly what we're dealing with. Emily's right. This isn't a time to mess around without a plan." Mark looked over toward her. She turned her head back toward the door and nodded in agreement.

"So, we're goin' out there to get Jonny's phone? That's it? How-sabout to look for other people that survived from last night?" Dan said, scratching his matted, dirty-blonde hair under his John Deere cap.

"Of course, we aren't just getting his phone. We can all get our belongings. We can see who else is out there but it's probably not best to take our time with it," Mark said to Dan. "If you come with us, you can look to see who's around. Okay? Just make sure you follow close to us. Same goes for you Shawn if you wanna come."

Dan fixed his cap and nodded.

Shawn sighed and said, "Aight then, let's go."

"Kevin and Emily, do you guys wanna come along or stay back?" Mark asked.

"Yeah, I'm not going out there unless I absolutely have to," Emily said, pulling out her pink phone from her back pocket.

"Yup. Agreed," Kevin said, not looking away from the news.

"Alright, three of us have our phones. Call if anyone comes by but do not leave the library, okay? Kev will you lock us out?"

"Sure thing." Kevin sprung up from his chair and followed Mark, Jon, Dan, and Shawn to the front door of the library. Dan turned around and handed him the key from his pocket.

Emily said, "We should have a special knocking code. You know, in case anything may happen to you guys. We should know that you're not mental patients trying to get back in. We don't know if this is some traveling virus or contagious brain disease. I don't want you in here with us."

"You're right," Mark said. He looked at the other three guys and put his fist up against the windowed entrance door. The bloodstain was on the other side of his hand. "How about we use a code like *Knock Knock Knock KNOCK KNOCK?"*

Everyone nodded their heads in agreement.

"And if we find any other ladies or gents out there that want in, we will tell 'em to do that code. The special knock," Dan said, repeating that knock on the door beside it.

"You sure you guys wanna do this? Shouldn't you each take a weapon or something?" Kevin asked them. That reminded Jon of his scissors which he forgot he placed in his back pocket.

"I have this," Jon said, pulling the scissors out like he was unsheathing a sword from his jeans. They all laughed a little, even Emily.

"Great idea," Dan said. "We should all have a pair of scissors with us!"

Emily turned around and began looking around the help desk. This was the first she had changed her position on her post. She looked down by the computer monitor, then hopped around on top of the opposite side of the desk. "Here," she said and pulled two sturdy-looking scissors from a black metal cup. "I've got two weapons right here." Dan and Shawn grabbed them from her.

"Thanks, Emily, we appreciate it, sweetheart," Dan said in a charming southern voice. He tipped his John Deere cap and winked.

"I'll stick with Jon and use his scissors if anything goes down," Mark said. "Kevin, you ready? On the count of three. We will go out the door and you close it and lock it as fast as you can. Ready?"

Kevin nodded, but his face read uncertainty at the plan. He kept his mouth shut. The library group had been arguing all morning about the situation and Kevin held the philosophy that whatever these folks wanted to say or do was their business. He didn't want to get in the way. He'd only help where he could.

"And don't forget the code alright?" Mark did the knocking on the window again. Kevin was beside the door now, ready.

Mark was in front. "One. Two. THREE!" The door swung open and the four guys ran out of the library onto the barren White Haven campus. Kevin slammed the door shut behind them. They heard the *CLICK CLANK* of the lock.

TWELVE

The Dorm Just Across Hell

The morning sun still shone its warm rays down on the silent campus. There was no trace of anyone traveling along the walkways towards the library or any of the other surrounding buildings.

They traveled with Mark and Jon in the front and Dan and Shawn in the back. Soon it would be just Dan in the back as Shawn began making a break for it toward the parking lot behind the library.

"No! No! Shawn, what the hell are ya doin'?" Dan said while trying to grab Shawn's shirt. No success. Mark and Jon turned around to see Shawn sprinting like a mad man down the pathway beside the library. Scissors in-hand.

"Hey! Shawn! Wait!" Mark shouted at him. He got no response. Shawn was running full force toward the cars as his life depended on it, which it did. How much longer could he be cooped-up on campus? That was the question that the other three thought to themselves as they stood there, not daring to go after him. There was no reason to run and try to stop him. Shawn already made up his mind and if he wanted to, he could kick all three of their asses if they got in his way.

"I guess that's it then," Dan said, scratching his head under his hat before re-adjusting it.

Shawn's head was now bouncing up and down as he raced through the rows of cars. Then, he vanished. The sound of a car's engine blared out through the morning air. A silver Volkswagen skidded out from one of the rows and drove down to the roadway beside the parking lot, blowing right through the stop sign. Shawn didn't even glance back up at them as his car went out of sight behind the library building. *Vrooooom.*

"Nothing we can do about it, guys. Might as well keep going. A man's gotta make his own decisions and Shawn clearly made his," Mark said, turning around from looking at the lot. The sound of the car's engine faded in the distance.

"You think he'll make it? Back to Philly, I mean?" Jon asked.

"Who the hell knows, man. The last place I wanna be is in a major city with all this shit goin' on," Dan said. He sounded angry.

"C'mon," Mark said. He motioned to Jon and Dan, trying to get them moving again.

"I just can't believe he pulled one on us! Took our scissors and everything!" Dan said, adjusting his hat back on. He was always moving his big, green hat. Now, he and Jon were following behind Mark across campus as they continued their quest.

As the three of them approached the crosswalk toward the dorm buildings, Mark's phone made a *ding* noise. Jon's heart pounded as he thought it was his mom or dad calling back. "Is it them?" he asked, even before Mark could react to the noise and vibration of the phone. Mark pulled it out of his pocket.

"Oh sorry, that's my sister. She's been texting me updates from her place," Mark said. "I wish it had been your parents. I'm sure they'll call any second. I'm sorry."

"So, your family's alright then?" Jon asked, trying not to act upset it wasn't a call for him.

"My sister, yes. The rest of my family, I'm not sure. I couldn't get a hold of anyone else. My sister's safe at her apartment in Maryland. She couldn't get a hold of anyone either." Mark squinted at his phone. The sun's glare made it hard for him to read it. "She says she hasn't heard from her roommate at all. She's been gone for the past day. The news is getting her upset thinking about mom and dad. Every call has gone to voice mail."

"That ain't good," Dan said.

"Are you from the area, Jon?" Mark asked, typing a message back to his sister and then returning the phone to his pocket.

"Sort of, I live about an hour away in Springsdale."

"Really? Springsdale? Interesting. I've definitely heard the name before, but I can't say that I've ever been," Mark said. "My parents live in Camp Valley, have you ever heard of it?"

Jon nodded his head with heightened interest. "I have! That's where my grandparents on my dad's side live. Outside of town. That's about half an hour from me."

"That's not too bad of a trip."

"Yeah, it's a small town off the turnpike. Typical suburbia, nothing special," Jon said. "Camp Valley is almost the entire opposite.

Although it has that building with the big red and blue race car on top of it. Slick Willy's."

Mark blew air from his nose; the same way Jon does when he wants to laugh but can't. "Yep, that's right! Slick Willy's Wings. That's pretty much how anyone remembers Camp Valley. They usually come for Willy's and then go home." He blew air again. "Dan, did you get a hold of anyone?"

What Dan pulled from his pocket seemed like an ancient artifact to Jon. It was a flip phone.

Dan flipped it open and then slapped it down in an instant. "Nothin' man." He opened his pocket and threw it down inside. "Yeah, I'm from a little place called Wells Mountain. That's about an hour away from here too but in the opposite direction. More East. I called my dad. He didn't pick up. I figured at least I'd get my stepmom, but she didn't pick up either. My brother doesn't have a phone. Sonofabitch never did. Can you believe that? Then again, these things aren't that useful anyhow."

Jon was still mesmerized by the site of Dan's phone that resembled the kind his grandparents used. A small flip phone with gigantic, numbered buttons that made it easy for senior citizens with poor vision to easily make a call. *Does Dan have poor vision? Was Dan poor? Or does Dan just not give a shit about smartphone technology?* Jon was going to make a joke about Dan's piece of history but figured now wouldn't be the best time. His mind returned to his mom and dad.

They were approaching Officer Cherry's cruiser and the ambulance. The lights were still flashing on both vehicles. He then remembered Michael and got in front of the group to get to the backseat window. He peered in. Michael was still fast asleep. His chest rose and fell just as it did before.

"Someone in there?" Dan asked as he stepped up next to Jon to peer in the window. "Holy hell, he's alive and breathin'!"

Dan put his hand down on the door handle and gave it a jiggle. He went to knock but Mark came up from behind and slapped his fist away. "I wouldn't do that. That guy tried to kill Jon's buddies last night," he said.

Jon nodded. "Yeah, he went ballistic on us. Took a bite out of a guy's hand and-"

"Oh shit, issat right? I'm sorry. I didn't know. I thought he was just havin' a snooze," Dan said with genuine surprise.

They kept moving across the crosswalk and Dan was asking Jon more questions about what happened overnight, but the site of Brandon's body kept him quiet. Officer Cherry's corpse didn't help either. There was nothing Jon could say. The bodies said it all.

There seemed to be a scent in the air as they got closer to the larger pile of bodies in the quad. It was a metallic smell. All of the splattered blood on the scattered bodies gave off an aroma that got harsher as the group got closer.

"Fuck me, I didn't know it got this bad," Dan said. He pulled his shirt collar up over his nose and mouth. His eyes got larger as he took in the scene. "Sheesh."

"Jesus," Mark said in a soft breath. His eyes gaped with the sight of death multiplied.

The three of them walked on the asphalt path, trying to look away. But the morbid intensity had its grip on them, making their eyes widen and hearts pound. Their stomachs began to churn. The three of them moved along as Jon turned away and focused on the dorm building in front of him.

"I'm right up here at Washington House in room 207," Jon said, trying to ignore the pyramids of the deceased. He breathed slowly out of his nose, anything to prevent taking a big whiff of the metallic air.

"Hey, I think I see some of them breathin'! Look there!" Dan pointed out two bodies lying on the edge of the grass. A girl in sweatpants with her hair tied and a guy wearing a flat-brimmed hat lay with their chests rising and falling. Just like Michael. "You see that? We oughta check on them or somethin'. Any of them try to attack you guys last night?"

"Can we please get my phone before we check on anyone? Please?" Jon was getting upset. He still refused to turn his head to the bodies. His eyes locked on to the Washington Building. He tried not to inhale through his nostrils.

"Sure, let's get your phone. Dan, I think we should wait. You don't know if you'll get sick or something from these people. You already look like you're gonna vomit," Mark said as he plugged his nose after a strong whiff himself.

Jon ran up the steps to the second floor of Washington House while Mark and Dan followed with their noses still covered. Their eyes were fixed on the bodies as they each pointed out more people that appeared to be sleeping. Jon pulled out the keys from his pocket that hung on a black and white lanyard. The lanyard that Brandon always wore around his neck. Now Brandon was dead.

He opened the door slowly after he unlocked it. Even though the door appeared to have been locked all night, Jon still had to be careful. The scissors came out from his back pocket. *There could be a maniac in here waiting for me.*

Click. Jon turned on the lights. The dorm looked the same as it did the night before. The living area appeared well kept except for a couple of pieces of paper and pens on the coffee table and the kitchen counter had a box of granola bars sitting on it with the top opened. Nothing seemed out of place as Jon scanned the area while walking back into the hallway.

His heart skipped a beat and he clenched the scissors as he noticed a light shining onto the open door to his bedroom. He approached, ready for an attack until he peered inside.

It was just the desk lamp. Since Brandon convinced Jon that they would only be an hour at Melissa's place last night, he didn't think to turn it off. *Click.* He turned on the overhead lights to show his unmade bed and cluttered desk. The phone was still plugged into the side of his laptop. He yanked it from the charging cable, almost pulling the entire computer off his desk with the motion.

The lock screen on his phone displayed NEW VOICEMAIL. 2 MISSED CALLS below it. Jon entered his passcode and dialed his home phone. His mother's voice mail message played again but he didn't leave a message this time. He opened his contacts list until he found DAD and called his new cell phone number. It rang and rang until he heard a robot woman's voice.

I'm sorry, but the person you're trying to call has a voice mailbox that has not been set up yet. Please hang up and try again. Goodbye.

Jon went back and scrolled down his contact list until he found MOM. He now tried her cell.

Hi, you've reached Catherine Barnes. I'm sorry I missed your call but if you leave your name and message, I will get back to you. Thank you!

"Mom! It's Jon! Dad didn't pick up his phone, I hope he's with you. Please call me as soon as you get this. I am okay! I haven't been injured or anything. Brandon's dead, Mom. A lot of people are dead. I left a message on the home phone." Jon was getting out of breath again as he spoke into the phone with his hands running through his sweaty hair. "Please, PLEASE call my cell. I love you."

Jon pressed back to the home screen and pressed on the phone icon that had a little red-colored number 2 on the corner. One missed call from his home phone, the other from his father's cell.

There was a voice mail from him from 11:03 the night before. He pressed the play icon.

Son, this is your father. I know we're calling you late, but your mother and I are going over to your grandparent's house. Grandma's been acting up, must be sick. Pappy said she'd been feeling ill and acting out. He called worried so we're just going to swing by to check on them, maybe bring them back to the house for the night. Just wanted to let you know. We will keep you posted. Call us when you get the chance, okay? I'll call you in the morning. Buh-bye.

Jon tried calling his father's phone again. No success. Then he tried calling his grandparent's house phone. All he got was their voice mail which consisted of them asking you to leave a message and then becoming confused on how to end the recording. He left a message like the ones he'd left before, asking them to please call his phone as soon as possible.

He tried to hold back the tears as he scrambled through his contacts list calling everyone he could. Friends. Cousins. His other grandparents in Pittsburgh. Nothing. Not one person picked up their phone.

Then the tears came. There was no stopping the pent-up emotion that Jon felt since he got out of the night from hell. In an instant, his eyes welled and spilled hot tears.

Mark and Dan stood in the doorway of Jon's room as he sat and wept on the edge of his bed. The world spun around him, making him dizzy in an overwhelming feeling of depression and hopelessness. A sad sickness.

THIRTEEN

Friday Night

Little Jon sat on the floor of his room, playing PlayStation late one Friday night. His room was lit only by the hue of his TV that reflected some shooting game off of his glasses.

Beside the TV, was a rack of DVDs and games. Darkened posters of his favorite bands and movies covered the walls. Behind him was a desk with a computer and scattered papers over the wooden surface. An unmade bed to his left. Various articles of clothing littered the carpeted floor. A dresser held different scented deodorants and body sprays on top of it. An empty hamper between it and the door. This was the room of a typical teenage boy.

He'd spent a lot of time in his room. Too much if you asked his father, but Little Jon liked his alone time. He felt safe in his room and all the stuff he needed was there. It was his room of solitude.

Knock. Knock. Knock.

Little Jon's mother opened the door a crack and stuck her head through. The light of the hallway behind her kept her face in a shadow.

"Don't stay up too late tonight, okay?" she said.

Little Jon paused the game and looked behind him at the digital clock on his desk. 10:21. Still early in his mind. Sometimes he'd play games or watch movies for hours and time would fly by without him knowing it. It's even worse when he'd have friends stay over. They'd stay awake until the birds were chirping the following morning. He could only get away with that in the summer though. If he did that on a regular weekend, he'd be toast.

"I know, I won't. It's Friday night anyway," he replied.

"I know but still," she said, smiling, "if you stay up all night tonight you'll screw up your sleeping schedule and I bet you won't like that when it's time to go back to school on Monday."

"Yeah, yeah."

"Don't worry. Before you know it, you'll be off for Thanksgiving break and you can play all the games you want all night long."

"Can't wait for that," Little Jon said, turning back to the TV to continue his gunplay.

"You want any light in here?" she asked.

"No thanks, I like it dark."

"I don't want you going blind."

"I'm alright. I never turn the light on."

"And you're sitting so close to the TV."

"It's a small TV! What do you want me to do?"

"Well maybe if you're lucky, Santa will bring you a bigger one for Christmas."

"I wish. Christmas seems so far away though."

"Hey!" she said, coming more into the room and turning on the light. Little Jon's eyes squinted, and he held his hand up to the fan-light on the ceiling.

"What are you doing? I said no lights!" he said.

"Look at this room! You have clothes everywhere, Jon!" She started to pick up the socks and shirts from the floor and tossing them into the hamper by the dresser.

"Mom, I'll take care of it this weekend! Please turn off my light!"

She laughed a little laugh and threw another sock into the hamper. "Ok, I'll see you tomorrow. Have a good night. Don't stay up late." She flicked off the lights and stepped into the hall, shutting the door behind her. "Your father must be working late tonight," she said, walking down the hall toward her room.

Little Jon sat in his darkened room, playing his game as the night grew longer around him.

FOURTEEN

A Helping Hand

It seemed like hours had passed before anyone said a word.

Mark was the first to speak after he took a deep breath. "I'm sorry, man."

Jon didn't reply. His hands were covering his face. It was quiet for another minute or two.

"Hey, they might be alright," Dan said. "Ya never know, they could be safe somewhere just without their phones is all."

Jon heard what Dan said but didn't pay it any mind. He was already convinced it was too late for his parents. The tears soaked his hands and his face was as red as a lobster.

"If they were still alive, they would've picked up or called back by now," Jon said into his hands.

"C'mon, Jon. That's not completely true," Mark said. "Dan's right. They could've got caught up somewhere and don't have access to a-"

"They're fucking dead!" Jon cried with fresh tears coming from his eyes. "My dad always has his phone clipped on him. He would've called. My mom would've. Grandpa and Grandma. Somebody would have! Why wouldn't any of them call this morning?"

Mark and Dan stood, making glances over at each other. What else could they say to Jon? After all, he had a strong case. His parents might as well be dead. Neither of them had made contact with their parents either. That fact made them feel like Jon for a moment. Hopeless.

"We can give you some time alone," Mark said. "Dan and I will head back down and see if any of those people are alive. Gather all the stuff you need and meet us outside whenever you're ready, alright?"

Jon didn't know if it was alright. He didn't know if *anything* was alright or ever would be again. But in the off chance that Dan was right, that his parents may still be alive somewhere without their phones, he had to find out.

Jon nodded, trying to compose himself.

"Then we can stop by Dan and I's room to get our stuff. Are you able to do that or do you want to go back to the library?" Mark asked.

"No, I'll come with you guys," Jon said, wiping his nose with his wrist.

"Ok. Take your time. We'll be right outside checking out the bodies," Mark said, leaving the dorm with Dan.

Jon heard the door close. He was alone. But he didn't feel alone like he did the night before. This time he felt it more than ever. It was as if he was the only person on campus. Maybe even in the world. Sitting on the edge of his bed with his wet and red face staring down at the carpeted floor, the waves of dread knocking him round and round.

***

Mark and Dan made their way back down the dorm building steps and out to the quad of bodies. That metallic blood scent returned, but they were less sickened by it. They were almost used to the smell by now.

The chests of the guy with the flat-brimmed hat and the girl with sweatpants still rose and fell as if they were fast asleep.

"They're breathin'," Dan said. He grabbed the wrist of the girl, then the guy. "And they gotta pulse alright."

"How about over here?" Mark asked, stepping over lifeless bodies and toward another girl wearing pants and a bra with no shirt that appeared to be breathing. He grabbed her wrist. "Her heart's beating. She's alive." Mark tried shaking her to see if she'd wake up. She didn't respond but kept a steady breath.

"You think they're in a coma or somethin'?" Dan pondered, looking up at Mark and noticing a few more breathing bodies. He also tried waking up the girl and the guy with no success.

"It sure seems like it." Mark looked around to see the other sleeping bodies that Dan noticed. "Only some are asleep. The rest look lifeless to me. Why do you think that is?"

"Not sure. Maybe those crazy ones only knocked some of them out. Didn't get a chance to kill them all in one swoop."

Mark nodded as if that was a reasonable explanation. "You think we even want to wake them up? You think these guys are hostile? Knocked out from someone trying to defend themselves?"

"Could be, no ways a tellin' just yet. Either way, I think we shouldn't bother with them. At least we know some are still breathin'. Might be better to have a professional take a look."

"You mean like them?" Mark nodded over to the scene of the two dead EMTs.

"Shit," Dan said, forgetting that they'd passed their bodies on the way over to the dorm buildings. "Yeah, I guess there won't be any professionals around here anytime soon huh?"

"Ah fuck!" Mark shouted.

"What? What is it?"

"Look, over there. It's another cop," Mark said, inching over toward an officer's body that lay underneath one of the light poles between two dead jocks. The navy uniform stood out.

"Holy hell. They got two cops in one night?" Dan said, making his way over.

"Shit man, I guess so." Mark had his hands on his head. He was stressed out.

The cop had a nice set of black hair that was now gelled with blood as he lay face down.

"He got his gun on him?" David asked.

"Yeah." Mark paused then said, "You think it's safe to pick up?"

"I don't see no blood on it. Go ahead."

"You do it."

"Alright then." Dan hunched over and used his fingers to pick up the officer's Glock 22 that lay propped up on his right shoulder. It spun as Dan eyed every inch to see if the gun was contaminated with anything that could drive him mad.

"Is it loaded?" Mark asked.

Click. Dan unloaded the magazine from the gun. No bullets inside. Not even one in the chamber.

"Dammit, it's spent," Dan said.

The sound of a door slamming shut made Mark and Dan stand up immediately. At first, they didn't know which direction the sound came from until they saw Jon walk down the outside steps of Washington House with his backpack on.

Jon looked different as he walked up to Mark and Dan. A clean, dark-grey T-shirt with HILLCREST HIGH SCHOOL written on it in white and red text replaced his blood-stained shirt. New blue jeans with his same Vans that had slight grass staining on the bottoms. His face looked washed from the splattered blood that once painted his face.

"How are you? Are you doing ok?" Mark asked as he and Dan approached.

"Yeah, I'm ok for now." Jon wasn't ok, but he composed himself for the time being. "But I think I'm gonna try to head back to my house in Springsdale. If my parents are alive then they must be there or at my grandparent's place in Camp Valley. I might stop there on the way." He still held the navy colored luggage bag by its handle. "I packed as much as I could. I think I should be fine getting back."

Mark and Dan understood as they nodded their heads in sync. They explained how there were bodies breathing among the dead but were unable to wake from their sleep. The empty Glock they found on the second officer made Jon step back for a second.

"What about Officer Cherry's gun?" Jon asked.

"Man, someone took his last night. Whoever has it might be in the pile somewhere, who knows. It would be like finding a needle in a haystack," Dan replied.

Jon sighed. "You're saying you couldn't get any rise out of them? Nothing would wake them up?"

"No, they're in a coma or some really deep sleep. It's strange," Mark said.

Jon took another glance at the bodies. His face was so sore from the stream of tears, he was almost numbed to the sight, unable to feel at the moment. "I guess there's nothing we can do then."

"You think there's an EMT manual in that ambulance?" Dan asked the guys. Neither Jon nor Mark replied to that.

"Are you guys planning on leaving?" Jon asked.

"Yeah. We are all probably going to be heading out at some point. Go our separate ways. You think you can stick around for a bit and help us get our stuff from our dorms though? We will have to help Kevin and Emily too. We don't all have our car keys. But if you don't want to stick around, we'd understand. At least you were here longer than Shawn was," Mark said with a smile that masked his disappointment in the runaway.

"That sonofabitch took our scissors! Didn't even apologize," Dan added.

If my parents are dead, then it wouldn't matter. If they're alive, I don't want to be wasting any more time. But these guys helped me. The least I could do is help them before I go.

"Sure," Jon replied.

"Thanks, man. Dan and I will get our belongings and we'll head back to the library then," Mark said.

"You guys should also take a quick shower too. It definitely helps," Jon said. "Gets all the blood off."

"We appreciate ya, Jon!" Dan said, smiling and squinting. "This whole thing is fucked up, but we're gonna get out of here and get you back home. We'll *all* get back home to find our families!"

The sun was shining higher in the sky.

FIFTEEN

Lunch

Knock Knock Knock KNOCK KNOCK.

Kevin used his library key to let Mark, Dan, and Jon back through the door. All three of them carried in backpacks filled with their clothing and items. Their bodies were re-clothed, faces washed.

"How did it go, guys? Anything out there?" Kevin asked. The door shut and locked behind them. *CLICK. CLANK.* Then, he realized Shawn wasn't with them. "What happened to Shawn?"

Dan let out a breath, still upset at what happened. "That dude ran off almost as soon as you let us out! Ran out to his car and sped off. Didn't bother going after him, we just kept goin'."

"Damn," Kevin said. "You think he made it?"

"Hell if I know!" Dan replied.

"We got as much as we could from our dorms. Most importantly, our keys," Mark said, putting down his backpack in front of the help desk. He stood up and *jangled* a key ring with a Pontiac remote before putting them back in his pocket. "We found a decent amount of people sleeping outside of the dorm buildings though."

"Like some of the ones in New York?" Kevin said, referencing the news footage from earlier of the emergency responders walking through the bodies in Time Square. The news played in the background.

"Exactly. They're alive. They have a pulse and everything, but they can't wake up. Dan and I tried. Have you guys seen anything at all while we were out there? Heard from your families?" Mark asked.

"Nope, nothing. We've just been keeping an eye on the news. The riots in LA seemed to die down. No word on how many bodies though. Did Jon get to call his parents?" Kevin said.

Jon kept his head down as he replied. "Yeah, I couldn't get a hold of them. I thi-"

"We can take you and Emily to your dorms," Mark said, interrupting Jon, stopping him from making himself upset. "It's safe as far as we know. You can get your things if you need them. Jon said he will stick around with us to help."

Jon's eyes went over to the analog clock on the wall by the bookshelves. 11:12 A.M. *Wow, time's moving quickly. I hope this doesn't take too long.* Then after that thought, *I shouldn't think this way.*

"Yeah, that would be great. We can go after we just have a little something to eat. Emily and I broke into the vending machine if you guys are hungry. We have the drink machine open too."

Mark, Dan, and Jon looked back beyond the help desk toward the hall where the bathrooms were. In front of it, Emily sat on the floor organizing bags of chips, candy bars, and plastic soda bottles beneath two shattered vending machines. One of the swivel desk chairs was beside it.

The group started heading over toward Emily and the snacks. Jon reached down and unzipped his backpack and took out the box of granola bars from his dorm. It was crammed into the bag so tightly, that the box looked flattened. "I also have these if anyone wants some."

"Thanks," Dan said, turning around to grab a bar. It crumbled coming out of the package, but Dan poured it into his mouth without out a problem.

"Take your pick boys," Emily said after taking a sip from a bottle of Pepsi. She moved her hands over the piles of Doritos and Lays chips. Hershey's chocolate products were in the mix. "We also have soda and water here. Just watch the glass, we don't want any more injuries." Emily seemed more energetic than she had been earlier that morning. Perhaps it was the sugary food and soda that gave her that pep.

Mark crouched down and picked up a bag of sour cream and onion chips and a bottle of water. "Thanks, Emily. Who broke the glass?"

Emily took another sip of Pepsi and almost burped her response. "I did! Kevin didn't want me too, but I was getting a headache."

Headache.

Jon had a headache that felt like it wrapped around his skull. The morning had been so upsetting that he'd forgotten that he hadn't eaten or drank in a while.

"Jon, did you call your parents?" Emily asked.

Of course, I called my parents! I called, and I called but no one picked up! Don't you understand!?

"I did but uh. . . no one answered." Jon didn't look her in the eyes when he said it. He kept his focus on the drinks, then got down by the shattered glass and picked up a bottle of Mountain Dew. A soda that always gave him the energy, aka sugar, to keep him going.

"Good thinkin' Jonny, I think I'm gonna have a Dew myself," Dan said, picking up a bottle, uncapping it, and washing down the crumbs from the granola bar. "Ahh, that's the stuff right there."

"If it makes you feel any better, my mom called me and said my dad never came back from drinking with his buddies last night," Emily said.

That doesn't make me feel any better.

"I'm sorry," Jon said and found enough strength to look back a little at her this time. She was attractive to him right then with her blue streaked hair that matched with the blue on her tie-dye top. Even the nose ring, which Jon was never a fan of, looked cute. "Where does your family live?"

"Up in place called East Gap. Waaaay up north. I actually came all the way here to get away from my dad." Emily almost smiled when she said that, but the current circumstances stopped it. This was no time to bring up daddy issues. "Where do your folks live?" she asked.

"Springsdale."

"Oh ok. I've never heard of that place. Is it far from here?"

"About an hour," Jon said. He didn't want to talk about it.

Everyone had their snacks and drinks and regrouped back at the help desk where Kevin watched the news and sipped his bottle of water. Now there was a brown-haired anchorwoman on the screen talking with those same images split screened beside her.

"It appears that the rioting has ceased at this moment," the woman said. "As you can see from our live footage, there are mass casualties not only in Los Angeles but also in other major cities around the country. There are also reports coming from Europe. We urge all of our American viewers to remain inside as we have yet to find a definite cause for all of this. We're not sure how this happened or if it's come to a permanent end so please stay with us as we bring you more information. The White House has released an official statement. . . "

"So still no answers huh?" Dan said as he failed to get a hold of his dad or stepmom on the phone. He slammed the flip phone's top down again.

"Nope. Nothing. I've been watching it all morning. I even switched between news stations and none of them seem to have a clue what's going on," Kevin said and took a big swig of water. "I think if we go to Emily and I's dorm rooms, we should either come back here and stay for the night or all try to drive. What do you guys think?"

Jon wanted to scream *LET'S GO HOME! LET'S ALL GO HOME AND FIND OUR FAMILIES!* The library was a prison and Jon was desperate to get out. But he kept his mouth shut and let the others speak instead. They each seemed level-headed enough and Jon needed to act the same.

"Do we know if the roads are safe?" Emily asked.

"Good question," Mark said. "When we head out again, we should head out of the parking lot and see what the road looks like. Shawn seemed to get out alright. I'd imagine it's gotta be safe on the main road for a little bit. Remember we heard his engine fade away? He might have been able to get on the turnpike at least."

"Yeah," Dan said, "and if it was blocked or somethin' he probably would have come back to us."

"I don't know. I saw some pictures of highways stopped. Cars backed up for miles on major roadways," Kevin said while he pulled out his iPhone. "Look at this." He had the Facebook app open now and it showed a picture posted from behind the wheel of a car stuck in stopped traffic. Bumper to bumper as far as the eye could see. "A guy I went to grade school with lives in Atlanta and this is right outside of the city, headed south."

"Holy smokes," Dan said as he ate at another crumbly granola bar.

Jon, Mark, and Emily all pulled out their phones and opened their own Facebook feeds to reveal similar posts. Dan was the odd one out as his flip phone had no features other than a calculator and a stopwatch. He sat and feasted on his snacks as the rest of them showed pictures and told the tales of their online friends. Traffic. Death. Fires. Blood. Bodies. It was all on display for social media and they each had a front-row seat.

"It can't be as bad as Atlanta or LA. I mean, this is central PA we're talking about. None of us are going to Philadelphia or Pittsburgh, right?" Emily asked. Her phone shook in her trembling hand. The graphic posts seemed to pull her back into her frightened phase.

"No, but Camp Valley doesn't look good either," Mark said, showing a photo someone posted of Slick Willy's Wings parking lot stained in red as bodies lay thrown on the asphalt.

They all took deep, sickening breaths.

"It's only gonna get worse, isn't it?" Emily said to herself with her eyes looking past her phone and into the void.

"Only if we stay here," Jon said. "The roads may be good enough to travel if we stay off the major highways and only use the back roads."

"If that's the case, then we should leave soon. Ya know, before the sun goes down," Kevin said with his eyes still on his phone with his finger swiping up on the screen. "It wouldn't be wise to be outside at night it seems. Based on the news and the pictures on here."

Perfect.

Jon finished his bag of Doritos and crumpled it up. He tossed it in the trash bin underneath the help desk. His fingertips were covered in orange dust. "I'll be right back guys. I'm gonna wash my hands."

The rest of the group stayed and talked about their plan to leave while Jon walked past the shattered vending machines toward the men's room. He pushed the door open. The scent of urinal cakes filled his nostrils as he stepped on the wet floor underneath the florescent lights. Three urinals lined the wall next to three tan-colored stalls.

Jon pushed the cold-water handle with the base of his palm. The water came out unevenly. He wet his hands and went to pump some soap from the wall-mounted dispenser but stopped as his eyes looked into the mirror. His heart stopped. Behind him in the farthest stall, the handicapped stall, he could see shoes beneath the metal door. A pair of jeans and underwear were pulled down around sneakers. Jon's mouth moved but words didn't come out at first. He froze with his hand still underneath the soap dispenser.

"He-he-hello?" he uttered.

No reply. Jon pumped the soap and finished washing his hands with his eyes fixated to the mirror, not looking away from the stall.

"Hello?" He said it louder now.

Still no reply.

"Are you ok in there? Hello?"

Jon turned off the water and pulled loads of paper towels out of the dispenser with his head turned almost all the way around at the stall. Like an owl. He knew he didn't want to, and the idea seemed disgusting, but he approached the door to the stall and peeked into the crack between the door and the stall wall.

It looked like a large-bellied guy had fallen asleep on the toilet. He was wearing a white polo shirt with red and green stripes on it and a blue ball cap on his head. His eyes were closed, and his mouth hung open. Jon could hear him breathing. Fast asleep. Just like Michael in the cruiser and the others by the dorm buildings. *Fast asleep or in a coma.*

Jon walked backward from the stall and left. He swung the bathroom door open and was fast walking back to the group, who all turned around at the sound of his quick steps.

"Everything come out okay?" Dan asked.

"There's a guy in one of the stalls. He's asleep on the toilet," Jon replied.

"Are you serious?" Mark looked puzzled for a moment, checking to see if Jon was messing with them.

"I am. You want to see for yourself?" A look of worry popped on everyone's face as Jon projected his fear onto them.

Mark and Dan both got up and ran by Jon toward the bathroom. Jon followed.

SIXTEEN

What Comes Next

"How do you think he got in there?" Emily asked. She was now speaking without that fun and pep in the step attitude. She held her knees against her chest as she sat on top of the help desk again.

"He must've been in there before we got in last night," Mark said.

"If that's the case, he must've been in there long before we showed up," Kevin proclaimed. "The library closes at ten o'clock. We weren't in here until after eleven, almost twelve I think. He was in that stall while this place was being closed down."

"Where was the janitor? Isn't he usually here at night? Wouldn't he have had made the rounds in the bathrooms and noticed him there?" Dan asked.

"Yeah," Kevin replied. "Maybe the janitor wasn't around yesterday. I don't remember seeing him."

Mark was shaking his head. "I can't believe it. I took a piss in that bathroom and I didn't even notice. No clue someone was in there."

"I wouldn't have noticed either, but I saw his feet in the corner of my eye when I looked in the mirror," Jon said. "If you were using the urinals you probably wouldn't have even guessed someone was there."

The group went quiet for a moment. All of them were thinking of what to do next.

"What if he wakes up?" Emily asked, breaking the silence. She was running her fingers through her hair right by the blue-dyed streak.

"Well." Mark sighed again. "We might have to lock him in there somehow. Keep the bathroom door shut so he can't get out."

"How we gonna do that?" Dan was scratching his matted hair again. Even though he showered, the John Deere hat made his hair look unkempt. "Does Kev have a key for that?"

Kevin shook his head. "The janitor has those sorts of keys. My keys only work for the regular doors."

"Shit," Mark said with gritted teeth.

"Sorry." Kevin shrugged his shoulders. "What can we do?"

The news kept on playing in the background. Those same images and video replays were being shown. The volume was down, almost to a mute. Mark looked at it and let out another sigh. He pitched his plan. "We better head outside now and see if it's clear to drive. Dan and I will run and check the road. The rest of you get Kevin and Emily's stuff and start bringing it back here. Then, if the road is cleared, we will call you so you can head straight to your cars and gun it out of here. What do you guys think? I don't think it'd be a good idea to be in here with that big boy in the stall much longer. Just another problem to worry about."

"Sounds good to me," Dan said.

"Wait," Kevin said. "We're just going to leave him here?"

"What else are we going to do? If the police or somebody eventually shows up, they'll find him," Emily said. "Besides, Mark and Dan said they couldn't get the other sleeping people outside to wake up, right? I'm not gonna touch the guy with his pants down. I'm not a doctor. He's not my responsibility or any of yours."

Emily's words met no argument. Not because they weren't empathetic, but because they came out of fear and exhaustion. There would be no use going back and forth. Besides, what *would* they do with him? The idea of waiting for him to wake up was not an attractive thought for anyone.

The rest of the group agreed with leaving the mysterious toilet man behind. They all began to get up from where they were, brushing off the chip and pretzel crumbs. Kevin took a final swig from his bottle of water. Mark, Dan, and Jon moved all their bags closer to the doors to the library, making it easier for them to grab when they came back.

Finally, time to go home.

SEVENTEEN

Workin' Late

The clock read 12:46 AM when the headlights of Big Jon's Ford Escape beamed up and made shadows streak on the poster of *Blade* in Little Jon's bedroom. Little Jon paused his game and peeked out the window. He glanced down to see the black Ford parked in the driveway beneath a spotlight of one of the many orange glowing streetlamps that lined the cul-de-sac. The engine was *humming*.

Little Jon squinted through his tired and video gamed eyes to see his father fetching something from the trunk. A large, plastic bag with a long, brown cardboard box hanging half outside of it. Little Jon tried to read the lettering on the bag, but Big Jon put it back into the trunk and took the entire box out before Little Jon could decipher it.

Big Jon shut the trunk of the Escape slowly so as to not wake the neighbors or their dogs. Holding the long box on his side, he walked up the little concrete pathway from the driveway to the porch.

With the video game paused, the Barnes' house was silent. That was until the faint *jingle* and *jangle* of keys came from the other side of the front door. There was nothing quite as familiar as the sound of his father's keys *jangling* as he bounced them in his palm looking for the right one. A brass key with a circular top, covered in a green, rubber protector.

Little Jon knew that when he heard that sound, his father was home and everything and everyone would be fine. Safe.

EIGHTEEN

A Good Snooze

The sky above began to turn grey as clouds formed over the blue. The sun shined down through the holes in the puffs above. It was hot outside.

Mark and Dan weren't even halfway to their cars before Mark started to get tired. His eyes became heavy like they had iron lids. It was taking more and more strength to keep them open as he and Dan ran on the asphalt roadway that Shawn's Volkswagen sped down only a few hours ago.

"When we get out there on the road, I'll drive east if you wanna to go west. That way we can get an idea of what our options are. It'll be quick, and if we're fast enough, we might have time to help the rest of the guys out," Dan said without looking over to Mark.

"Uh-huh. That works," Mark sluggishly said in response.

"You alright, man? Everything good?" Dan asked after noticing Mark's pace was slowing down. Dan was now a couple of feet ahead of him.

"Yeah, yeah. I'm good. I'm just a. . . I don't know. Maybe I didn't eat enough. Blood sugar must be low. . . or something. My energy's a little low. Just a little low." Mark tried to speed up his walking but found his knees getting weaker. His running was transitioning into sloppy motions. "Hold on. Hold on," he said, now sounding out of breath.

"You wanna sit down for a sec? You need some water?" Dan asked as he stopped running and turned back toward Mark.

"Yeah, let me just catch my breath. Hold on. Whew." Mark walked over to the concrete curb as if he were walking on two accordions. Sitting down the curb, he let out another exhausted breath and lay back on the warm grass.

"It *is* heatin' up out here. Maybe a storm's comin'. What did you eat? A bag of chips? I saw you drinkin' water," Dan said, removing his John Deere hat for a moment to move his hair around. He squinted at Mark, who nodded back to him.

"Just go ahead. I-I'll catch up," Mark uttered.

"If you wanna take a breather for a sec, we can get you back into the library. Maybe you wanna rest in my truck? I'll pull it right up for ya."

Mark nodded his head again in response. "Yeah go ahead. I will be right there." His eyes struggled to stay open. It wasn't the heat from the sun that popped its head through the clouds, but sudden exhaustion from within. Genuine tiredness. He wanted to lay back on the green grass behind the curb and close his eyes all the way for the moment. Just a moment. A second really. And that's what he did as Dan said something again to him. Mark couldn't make it out. It didn't sound like words. *Womp womp womp womp,* Dan said to him, just like the parents from the old Charlie Brown cartoons.

All Mark could see before he fell into sleep was the wavy vision of Dan running away from him, toward the rows of cars to fetch his pickup. The bright sun spun behind a cumulonimbus. It rotated around in the sky until the darkness of his eyelids covered the day with a heavy sheet of black.

The phone in Mark's pocket began to vibrate while it played a ringtone, a rhythm of *beeps* and *boops.* Dan's truck *revved* in the distance as Mark lay there, fast asleep with his back on the grassy hill behind the library. The heels of his flip flops were resting on the curb. He was unaffected by the feeling or sound of the phone coming from his shorts or the engine from the lot. The phone rang and buzzed for half a minute until it stopped. Mark's chest rose and fell under the bright and heat-filled sun. A cloud passed by the rays, casting a shadow on everything for a moment.

Dan pulled up by the curb behind the wheel of his green, 1999 Chevy pickup. It looked well taken care of even though it was two decades old. Unchipped and pristine green glistened in the last of the shiny sunlight before another cloud took over. You'd think this country boy would have a mud-splattered and dirt-stained truck, but it looked like it could've traveled in time from the 90s. Straight off the car lot and into the 21st century.

Bringing the truck up to the curb, Dan saw Mark was fast asleep. His body didn't stir when Dan's green machine pulled up with a country CD spilling out a song about girls and beer.

"Buddy, yalright?" Dan asked through the open window of the driver's side.

Mark could only respond with his sleeping silence.

Dan jumped out of the pickup and began poking and shaking Mark's body, failing to get any rise out of him. He put his head on his chest. *Thump thump. Thump thump.* There was a regular pulse on his wrist. He was alive.

"Mark, c'mon man. Wake up! We gotta get movin'!" Dan gave his friend a gentle slap on the face. It didn't stir him.

Dan drew a long breath and blew it out from his dried lips. He hunched over behind Mark and picked him up from under his armpits. Like a dead deer, Mark provided no help. Dan shuffled back and forth as Mark's body dangled from head to toe.

The flip flops on Mark's feet skidded on the asphalt as the blacktop stained his heels. Dan brought him around the truck and lifted with all his might to bring Mark's body onto the passenger seat. He was heavy, but Dan had wrestled with pigs and cows that were double Mark's size.

"There you go. Now let's get you strapped in," Dan said, patting Mark's chest. He pulled across the seatbelt and *clicked* it in the red latch.

***

The road seemed clear to the east as far he could tell, but the west was another story. When Dan drove in that direction, near the White Haven town itself, he found two cars crashed head-on into one another. Broken windows and splattered blood. He hopped out and peered inside. One car looked like it had a family of four inside. All dead. The other had a man and woman in the front seats. Also dead. A little further up he saw a cop car on the side of the road with its lights still on. No cop in sight.

The driver door to the cop car was unlocked. Dan looked around the seats in search of a gun. No luck. Then, he noticed the radio receiver was on the hook and powered on. *Click.* "Hello? Is anyone out there?" No response. *Click.* "Hello, hello? Anyone read me? Hello?" Nothing. Only the faint sound of static.

He didn't drive much further west as it would take him into the town that, from a distance, looked like it had more crashed cars and mayhem that took place from last night. Part of Dan's mind told him to see if there were any other living people in White Haven while the other part said to turn back now.

Thunder rolled in the distance.

If the east was clear, they could all make it onto the turnpike and have an easy route to their homes. Dan spun the truck's wheel around to head back toward the campus entrance where the sign stood wrapped in shrubbery.

Suddenly, a female voice cried out. "DAN! DAN!"

Then, a male voice. "DAN!"

It sounded like it was just up the path toward campus and, just as Dan started pushing his foot down deeper on the gas pedal toward the parking lot, Emily and Jon appeared from around the bend.

"Hey guys, the road is clear toward the east!" Dan yelled out as he eased off the gas and turned the black dial on the dash, bringing Luke Bryan to a mute.

Emily and Jon sprinted up to the window, both out of breath.

"Dan! Kevin's passed out!" Emily said, just before noticing Mark sitting in the passenger seat. Her eyebrows curled.

"What happened to Kev?" Dan asked.

"We were walking back to the dorms when he said he felt really tired and needed to stop. Then, he collapsed onto the ground by the crosswalk. Mark didn't pick up his phone. We thought you left us!" Emily explained between breaths. Her eyes were jumping from Dan to Mark.

"Shit!" Dan cursed as he gave his steering wheel a slap. "Mark was saying he was tired, too. I thought he'd just lay down for a sec on the curb there, but I had to drag him in the truck myself. You're sayin' the same happened to Kev? All a sudden lost his energy?"

They both nodded.

"Where is he?" Dan asked.

The thunder was approaching.

"By the ambulance on the crosswalk," Jon said.

"Alright, alright. I'm gonna pull up by the walkway to the library there. We gotta take Mark back to the library. Same with Kev. C'mon, let's go!"

Jon and Emily ran ahead as Dan followed. Mark didn't utter a word. Not even a snore as the truck stopped in front of the white, concrete path.

"Jon, can you grab his legs?" Dan requested. He *clicked* off the seatbelt, making it whip around Mark. Then, he placed tight grips on Mark's limp wrists. Jon held Mark's ankles as he stepped up on the truck's bar, waiting for Dan to slide him off the seat.

"Ready, Jonny?" Dan asked.

Jon nodded. His heart was going a mile a minute.

"Ok. One. Two. Three!"

Dan and Jon lifted Mark's body down from the seat. It was a little heavy for Jon, but Dan was strong enough to take most of the slack. *Let's make this quick.*

"You guys need any help?" Emily asked. Her eyes focused on Mark to see if he was waking up during any of this. He wasn't.

"No, thanks. We got 'em," Dan replied. "But howsabout you grab the baseball bat from the bed? It's in that box, just click the handles out."

Emily climbed up on the back of Dan's pickup. Inside the large titanium container was a toolbox, some pieces of 2x4, and a baseball bat with LOUISVILLE SLUGGER written in chipped and almost illegible black ink.

"Is the library door unlocked?" Dan asked.

"No," Jon said. "Kevin locked it."

"You get his key?" Dan asked.

"Oh, dammit! No. It's in his pocket," Emily answered, feeling dumb that she didn't think to grab it. She let out a breath and smacked the bat into the palm of her other hand. "When Kevin fell down, Jon and I panicked!"

"Ah, shit! Well, we will have to drop him off first and grab Kev then," Dan grunted.

They were now coming up the concrete path that connected the parking lot to the campus as small droplets of rain began their descent. Dan was walking backward with his grip on Mark's arms. Jon was keeping up the pace as best he could. Emily started sprinting up ahead of them. She headed for Kevin with the bat swinging around in her hand.

"Did you say the roads were clear?" Jon asked Dan between adjusting his grip.

"Yeah. We should be able to get to the turnpike at least. I didn't go too close to White Haven. Looked pretty much taken over. The whole place looks turned on its ass."

"I'm guessing you didn't see any other survivors?"

"No, I didn't. A couple of crashed cars though. People were all dead inside. Wasn't too pretty."

Dan and Jon walked up around the concrete path and were now standing in front of the library doors. The blood-stained glass and doorknob dried to an almost black color. They placed Mark's body on the ground. When they released their grips, his body slumped but remained breathing at its regular pattern. The two of them started toward Emily and where Kevin's body lay.

"What do you think happened to him?" Jon asked while wiping sweat from his forehead, using the bottom of his T-shirt. The cool water droplets from the sky felt nice.

"He said he just needed to sit down for a moment. Said he had some chips and water but that wouldn't make someone react that way. I mean he's out cold."

"Yeah, that's strange. Kevin didn't even respond to us. We asked if he was ok but before we knew it, he was face down in the road. He almost hit his head on the side of the ambulance."

Emily was digging into Kevin's pocket when Dan and Jon arrived at the crosswalk that connected the campus to the dorms. The lights on the police car and ambulance, which now seemed faded, still flashed underneath the clouded sky. Kevin was face-down on the asphalt with his head just a few inches away from the ambulance's tire. No one checked again, but Michael's body was still in the back of police cruiser.

"Alright, I got the keys. You sure I can't help lift him up?" Emily asked pointing with the bat, the keys clutched in her other hand.

"No thanks, we will be ok," Jon replied.

Before they picked him up, Dan rolled Kevin's body over. His glasses were smashed inward and there was blood coming from his nose. As he slept and breathed through his nose, more blood seeped out of his nostrils. Dan looked over by the tire to see that his nose bleed formed a small puddle of red.

"Ready, Jonny?" Dan said. "One. Two. Three!"

Kevin's body was limp. Like Mark, he was breathing and not reacting to anything they did. The body seemed lighter to Jon because Mark had more muscle on him, and Kevin matched Jon's slim physique. *Weird. It's like I'm carrying myself. Kevin looks like my long-lost twin brother.*

Emily led the way as Jon and Dan took Kevin's body back to the library.

"This shit's gettin' worse by the second, huh?" Dan said. "You think we're gonna pass out next?"

Jon didn't know, but the thought of going down wasn't helping his crazy anxiety.

The rain now fell steadily as thunder *cracked* over the air.

NINETEEN

A Late Night Surprise

"Don't tell your mother about this, okay? Let me be the one to bring it up to her. If she finds out how much I paid for this, my ass is grass. Got it?" Big Jon whispered.

Little Jon nodded.

It was almost one o'clock in the morning. Little Jon was still in his T-shirt and jeans that he wore to school and Big Jon was in his khaki slacks and dress shirt with his health insurance company's logo above the front pocket. Blue and red swirls around GUIDING LIGHT INSURANCE.

They were both standing underneath a white chandelier that dangled over the dining table outside of the kitchen. The long cardboard box sat in the center. It read REMINGTON in black lettering on top. Packaging tape covered every side.

Big Jon began to cut into the tape using a knife he got from one of the kitchen drawers. He sliced straight lines along the middle of each piece. He cut right through to the folds of the cardboard case. When he finished, he placed his fingers on the sides of the box and brought them up so it would open nice and clean.

"You wanna open it?" Big Jon whispered while nudging Little Jon with his elbow.

"Sure," Little Jon replied. He placed his fingers on the sides and lifted the cardboard top.

TWENTY

Back at the Library

Mark and Kevin's bodies lay behind the help desk. Emily propped backpacks behind their heads to keep them elevated and took Kevin's smashed glasses off of his face. She placed them on the help desk and shoved wads of tissues into Kevin's dripping nostrils. Both guys were sound asleep. They looked identical to the bodies out the by dorms, Michael's body in the police cruiser, and the fat guy in the bathroom stall.

"You think they caught something from the rest of them out there?" Emily asked.

"I don't think so. If they're sick, I would be too. I was touchin' those bodies out there more than he was. It wouldn't make sense I don't think," Dan replied. Then, he thought for a moment. "Howsabout allergies? Anything they ate or drank that caused a reaction?"

"All I saw him have was a bottle of water. If he ate or drank anything else, I didn't see it," Emily replied. Jon had the same response.

"Hmm." Dan rubbed the bottom of his scruffy chin hair. Then he took his hat off to scratch his sweaty head as he pondered what would cure this uncertainty.

It was silent for a moment, except for the sound of heavy raindrops landing on the roof of the library.

"What do we do now?" Emily asked, and that was a great question.

Dan answered by asking another question. "Well, shouldn't we wait until they wake up or somethin'? I mean, we've been with em both the whole time. They didn't get bit or anything. Maybe they're just out cold for the time bein'. They gotta wake up at some point, right?"

"What about the guy in the bathroom?" Jon asked. "What do you think he'll be like if *he* wakes up?"

"That's what the bat's for." Dan chuckled, but not in a good way. "But we can't just let these two guys lie here. We oughta stay with em here or put em in our cars and go." Dan was making good points, but neither Emily nor Jon could decide what to do. Another episode of silence came as the three of them sat by the bodies. Their hearts pumped with anxiety.

"What if we wait until tonight?" Emily asked. "We can still eat and drink from the vending machine. The doors are locked. We got your bat. How about that?"

"You think that's such a good idea? Maybe we've already spent too much time here," Jon said. He was hoping more for putting the bodies in the cars and leaving. Better yet, leaving without the bodies. *No, no. That's not right. They helped me.* His mind went back to his parents and wondered if they were still alive. His phone hadn't rung and there were no other notifications or emails on the screen.

"You got a better one?" Emily asked, pointing the end of the bat at Jon. Her eyes became fierce for a moment. The cuteness lost. Jon's lip quivered, but he couldn't muster up a response before Dan chimed in.

"We can carry them to your truck. We can even use my car," Jon replied.

"Jonny, I understand if you want to leave but we have no idea what's happened to 'em. We oughta wait and see. I know you want to get back to your folks, but it seems we are safer here than out there. I mean, who knows what triggered this. Could be somethin' in the air!"

Jon didn't argue.

Dan continued. "I figure all of us want nothing more than get our asses out of this fuckin' place, but it wouldn't be fair to have Mark and Kev not get their chance. Alright? What if it was us? You wouldn't want to wake up to find yourself all alone, right? I can't guarantee we can make it all the way to our places outside of the turnpike. Our best bet is to wait for these fellas to get up. We can give it a few more hours and that's it. Then we will get right the hell outta here regardless. Alright? But we can't just throw 'em in the back of the truck like they're slabs of hog. Hell, even if piggy boy in the bathroom stall wakes up, and he doesn't wanna tear our heads off, we can take him with us!"

"You're right, you're right," Jon said, and Dan *was* right. Jon wouldn't want to be left alone in the library or thrown in the back of some pickup truck as he napped in a bizarre slumber. "What if something like last night happens again?" He motioned over to the quiet news broadcast that displayed what it had been like since he got to the library.

"The doors are locked and we're well protected. As far as I can tell, if we don't let anyone in, we will be ok. Right, Em?" Dan asked, winking over at Emily.

"Hell yeah, we are!" Emily smiled. She looked cute again.

TWENTY-ONE

It Starts Again

The hours passed as the storm raged on. Outside, the grey sky began to fade darker as the sun was of no more help for the day. The three students sat on the carpeted library floor beside the sleeping bodies of Mark and Kevin. The news still played on the computer screen, but the volume was too low for them to listen to it. Last they paid attention, the news people reported that last night's events were happening worldwide. Paris, France was being overrun with maniacs. Countries in Africa were in utter chaos.

Then, the power went out. CNN cut to black for good. Darkness fell all around the three college students.

"Shit!" Emily cried out.

Click. The emergency lights came on. Above the entrance, in the corners of the first floor, and in the back by the vending machines and bathrooms were circular, florescent lights that beamed from plastic mounts.

"It's alright, least we ain't in pitch-black," Dan said.

Jon wanted nothing more than to get back to his house, but for the time being, it felt kind of calm. Faint lights and sounds of water outside mixed with thunderstorms. Relaxing. Mark and Kevin remained at ease.

The group indulged in more snacks and drinks. Perhaps staying was the right decision.

All three of them tried to call their families from their cell phones but without success. They had been trying all day with the same, depressing results. Dan even tried calling Kevin's parents from his phone, but it was password protected. No way in. Then, they tried 911 a few more times but still that automated message played. It told them there were too many incoming calls.

Mark's phone buzzed a few times in his pocket. He was getting more text messages from his sister, Jessica, who left her Maryland apartment to drive up to White Haven College to get her brother. She couldn't get a hold of her other family members, and when

Emily texted her back explaining what had happened, she called panicked.

"What do you mean you can't wake him up!?" Jessica shouted from the phone. She was behind the wheel. An occasional *ticking* sound of a turn signal could be heard behind her impatient tone.

"He collapsed all of a sudden while we were outside. We're safe in the library at the moment and are gonna wait and see if he'll–"

Jessica's shouting interrupted Emily.

"That's unbelievable! Jesus Christ!" A car's horn blared on Jessica's end of the call. "Get off my fucking ass!" There was a pause. "I'm sorry. Hello?"

"We're still here. Is everything ok?" Emily replied.

"These assholes behind me are tailgating way too close and they won't go around. Hang on." It sounded like Jessica put the phone down. She screamed out of her window at the car that was closing in behind her. "Go around! AROUND! HEY SHITHEAD!"

HONK. Then a loud *CRASH* blared from the phone. *BANG BANG SMACK RUMBLE SKID.* Jessica's phone sounded like someone put it in a blender, making it bounce and smash around. The noises ended after a few a moments and Emily, Dan, and Jon all looked at each other with their eyes wide. It was silent. They kept looking back and forth between one another. No more noises came from Jessica's end of the call. *A car wreck,* Jon thought. *The person behind her must've slammed into the back of her car and sent her into a spin. She must be…*

"Jessica, are you there?" Dan asked, trying to be calm. But Jon could tell in their eyes that both Dan and Emily knew what had happened. There was still silence. No sound coming from the phone. The three of them remained in locked eyes until Jon looked over and saw the large man from the bathroom stall standing before the shattered glass of the vending machines. He was a shadow beneath the emergency lights.

Thunder *rumbled.*

"Woah man! Are you alright?" Dan asked the large man as the three of them jumped up from the floor. You could hear all three of their hearts racing in their chests.

"What the hell happened? Why'd you leave me in the bathroom stall?" the fat man said. He spoke in an irritated voice. His face was red and moist with sweat that caked his forehead. It glistened beneath the lights.

"We didn't leave you in there. You were there when we got here, sleepin'," Dan replied. Fear was injecting itself into his words, which made his voice start to sound like he was laughing a little. "Why were you sleepin' on the toilet all day?"

The fat man began to walk closer toward the three of them. "You got some problem with me? Huh? You gonna punish me for what I did to the window? You leave me in there so you could wait for the cops to show? JUST TRY AND TAKE ME!" The irritated tone was now moving up to a rage-filled level.

Emily walked backward with her eyes still fixed on the large man. She lifted her hand behind her and grabbed Dan's wooden baseball bat that leaned up against the back of the help desk. The large man stepped closer.

"What are you talkin' about?" Dan asked. The man stepped even closer now. "Hey, look we don't want any trouble alright? There's enough going on out there in the world. Let us help you out." Dan extended his hands out like he was trying to ease the situation and to calm the fat man down. It wasn't working. Especially not when the fat man threw a punch at Dan, which Dan blocked most of with his hands. "Hey! Hey! Calm down now!"

Emily *CRACKED* the baseball bat on top of the fat man's head. Jon closed his eyes tight and gritted his teeth. Dan pulled his head back. The wood came down in a vertical slam like she was playing that game at the carnival where you hit the scale with a hammer, hoping to send that piece of metal up to ring the bell. She rang his bell with a loud *THWACK*. The fat man's body hit the floor. Soon after, blood began to pour out from the top of his head through his baseball cap and onto the grey and blue patterns of the carpeted floor.

"Holy hell Em, you just killed him in one swing!" Dan said, more surprised at her strength than the fact that the large man was spilling the contents of his skull onto the carpet. Emily *SLAMMED* the bat down again. This time onto his face, breaking his nose and teeth.

More thunder came from above.

"Are you hurt?" Emily asked Dan, who was looking at what she had done. Shocked and mortified.

Just then, a loud *KNOCK KNOCK KNOCK* came from the front door of the library. It came between the rolling thunder. The three of them turned around at the same time. It played out in slow motion as they turned their heads toward the door to see a man knocking. The fading lights of the police cruiser and ambulance behind him made out a vague shadow of his face. Jon could make out he was wearing a flat-brimmed hat.

Holy shit. It was the man in sweatpants who was asleep on the ground next to that girl by the dorms. Mark, Dan, and Jon passed by him when they went to get Jon's cell phone. Now, he was awake and banging on the door. The computer that once showed CNN blocked off the lower half of the flat-brimmed man's body, but Jon knew he was wearing those sweatpants.

The man outside started making demands on the other side of the blood-stained door. "You idiots! Let me in! They're gonna kill me out here! C'mon, open up! RIGHT NOW!" The three remained frozen looking at him. The knocking never seemed to stop. "Open it up or I'll FUCKING kill you! Got it? OPEN IT UP!"

"Guys," Jon said, breaking the frozen silence that trapped all three of them yet again, "look behind him."

There were more people coming up behind the flat-brimmed man through the blue and red flashing lights. Each time the lights flashed, the bodies came closer. One of them grabbed the flat-brimmed man. It looked like a fight was breaking out between the two.

KNOCK KNOCK KNOCK KNOCK KNOCK.

Now, two people were pounding on the glass door. The flat-brimmed man was no longer there. Instead, a young woman with glasses and a man with a white undershirt banged their fists.

"Let us in ASSHOLES!" the woman yelled.

"OPEN the door up or we'll BREAK it down! I swear to GOD!" the man said soon after. Behind them, more lingered. Some appeared to be in fistfights while others were standing still, giving the thirty-yard stare.

Jon, Emily, and Dan were made of stone. Between the rage that stood outside the library door, and now the darkness that almost covered them all, it appeared they were trapped. But little did they know, they weren't trapped inside by those who wanted in from the outside. They were trapped from the *inside* by Mark and Kevin.

TWENTY-TWO

The Rifle

Beneath the light of the dining room chandelier, the rifle sat in the cardboard case, gleaming up at Little Jon and his father. A smooth, brown wooden stock with a long, black barrel that shined. Atop sat a black scope. Other than the old guns Big Jon had in the basement and the virtual shooting machines on Xbox and PlayStation, Little Jon had never seen such a pristine firearm.

"What do you think? You wanna hold it?" Big Jon asked, placing his arm on Little Jon's shoulder. A smile painted his face as he caught his son's reaction.

"Sure."

Little Jon wrapped his fingers around the stock of the rifle and pulled it from its box. Heavy. He admired its beauty up close, feeling the glide of the wood. The end of the stock leveraged into his armpit as he focused one eye down the scope, pointing the barrel at the door to the garage. His finger was on the trigger.

"Just be careful there, Jon. You must treat every gun as if it's loaded. There are not any bullets in it, but you must follow proper trigger discipline, ok?" Big Jon said, still smiling at his son enjoying himself.

"Whoops!" Little Jon said, releasing his trigger finger. He handed the rifle to his father. "I guess I have a lot to learn, huh? I don't think I've held a rifle like this before. It's nice."

"You sure do, that's why we're going to take this bad boy out in the woods as soon as deer season starts. We'll get you trained and everything. Get you some camo. What do you think? I believe you're old enough to get a buck with your old man."

"Let's do it! You think I can do it?" Little Jon asked. His eyes still stuck to the rifle.

"Oh, I have no doubt in my mind. My father taught me, and if I can do it, you most certainly could!"

Little Jon smiled a genuine smile. So did his father. Big Jon couldn't remember the last time that his son was so quick to liking something he'd brought home. Papers to sign up for middle school basketball was a bust. The fishing poles didn't start a fire in his belly. *A gun. A Remington 700 is all it took huh?* Big Jon thought to himself as he smiled back and shook his head in a manner of near disbelief. There was finally something that the two of them could agree on with a shared amount of excitement.

TWENTY-THREE

Knock Knock

Kevin was the first one to wake up.

As his body rose from the ground, he scratched his eyes and felt around the carpet for his glasses. Dried blood stained above his lip and his eyes were crusty. His nose was stuffed with tissues. "Where are they?" he asked with a congested sound. "Where are my glasses? Why's it so dark in here?"

"Kev, are you alright? We got your glasses right here," Dan said, grabbing them off the help desk and handing them to Kevin. Kevin snatched them right out of his hand and put them on.

"They're broken!" Kevin shouted. "You broke my glasses! Why'd you do that?"

"Kevin, you passed out on the crosswalk. You fell right onto them!" Emily explained. Her eyes were darting back and forth between the door and Kevin.

"Don't lie to me, you bitch! You broke my glasses!" Kevin stood up. His eyebrows were curled, making an angered facial expression that no one would've thought he was capable of. His normal, innocent face looked contorted. It didn't look like Kevin at all. "Come here!"

Kevin tried to grab Emily, but Dan intervened and pushed him back. "Whoa Kev, you better chill buddy. What's gotten into you?" Kevin shoved back at Dan, but he didn't have the same strength as the country boy. "Kev, I'm warning you. Don't do this."

"DON'T TOUCH ME!" Kevin screeched. The sound of his voice was frightening. So strange to hear that volume coming from him. "You broke my glasses and now I'm gonna break you!" He shoved at Dan again with greater might, making Dan move backward a little bit. The surprising strength came out of nowhere.

Emily held up the bat, pointing the tip to Kevin's face, trying to intimidate him. "You callin' me a bitch? You want some of this, Kevin? You wanna try me? Don't do that again!" Kevin grabbed the bat with both hands and started a tug-of-war with it. "Fuck you,

Kevin!" Emily shouted, yanking. Dan got on Emily's side and helped her in the struggle. The two of them pulled the bat from Kevin's tight grip.

As Jon stood to the side, unsure of what to do, he felt a hand wrap around the bottom of his leg. He looked down. It was Mark. He had his hand gripped onto the bottom of Jon's leg, above his shoe. His eyes were open, but they didn't blink. They just stared up at Jon.

"Mark? What are you doing?" Jon asked, starting to wiggle his foot. Mark's hand squeezed tighter.

"Mark? Stop that!" But Mark didn't answer nor cease his vine-like grip.

KNOCK KNOCK KNOCK KNOCK KNOCK. The man and woman were still right outside the doors. It was now background noise that played between bouts of *rumbling* thunder.

"Kev! Man, I don't want to hurt you!" Dan said, raising his voice. "Just calm down, let's all relax for a sec!"

Kevin took a swing at Emily, but she blocked with the bat. Dan stepped in and *SOCKED* Kevin in the face, sending him back in a tizzy. The tissues fell from Kevin's nose, onto the carpeted floor.

Emily wound up the bat.

"Wait a sec, Em! Don't!" Dan shouted, trying to stop her. But she continued and hit the side of Kevin's head as if it were a baseball. *WAM*. His body was the tee. The sound of hardwood *CRACKING* against bone rang out into the library. Kevin's head jerked to the side. The broken glasses flew right off his face and soared a few feet in the air. His body collapsed backward onto the backside of the help desk. Blood came oozing from his right ear and nose again. Both nostrils streaked bright-red blood onto his blue shirt. A tooth came out from between his lips.

"Jesus Christ!" Jon shouted. Vomit was rising in his throat.

Mark released his grip from Jon's leg and turned to see what had happened. "What the fuck, guys? You killed Kevin!"

"Fuck!" Emily's face became red and wet as she started to cry. "He was coming at me and I. . . fuck, oh fuck!"

"Holy hell, Em!" Dan said with his hands on his head, pushing his John Deere cap upwards. Heart pumping. Adrenaline streaming. No one spoke for a few moments.

KNOCK KNOCK KNOCK KNOCK KNOCK.

Kevin was still alive. He shifted his body back and forth as he clutched his face to stop the bleeding. There was no way he was getting back up as he spit another tooth from his bloodied mouth onto the carpet. "Why you bfff I ougtttt fu fu-" He tried to speak, but nothing intelligent could come from him now. Only blood and teeth, filling his mouth with disgusting drivel.

Thunder *crashed* overhead.

Mark stood up and leaned over Kevin's body. His eyes scanned over Kevin's face, taking in all the gore. He turned back at Emily. "You're a real bitch you know that? What kind of person swings a bat at my friend like that? LOOK AT HIM!"

Emily couldn't speak or curse, she was so upset. The whole situation was out of control.

"Hey man, we didn't mean to! He was coming at us, you saw it! Emily was scared, alright? Don't do anything crazy now," Dan said with his arms extended out again.

"You're a hillbilly moron fuck, Dan. Always were," Mark said in a calm but sinister manner. The tone struck Dan as it appeared to have hurt his feelings at the moment.

"Mark, c'mon. Please, what's happening?" Emily asked, wiping her eyes.

"Shut up!" Mark shouted, wide awake. He continued with his angered ranting. "Dan's a real mess. I'm always the one that has to help him get through his classes while he's busy bullshitting around all day. You think I'm gonna listen to him now? Think I'm just gonna stand here and let you two beat the hell out of us? You KILLED Kevin. THAT'S RIGHT! You KILLED him, you BITCH! FUCK-ING BITCH!"

Mark charged toward Emily, but Jon grabbed him from behind, holding onto both of his arms. Dan got in front and placed both of his arms on Mark's chest.

"Kevin's still alive!" Emily sobbed. "I'm sorry!" She was crying hot tears. They burned her eyes. Her brain was operating at one hundred miles per hour and had no time to react again to the insult of the B-word.

Mark irked around, trying to free himself from Jon and Dan's hold. "Get off of me! Right now! BOTH OF YOU, OFF!"

KNOCK KNOCK KNOCK KNOCK KNOCK.

Both of Mark's elbows pushed back and into Jon's stomach. Mark turned and swung at Jon but tripped over Kevin's feet. His body fell to the ground and Dan jumped on top of him to hold him down to the floor. Kevin jumped up and grabbed on the back of Dan. Punches began raining down onto Dan's spine from Kevin's blood-soaked fists.

Another *CRACK* of the bat came down onto Kevin's head. His body plopped backwards onto the library carpet with his head leaning on the backside of the help desk. Blood splattered all over the wood. Jon's vomit let loose and spewed onto the side of a bookshelf he was standing near. The gore was too much. The blood was everywhere. His stomach couldn't handle it.

The bat swing stopped the fight between Mark and Dan for a moment until the site of Kevin's now dead body on the ground brought more rage out of Mark. He pushed Dan off him with a punch to the face.

"Dan, watch out!" Jon yelled as Emily was about to strike down the bat again. Only this time, it was above Mark's head.

Dan gathered himself and crawled back away from Mark. Emily brought the bat down, but Mark moved his head out of the way, causing her to slam it into the carpet beside him. *Thud.* Then, he brought his leg up behind Emily's. It made her knee bend inward and she fell right next to him on the floor. The baseball bat rolled over by Jon's feet. Mark scrambled on top of Emily and grabbed her neck, strangling her. As she fought back, Mark began to hit her head hard onto the floor, rubbing and brushing her face with carpet burns.

"Get that bat! Get that bat!" Dan shouted at Jon. His eyes were blinking fast, still in a daze from the punch. Jon was still gathering himself from his sickness. He felt like those old cartoons where birds and stars circled around the head of Wile E. Coyote. "C'mon man! Pick it up!"

In the brutal haze all around him, a voice spoke to Jon in his mind. For a moment, it was the only sound that could fill his thoughts.

If you're gonna do it, you gotta do it now.

The room spun. The voice remained.

Now, Jon.

Everything whirled back into focus as Jon grabbed the bat with both of his shaking hands. He wanted nothing more than for Dan to have to do this, but it was what it was. No time to waste. Mark was now a maniac who was strangling this poor girl on the floor of the library and it was up to Jon to put an end to it all.

I don't want to kill him he thought to himself, *but I have no choice. Now.*

Time slowed for the moment. Jon brought the wooden bat down upon the back of Mark's head in a fearful, adrenaline-filled slam. Jon's heart was beating so fast in his ears he didn't quite hear the *CRACK* of the wood hitting skull. Pure blunt force. Mark's body slumped down on top of Emily's. She screamed as the grip of Mark's hands went limp and his body lay heavy, almost kissing the back of her head with his loose, open lips.

Dan was up again and was quick to grab Mark's body off of her. Mark fell to the side and it looked like there were no signs of breathing. No signs of life. Jon hit him hard enough in the back of the head to kill him in an instant.

"Em, are you ok?" Dan asked while he and Jon pulled her up from the floor. He wheeled out a chair from the help desk so she could sit down, which she did as she caught her breath and rubbed her neck. Her face was red. By the looks of her messy hair, she appeared to have just gotten off a roller coaster.

"I'm ok! I'm ok! I just need a moment," she coughed. "Thank you, guys. Holy shit." She coughed again and wiped her eyes with her tie-dye shirt. "Thank you so much! I owe you guys my life! I thought I was dead. Honestly, the scariest moment of my whole fucking life. Holy shit. Fuck!"

KNOCK KNOCK KNOCK KNOCK KNOCK.
KNOCK KNOCK KNOCK KNOCK KNOCK.
KNOCK KNOCK KNOCK KNOCK KNOCK.

Dan and Jon looked up at the door which now had more people banging to get in. Two girls and another guy joined the flat-brimmed man and were mashing their fists. Through the dark, they could see the glass shaking. The people outside looked soaked from the rain. The red and blue lights from the emergency vehicles were blocked out now.

"OPEN IT UP!" one would say.

"Let us IN!" another would follow. Almost chanting now.

"WE'LL KILL YOU!"

Emily sat, leaning over the computer swivel chair. She was paying no mind to the constant knocking from outside. Her eyes traveled from Kevin's body to Mark's, then to the fat man's body by the vending machines. "I can't believe this you guys," she said, still sounding out of breath. "I can't believe we killed them. All three of them." Now her tears made their way back into her eyes. "What got into them?" Emily wept and covered her face with her shaking hands.

A loud *BANG* came from the front doors. It was so loud and startling, that it snapped Emily's head up from her sobs as she shrieked. The three of them were now all standing and facing the door to the library. It had a large gash in the glass. At first, they couldn't tell what the maniacs had done to cause this until the red and blue lights illuminated two of the people outside running at the blood-stained door, holding a bench.

BANG. CRACK.

"Oh shit! They're trying to break their way in!" Dan shouted as he pointed out the use of the bench. "We gotta get the hell outta here. No way are we gonna be able to take them all on. They'll rip us to shreds! Shit!"

"Upstairs!" Emily screamed as another *BANG* and *CRACK* rang from the door. "C'mon!"

The three of them bolted to the stairs that sat to the left of the front doors. Jon grabbed his backpack and held it by the handle on the top. No time to grab anything else.

As they approached the steps, they each took a glance at the evil and horror that lay only a few feet away from them behind a now deteriorating shield. Even though the darkness of the library and the cover of nightfall and pouring rain, they could each see out into the eyes of rage, the hunger waiting to come inside. None of their once former classmates looked human. They looked as furious as demons.

There were two sets of stairs and at the top of them was a wooden door, similar to the ones used for the bathrooms. Except this door had a vertical window in the middle of it and a silver plating on the right-center with a circular key lock. Usually, this door was propped open. Now, it was shut and locked from the night before. The three of them pushed and pushed until they realized that Kevin's key would be the only way to get in.

"Em, where's the key?" Dan asked with a face that read *no time to waste.*

She patted her pockets. "Shit! I don't have them. Fuck! They gotta be downstairs!"

Dan pushed her aside. "I'll go! Is it on the help desk?" he shouted as he flew down the set of steps, back down into Hell.

Emily's voice shook. "It might be. It could also be by Mark or Kevin. I don't know! Just hurry, please!" Her legs buckled. "Try Kevin's pockets!"

BANG. CRACK. CRACK.

That doesn't sound good.

"Dan, hurry! Get your ass back up here!" Emily screamed as she stepped down onto the landing, facing the steps down to the first floor. Jon stood by the locked door, heart beating fast with the weight of a sledgehammer into his ribcage. He watched Emily as she looked down the steps, waiting for Dan's return with the keys.

BANG. CRACK. CRACK.

The bench was being pushed into the door faster now and jagged pieces of glass were peppering the carpet beneath the spotlight of the emergency light beams.

"Dan! C'mon!" Emily shouted.

"One sec, I'm grabbin' the bat!" Dan shouted back up at her.

BANG. CRACK. SHATTER.

Emily saw the end of the bench break through the door. Glass blasted into the library. Cool, wet air flowed in and the sound of rain became more audible. She could see the maniacs outside start to funnel inside. Emily recognized the flat-brimmed man among the few coming in.

Dan appeared at the bottom of the steps, walking backward with the bat held out against the three people that were now walking toward him. The flat-brimmed man and two girls wore wet clothes. One wore a gym outfit and the other a black pair of yoga pants and white bra. More were getting through the shattered hole in the door behind them. They were dripping-wet maniacs.

"Stay back! I don't want any trouble, alright?" Dan said to the three psychos. They were approaching him with furious and focused faces.

The flat-brimmed hatted man spoke. "Why didn't you let us in? We were knocking and knocking and knocking. Now you're gonna pay. YOU'RE GONNA PAY!"

Dan quick looked behind him, up the stairs. He saw that Emily was standing on the landing and removed one of his hands from the bat. He had Kevin's key. "Em!" he shouted up at her, keeping his eyes fixed on the now four maniacs coming at him. Another man wearing shorts and a red shirt that said WHITE HAVEN HONOR SOCIETY on it was gazing at Dan with gritted teeth. "I'm gonna throw you the key."

"What are you gonna do with that bat, huh? Kill us? You wanna FUCKING kill us?" the woman in the drenched gym outfit said.

"Dan, it's too dark. I can't see it. Just run back up here! C'mon!" Emily cried out to him. There was no time for more tears. "Get away from him!" Her legs felt as if they would give out any minute.

Jon stood frozen by the locked, wooden door, too afraid to move. What could he do? His heart couldn't beat any faster. *Please, Dan. Get up here.* His hand moistened as it remained gripping the handle of his backpack.

Dan gave it his best shot to run up the stairs, but the four maniacs grabbed his legs and pulled him back down to the first floor. He tried to swing his bat to shoo them away, but once it made contact with the flat-brimmed man's arm and knocked him back into the others, he was overrun as the horde let loose. The flat-brimmed man grabbed the bat. Dan tried with all his might to climb back up the steps, but the bat came down onto his back. *CRACK.* It made Dan scream. Emily ran down after him, but Dan shouted, "Stop! Emily, stay back. Take the key and go!" The four lunatics tugged and pulled on him as he tried to climb up the steps with only his hands. *CRACK.* Another hit to his back. His body squirmed. The maniacs yelled but the words were lost within all the chaos.

"You monsters! STOP!" Emily shouted as her hands tried to cover her face from the slaughter below.

Jon dropped his backpack and ran down to the landing by Emily to see the horror that he wished he didn't have to see. Four maniacs were on top of Dan. A fifth one came up behind the fighting and stared up at Emily and Jon.

"Take the key! Go!" Dan yelled as best as he could and flung Kevin's little, golden key up a few of the steps. It *dinged* on the step before the landing and Jon picked it up without hesitation.

He grabbed Emily by the arm. "C'mon!" he shouted. Emily moved with him, but her eyes kept on Dan for one last moment.

Dan now had his hands covering his head as the maniacs punched and beat him with his own wooden bat. The Louisville Slugger rained down on his spine. All Emily could make out was the green and yellow John Deere logo on his hat as the violence overtook him. *PUNCH. CRACK. PUNCH. CRACK.*

With hands trembling, Jon unlocked the second-floor door and picked up his backpack. He grabbed Emily and the two of them entered and locked it behind them.

Lightning flashed outside.

TWENTY-FOUR

One Way Out

"Oh my God!" Emily shrieked.

She and Jon were now shaking and alone on the second floor of the White Haven College library. The lights from outside beamed up through the water droplet covered windows, casting their blue and red flashes onto the still bookcases and the single-person study booths that surrounded them. The emergency lights were still lit on the corners of the ceiling up here.

Emily and Jon knelt together against the locked door.

"I can't believe this," Jon said, wanting to cry. But he knew he couldn't now. The night had just begun, and once the maniacs finished with Dan, they'd be up to the wooden door, ready to bust it down, ready to kill Jon and Emily without hesitation.

"We're gonna fucking die up here, Jon. This is it," Emily said with her familiar tears winning her over again. Her black hair was covering her face now and the messiness made it hard to see the blue streak in the dark. She put her head into Jon's chest and wept. Jon placed an arm around her. He wanted to hold her forever and cry with her.

No time for that.

It didn't take long for one of the maniacs to *BANG* on the wooden door. It made Emily clutch onto Jon's arm tighter.

"I know you're in there!" a shadowy man shouted from the other side of the vertical glass window. Jon looked up to the window on the door, convinced the psycho couldn't see him. It was as if the man on the other side had no face and was nothing more than a rage-filled entity. A phantom banging at the door, wanting nothing more than to come in and let loose on them.

Behind his *BANGS* were the sound of footsteps coming up the stairs. Thunder.

Dan's dead, Jon thought to himself, but it came out as a slight whisper.

"Now they're coming for us," Emily said in response, also in a frightened whisper.

"We can't stay here," Jon whispered back to her. He put his backpack over his shoulder.

They had no other choice but to run into the aisles of bookcases. Jon went ahead with Emily behind him. He was holding her arm as he guided them through the infinite pieces of literature. The backpack's zippers *jangled* as they bounced on Jon's back. The *BANGS* on the wooden door were almost in sync with their footsteps that ran through the rows of textbooks. They both knew at any second that those *BANGS* would be followed by *CRACKS* and then the *THUD* of the door falling to the floor. God knows how many maniacs are on the other side, waiting to come in. It made them run even faster. But to where were they running?

The emergency lights beamed lines of white through the rows of books, casting shadows on the thick stacks of pages.

They got to the end of the bookcases and took a left toward the back-right corner of the second floor, beneath another emergency light. Jon wasn't sure what he was doing, but he wanted to get as far away from that wooden door as possible. They both stood with their hearts pounding. Somehow, Jon could smell a hint of that metallic scent from before. It mixed with the cool, stormy night's air. He made loud sniffs in between breaths.

"Do you smell that?" he whispered.

"What?" Emily tried to compose herself and take a whiff. "Smell what?"

Jon sniffed again and started walking forward, between the rows of study booths that sat along the windows to his left. The smell became stronger as he walked with the red and blue lights streaming up, making him a shadow to Emily. The *bangs* still came but weren't as loud now.

"Where are you going? Don't leave me here!" Emily said in a rising whisper. She wiped her nose and began to follow behind Jon. Her nose was too stuffy from all the crying to pick-up any scents.

Jon stopped when he felt that he was walking into a slight breeze. The smell came with it. He came to a window with a large piece of tarp covering it. It was between two study booths and swaying in the storm. *The broken window. The popped glass.* Sure enough, Jon could make out a big, rectangular pane of glass leaning up against the back of one of the study booth chairs that were smaller versions of the ones they had in the dorm rooms. Little, blue-colored cushions on wood.

"Over here," Jon whispered back to Emily, who was several feet behind him. She hurried up and was now standing over his shoulder. Jon pulled up the tarp, making the cool breeze and metallic scent flow over them. Emily still couldn't smell it, but Jon could. He tore the entire tarp off. It made a *ripping* sound.

"What the hell?" Emily sniffed.

They both looked out toward the night sky that shed no moonlight beyond the storm clouds. Rain pelted their heads. Water streaked Jon's lenses.

There was no one below them or toward the parking lot, but when they turned their heads to the right, they saw a couple of people fighting in the middle of the campus grounds. Two guys pushing and shoving one another. Bodies were scattered around between puddles of blood. The concrete paths were all dark from being soaked with rain and gore.

Beyond that was the police cruiser and the ambulance still flashing beams of light. Jon couldn't see exactly, but the rear door of the police cruiser was open, and Michael was gone. The dorm area in the backdrop still had bodies lying in piles beneath the now inoperable orange-colored streetlamps.

It was quiet for a moment as Jon and Emily looked over the wet, bloody and night-covered campus. It seemed like another dimension to Jon, a more sinister version of White Haven College. The quietness ended when Emily asked if they could survive a jump from the second floor.

"I don't know." Jon took a deep breath. "But it seems like we don't have a choice. What do you think?"

"We either die from the fall or die from those psychos. Which one do you think will be better?"

Jon leaned out of the open window as far as he could to get a better grasp of the length of the drop. *Twenty feet? Thirty?* There was shrubbery below them that sat along the brick of the building, separating it from the walkway which had grass on the other side of it. "Jumping would be better."

Another distant *bang* came from the wooden door.

"I got an idea," Jon said. He turned to the chair under one of the single study booths and snagged the blue, square-shaped cushion from the seat. "If we throw enough of these down there, we can soften the drop."

"Jon, you're a genius!" Emily almost broke from her whisper.

Jon smiled and nodded. "Help me gather more cushions." He took off his backpack and put it down by the booth. The two of them worked and ran up and down the side of the second floor, taking as many cushions as they could, using the harsh emergency lights to guide them. The *BANGING* continued, louder now. Soon enough, they had stacked up a few piles of cushions by the open window. One by one, Jon and Emily would let go of the cushions by extending both of their arms out and releasing the grip so that each would fall flat. A couple had got caught in the shrubbery and rustled the leaves on it. Jon stuck his head out of the window to see if the two fighting men heard it. They hadn't.

"We have to aim for the walkway and grass. As long we throw enough of them close together, we can jump down and it won't hurt as much," Jon said as he demonstrated his dropping technique. The cushion fell to the walkway. It made a soft, wet *clap* sound and bounced. The two men fighting on campus remained in their duel.

Emily dropped the last cushion they had down onto the cushioned-covered walkway below. Not all the cushions were side by side but there were enough of them on the path and grass that it created a puzzle-like blanket over the ground.

"Good work," Jon said. "Let's test it out." He picked up his backpack and brought it up to the edge of the window. With all the commotion, he didn't realize how heavy it was. But then again, Jon always had a filled bag. He never forgot his supplies. The main compartments held his laptop, textbooks, a few shirts, and notebooks. But the small pocket in the front held the most important item of all: car keys.

Jon's bag with most of his wardrobe sat downstairs by the door of the library. He'd have to go on without them. Good thing he showered and changed.

The weight of the backpack allowed for a better test of the cushions' safety below. Jon threw the backpack outwards and toward the left where the grass met the concrete and where most of the cushions had landed together. It dropped and landed against the cushions. The laptop and books rattled against each other inside, the keys making a hard jangling noise on top. Still, the maniacs fought on, unaware of Jon testing his escape plan.

"Alright, perfect," Jon said. "We're going to aim for my backpack. Are you ready?" His right foot was already resting on the ledge. Emily nodded. "I'll go first, okay? If I survive, I'll give you a thumbs up to signal you to jump and I'll catch you," Jon said with a crooked smile. He didn't even realize he had smiled until Emily gave a slight one back. It was a moment that took Jon out of the madness for a moment.

I'll catch you.

"Ok," she whispered. Then she pulled her hair back away from her face and wiped her nose. "Be careful."

Both of them turned their heads back toward the darkness to hear one last *BANG* echoing through the lonely bookshelves. Jon stepped up on the ledge, crouching. Metallic air blew over his face and moved his messy brown hair. *Here we go.* His heart raced, but his mind was focused on landing. *A little to the left, right by the backpack.*

Now, Jon.

When he pushed off the ledge from the second floor of the library, he extended his body to maneuver himself toward the backpack and cushions on the left side. What he hoped would play out like the slow-motion instant replays before, turned out to be only instant. No slow motion. He fell as his backpack had. Before he knew it, Jon was face down in a blue cushion on the rain painted grass beside it with his legs *smacking* on the concrete. His glasses flew off his head and landed in the wet grass.

It didn't hurt at first, but as soon as he composed himself, he wanted to scream out in pain. He thought he broke his leg.

"Jon, are you okay?" Emily asked, sticking her head out of the window. Her voice was a yell now.

Jon squinted his eyes in pain and clutched his left knee. He gritted his teeth and felt around, expecting to feel a bone sticking out from it. But he didn't. Then, he extended his leg all the way out and felt the sting of pain right on the kneecap.

"Jon?" Emily's voice was getting louder now and when Jon opened his eyes, he turned his head to see Emily crouched on the ledge, ready to plummet. He wanted a few more minutes to lay there on the ground, but he caught a glance over at the two fighting guys and noticed they were returning the gesture at him. *Get up.* He squinted his eyes hard and felt around the surrounding grass until he felt his glasses. Placing them on his face, he saw slimy dirt and bits of green on them. No time to wipe them down.

The rain continued to pour.

"I'm alright! I'm alright!" Jon said back up to her, trying to keep his voice low. He stood up as best as he could without limping. No way did he want to seem weak right before Emily jumped down. "Don't jump yet! Let me move these cushions closer together."

Jon gathered the surrounding cushions the best as he could with his injured knee. Every time he glanced over to the two guys, they were closer. One was wearing a blood-stained, yellow soccer jersey and the other a ripped up, plain white undershirt. Both wore shorts but no shoes or socks. They were walking over from the center of campus with their bare feet *slapping* wet concrete.

"Jon, are you sure you're alright? Did you land on your leg wrong?" Emily asked. She saw Jon's limp, but her focus changed as she caught sight of the two men making their way towards him. "Jon! They're coming!" Emily said, pointing over to them. She hesitated on what to do next. Her head went back and forth between the two men and Jon.

"I know! Get ready to jump down," Jon said as he placed the last soaked cushion, creating a double-layered square of them beneath the window. A landing pad for Emily. He looked over his shoulder at the two men as they continued their pace toward him. "C'mon, Emily. We gotta go!" Jon said, waving for her to come down.

Emily was nervous, but she moved closer to the edge of the window. "Ok. I'm coming down now. You're gonna catch me, right?"

"Yes! I will!" Jon said, glancing back at the two approaching men with his arms extended over the layers of cushions. "I'm right here. C'mon Emily!"

Emily looked back once more and saw a figure running toward her through a row of books, only seeing the whites of the eyes staring her down. She pushed off the edge of the window and her arms flailed in the night's rain. Her thin body dropped as fast as Jon and his backpack had and she landed onto the padded square.

"Oh my God," Emily said, breathing with her messy hair covering her face. "I made it!"

"Are you alright?" Jon asked. The rain fell like a shower.

"I'm okay!" She stood up from the cushions and straightened her shirt and tight, hole-covered jeans. Her fingers pressed upon her nose ring to see if it was still intact. It was. "Let's get the hell out of here, there was someone on the second floor!" she said. This time, she grabbed Jon's arm.

"Wait!" Jon shouted and picked up his backpack off the ground and slung one strap over his shoulder. The bottom was wet. The two men were almost to them. "Alright, let's move!"

Emily and Jon ran down the concrete path and into the darkened parking lot. They were kicking up puddles. With the power out, they had no source of light coming from the giant light poles that hung over different lettered rows.

"Do you know where you're parked?" Emily asked as they ran.

Jon didn't know. The last time he was in his car was when he drove back from visiting his parents during Easter and he parked in a different spot each time. There were no set parking spots for the students. *Think.*

"Uhh. . . " Jon tried to remember back to April. "I. . . ." The two maniacs were almost behind them now. One of them began to speak but neither Jon nor Emily saw which one it was.

"Hey! Stop!" one of the two men said. "Don't run from us! Come back here!"

"It doesn't matter, let's just get to mine. I'm back in row G," Emily said to Jon as she pulled out a set of keys from her front-left pocket. They took a right at the bottom of the concrete path, running a little bit faster now to add a couple more inches between them and the two lunatics. The adrenaline coursed through Jon's body, injecting a natural painkiller to his once aching leg. Emily was frantic.

The sign hanging from the middle of the dead light pole read ROW G in the dark. Emily *clicked* her car key remote and the bright, white headlights of her Nissan Ultima lit up in the middle of the row, facing out and illuminating cars as if it were a beacon of hope. The only bit of light in the darkness. *Cerclink.* Emily unlocked it with another *click.* "C'mon Jon, get in!" she said as she looked back at the two men who were now catching back up with them, still commanding them to stop.

Emily flung the driver door open and fell into the seat. Jon jumped in the passenger side with his backpack resting on his lap. *Cerclink.* The doors locked and Emily pressed the key into the ignition, firing up the engine. "We're getting the fuck out of he–" The two men ran up on Emily's side of the car and *BANGED* on the window. "Fuck!" Emily shouted.

"Open it up, you BITCH!" one of them said and then tried the door handle. The other one went over to Jon's side and did the same. "You better open it you dumb CUNT, we're gonna beat the shit out of you and your boyfriend!"

"Emily, go! Drive!" Jon cried out.

Emily brought the shift gear up to DRIVE. *SKRRRR.* Her foot *SLAMMED* down onto the pedal and the car peeled out of its parking space, almost ripping the arm off the one who had his grip on the passenger door. The wet asphalt almost spun the car. She took a left, toward the roadway they came from. That would lead them straight out onto College Hill Avenue and away from White Haven College. She turned on the windshield wipers. They made a *squeaking* sound as they pushed away the falling droplets. The two men chased after the car as fast as they could. Emily looked up into the rearview mirror and stopped the car. Rain droplets covered the back windshield, making the maniacs look like two, dotted figures.

"What are you doing? They're coming for us!" Jon shouted.

"One second," Emily said in a flat tone. Her eyes fixed on the rearview mirror.

As the two men ran closer, Emily shifted the gear from DRIVE to REVERSE and *SLAMMED* her foot on the pedal again. Jon's head swung forward in the motion as the car sped backwards toward the two men, *PLOWING* into them. *BUMP. BUMP.* The car drove back over the bodies like they were speed bumps.

"Jesus Christ!" Jon shouted again, voice cracking. "What are you doing?"

The two men lay motionless on the asphalt path. One of their heads looked crushed inwards. Blood was pooling around it.

"Em–" Jon couldn't finish his sentence as Emily placed the gear back into DRIVE and the tires *SKRRRRED* again. Jon's head swung back this time, into the seat's headrest. The Nissan barreled up the roadway and over the bodies once more, this time faster. *BUMP.* The bodies went under the two sets of tires again.

"I HATE the word cunt!" Emily shouted. "My dad would scream it at me and my mom all the time and I swore the next time I heard that word, I'd kill whoever said it. Even if it was my own goddamn father!"

Jon sat sunken into the passenger seat, breathing heavily. The car stunk with the smell of old cigarettes. He wanted to say something, but the words couldn't manifest. His stomach was in his throat and his heartbeat in his ears.

TWENTY-FIVE

Tradition

The cold morning air of November felt like a winter tundra to Little Jon as he could see his breath come out from his mouth. He looked like a steam engine.

He crouched beside a cracked and leafless tree with Big Jon, who was securing a post for his bolt action Remington. .308 caliber. It would be the first time Little Jon could shoot a deer and his father wasted no time getting him geared up as both of them were wearing matching outfits of bright-orange hats and vests atop full camouflaged suits with gloves.

Little Jon remembered seeing photographs of his father posing with his first buck. His dad was twelve years old, around the same age as Little Jon. It was an old Polaroid picture from the 70s of Big Jon sitting on the wooded ground, clutching the antlers of a freshly shot creature. The lifeless face of the deer with its tongue hanging out of its dead mouth in contrast with the beaming smile of his young father always struck Little Jon. He figured it was just part of the Barnes' family tradition to kill wild animals and get a photo taken with them.

All those years ago, Grandpa Jon woke up his son early during a freezing-cold morning to find an unsuspecting deer to hunt. A tradition that must've been passed down from generation to generation. *What a life.* Now, it was Little Jon's turn.

School's Out

It was quiet after Emily's stunt, except for the steady, heavy rain. There were no other maniacs coming for them that they could see. And the two on the ground behind them were not getting up after being crushed twice. The car stopped in the middle of the parking lot. It was still in DRIVE, but Emily had her foot on the brake.

Jon began to unzip the front compartment of his backpack to retrieve his car keys. Emily *clicked* on the plastic overhead lights to help him. The lights also illuminated how much of a mess there was of Emily's Nissan. Papers and bottles were scattered on stained floor mats. An empty pack of cigarettes filled one of the cup holders.

"Emily," Jon started, "you said you live way up north right? East Gap was it?"

"Yep. It's quite a hike, but–"

"Maybe I should get my car."

"Are you crazy? We gotta get the fuck out of here! It would be best if we just stuck together, alright?"

Emily took her foot off the brake pedal and pressed on the gas.

Jon was silent. His clothes were drenched, and his heart thudded in his chest. He wanted nothing more than to stay with Emily, stay with her in her little, dirty car that smelled like smoke. It was better that way. Safer. Two minds are better than one. She was right about that. But the reality in Jon's mind was that they had families in two places. Whether they were dead or alive, the equation remained the same. He had to go his own way.

"It's out of the way, Emily. I–"

"Look," Emily said, interrupting, "we don't know what the hell is out there, okay? Did you not see those lunatics kill Dan? How fucked up Kevin and Mark were? The two freaks that nearly got us?" Emily grabbed at the empty pack of cigarettes and shook it around, looking for a smoke. Empty. She threw it against the dashboard. "Holy shit. We just have to go. We just have to drive and hope some other people like us are out there and will let us get back home." She *clicked* off the overhead light. "You don't even remember where you parked!"

Jon remained silent as his eyes looked straight ahead, into the rest of the darkened lot. The headlights illuminated only a couple feet ahead.

"I could hit the panic button. We'd find it in a second," he said.

"Oh yeah? And then what? Get the rest of those guys to come down and finish us?"

"I'll go quick!" Jon said, pulling his keys out. His thumb pressed the red speaker icon on his key remote.

"Forget it! Forget it! Stop!" Emily shouted, trying to watch both the parking lot and Jon. But it was too late.

The car alarm *BLARED* out into the night. It sounded like it was coming from behind them, but Emily didn't give Jon a second to turn around and look. Her foot hit the pedal harder to the floor, sending Jon's head back into the headrest again.

Emily sped by the trees and peeled out of the White Haven College entrance, towards the turnpike. Almost skidding out of control, she made the left turn without even looking to see if any cars were coming. The road was clear just as Dan had said before, but Jon didn't feel safe as the night brought sinister possibilities. *It won't be an easy drive for long,* Jon thought. *What the hell are we gonna do?*

The Nissan flew up the roadway, passing by crashed cars. Some were slammed into each other while others were smashed into the trees and utility poles.

The wipers were going full speed. Emily was whispering curse words under her breath as she drove around the vehicles in the middle of the road. Her headlights illuminated each scene.

As they approached the bend that would put them on the Pennsylvania Turnpike, a blue and yellow metal sign with flashing lights above it caught their eyes. It read:

URGENT MESSAGE WHEN FLASHING
TRAVELER INFO: TUNE RADIO TO 1640 AM

Without saying a word, Emily turned on the dashboard radio. Little green text popped up, showing a popular radio station. No music played. She felt around the buttons, pressed AM, and turned up the volume dial. A robotic woman's voice played a recorded message with a slight static sound behind it.

Drivers, please be advised. The turnpike is experiencing stopped traffic and heavy delays going east and westbound. We are advising all drivers to exit the turnpike and to take alternative routes. This is the Pennsylvania Turnpike broadcasting system. Drivers, ple- Emily cut it off as the voice began to repeat itself.

Emily turned the radio back to the FM channels. Silence. She pressed through the numbered radio presets until classical music played from one of the lower channels. It was the only station with a sound other than faint static.

"Well," Emily said with a sigh, "shall we take a look?"

"Nothing else we can do but try," he answered. "I'm sorry about what happened in the parking lot. I got scared, I guess. With everything going on, I wasn't sure what to do."

"It's alright," Emily said, giving glances over to Jon. "I understand. I'm scared too. I'd probably have done the same thing if I were you."

Jon nodded and blew air from his nose. *Squeak* went the wipers.

"We're gonna get back to our homes ok? We'll head to Springsdale first. Do you know which exit we need to take? I haven't been that way before and we can't afford to fuck this up."

"Yeah, we need to go west. It's the Simpsonville exit. From there it's only about ten minutes to my neighborhood off the highway."

"Ok." Emily nodded and swiped the hair away from her eyes, focusing on the upcoming on-ramp to the pike. "Ok, we can do that."

Jon turned on the screen to his cell phone. The time read 10:41 P.M. His confidence was low, but he figured he'd try calling his family again. First, the house. Then, his parents' cell phones. Then, grandparents. Nothing. He left new voice mails for all of them.

"What's your phone's charge at?" Emily asked with her eyes fixated to the road.

"It's at eighty-eight percent."

"Good," Emily said while *clicking* on the overhead light again. She drove with one hand as she reached behind her and made quick glances at the back seat. She reached. A white car adapter appeared, and she plugged it into the cigarette outlet. She lifted her butt up from the seat and pulled out her cell phone from the back-left pocket of her tight, ripped jeans. It had a white and pink plastic casing around it with flower pedals. Cute.

"I haven't charged mine in a while. Better get some juice in it while I still can."

Emily made a couple of calls to her family members.

No one answered.

Road Trip

Emily and Jon should have listened to the robotic woman's message on the radio to take an alternative route.

Coming around the bend to get onto the turnpike, Emily slowed the Nissan as they saw the toll booths to the turnpike were all filled with cars pushed into each other on both opposing lanes. Their headlight beams struck the booths. A couple of bodies lay outside opened car doors with their heads on the soaked road.

One lane on their side was closed for construction as red lights flashed above the CASH ONLY sign. Cars had crashed into it with their hoods smoking. The EZ PASS lane was the worst of them all with cars lined up and scattered around one another, making it impossible to get through.

From what they could see beyond the booths and rain, cars had pulled over to the side of the road. Two were smashed and the third was just stopped with its four-way flashers on. Beyond that, there was a car traveling alone. There wasn't as much clutter on the other side of the booths. It seemed possible for them to travel on the turnpike if they were careful to get by the blockage.

"Look there," Jon said, pointing in the darkness. "There's somebody down there."

Emily squinted her eyes and moved the Nissan a little closer. The headlights lit the scene up.

It was a big-bellied man with a neon vest and flashlight. He was walking along the cars and looking inside them. The vested man was tapping on a window and saying something, but neither Jon nor Emily could make it out.

"He must be one of the toll workers. Do you think he's alright? I mean, normal?" Jon asked.

Emily didn't answer but kept inching the Nissan closer and closer until they could see the man tapping on the window of a maroon SUV, trying to get the attention of a woman whose head was lying down on the dashboard. Emily moved a little closer until the neon vest man noticed the headlights. He turned his head toward them, lifted an eyebrow, and started heading toward the Nissan. There was blood on his vest and hands. Rain bounced off his head.

"What are you doing, Emily?" Jon asked with clear fear.

"Hang on," she replied. "He might be ok."

Jon froze. He tried to think about what he would do if things started to get worse. *Would I run out of the car? Where would I go?*

The man approached Emily's side of the Nissan before Jon could think up a good escape plan. The man motioned for her to put down her window. He didn't pound or shout. Emily pressed the button and the window slid down, bringing in the warm breeze of burnt rubber, smoke, rain, and a hint of blood.

"Are you two alright?" the man asked, leaning down with a shaky, frightful voice. He shined his flashlight into the car, making Emily and Jon squint. They nodded at the same time and Emily put a hand over her face to block the rays. Rain danced into the driver's side door.

"What the hell is going on?" Emily asked, sounding like she wanted to cry. Inside, she felt relieved to find someone else who seemed to not have lost it.

"I don't know, Miss." The man sniffed as if he wanted to cry himself. He lowered his flashlight. "We can't get any police or ambulances down here. I've been calling 911 for the past hour. I can't get a hold of any of my guys and we have families and children hurt and…" He stopped and looked up like he heard a noise. He pointed his flashlight at the cars behind him. Emily and Jon looked around but didn't see or hear anything except for the quiet classical music that remained playing on the radio. Thunder maybe? "You folks might want to turn around. Where are you trying to go?"

"We're going west to the Simpsonville exit to get to Springsdale. She needs to get to East Gap. Up north. We need to get back to our families. They aren't picking up their phones and this is the fastest way," Jon said.

The man lifted a brow and wiped his nose. "Hold on a second, guys. Stay right here."

He turned and began running back toward the toll booths. Emily and Jon sat, watching him go with his vest waving with every stride. They turned to each other and then back toward him. No words were spoken. They both breathed heavily. All the two of them could see was the man's flashlight inside one of the booths. He was rummaging around papers.

"Did you hear that?" Emily asked, turning to Jon with questioning eyes.

"What? What is it?"

"Sounded like a horn or something. Maybe a person in one of those cars up there."

Jon shrugged. With a head full of racing thoughts, he had no room for any new stimuli. It was already too much. Plus, his shirt stuck to his back with rain and sweat. Not an inch of him was at ease.

Suddenly, the row of the booths was lighting up more than all the headlights shining together. Something was approaching.

The man left the booth and was walking back around the piles of cars. He was holding a giant piece of paper of some sort. As he got closer, Emily and Jon realized it was a map.

"Hey, I think I heard it too, just now," Jon said over to Emily. "It *does* sound like a horn." But Jon couldn't see any movement coming from the cars ahead.

As soon as Jon spoke, the man stopped in his tracks as his fearful face looked down the road at the now fully formed bright light that was filling up the entire scene, overpowering all the other light sources. It looked as if he just walked out on stage for a play he had forgotten his lines for. Emily and Jon turned their heads around to see a white tractor-trailer with the words PREMIUM ELITE on the side, barreling toward the man.

HONK. HONK.

The man tried to move from the tractor-trailer's speeding path. Too late. *BOOM.* It smashed into him and the surrounding cars. His body was obliterated in a second. An explosion erupted as the gigantic metal machine slammed into the gas tanks of the piled vehicles, causing each of them to ignite one by one, sending metal and debris into the air at every angle like a firework show.

The windshield of the Nissan shattered. Emily screamed. She and Jon covered their heads and ducked under the dashboard, just in time to miss face-fulls of glass. Jon flung his backpack up to cover his face. The windshield wipers *CRACKED* off and flew into the backseat of the car.

Bits and pieces of cars and body parts flew by the now wide-open windshield. Jon's eyes shut tight. A rear bumper of a black Cadillac flew and ripped off Emily's side-view mirror. She screamed again. Jon squeezed his eyes shut tighter. Chunks of glass and metal rained down on the Nissan like daggers. It sounded like a hailstorm.

This is it, Jon thought. *I'm fucking dead! Please God…God!*

The sound of the explosions faded to an end and the remaining debris fell over the road after the white tractor's trailer slid on the concrete beyond the tolls. Sparks danced all around. Then, after what seemed like an eternity, it was quiet. Rain was pouring into the car, filling it up like a cup. Jon wasn't sure if he was dead or alive, so he remained in his duck and cover position until Emily started to speak.

"Jon?" Emily said all shook up. Her body vibrated. "Jon, are you alright?"

Jon lowered his backpack with the speed of a hostage during a bank robbery. His eyes were still closed, hair still messed up. Bits of windshield covered him. "I think so," he said. He opened his eyelids and adjusted his glasses to see the bonfire of cars and the road in ruins. The flames. The wreckage. The gates of Hell had opened up right here on Earth. "Jesus Christ!" With eyes fixed at the scene, he took short, quick breaths. "Are you ok?"

Burnt rubber and metal smoke poured into the car. The night's air was contaminated with death and bloody rain. A scent you couldn't forget. A smell that would stick in their nostrils forever.

"Yeah." Emily swallowed, making a noise in her throat. She fought nausea. She coughed and so did Jon. Her eyes locked onto the scene. Jon could tell she was adjusting her nose ring, making sure it was still intact. "We have to go through there. Okay? We have to go. We can't stop now this is the only way out of here."

"What? Where?" Jon asked. He was almost angered at what she'd just said. He coughed again. *Forward? Into that?*

"There." Emily pointed at the flaming and smoking cars that surrounded the now opened pathway. It was the EZ PASS lane that the white tractor-trailer ran through with a force so strong that it cleared everything in its path, including the roof above it. The top was torn apart like a crumpled piece of paper. The metal beast lay dead just after it. There was debris scattered around it, but Emily and Jon couldn't tell what it was. It appeared to be like piles of Frisbees.

Jon was quiet. He wanted to ask if she was crazy, but there was no point in asking. This whole situation was crazy. The world was crazy. *If we would've pulled up closer to the man in the vest, we would've been fried.* That thought was too much to say out loud. It made him sweaty and nauseous. He coughed hard into his elbow.

There weren't any rules anymore. Anything goes at this point. You either get killed trying to get home or get killed waiting around, fetching a map from a turnpike tollbooth.

"If you're gonna do it, you gotta do it now," Jon said, pulling the collar of his shirt over his nose and mouth.

Emily waved away the fumes from the front of her face and hit the gas pedal. She sent the Nissan through the flames and rubble with no interest in checking for anyone else on the road despite having witnessed the worst vehicle collision known to man. Jon checked again for Emily. He looked behind them to make sure that no more tractor-trailers were coming. They were safe. . . for now.

As the Nissan drove through the destroyed and smoldering EZ PASS lane, the flames whipped at them, making Emily put more weight on the pedal. Pulsating heat beat upon them. The rain fought it. They sped around the tipped tractor-trailer that killed the vested man and saw that the Frisbees were actually frozen pizzas. In fact, those pizzas were something Jon enjoyed eating, but now the thought of eating anything made him feel sick to his stomach. Sick. Tired. He needed to, but he didn't want to eat or sleep. He just wanted to get home.

The Nissan, which was now a convertible, sped off onto the turn-pike. Into the wet, dark night.

TWENTY-EIGHT

Patience

Big Jon finished setting up the rifle on its tripod, which rested on a tree stump. Its long, black barrel looked out over a field far from the road. Woods surrounded the field in a U-shape. He peeked into the scope and adjusted it, then scratched his heavy mustache. All clear. Silent, except for the occasional sniffle coming from Little Jon.

"Don't worry, son," Big Jon whispered, not wanting to make too much noise in the chilly silence. "Any second now we're gonna get you a buck. It's all about patience."

Little Jon was nervous. As exciting as it was to be on his first real hunting trip with his dad, he worried if he'd be able to steady the shot and pull the trigger when the time came. Part of him wanted a deer to pop out right now so he could get it over with, and the other part of him wanted to give up and go back home to his nice, warm bed. It was the weekend after all. He would normally be asleep at this time, away in dreamland, not worried about freezing to death and waiting for something to happen.

TWENTY-NINE

Night Drive

The further they drove, the more they discovered that the turnpike was covered with carnage. Smashed up cars with cracked bumpers and broken headlights littered the road. Some were on fire. Others had cobwebbed windshields. There were people inside, thrown around and contorted. Some of them burning. Tractor-trailers were on the side of the road with their back doors flung open and crates spilling out. There were knocked down light poles and torn up guide rails. Bodies and blood. Emily did her best to maneuver around it all, even driving onto the dividing grass patch and into the opposite lane. The wreckage seemed to be infinite on both sides.

The rain was slowing down. But what would wash away this gritty mess?

Jon tried to see if his parents were in any of the wrecks. *The black Ford Escape or maybe they were in the blue Chevy.* He wondered if they tried to drive on the turnpike and got caught up in this mess, trying to get to him. But it was no use. It was hard for Jon to focus because there was so much destruction. He thought back to the news footage of Los Angeles where that airplane crashed onto Route 45. *No airplanes here. But what would that matter? The turnpike is so fucked up, it might as well be the same place.*

The lanes split off as the road rose and approached a short overpass. The left lane was where they needed to be. It would take them back down to the ground, headed west. They glanced down at the dark road that had a concrete barrier separating the opposing sides. *Thank God,* Jon thought. At least a little something to protect them from the oncoming traffic. But there were still cars. Some moving up the way and others stopped. Crashed. Similar to what they've just been through, but more spread out it seemed. More room for comfort and moving faster. As long as they could avoid being fried like the man back at the tolls, it would only take about an hour for them to get to Jon's exit.

"You think we'll make it through this fucking mess tonight?" Emily asked.

"I think so. Are you comfortable driving? I could take over if you'd like."

Emily thought for a moment as she drove down the bend and onto the next part of the turnpike. Her hair was soaked to a darker black. The cool night's air flowed through the blasted-off windshield, fighting against the smell of hot metal and rubber.

"I…" Emily got interrupted by a *ding* sound coming from the dashboard. She peeked over the wheel and saw an orange-lit gas pump icon pop up beside the odometer. "Well isn't that just fucking perfect?"

"Oh no. Are we low on gas?" Jon asked, feeling a sweat come across his face beneath the rain coating.

Emily sighed. "Yeah. Fifty miles until empty. Goddammit!" She *slapped* the steering wheel. "I didn't even think to fill it up. I mean, I didn't know all this was going to happen. God, I'm such a mess! What the fuck is going on?"

"It's alright! How would you even know? This whole thing just happened overnight. Neither of us could've guessed we'd be having to do this," Jon said, trying to calm her down a little. The truth was Jon was upset too. *Fifty miles left? Shit!* His thoughts wouldn't help the situation. Only worsen it.

"We just have to keep going," Emily said with another angered sigh. "Can't stop now. We will just have to see how far we can get. Do you know how many miles away your house is?"

"I can check on my phone, give me a sec."

Jon leaned upwards and pulled out his iPhone, careful not to cut his hand on the pieces of windshield glass that were covering just about every inch of the car. He turned on the screen and pressed on the app that read GOOGLE MAPS. After a short load, a virtual map of their location popped up with a red triangle moving along with the Nissan. He slid up the bottom of the map with his thumb and entered his address. 524 Franklin Court, Springsdale, Pennsylvania. Jon's face became sweatier now, redder too. He didn't want to tell her how many miles it would take. They wouldn't have enough gas for the trip.

"About sixty-eight miles," Jon said, now sighing himself. It was out there. *Sixty-eight goddamn miles. At least the Verizon satellites still work. The maniacs haven't gone to space yet.*

"Are you serious?" Emily ran her fingers through the top of her hair.

"Yeah. Approximately an hour and two minutes at this rate it says."

Emily gripped the steering wheel tighter, looking more focused now. "Sixty-eight miles, huh? Isn't that a fucking blessing?"

Jon didn't say another word but nodded in silence as his eyes remained on the screen of his phone. He hit a little plus icon on the app, and it brought up options for local places. Restaurants. Hotels. Gas stations. He hit the pump and nozzle icon and the virtual map zoomed-out from their exact location and showed red blimps that pinpointed the different stations surrounding them. He pressed on the closest blimp, a Speedway. Five miles away. A robotic woman's voice spoke from Jon's phone. It was loud and clear.

STARTING ROUTE TO SPEEDWAY IN HUNTINGTON, PENNSYLVANIA.

IN FOUR AND A HALF MILES, KEEP RIGHT TO TAKE EXIT THIRTY-THREE TOWARD HUNTINGTON.

"If we follow this, it'll take us right to a gas station," Jon said, looking up. They were approaching figures on the side of the road. Two people who were waving their arms up and down, trying to get Emily and Jon's attention. They were drenched.

"We can't stop for them," Emily said without taking her eyes away from the road. It was as if she knew the people were there without seeing them. "It's not safe. We can't risk it."

Jon agreed but didn't say anything as he made out two women wearing tank tops and short shorts, jumping and looking terrified as they waved their arms harder and higher as the car approached closer. Their breasts bounced. Then, they started to move closer to the road, almost putting themselves in front of the car.

"Hey!" the two women shouted. "Hey! Please help us! Please! Hey! Pullover! Please!"

Emily HONKED the horn. The two women backed away to the side of the road again, still shouting. Emily sped up and the two women continued to wave and scream as Jon looked back at them through the only side view mirror that remained on the Nissan. They put their arms down and looked disappointed. They started to shout and curse, but their voices faded away.

"I guess we have no choice, right?" Emily asked, wiping her nose with the back of her wrist. "We *have* to get gas, or we're fucked. I really hope we can get some juice in this thing or I don't know what we'll do. We might have to steal a car or something. *SOMETHING.* God, I need a cigarette. I don't care if I have to rob the place. Where are we going again?"

"Speedway. Only three miles now."

"I don't think we even have Speedways in East Gap. Hess or Sunoco. Do they sell cigarettes there?"

"I'd imagine so. They have them at all the other ones I think."

"They better." Emily let out another sigh and rubbed her nose ring. "You think there's even a gas station left? For all we know, there could be nothing but a pile of ashes when we get there. Then what?"

"Then we'd just keep going to the next gas station. There's gotta be one still standing. They can't all be wiped out ya know?"

"True."

"Would you know how to steal a car? Hotwire, I mean."

Kind of. I have a cousin who had a boyfriend show us one time how to do it. He was homeless or something at one point and was able to get the job done with only a screwdriver."

"Wow."

"He did it though. A screwdriver was all it took. He was fuckin' nuts but he got the job done. Yeah, interesting folks up at East Gap, let me tell ya. A fun bunch. A lot of wackos and creeps, but with all of this shit going on, I would take them over whatever the fuck these things are any day. Hell, even my father wasn't this shitty to me and he was quite the shithead."

Jon blew air from his nose. Now didn't seem to be the appropriate time to bring up daddy issues, but Emily got right into it.

"Who would've thought getting away from one abusive relationship would lead me right into another one? The only difference is I don't think these monsters are fueled by alcohol, at least not all of them." She gave a depressing chuckle.

"Yeah, I think there's something more sinister going on here," Jon said, trying to change the subject back to the current state of affairs.

"I could use some alcohol myself. Strong shit, too. Like Jack Daniels. God, I sound like my dad. He'd down bottles of Jack like they were water, slap my mom around, and then take a nap on the couch like it was nothing," Emily said.

"Jesus," John said.

"Yep, then he'd wake up hours later, forgetting he ever laid a finger on her. She'd yell and scream until his hangover got him pissed off all over again. Chairs, plates, the vases. He'd throw them all over the house without an ounce of regret afterward. One time, he hit me right above the eye with one of my mom's high heels. I had to get stitches and the bastard never once apologized for it."

"I'm sorry to hear that. That's terrible." *Is this necessary right now?* Jon thought.

"Now you know why I smoke, huh? All I wanted to do was get away. I figured if I came to White Haven, I could figure out what I wanted to do with my life, but the truth is I still don't have a fucking clue," Emily said, glancing over at Jon with a little side smile. "Do you smoke or drink, Jon?"

"Nah, that's not really my scene."

"Well, good for you. They're not habits you want to pick up. Then again, at this point it wouldn't really matter, would it? Might as well drink and smoke as much as you'd like! I don't imagine any of this getting any better."

Ebola? No, couldn't be. Swine flu? Jon tried to make sense of it all. The behavior from his classmates was shocking. Unreal. *What would make people do this? Drive a two-ton truck into somebody? Was Grandma sick with the same thing? My parents? Please, no. . .*

"I think you're right. Maybe I'll try a smoke with you if we get out of this alive," Jon said.

"You never even tried a cig before?"

"No, never."

"What a nice, innocent boy," Emily said. "What were you studying to be?"

"A psychologist. Maybe have a career as a therapist or counselor. I don't know. I feel the same way you do. Some days I don't have a clue myself."

IN TWO MILES. KEEP RIGHT AND TAKE EXIT THIRTY-THREE TOWARDS HUNTINGTON.

Emily did a great job maneuvering through obstacles on the road while maintaining a speed between fifty and sixty miles per hour.

There were more overturned cars. Cars stopped in the middle of the road. A knocked over tractor-trailer. It seemed they were the only ones going west. An occasional set of headlights would shine from the opposite lane, but no one tried to plow through the barrier.

No more tractor-trailers. No more explosions. They didn't even find any more people on the side of the road waving for help. It all seemed so easy. Too easy. *What's going to happen? Something's got to happen,* Jon thought.

And, just before he could think another thought, something did happen.

THIRTY

Movement

There was movement in the woods across the field. Shrubbery *shook*. Twigs *snapped*. It made Little Jon's heart race. A shadow flashed between the trees. Big Jon looked into the scope. *Here we go. This is it.* Little Jon leaned in closer to his father, ready to take hold of the trigger.

But time passed and nothing happened. No sign of a deer or any animal coming out of the trees. Big Jon leaned back from the scope. Cold breath poured from his mouth beneath his mustache. His eyes darted left and right over the field, scanning the woods.

"Did you see where it went?" Big Jon whispered.

"No, I-I lost it. I think I saw its tail though."

Big Jon reached down into his camouflage backpack that lay just beside the rifle. He unzipped the side pouch and pulled out a deer call, or as Little Jon called it, the giant straw. The top of it was a wooden cylinder with the words HARDWOOD GRUNTER on it. The bottom half looked to Little Jon like a big, black bendy straw, shaped and flexible like the ones he'd get at restaurants when he was really young.

"I want you to call it," Big Jon said, handing over the giant straw. "Remember the breeding grunt we learned about?"

Little Jon nodded. He took the straw and puckered his mouth around the top wooden part. Then, he cupped his hand around the opened bottom of the bendy end. Big Jon looked back into the scope as the breeding grunt call played. The sound always made Little Jon think of a frog or toad. A strange sound. His hand opened and then closed and then opened again as he repeated the noise for a few seconds, cupping the sound. Big Jon went back to the backpack and pulled out binoculars.

God, it's cold. Where are you, you stupid deer?

THIRTY-ONE

The Cyclops

The map app's voice was saying to keep to the right to take Exit 33 in one mile when Jon noticed a big flash of light bouncing off the dashboard of the car. He looked around, confused. Emily didn't seem to notice it. Then, it flashed again. Brighter now. Jon looked into the side-view mirror that somehow survived the explosion and saw headlights beaming right at them. It looked like a Jeep based on the lines of the grill and the way the circular headlights sat on either side. His chest started to hurt and sweat began to form over his face again.

"Emily! There's somebody behind us!" he said.

Emily went to look into the rearview mirror, forgetting that it had been destroyed from the windshield blasting off. She kept her foot on the gas and turned her head around to look out the back window. Bright lights shined into her eyes from the vehicle as it approached the Nissan, evading the obstacles of debris just as Emily did.

"I'm gonna pull over and let them pass," she said. "We don't want any trouble."

Emily slowed the Nissan down and pulled it off to the right side of the road, onto a strip of grass before the line of trees. A red Dodge Challenger lay sideways just behind them. Neither Emily nor Jon checked to see if anybody lay inside as they waited for the Jeep to pass them. They sat with their breaths heavy and hearts pounding. They looked over their headrests, out the back window, beyond the flipped Challenger at the oncoming car.

The rain was a tinkle now.

As the Jeep got closer, the headlights remained locked on them. Not the road. They both realized that the Jeep was driving straight toward their direction and not looking to go around. Emily said she didn't want any trouble, but that's what she got.

It was lucky that Emily pulled in front of the flipped Challenger as it made a nice buffer when the Jeep *SLAMMED* into the back of it. Emily and Jon squeezed their eyes shut and held their heads against the headrests. Glass blasted from the rear window as the Challenger shoved into the back of Emily's Nissan. *SMASH*. Metal collided with metal, rocking the car like a boat out at sea. The grill of the Challenger dented the back of the Nissan's trunk, causing it to open, blocking Emily and Jon's view.

"Emily!" Jon shouted without moving his head. "Emily! We have to get out of here! You have to drive!"

The Jeep was smoking with its engine still *humming*. It reversed from the collision and the plastic taillight pieces *crackled* underneath its tires as it pulled back from the grass to the concrete road. Jon could hear the tires moving and adjusting, trying to place itself so the Nissan was right in line for the second ramming.

"Emily!" Jon cried.

Emily twisted and turned herself. She *SLAMMED* her foot on the gas pedal as hard as she could. The Nissan shook and skidded as bits of wet grass and mud flung from underneath the tires before it shot forward towards the exit ramp, which was now only half a mile away. A clear shot if they stayed in the grass strip. But neither of them could get a look at where the Jeep was since the trunk covered up the entire back window. *Shit!* The side-view mirror was of no use now as it could only see the Challenger fade off into the distance.

A light streamed onto Emily's left side and up the side of the driver's door.

"Emily! It's coming up on your side!"

"Fuck! Fuck!" she screamed and tried to put her head out the window to see. The Jeep, now with only one headlight on the right side, was speeding its way up the concrete lane. The streaming light became brighter and illuminated Emily's side of the car. The hood of the car came into view and the smoking, dark Jeep was parallel with the Nissan. With its tinted windows, there was no way to see who was behind the wheel. It kept its pace with Emily and Jon before speeding up ahead and turning right in front of the Nissan.

"Fuck! AHHH! Fuck!" Emily shouted as she jerked the wheel to the right and *SLAMMED* both of her feet onto the brake pedal. The Nissan spun with the Jeep. Swirling. Skidding. A tornado of metal and rubber dancing through the darkness.

Jon shut his eyes and braced for death.

THIRTY-TWO

Face to Face

Both Big Jon and Little Jon inhaled when they saw it. A young buck with white fur on its underside and tail pranced out of the woods across the field toward their direction. *Here I am* it seemed to answer. It stopped only a few feet from where it appeared from the trees, looking around to find the source of the breeding call.

"Look at that, son. He's only got one antler there," Big Jon whispered, handing over the binoculars.

Little Jon held them up to his face. The deer's right antler was just a boney stump on its head. Cracked off it seemed. The left was intact but appeared to be short and chipped like he was in some back-alley brawl in the woods and only one antler made it out alive. It moved closer to them now but not enough to get the shot in.

Stillness.

Big Jon patted Little Jon on the knee and pointed at the Hardwood Grunter.

"Just one more little one," Big Jon mouthed.

Little Jon placed the wooden top back to his lips and cupped his hand on the bottom of the giant straw. He blew as gently as he could and made the toad sound, but only for a half a second. The deer's eyes shot up. It came closer and stopped. Its eyes were wide, ears pointed up. Its nose pointed toward them. Cold, late-autumn air puffed from it.

Big Jon leaned to the side so Little Jon could grab onto the trigger. The deer stared ahead, frozen. Little Jon took a hold of the rifle and squinted his right eye with his other looking through the scope at the creature. The statue.

His little finger wrapped around the front of the trigger. The crosshairs aligned right on the deer's left shoulder. All he had to do was squeeze and it would all be over.

"Go on, son. Pull," Big Jon whispered in his son's ear.

Little Jon couldn't hear his father as the thumping of his heart pounded in his ears. There were no thoughts, no shots fired. Just a twelve-year-old boy and a young buck staring at one another. Motionless. Both statues sitting in the freezing November morning. The frozen stillness.

"If you're gonna do it, you gotta do it now," Big Jon whispered.

Little Jon pulled the trigger.

THIRTY-THREE

A Walk in the Woods

Jon woke up with his face mashed into the top of his backpack that acted as an airbag. His glasses were broken right down the middle with the lenses cracked like cobwebs. Both sides separated and fell to the floor as he went to adjust them. His head was aching, and he felt a dizziness like no other. He wanted to vomit.

With blurred vision, he blinked, rubbed his eyes, then blinked again, trying to bring any bit of focus. In front of him was the light-blue hood of the Nissan beneath the morning light. It was wrapped around a tree, which looked like a brown blob. He rubbed his eyes again and felt his face. Dried blood was under both of his nostrils. On his bottom lip too. He could taste it.

The only sounds were the *chirps* of early birds. No more rain or thunder.

"E-E-Emily?" He barely got it out. "Ar-ar-are…" He coughed and tasted blood. He choked on his own words. "You…alright?"

He turned his head toward the driver's side and saw what he could make out of Emily's tie-dyed shirt and the long messy black hair. She was in the corner between the steering wheel and the door. Jon leaned toward her and touched her back. No movement. No sound. Beyond her was the grey and black, out of focus Jeep that looked to be slammed into a tree.

"Em-Emily?" Jon said, breathing quicker now as the present time started to become clearer. He nudged her back but still got no response.

"EMILY!" he cried out. "EMILY!" But there was nothing. Jon was shouting at a dead girl.

Jon felt around his backpack, flipped it around and began unzipping compartments. Old bits of his glasses slid off from it. *Zip. Zip. Zip.* His heart was beating in his ears and sweat caked his face.

He opened the bottom pouch on the front of the backpack and felt around pencils, pens, and folded papers until his fingers found a plastic case. He pulled it out and flipped it open to reveal a pair of silver, square-wired glasses. His backup pair.

The glasses were dirty and small for his face. Jon hadn't worn them in God knew how long since he'd always taken great care of his black-framed ones. He hated these backup glasses. He wished he'd never have to wear them again. Now, he wished he couldn't see at all as the sight of Emily's lifeless body slumped in the corner of the driver's side of the Nissan burned through his retinas and sent a striking pain to his stomach.

"EMILY!" he shouted again, voice cracking at the now in-focus horror.

The dashboard and the tan wrap of the steering wheel were dyed in a dark, bloodied stain. Trying to be as careful as possible, Jon pulled on her shoulders. Her head made a slight *peeling* sound as it separated from the side of the dashboard where more of the blackened blood spotted. Jon leaned her body back into the seat.

A large gash from her left eyebrow up to Emily's hairline seeped with dark-red and scabbing flesh. Her face bloodied and beaten with a blackened left eye bulging. The nose ring was ripped off, with skin from her nostril taken along with it. The colors on her tie-dyed shirt now featured her own blood. The once cute girl with the black hair and blue stripe down the side was now ugly and ravaged by death. Pure, unmerciful death.

Jesus Christ. Jesus FUCKING Christ!

Jon covered his mouth. His face was wet with sweat like the condensation on a glass of Coke at a diner. He grabbed his backpack and pushed himself out of the Nissan. Throwing his backpack on the ground beside him, he bent over with his hands on his jeans. His eyes squeezed shut. He gagged and heaved underneath the warmth of the morning rays that dried the damp grass. The stench of blood, metal, and rubber filled his nostrils, causing strong nausea. But no puke came. He sat and spat up bitter saliva onto the grass that stained his knees with a moist brown and green.

The weight of the world felt unbearable on him. Things were getting worse by the moment and Jon felt like giving up just then. If he couldn't even stay the course on the turnpike, just what in the hell was he going to do on-foot?

I need some water. Something to drink. Anything.

He tried to distract his mind from Emily, but when he gave her lifeless body another glance, his body seemed to implode on itself. He felt such utter sickness, despair like nothing he had ever felt before. Jon hadn't known the girl well, but his heart yearned to have her back. He needed her. He needed someone to help him. The college boy was alone and pressing on by himself seemed so useless.

The waves of nausea crushed him, but Jon stayed steady on his feet, forcing his puke to stay down.

He walked back to his backpack, trying to keep his eyes away from Emily and keep his sickness at bay. *Zip.* He looked through the top, biggest pouch and found the flattened box of granola bars sitting atop the books and supplies from his dorm room. He tore off one of the green wrappers to reveal the bar had been smashed into crumbs. Jon shoved them into his mouth, moving them around his tongue, trying to scrape the granola onto his taste buds to remove the bile flavor in his mouth. It almost did the trick, but he needed liquid to wash it all down.

No luck in his backpack as he spilled all of his textbooks and the laptop from it. Nothing in Emily's car except for an empty Starbucks paper cup that was rolling around in the back seat. Not even a drop of coffee left. The taste of granola and unspewed vomit was getting sickening as it marinated in Jon's mouth. *Anything.* Then, he glanced over at the crashed grey Jeep against the tree.

The windshield was shattered, and the hood looked like an accordion. From what he could see with his hands pressed up against the tinted passenger side window, there was a man's head lying on the wheel.

He noticed an arm behind the driver seat, so he moved to the left and pressed his hands and face up to the rear passenger side window. It looked to be two people lying against each other. Half on the seats and half on the floor, tangled up by their arms and legs. Long hair was everywhere. *Two sisters maybe? A father and his daughters?* Jon tried the handle. Locked. *So thirsty.* He stepped back and looked around and saw no movement around him. No cars. No sounds. No life. *What the fuck am I supposed to do now?* His head was pounding his skull like a drum.

He coughed up more mixture of sickening spit and granola. Birds *chirped* from above the trees and Jon turned his head, trying to find them, squinting his eyes as the sun beat down. Everything hurt.

The woods. I can't be far from Huntington. With that thought, he quick-stepped back to the Nissan, eyes looking away from the driver side. He still couldn't look at Emily. How could he? How would it help him?

He rounded the car and picked up his backpack, placing it over his shoulders. Then, he closed his eyes and reached around the passenger side for his phone. The smell of death was teasing at his nose, begging him to vomit at once but Jon resisted and pulled out his phone from under the dashboard. He wiped pieces of the windshield from it and noticed a prominent crack going along the side of the screen. It still turned on.

7:58 A.M.

The battery icon displayed 59%.

Jon opened the maps app and saw that he would be in Huntington in just over a mile after getting off the exit. *The woods,* Jon thought again. *The woods have to pop out somewhere by Huntington.* There was no way Jon could walk the turnpike, not after the shit show last night. *Look at Emily. Just one more time.* But he couldn't. Emily was dead and there was nothing else he could do about it. *Put a blanket over her face or something.* But what blanket? There were no blankets or covers available. *It's the right thing to do, cover her up.* He decided one of his wrinkled shirts from his backpack would have to do for now.

Jon placed a *Pulp Fiction* shirt over Emily's face as she lay slumped back in the seat of her Nissan. Jon's chest ached as he looked at her for the final time. A poor, troubled girl whose life had been cut short. Not from rebelling against her abusive father, but from freaks with an unknown motive for destruction.

He wasn't sure if he should pray or say anything. A part of him wanted to make the promise of returning after he found his parents or someone to help him. He wondered if it would matter or if he'd even be alive long enough to return to this spot. The thought of her body being forgotten and left here for the rest of time, haunted him.

For now, he could only cry.

***

Jon walked through the woods. He called his family again. No answer. What else did Jon expect at this point? *How much time has passed since the night everything went to hell?* Then, he started to call all the numbers in his phone. Old friends. Relatives. Everything went to voice mail. 911 went to the automated machine as it did before. *Useless. Everything's useless. God, I'm thirsty.*

Twigs *snapped* and leaves *crunched* underneath Jon's sneakers as he made his way through the woods beside the turnpike. Although he moved at a sluggish pace, Jon made his way as the phone went from 1.1 miles left to 1.0. Progress.

But Jon already felt exhausted. He hadn't slept well or ate anything of substance in a long time. Thoughts of passing out and dehydration played in his mind. *Maybe that's how I'll go. Right here in the woods. Alone. Ugh, my head. I should've died in that crash. I'm sorry, Emily. Emily, please forgive me. I should've gotten my car. You could still be alive right now. I'm so sorry.*

The sound of a car driving by pulled Jon from his thoughts and he ran to his left. The woods were now above the turnpike and tall, metal barriers separated the nature from the gravel. Jon looked all around but couldn't see a moving vehicle, only the same debris and wreckage as he's always seen. *Was it all in my head?* But he swore he heard it. A car driving, maybe even listening to loud music. *Perhaps it was really flying up the road.* He stood still at the top of the hill, looking down at the roadway. Nothing came or went. He decided he would walk at the edge of the wooded hill until he got to Huntington.

Granola and vomit swirled in the back of his throat. His face convulsed. He gagged. He never saw or heard any other cars go by.

Jon's mind bounced all around as he thought about Emily, his parents, and what happened at college. Everything. *What started it all? What happened? Is there something in the air? The water? Is the food poisoned? Why? Who did this? Kevin. Mark. They tried to kill us. Everyone tried to kill us. But it all happened overnight. Nighttime. Why the night? Why not the day? Why were they sleeping in the day and up at night, trying to tear us apart?* He couldn't come up with a theory of any substance. Only more questions. It was too much to handle. The questions in Jon's brain got him distracted enough from his ailments. Before he knew it, he was coming up to Huntington as the phone's voice said:

KEEP RIGHT AND IN A QUARTER MILE, YOUR DESTINATION WILL BE ON YOUR LEFT.

The woods sloped down, which helped as Jon approached the tolls. They were clear, except for a car or two. Jon had to stay to the right as the lady on the phone said. Beyond it, if he went straight, the overpass curved to the left and went to who knows where on Interstate 83.

His legs were weak, and his body ached. Especially his head. A pounding ring wrapped around his skull. He turned the maps app off to conserve battery power. 47% now. If Huntington still had power, which at this point seemed doubtful, he could get it all the way back to 100% if he could find an outlet. His body needed a recharge as well.

Sniff, sniff. There was an odor of char in the air. A burnt stench that made Jon's nostrils rise, cracking the dried blood beneath them. He coughed granola up.

As Jon finished the slope, the trees began to dwindle from his right side as he walked over the patchy grass. He was walking along the guide rail outside of the exit ramp from the turnpike that curved to the right and he could see dead traffic lights above where the concrete turned into the asphalt road up ahead. The stench became stronger as he walked alongside the curving rail and the last of the trees until he saw it.

The Speedway gas station was burned to a blackness.

Huntington

Jon didn't get any closer than the side of the road, which was brushed with black ash. The stench was harsh. His lungs wept.

Blackened rubble and warped metal were all that remained of the Speedway gas station. It looked as if a missile had struck it. The four pumps were fried and covered in ash. The metal roofing was completely blackened and ripped on the right-end, exposing the metal skeleton inside. Three cars, two of them pickups and the other a tiny little four-door, were burnt and shriveled. The gas station didn't look much better as the entire storefront was blackened from the fire's wrath. It was hard to see the letter S across the top of the roof. It was nothing more than a filthy imprint of what the lettering used to be.

The scene was something from a post-apocalyptic movie, but Jon's shock didn't last long as his thoughts returned to the night before. He'd seen worse than this. He saw that tractor-trailer plow into that man and light up the entire turnpike with its crushing speed. *The same thing probably happened here. But where's the tractor-trailer?* It didn't matter. Jon didn't have a car. Gas was no longer on his list. Neither were cigarettes. *I'm sorry, Emily.*

Speedway's remnants were so black in contrast to the morning's bright and blue sky, that Jon hadn't noticed the McDonald's standing to the right of it. Not as rattled from the fate of its neighbor, the Golden Arches stood with its darkened windows reflecting light. One window, however, looked smashed open.

A couple of cars were in the parking lot. A tractor-trailer parked behind it with its front facing out toward the west. No movement from what Jon could see.

He approached McDonald's and found no signs of life outside.

All of the cars were locked. No one was inside any of them, not even the tractor-trailer around back. It was a lonely lot. There was only one other place to go as Jon hopped through the shattered window and into the eating area inside.

THIRTY FIVE

McDonald's

The McDonald's eating area was lit only by the daylight through the windows. Behind the counter, light streamed through the vacant drive-thru. There was a man in a trucker cap lying face-down between two tables. A stain on the brown tiles surrounded his head. His white tank top shirt had stains of what looked like a blast of Coca-Cola.

An older man in a jacket sat in the corner at one of the tables, fast asleep. His head rested on the window behind him as his breakfast sandwich lay cold on a yellow wrapper.

Jon approached both men and found they weren't interested in talking or moving an inch from their places of rest.

Damn it.

The soda fountain wasn't working. No power. Jon turned toward the counter, which was stained with either blood or soda, maybe both.

There were napkins and cups thrown around. A harsh stench of meat filled the air. Rotten meat. It emanated from beyond the counter and silver shelves that fenced off the cooking area. A door in the back was open to the morning air, but it wasn't enough to flush out the smell of rotting food that stung Jon's nose.

Behind the counter, and just before the silver shelving, Jon could see a darkened, little refrigerator with two bottles of white milk inside. He walked around the side of the cash register and saw a young, fat female employee lying dead on the ground with her headset smashed into her face. Jon looked away just after noticing her silver name tag displaying COURTNEY. The rotten meat was stabbing into his nose. He sucked his upper lip to his nostrils to shield the smell. Flies *buzzed* around. One flew on Jon's arm and he shook it off.

Not much further behind Courtney was another employee, face-down by the drive-thru window. He was next to the fryolator that had a brownish liquid settled inside. Grease. A big vat of grease.

It was a Black man with burns on the side of his face that seemed to have fused with the tiles on the floor. Jon didn't dare turn him over to see the damage.

The flies *buzzed.*

He leaned over Courtney to open the refrigerator. No coolness came from it and the bottles seemed to be room temperature. Jon wasn't sure how long ago the place had power, but he didn't care. He grabbed the bottles and shook them. Then, he twisted the cap of one of the bottles and drank lukewarm milk. Not spoiled yet. It was almost refreshing. It helped the taste of vomit and granola for a moment as he drank and moved back into the eating area, trying not to make any eye contact with Courtney or the burnt man, or get another whiff of that putrid meat.

After downing the second bottle of milk, Jon had to use the bathroom. Perhaps it was the warm milk that was stewing up something in his stomach along with whatever he last ate before the granola. *Doritos? Chocolate? What did I eat before that?* He couldn't remember for sure what he had eaten from the vending machine back at the library. It wasn't whatever Mark and Kevin must have eaten, thank God. If that was even the reason for their sleep and insanity. The thought of those two, and now thoughts of Dan and Emily, made his stomach churn. The *THWACK* of the bat against Mark's head. Thinking about the sound made Jon cringe. That scene replayed in his mind for a moment. It made him feel sick, but he tried to shake it as he moved away from the cooking area.

The men's bathroom was pitch-black. Jon used the light from the flash of his iPhone camera to look around. No bodies. No trash. Just a quiet public restroom that smelled like urinal cakes with a hint of excrement. There were more flies in here, climbing on the white walls with their little black legs. Jon shined the phone's light over the toilet and saw yellow in the bowl from the previous user.

He did his business and flushed with his shoe. He was surprised to see the bowl flush without a problem. *The water must still be working.* He came out of the stall and turned on the sink below a fingerprint-covered mirror. Cold water spurted out. Jon propped his phone on top of the paper towel dispenser and cupped some water in his hand, sniffed it, and splashed it on his bloodied and dried face and hair. He even cupped some into his mouth to rid the taste of the old milk.

Then he had an idea.

Jon returned to the eating area and grabbed the two empty milk bottles off the table. He went behind the counter, grabbed a large paper cup from the line of circular cup dispensers, and walked to the soda fountain for a large lid and a straw.

Jon brought them into the bathroom and first rinsed out the milk bottles with the sink water, pouring whitish water out and down the rusty-ringed drain. He filled one all the way up with water and drank it. Water splashed out of the sides of his mouth and dripped on his chin and shirt. *Ahhh.* He refilled it and then filled the other. After making sure the lids were screwed on tight, he pushed them in his backpack on top of the granola bar box and clothes and zipped it up. Then, he filled the large-sized paper cup all the way to the top, pressed on the clear plastic lid, and inserted the straw through the hole. He took a sip.

Ahhh. It was the finest water that Jon had ever drank.

Now with his holy grail of McDonald's bathroom sink water, Jon ate the rest of his granola crumbs. He ruled out dehydration as his inevitable cause of death, but hunger still lingered. The crumbs weren't much but were enough to give him the energy to keep him going for a little longer. They wouldn't be able to carry him for the entire day. Too bad McDonald's was filled with rotting meat, Jon would've loved nothing more than a Big Mac, large fries, and a chocolate milkshake.

Jon was about to step out through the window when he remembered the cars and tractor-trailer that were parked around the building. A Honda and a Pontiac were out front. *Keys. I need keys.* He glanced back at the dead trucker. *I can't drive a fucking tractor-trailer.* Then, his eyes moved over to the counter where he knew those two dead employees lay just behind it. *Shit.* No way did he want to get up close and personal with those bodies, but he knew for sure that the two cars in the front lot belonged to them. One of them at least. It had to be true. Just as true as the keys were in their pockets. Their cold, dead pockets.

Jon sighed and walked behind the counter to see Courtney still lying there. Dead. Her fat-cheeked face looked punched inward, and her microphone headset was shoved up her bloodied nose. Jon held his breath. *Fuck it, here we go.* He crouched down and felt around the pockets of her black work pants.

A bulge from her left pocket felt like keys and Jon shoved the top of his hand into it. Tight. His middle finger got to the keyring and he almost fell backward with them popping from the skin-tight pocket. A large set of keys around a pink ring *jingled* and *jangled.* He fumbled around with them until he found a car remote with a Honda logo. A silver button *clicked* out a key. *Perfect.* With no need to work with the burnt Black man, Jon got up, grabbed his large cup of water, and left the restaurant through the broken window.

Courtney's white Honda reminded him of Emily's Nissan. An older, used model that doubled as a personal trash can. It also had an aroma like Emily's car, except that it was McDonald's food. Courtney must have taken her work home with her every day.

Jon put his backpack in the passenger seat and twisted the ignition. Half a tank of gas, what a pleasant surprise! *Thank you, Jesus.* That was enough to get him home.

He fetched his phone from his pocket. 42%. The screen popped up the map app and Jon punched in his home address again. 524 Franklin Court, Springsdale, Pennsylvania. He clicked START ROUTE, bringing back the robot woman's voice.

STARTING ROUTE TO 524 FRANKLIN COURT IN SPRINGSDALE, PENNSYLVANIA. TURN RIGHT ONTO VALLEY ROAD, AND IN ONE AND A HALF MILE, KEEP RIGHT TO MERGE ONTO THE PENNSYLVANIA TURN-PIKE.

A *growl* in Jon's stomach made him check around the car for any form of food. No success. Not even a left-over scrap of a quarter pounder or a flake of a fry. Nothing. He thought for a moment about getting the keys from the Black man or even the trucker or old man to see if they had any snacks in their vehicles, but he couldn't waste time. The sunlight wouldn't last forever, so he put the car in reverse and backed out of the spot, turning right onto Valley Road.

THIRTY-SIX

Mirch's Motel

The Honda drove under the overpass as Jon listened to the only station that remained on air: 91.7. Classical music. Orchestral tunes played without interruption from a radio host or commercials. Just a constant stream of Vivaldi and Beethoven.

IN ONE MILE, KEEP RIGHT TO MERGE ONTO THE PENNSYLVANIA TURNPIKE.

Jon's stomach growled again. Going number two in the bathroom must have emptied him out, and with all the water he downed in a short period of time, he felt like he would have to piss again soon. But Jon didn't worry as there were plenty of trees around him to pull over and take a leak on.

The woods were on either side of the road as the Honda glided through the empty road toward an upcoming bend. As Jon approached it, he saw the woods break away to reveal a brick building with MIRCH'S MOTEL displayed in red lettering on top of a long, grey roof. The lot was empty.

Jon would've kept driving, but the sight of a snack and soda machine outside of the place caused him to slow the Honda down and turn left into the lot. His stomach did the driving.

It was a quiet, old motel. The sign on the check-in door said SORRY, WE ARE CLOSED.

Dark-red bricks and white doors that looked like they had taken a beating off of their hinges more than once lined the front. Small porches sat at each door with plastic chairs and tables holding ashtrays on top. The parking lot looked like one big ashtray. It smelled smokey and looked dirty. Murders. Drug deals. Who knows what had gone down in this backwoods motel? None of that mattered to Jon. The only thing on his mind was getting into those machines.

The soda machine was a newer model that just had the big plastic buttons that dispensed the drinks. There was no glass to break except for the vintage snack machine that shelved chocolates and chips behind glass.

Jon tried using one of the plastic chairs to break it. No use, it only wobbled the glass and cracked the plastic. Then, he grabbed one of the ashtrays and smashed as hard as he could against the machine. *CRACK*. It put a big, X-shaped smash across the glass in an instant. *CRACK*. *SMASH*. Jon squeezed his eyes and covered his face as the glass dropped from the machine and onto the asphalt.

He grabbed little bags of Cheetos and Lays sour cream and onion chips, Reese's Cups and Twix Bars. He pulled out as much as he could carry and threw them into the backseat of the Honda. More and more he grabbed. He tore open a bag of Doritos and ate it within seconds. His fingers were covered in orange. He licked them off and opened a cinnamon bun. He devoured it and went back to take more. The plan was to empty the whole goddamn machine.

Jon was an animal between eating and stealing. He dumped another batch into the car and was about to turn up from the backseat door to grab the last row of chocolates when he felt something hard sticking into his back.

Interrogation

"Don't move an inch. Put both yer hands up right now," a man commanded in a loud, backwoods accent. It reminded Jon of Dan, but even more hillbillyish. Part of him hoped he'd turn around and it would be Dan, alive and well. Although, the tone was not fit for a friendly reunion. It sounded like Dan's evil twin.

"What are you doin' here? Lookin' for trouble?" the man asked.

Jon swallowed hard. His arms shook as he held them up like a football goal post. He could only assume the jabbing in his backside was the barrel of a gun. "No, sir."

"Then what are you after then? Lookin' to rob an old man's place?" The way he said the word *you* sounded like *yew*.

"No, sir. I was just looking for some help."

"What kindsa help you lookin' for?"

"My friend and I were in an accident on the turnpike and I had to walk to Huntington, sir. I was trying to find some food and get back on the road to get to my family." He felt sick. Regretful.

"Where'd you get this car?" the countryman asked.

"I got it from McDonald's, just up the road." Jon's voice trembled.

"You steal it?"

"Yes, sir."

"Where's yer friend?"

"She's dead." Jon swallowed again. A slight sourness of milk crept up from his throat despite all the water he had downed. "She died in the car crash." Jon closed his eyes when he said it.

"Hmm. You ain't one of them lunatics, are ya?"

Jon shook his head.

"Turn around. Slowly now," the man commanded.

With arms still trembling, Jon turned his body to face the mysterious hillbilly man who was neither large nor frightening, if you didn't count the hunting rifle now pointed at Jon's face. He was young and thin, maybe Jon's age.

The man had buzzed brown hair. A stern face. Cold, brown eyes. There was gauze wrapped around his left forearm. He was wearing a plain, white T-shirt tucked into navy slacks that looked too big around the waist and too short for him. They sat atop shined, black oxford shoes. Something shone behind him. Handcuffs. He looked like a cop in the middle of getting dressed for work. Perhaps he was a rookie with clothes that didn't fit.

"How'd you get all that blood on yer face? Car crash?" His voice didn't match his appearance.

"Yes, sir."

"You ever kill somebody before?"

"No…well…" Jon didn't want to talk about what happened with Mark.

"Tell me!" the man shouted and inched the barrel closer to Jon's frightened face.

"Uh…well…" Jon swallowed hard. His mouth and throat were bone-dry. "I had to kill one of the… maniacs… or whatever they are…he was attacking my friend and I had no choice. I used a base-ball bat to bash his head in…"

The man paused for a moment and then asked, "If I didn't have this gun, would you try to kill me?"

"No, I wouldn't."

"You tellin' me the truth?"

Jon was so nervous that his head was vibrating. He took too long to answer.

The man *RAMMED* the barrel of the rifle into Jon's head like he was trying to pop a balloon.

"Fuck!" Jon shouted and rubbed his forehead, feeling the blood drip right above his left brow. It stung like hell. The spot on his head began to throb. He could see red droplets dangling above his eyelash. Somehow, by the grace of God, his glasses were still intact.

"Don't you lie to me! And keep yer fuckin' hands up, I didn't tell you to move, you thief!" the man shouted. "How can I trust you when the whole world is run amok with liars and fuckin' psychos!?"

Jon stood silent with his eye twitching. A bloody raindrop fell into his eye and he blinked as the red covered his iris.

The man's stare remained. "Empty them pockets for me. Put eve-rything you got on the hood of the car there. Go on. Any quick movements and I'm blastin' yer ass, got it? That cut's just the beginning."

Jon pulled his phone from his pocket and placed it on the hood of the still-running Honda. He reached into his back pocket and pulled out his wallet.

"That's all I have in my pockets," Jon uttered.

"Alright, put them hands back up." The man kept the rifle pointed with his right hand as his left grabbed the wallet and flipped it open. Jon's license slid out into the man's fingers and he held the license up next to Jon. Jon could now see the gauze had a tiny red stain in the middle of it.

"What's yer name?" the man asked.

"Jonathan Barnes."

"Where you from?"

"Springsdale."

"What year were you born?"

Jon could feel the blood going down his cheek and dripping off his face, onto his shirt. "Nineteen ninety-eight."

The man's eyes danced between the license and Jon's face. He put it next to the wallet and pulled out Jon's college ID. "White Haven College, huh?"

"Yes, sir."

"What you studyin'?"

"Psychology."

"Studyin' the brain?"

"Yes, sir."

"You figure out what's been goin' on? Why these people are losing their damn minds? Can psychology give me an answer? Huh?" The barrel of the rifle came close again, making Jon flinch.

"No, I'm sorry. Your guess is as good as mine."

"What a waste. All that money yer payin' to learn about the brain and ya can't even give us a diagnosis. Guess those doctors don't really know what's what after all, huh?"

Jon didn't respond.

"Alright then. What you got in that there backpack?"

"My laptop. A phone charger. Some clothes."

"Let me see it. Take her out slowly and put it down on the ground there."

Jon's trembling arms lowered. He opened the passenger door, taking out the backpack without moving his hands any more than he had to. He placed the backpack on the asphalt and raised his arms again in the air.

"Now, step back. I don't want you movin' an inch ya hear me? I see you move at all I'm gonna shoot you no questions asked. Got that?" the man said.

Jon nodded and stepped back with his back toward the pile of snacks, hands still raised. Blood dripped off his chin. The man emptied the backpack. Everything inside spilled hard onto the asphalt. The two McDonald's milk bottles fell out and rolled around. A *snap* sound came from Jon's laptop as it fell. The rifle barrel sifted through the items as if they were contaminated. Shirts were picked up and examined. The man kicked the phone charger to the side and flipped over the laptop.

"Rusty!" an older man's voice shouted from behind Jon, but Jon didn't turn to look to see who it was. The old rifle was still aimed at him and he wasn't interested in getting shot.

"Why you pointin' my rifle at that boy?" the old man continued. The voice sounded aged but still as harsh as the gunman's backwoods drawl.

"Grandpa, this here sonofabitch was stealin' from our vendin' machine! Look there! He broke it and everything! Look at all this glass I gotta clean up! I was gonna shoot 'em in his ass!" Rusty replied.

"Put that damn rifle down right now!" the grandpa commanded.

Jon stood with his right eye widened as Rusty lowered his weapon. His heart relaxed a little, but his hands still shook like leaves. His forehead bled like a waterfall of red.

"You just wait till I get over there," the old man said. Jon could hear he was approaching but still refused to move his body. The old man walked around the front of the Honda, glanced down the contents on the hood, and then walked between Jon and Rusty. He grabbed the rifle.

At first, Jon thought it was his own grandfather. The wrinkly face. Short, all white hair combed to the side. Brown eyes underneath tired lids. He even wore an outfit similar to his grandfather. A short-sleeved, checkered button-up shirt with khakis and tan orthopedic sneakers. Velcro instead of laces. It was the go-to senior citizen attire.

Grandfathers all over the country looked like this, even in the unknown small town of Huntington.

"Jesus Christ, Rus, look at him!" the old man shouted as he reached in his back pocket and brought out a handkerchief. He wiped away the blood on Jon's face and held it on the gash, making Jon grit his teeth.

"Young man," the old man said to Jon. His old and angry eyes scanned Jon up and down, taking in his ruffled, brown hair, tired eyes, and bloodstained face and shirt. Jon could see an almost concerned look in his eyes. "You can put those hands down." His voice was stern and rural. "Now, I ain't gonna shoot ya unless you give me a reason to. Unlike Rus' here, I'm not gonna scare ya, alright? Can you hold this handkerchief there for me?"

"Ye-yes, sir." Jon was thankful for the old man's rescue of the situation, but still felt a great sense of unease.

"What exactly happened here? What's yer story?" the old man asked.

Rusty interjected. "He was tryin' to rob us! I seen him smash o—"

BANG. The old man shot a round into the sky, making a shattering echo in the air. Jon and Rusty both jolted. "Would you shut up! Now stop it! One more word outta you and I'll shoot YOU in YOUR ass!" the old man yelled.

Rusty looked away with a pissed-off look on his face. He crossed his arms and kept quiet.

The old man continued talking to Jon. "Now, young man, explain to me your situation here. Sit down, sit down."

Jon pushed away from the stolen goods and sat in the back of the Honda. He did his best to recount everything that happened. After a barrel to the head and being front and center to a rifle blast, Jon had to compose himself for a moment. His ears were ringing.

Jon explained the pain and horror that played out in White Haven College and the death of the others. He talked about how he couldn't reach his parents over the phone and how he only had the one voice mail from his father about heading to his grandparents' house since grandma had been "acting up." Jon almost cried explaining how much he wanted to get home. He also explained how he was so hungry and needed to find anything to fill his stomach so he wouldn't fall over on his journey back.

The old man's expression didn't move at all during the tale. Neither did Rusty's as he remained looking down at the asphalt like a child put in timeout.

"I'm sorry, sir, I didn't think anyone was around. I haven't found anyone else in the daytime that could help me. I'll give all this stuff back and be on my way. Okay? Please... I don't want any trouble. I just want to get to my family." Jon finished his story with his hand pressed on the hole above his eyebrow.

"Well. . . Jon, right? Issat yer name?" the old man asked.

Jon nodded. He was so exhausted.

"I sure am sorry to hear all this." The old man's eyes were still and as cold as Rusty's were. It must have run in the family. "All that's been happenin' ain't too pretty and I'll tell ya we've had a great loss ourselves. A tremendous loss to the family so I know that you must be hurtin' deep down. We know that pain."

Rusty nodded his head with his eyes still shooting downward. The old man's eyes remained focused on Jon.

"So, we'll let you get back home as none of us here can say where yer folks are or if they're livin'. And if what yer sayin' is true about all that happened to ya, and I believe it as you look quite rattled, I think you should come with Rus and me back to the house. Clean yerself up. Get you something better than all this here junk food. Hell, it's probably all expired anyhow. Not sure the last time we had the delivery boy around here."

Jon didn't know what to say, but his lips were saying *thank you* even though his mind was saying he was dying of blood loss.

"Turn your car off and follow us back to the homestead, alright? Can you walk?" the old man asked.

Jon nodded.

"Getcha cleaned up and on yer way before sundown. Least we could do as my grandson here doesn't know the first thing about hospitality. Speakin' a which, Rus, why dontcha clean up this young man's belongings." The old man turned around and glanced at Rusty as he started heading toward the check-in door of the motel. He spoke again, quieter now, almost to himself it seemed. "Your father would've been disappointed in you treating him like 'at with a gun. Yer wearin' his clothes and all. Whatsa matter with you?"

Rusty heard it as his body tightened. It was if he was out in the winter cold. He squeezed his eyes shut and then opened them, looking up at Jon. His eyes shined but no tears fell. "C'mon. Turn her off. Follow grandpa and me back to the house, alright?" He nodded his head over toward his grandfather and began scooping up Jon's things, shoving them into the backpack.

Jon nodded and closed the back door of the car where his stash of food was. His body still trembled in fear. The handkerchief shook but held its place on his beaten head. He went around to the driver's side and shut off the Honda, placing the pink-ringed set of keys in his pocket. Rusty finished filling back up his bag and handed it over to Jon without saying a word. Jon slipped it on and the two of them followed toward the old man, into the lobby where it smelled like the 70s, or at least what Jon thought the 70s smelled like. Musky.

The check-in area of Mirch's Motel looked stuck in the past, frozen in time four decades ago. A big, golden clock shaped like a sun was on one of the wood-paneled walls. Brown-striped carpeting covered the floor. The white corner counter had maps and a tan rotary phone. *Wow,* Jon thought in his pulsating pain, the last he saw a rotary phone was when he was little at his grandparents' house. That was way back before his dad made them switch to a modern phone with caller ID as they were being prank called over and over again one summer.

The three of them passed by a set of wooden furniture with orange cushions on them, toward a cracked door opposite the entrance. There was a framed oil painting of a town on the wall. It looked to be Huntington from back in the day. On the opposite wall there was a sign that read:

MIRCH'S MOTEL

HUNTINGTON'S FINEST

"The name's Hal Mirch," the old man said as they exited through the door and went back outside, now standing on a rocky path that cut up a wooded hill toward a white house. "Been runnin' this motel since I was round yer age." Hal turned and locked the door behind them with a key ring so large, Jon wasn't sure how he'd fit it in his pocket. "Time sure changes though, huh?"

Jon nodded. Rusty kept quiet.

Hal continued talking as they began walking up the rock path between the rows of trees. "We've had some evil stuff blow through Huntington, but never somethin' like we been seein' lately."

"Dad said it was the devil's work," Rusty said as he walked with his head down. His face looked aggravated.

"Yup," Hal said, "yer daddy's right. We thought we'd seen it all workin' this motel over the years. People cheatin', boozin', druggin', fightin'. But whatever's gotten into these folks that are tearin' each other apart for no God-given reason is beyond me. We were watchin' on the TV that people were driving cars into crowds. Killing children even. Devil worshipping whackos. . . Maniacs. . . That's why I hope you can someday forgive Rus for his actions. He's got his daddy's temper and he thought you were, well, one of those whackos ya see. One of those whackos that-"

"Stop! We don't have to talk about that! He don't need to hear it!" Rusty yelled with his eyes shut.

"Alright, I'm sorry. Jon, it's just we've had a tremendous loss in our family and-"

"ENOUGH!" Rusty shouted and ran off into the woods, kicking over shrubbery and *snapping* twigs with every step of his sprint. Jon and Hal stood watching him fade into the greenery until his white shirt vanished behind a fat tree trunk.

"Rus!" Hal screamed at him. "Rus, c'mon!" But it was no use. The only response was the sound of leaves *rustling* and distant branches *breaking*.

Hal turned back to Jon, who was still dabbing at his gash. "Jon, I'm sorry. He's been going through a lot, we all have. He just needs to be alone right now, he'll come around. Let's get you inside and clean that thing up."

"What happened?" Jon asked, almost in a whisper, not wanting Rusty to hear him and come rushing out of the woods with a sharp stone, looking to slice his throat open.

"I'll tell you once we get inside. Can't have him hear it, I don't think he can take it."

THIRTY-EIGHT

Ramblin' Man

Hal Mirch's house had no neighbors. The place was lonesome in a clearing. An old, two-story country home with paint peeling on the sides that used to be white but was now covered in a dark residue. The porch made a *squeaky* sound even from just looking at it. If the motel looked like it was from the 1970s, the Mirch residence looked like it was from the 1870s.

As Hal and Jon approached the house on the rocky path that led to the rotten porch, Jon noticed a plot of dark dirt on the ground with a cross made from sticks at one end. Just above it, a face stared at them from one of the side windows. The figure was shaded behind the screen of the window and Jon's heart began to race as he thought it was Rusty, already back at the house, waiting to shoot him with another gun they had. A pistol or another hunting rifle. But as they got closer, the figure seemed to have hair. Old woman hair. Glasses, too. Perhaps it was Mrs. Mirch.

"Watch yer step, this place is old. Older than me even," Hal said, but there wasn't a smile when he said it.

The porch *squeaked* just as you'd imagine and the front glass door *eeeeched* open from rusty, dirtied hinges. Hal popped out his enormous key ring and *jangled* them around to find the right key. He led Jon inside.

That musky smell didn't just find its home in the motel, it made itself comfortable here too.

There were black and white and faded photographs on the walls. Portraits of family members. Shots of picnics and fishing. They were all placed in brass and chipped frames that hung on teal-painted slats of wood. White wooden stairs headed to the second floor. A little study was on the left with a single vintage desk and two small oak chairs. To the right were two white steps that led down into a dining room with a mahogany table where the light shined in. *That's where that old woman was sitting,* Jon thought, but no one was there now.

"Can you make it upstairs?" Hal asked.

"Yeah, I can."

"I want you to head up there and go to the guest room, first room on yer left. Sit down there on the bed. I'll be right up with a wash-cloth and some bandages. Bathroom's across the hall."

Jon stepped up to the *creaky* second floor, which was lit only by the windows. An eerie place in the daytime, Jon wondered how spooky this place must be at nighttime.

The guestroom was plain with a white dresser and mirror. A brown end table with an uncovered lamp stood by a bed with flowery sheets. An armchair sat in the corner by a standing lamp that wore a dusty shade. In the middle of the room was a shaggy, brown rug. Nothing on the white walls but a cross by the closet door. There was a small window by the foot of the bed to provide some light.

Jon took off his backpack and placed it on the floor. He sat on the edge of the bed, holding on to the soaked handkerchief, trying to take in all that just happened. It was amazing his glasses weren't broken. He slid them off his face and placed them on the end table. The switch on the lamp did nothing.

The gash pounded away at his skull as dizziness returned. With one hand, he zipped open the top zipper of his backpack. Out came one of the McDonald's milk bottles filled with sink water. He was so shaken-up that he forgot to take his large cup of water from the car when they left the parking lot. Phone too.

Shit, the map app is probably draining the battery.

"If yer hungry, let me give you somethin' better than that old vending machine crap so yer stomachs full," Hal said from down-stairs. There were sounds of cupboards opening and closing. *Clinging* and *clanging* of tin followed. Then, water running.

I'm gonna drain my fucking head out at some strange old man's house with his crazy grandson. Jesus. I should've just kept going. God, I'm such an idiot.

Jon snapped out of his regretful thoughts when he Hal came marching up the loud stairs, holding a big, white porcelain bowl and a tall glass of water. An orange towel hung over his left shoulder.

"Howssat head holdin' up?" Hal asked, placing the porcelain bowl down by Jon's feet. Rolling around inside of it was a fat, grey bottle with a white cap. Rubbing alcohol. He put the glass of water on the end table and pulled down the towel off his shoulder.

"It's still hurting pretty good," Jon said.

Hal hunkered down. "Lean forward and move yer legs apart," he said, sliding the bowl between Jon's sneakers. "Lemme see now."

Jon pulled the soaked handkerchief from his head, trying not to rip off the scabbing blood and spill anymore out of his aching head. Fresh blood persisted from the gash, but Jon couldn't feel it. His left eye was shut since the parking lot.

"Oh, it's not so bad now. Looks like the hanky did its job," Hal said as he squinted through his thick lenses. The white cap of the rubbing alcohol came off under his shaky hands. "More blood than damage from what I can tell. Now, this'll sting ya a bit, alright?"

Jon nodded and Hal began to pour the rubbing alcohol just above the spot, holding the towel below Jon's chin. It sent a jolting sting, making Jon flinch. But he knew the pain was worth it. Blood and alcohol splashed and dribbled down onto the towel and into the bowl.

"I oughta tell ya, if I had a nickel for every time my boy had to have his daddy pour this on his cuts, well, I'd certainly wouldn't be livin' in this old place." Hal still didn't show any signs of emotion. Not even a smirk came from his old lips. "My son was always gettin' into trouble when he was young. Never much listened to me. Hell, who knows if he ever cared about what his momma thought."

Hal put the rubbing alcohol down by the bowl and dabbed the now cleaned gash. Another jolt went through Jon as the cloth made contact. Then, it moved down to his cheek as Hal cleaned off the streams of red tears.

"Oh, now that's not bad at all. With all that blood, you'd think Rus put a big ole' hole in yer brain. This here can't be more than a hair of a cut," Hal said as he fetched a Band-Aid from his breast pocket. His hands were too shaky to get a good grip on the thin seal.

"Let me get that," Jon said, now starting to open his left eye. He grabbed one of the Band-Aids and used his fingernails to rip open one end. Hal took it back and peeled off the remaining protected papers that covered the sticky side.

"I wanna apologize again for Rus. He takes after his father, who I guess took after me," Hal said as he placed the bandage diagonally across Jon's cut. Then he pulled another Band-Aid from his pocket. Jon tore it open for him and Hal placed it in the opposite direction, making an X-shape with the two bandages. "Good as new," he said without a change in expression.

Jon rubbed the bandages and grabbed the towel, flipping it to a dry side, and patting his left eye with it. He blinked, trying to get all the red out. It looked like he was seeing through a church's stained-glass window.

Mr. Mirch pulled a sealed pack of Tylenol from his breast pocket and placed it on the end table by the glass of water.

"What happened to Rusty's dad? Was it them? The maniacs?" Jon asked.

Hal nodded his head as his tired, old eyes looked down into the bowl of blood and rubbing alcohol. "Sure was." He paused a moment.

"If you can't tell me, I understand. I know how horrible it is out there. I've seen a lot of terrible things in the past twenty-four hours," Jon said.

Hal rubbed his chin. "Well...I suppose I should start from the beginnin' to give ya an idea of the Mirch family here. You see, Jon, my son Edward was the sheriff for the local department. Not sure where he got the idea to run around with the police, he was always such a troublemaker growin' up that I figured he'd be the one in jail, not puttin' other folks in there.

All a sudden he changed his attitude after years of stealin' and fightin'. I figured he came around when Rus was born. Course he wasn't married at the time. I thought he'd want nothin' to do with 'em, but it turns out Rus' momma was the one who wasn't interested. My wife yelled and screamed at our son for hookin' up with such a floozy." His head shook back and forth to show his disappointment all these years later. "I'm sorry, I don't mean to ramble."

"It's alright. Keep going," Jon said as he dabbed more on his eye. *Anything to help me understand what's going on.*

"Well, anyhow, little Rus' momma took off when he was just a baby and is off in who knows where. Eddie would yell and curse while runnin' down the street chasin' after young women that broke his heart, but not this time. I think at that moment, he realized it was just him and Rus in the world and that all those years of causin' mischief only attracted the least holy of people. You know what I'm sayin', Jon? You behave poorly, you're only gonna attract those same poor people into your life. Understand?"

Jon nodded.

"It was just him and that boy," Hal said. "Eddie, that's what we called Edward, tried his hardest to raise him right and I did my best with Margaret, God rest her soul. Eddie wanted nothing more than to raise him in a way so that Rus didn't cause all that trouble he did. Problem was, just like with Eddie and me, Rus rebelled against his dad and got in trouble anyhow."

"What did he do?"

"Oh, anything he damn well wanted. Skipped school. If he wanted something, he took it. If he had an issue with another fella, he punched him right in the jaw with no questions asked. Hell, yer lucky you didn't run into him back when his dad was around. You might not have made it out of that parking lot alive."

Hal rubbed his chin again and shook his head. "He loved his daddy, but he loved to make him angry, too. He loved to rebel. Boy, he got in so much trouble. Where on earth did I go wrong with my son? I only wanted to raise him right, but I guess it didn't work for him or his own baby boy. His momma was a stern Christian maybe I. . . I'm sorry I keep ramblin'."

Jon grabbed the glass of water from the end table and took a sip. It was nice and cold as it streamed down his desert-dry throat. A taste to which no McDonald's bathroom sink water could compare.

"Anyhow, what I was sayin' was that Rus was a troublemaker, even though his dad was climbin' the ranks of the police force. It was as if he wanted to get in even MORE trouble. I'd yell at Eddie and say 'howsabout you get your son in order before you police everybody else,' but he'd yell back, 'you never raised me right, never lettin' me do anything.' It was like we used to argue when he was younger. Jon, I tell ya, he would storm off just like Rus did a moment ago. Off into the woods and not come back until after supper. His momma would beat him with the big wooden spoon until he ran out into the woods again. Didn't come back until the sun came up. Sometimes I'd find him sleeping under a tree."

"Like father like son, huh?" Jon thought of his own father then. Where he was and whether he was alive. He hoped he was.

Hal nodded and stood up. The wooden floor *creaked* beneath his velcro shoes. He walked over to the reading chair in the corner and took a seat as he pulled up his khaki pants. "Yer right. Anyhow, where was I? Oh. You see even though Rus' dad was a police officer and was livin' in a whole new light, that troublesome spirit would still come out every now and again. Sometimes he had to rough up a perp or two in a way that wasn't protocol. Ya know, take the law into his own hands. They'd call him Shotgun Eddie. But hell, he put more guys in jail than anyone else had ever seen. Before ya knew, he was the sheriff and was runnin' things for a little while. That was before everything went to hell."

There was a pause. Jon took another sip of water and dabbed his eye. The red tint to the room was almost completely gone. Hal was looking down and rubbing his thumbs together between his cupped hands.

Hal began again. "At first it seemed odd. Eddie was tellin' me they were gettin' more calls than usual at the station. The phones were ringin' off the hooks and people were shoutin' to send help right away and that their husbands and wives were tryin' to kill them. Their kids were punching holes in the walls, kicking the dog, scratching their siblings. It was madness, especially at night. That's when it was the worst. I don't think Eddie even got to sleep most nights, had to snooze in the daytime with the curtains pulled. Made him sick. He couldn't even stand to watch the news anymore. All they showed were stories of the ongoing violence. It even seemed to be going on all around the country. Huntington was just the tip of the iceberg."

"Yeah, I saw on CNN that there were explosions and mass riots going on from coast to coast. They said it was going global," Jon said.

"That's right. Rus and I would get around the TV at the motel and watch with some of the guests. We'd all be shocked with our jaws on the floor at what we were seein'. Eddie always turned it off when he caught us watchin' the news. He had enough of it. Didn't wanna see any more of what was goin' on just outside our motel. All the while his son was still causin' trouble, but Eddie didn't have a second to deal with Rus. Bein' the sheriff and all, he's gotta be ready at all times. Anyhow, Eddie gets a call in the middle of the night to respond to a situation with a pregnant woman. Her husband was threatening violence against her, threatening to kill her and the baby."

Jon's eyebrows curled in reaction to the viciousness. It caused a little more blood to soak the bandages.

"I'm not sure what happened when he got there," Hal said. "I wasn't given any specifics, but I imagined it wasn't too pretty. One of Eddie's men called us and said they were doin' all they could, but the ambulances were runnin' all over the county to other calls. I had to block the door from Rus tryin' to drive to the scene himself. Wasn't til' the next mornin' we had an officer come to the house to inform us that Eddie was dead. Tryin' to do his job protectin' a young woman and her unborn baby, and he ended up gettin' murdered."

"I'm so sorry, Mr. Mirch," Jon said as the emotions of the story and the thoughts of his own family mixed together to form hot tears in his eyes. They flushed out the last drops of blood. "Did they get the guy who killed him?"

"Dunno, can't say. No one ever told us any more details. For all I know, the demon is still out there running with the other demons like a true troupe of evil. . . "

"That's horrible."

"Yup. I lost my wife, then I lost my son. By the grace of God, Margaret got to have a proper funeral. God rest her soul, she died just earlier this year after havin' a stroke. As hard as it is for me to say, I'm glad she died that way rather than having to be beatin' to a pulp by one of these heartless punks. Who knows what would've happened to her just going to the grocery store or down to the post office? God took her at the right time, Jon. The right time. I just wish he would've left Eddie with us, but I know they're lookin' down on us, protectin' us even though the devil's army is runnin' amuck."

Jon's heart leaped as the news of Margaret's passing registered in his mind. *The woman at the window. The dirt grave with the stick-made cross.* Sweat began to form around the gash of his head as a high dosage shot of anxiety injected itself into him.

"Mr. Mirch," Jon said with a shaky voice, "is your son buried outside the house? Underneath the window?"

"I'm afraid he is, Jon…I'm afraid he is. Had no choice either. Barry Henderson runs the funeral parlor and both he and his family are nowhere to be found. Tried callin' 911 with nothing but some lady sayin' we can't take the time help you. I don't think anyone will be helpin' us anytime soon. I s'pose we gotta take matters into our own hands."

"You're right," Jon said. He didn't want that to be the case.

"Jon, I tell ya it hasn't been easy. Rus has made it his life's goal to kill anybody and anything that he thinks is sick like the fella that killed his daddy. Not long before today, we had someone banging on the door of the motel. Rus took it to himself to take care of business on his own. He damn near got his arm cut off by a biker who was lookin' to spend the night. Course, the motel has been closed since Eddie passed. The biker man wasn't haven't it, so he drew a pocketknife and started swingin'. This is all accordin' to Rus of course.

"Rus had my rifle, my old Remington, and shot that sonofabitch right in the head. I couldn't believe he'd do something like that. He went too far, Jon. But I guess he was defendin' himself as far as I know. We had to put the body somewhere out in the woods there, I don't think anyone will be lookin' for him."

Jon was in disbelief both about Mrs. Mirch and the tale about Rusty.

"I still can't believe he didn't just pull the trigger on you, I guess that was some of his mercy comin' out for a moment. Yer lucky, Jon," Hal said.

Jon looked down into the bowl that mixed his blood with the alcohol. The emotions were swirling around in the blender of his mind with a thick misery. He was living in a world of murderous maniacs and ghosts of the dead. Emily was a ghost. Dan. Brandon. Maybe his own family were nothing more than spirits now. Better spirits than God knows whatever the fuck these pyschos were.

Hal seemed to pick up on Jon's body language and stood up as the wooden floor *creaked* again. He began to walk out of the room. "You take those pills and drink that water down, I'm gonna get you somethin' to eat. I'll be right back."

"Thank you, Mr. Mirch," Jon said.

"Call me Hal."

"Thank you, Hal."

"Oh, and one other thing," Hal said, stopping, turning back to Jon. "Poor Rus had his heart broken by a young girl. Rosaline? Rachel? I can't remember the name, but anyhow he's sensitive about that girl and I'd advise you don't ask about any females round him or his daddy, ok? Whoever that girl was broke it off with him and I don't think he's able to let her go. Just like his daddy, he wears his heart on his sleeve. That boy, I tell ya. Not sure what I'm gonna do with him… You got a girlfriend back home, Jon?"

"No girlfriend at the moment," Jon replied. He had girlfriends before, once back at White Haven even. A brown-haired girl named Veronica Gerhman. They had dated for a month or two before she decided to transfer schools. They had tried to keep in touch, but there were new boys at her campus that she wanted to get to know.

There had also been Jon's high school sweetheart, Jessica Mergo. His first kiss. A ginger. Jon broke up with her after he found out she smoked cigarettes. Mrs. Barnes wouldn't allow her in the house ever again after that.

"Well, I betcha you'll find somebody to take care of in all of this mess. Probably a girl out there looking for a young man to fix her head wounds, whaddya think?" Hal formed somewhat of a smile.

"Maybe you're right," Jon said.

As Hal stepped down the loud staircase, Jon sat as he was on the edge of the bed, trying to get himself under control from the panic in his mind. As he wiped the last of the bloodied tears off his face, he looked up at the wooden cross by the door. A wave of tiredness hit him.

"You like chicken, Jon?" Hal yelled from downstairs.

"Sure," Jon replied.

"Howsabout peaches?"

"That'd be great, thank you."

Rusty Returns

The old guestroom faded in from black as Jon awoke from his dreamless sleep. Long shadows from the sun streamed across the foot of the bed. In the corner, a figure sat in the armchair. Jon squinted for a moment and then grabbed his glasses from between the bowls of peach juice and chicken remnants on the end table. Putting them on, he saw the figure was Rusty, holding his grandfather's rifle across his lap. He was a shadow behind the curtain of the setting sun. Jon could see Rusty's eyes locked onto him and wondered how long he'd been staring.

Maybe enough to wake me up.

"I'm here to apologize," Rusty said, breaking the silence. "How's yer head feelin'?"

"It's ok. I'm alright now," Jon said, still aching. "Your grandpa took good care of me. Listen…he told me what happened. I'm sorry. I understand why you reacted the way you did out there, I can't say I wouldn't have done the same thing. . ."

Rusty was silent. All Jon could see was his shadowed face looking down at the rifle, breaking away the staring contest.

"What time is it?" Jon asked as he ran his fingers over his X-shaped bandage. The sunlight was a good indicator that he still had time to drive, but his heart still raced from the mystery of his slumber's length.

"You see my dad always said I oughta say how I feel," Rusty spoke without acknowledging that Jon had asked a question. His head was still hanging down with his finger rubbing the barrel. "Always bottlin' everything up inside is no good, makes a man all crazy in his head. Makes a man lash out and run away sometimes."

"Rusty, it's alright." Jon felt uncomfortable. He thought Rusty was going to do something crazy like pulling the trigger. Maybe snap and have a mental breakdown right here, either killing Jon or himself.

There was silence as Jon propped himself up by the elbows.

"I'm here to apologize," Rusty repeated. His voice was softer than it was before. "I'm sorry, Jon. I'm sorry I bashed yer head with my grandfather's rifle. Kinda thought you were like one of them other folks out there. It was wrong of me and I ask you to forgive me."

The time. What's the fucking time?

"Rusty, it's ok. I forgive you," Jon said.

"Grandpa said God would've sent me to Hell if I killed you. He said if I hurt somebody or killed somebody, that I'd be just like the man who killed my dad. I'd be one of them."

"Rus..."

"I want you to take this," Rusty said, standing up and pulling a weapon from behind his back. Jon's heart fluttered and his body jerked back as if Rusty was about to finish him right here in the guestroom. Instead, Rusty was holding out a Glock 22 towards Jon. His hand offered it like it was a holy sacrament or a form of a sacrificial gift.

Jon's head jerked back an inch in confusion. "You want me to have this?"

"Yes. I talked with my grandpa, he said it would be ok. Said I shouldn't be usin' it anymore and he's right. You ever fire a gun before?"

Jon swallowed a dry, scratchy swallow. "I have. I used to hunt with my dad when I was younger. That rifle sort of looks like the one I shot before actually. A handgun? No."

"Good, then this should be no problem for you. It's pretty much the same thing. You just don't have as much leverage ya see. No scope either." Rusty put down his grandfather's rifle and began aiming down the sights of the Glock, pointing the barrel at the wall. His one eye squinted shut. "You see somebody actin' up, just pretend they were a deer or a squirrel. But make sure they're sick in the head before you do. You make sure it's not a situation like you and me almost had," Rusty said as he placed the Glock on the foot of the bed, inside of the setting sun's rays like it was a gift from God himself. The weight of the gun pressed down on the floral sheets. The metal shined. It looked brand new to Jon. Pristine.

"Thank you. Are you sure your grandpa is ok with it? I mean, did this belong to your. . . "

"My dad?"

Jon nodded.

"It did and I sure am sure my gramps is okay with it." Rusty was staring at the gun in all its golden-lit glory, mesmerized by its gleam. There was a face on him that said he didn't want to give it away.

"We got plenty of ways to defend ourselves around here. But grandpa insisted you take one of my dad's guns. It wasn't the *exact* gun he used when he was on duty. One of his many backups. I also got some ammo downstairs, packed and ready for you to take on yer trip home. Grandpa also packed you a bag of more of that canned crap. Course you still got all our snacks from the vendin' machine waiting in yer car."

"I guess it's my turn to apologize to you Rusty," Jon said, turning to him. Rusty's eyes moved from the Glock to meet Jon's. Jon could see Rusty's eyes were swollen from crying. "I'm sorry about your grandpa's vending machine. I didn't mean to break it and rummage through it. If I'd a known about you and your family's situation, I would've kept going. I didn't think anyone was around. I'm sorry."

Rusty nodded his head and gave the gun one last glance before he started toward the door. Backup gun or not, it was still a part of his old man's collection. "I forgive you," he said, sounding like crying again. "Meet me and grandpa downstairs, we will help you get to where yer goin' whenever yer ready. The bathrooms just across the hall if you need it."

"Thanks," Jon said. "Oh, and what about the time?"

"Almost six," Rusty said as his boots *banged* down the wooden steps.

Damn.

"And another thing," Rusty said from downstairs, "make sure you handle that thing with care, alright? It's gotta loaded, full clip. Only point it when yer lookin' to kill. Take it from me. I coulda used that advice earlier..." He blew air from his snotty nose.

Jon sat up and wondered if he'd be able to drive home fast enough before the sky went dark. Then, he caught a glance at the gun again and sat up even more on the bed. He looked down at the heavenly handgun that lay within the sun's warm but fading light. The black, smooth barrel and the polished metal. He plucked it from the bed-sheets and felt the weight in his hands. Cold and heavy. Jon pointed and aimed like Rusty had a moment ago but kept his finger away from the trigger. *Trigger discipline* his dad taught him years ago. *Only point it when yer lookin' to kill* Rusty said a second ago.

With the floor *creaking* under his socked feet, Jon got up from the bed and headed to the bathroom.

On the edge of the stained sink were disposable razors, a rusted can of Barbasol shaving cream, and Bengay. Jon turned the nozzle and water spurted out. He ran some water through his hair and stared into the mirror at himself. His patchy facial hair had found its way out. Jon could never grow a full beard or mustache even if he wanted. Nothing would connect. How his father formed such a manly and bushy stache was beyond Jon. Why would his father have that kind of hair growth and not him? Still, as he stared at himself, he could see his father's eyes in his own.

Jon shut off the water.

FORTY

Leaving

It was an odd feeling to be leaving the Mirchs' place. You'd think after being bashed in the head with the barrel of a rifle, Jon would be eager to hightail it out of Huntington and never look back. But Jon could only feel sadness for Rusty. A sadness for Hal. The two of them had their family taken away from them. Rusty's mother walking out. Mrs. Mirch passing on. Ed Mirch being taken by one of the psychos. These people didn't deserve this.

"We packed you some supplies, Jon," Hal said, reaching down to a shabby white and green bag with REHOBOTH BEACH written on the front in faded letters. "Some more peaches and chicken. Even threw in a can of corn for ya. Also got Band-Aids, pain pills, and towels in there in case anything gets messy."

"Thank you, and thanks again for patching me up," Jon replied, rubbing on his bandages. He was wearing his backpack over his shoulders. It was stuffed to the brim with worn and wrinkled clothes, one of which he had changed into. A dark-grey undershirt. The Glock was clutched in his right hand. "Are you sure I can take this? I know Rusty said you insisted, but I want to make sure."

"Absolutely. I think you will have better use for it than Rusty will. I trust you'll have better judgment of who you point it at," Hal responded with his same tone, void of any emotion.

Rusty came up from the downstairs dining area, holding a stuffed school bag of his own. A maroon backpack that looked like it was about to pop.

"I stuffed this sucker with as much ammo that could fit," Rusty said, zipping up the last pouch on the front.

Jon almost laughed at the sight of it. "Don't you need any ammo for yourself?"

It was still hard for Rusty to maintain eye contact. "Oh, we got plenty of ammo. This is just the tip of the iceberg for the twenty-two. We got more than you'll ever know. It's all yers." He handed the bursting backpack over to Jon.

"Wow, thanks a lot. I really do appreciate all this," Jon said to Rusty and his grandpa.

"Welp, we best be taking all this stuff to yer car out there. Can't be wasting sunlight, unless you wanna stay the night. You got everything you need for the road, Jon?" Hal asked.

Jon couldn't believe he even had the thought, but a part of him considered staying with the Mirchs. Maybe it would be better that way since there was shelter, food, and, according to Rusty, plenty of weapons and ammo to defend themselves with.

"No, I better get going now. I think I have everything I need," Jon said.

"Alright. Rus you lead the way with the bullets, I'll get the food," Hal said as he picked up the worn beach bag. "Let's get Jon on his way."

The three of them walked out of the old house as the floor *creaked* one last time. The screen door *slammed* shut behind them. They stood on the porch as the spring evening brought a slight breeze through the woods.

Peaceful, Jon thought. *But for how long?*

Around the house, Ed Mirch's grave sat by the stick-made cross where his mother watched over him. Jon didn't look back, but he knew for sure that if he would have, he would see Mrs. Mirch's spirit staring out the window just as she was when Jon first walked up from the rocky path. Just then, as if Hal was thinking the same thing, he said himself, "I'll be right back, Marge."

The three men walked down the rocky path and through the 70s lobby of Mirch's Motel, out into the parking lot where the Honda remained parked and stocked with the vending machine snacks. Jon popped the trunk and Hal and Rusty placed their bags inside. The engine started and *rumbled* as Jon turned the ignition. He placed the Glock on the passenger seat.

"I guess we better let you go now. Suns goin' down," Hal said. He squinted up at the setting light. "You're headed to a town called Springsdale, that right?"

"That's right. My home. Springsdale, born and raised."

Rusty raised an eyebrow but didn't speak. There was something on his mind just then.

"Best of luck to you, Jon," Hal said. "May God bless ya."

"Thank you guys again. I'm so sorry about everything," Jon said.

Hal waved his hand. "Ain't nothin' you ever need to worry about again. You just get back to yer family, Jon. We'll be prayin' for you."

Rusty nodded. "Take care, Jon." His face still looked questioning. The eyebrow hadn't lowered after Jon mentioned his hometown.

Jon nodded back and said, "I hope you guys make it out alright."

Both Rusty and Hal nodded as they closed the trunk and moved away from the Honda's path. Jon got inside and saw the maps app still had his home address entered and ready to go.

524 Franklin Court, Springsdale, Pennsylvania.

Jon gripped the back of the passenger seat's headrest and reversed the car out onto the vacant road. He pushed the stick into drive and gave Rusty and Hal a final wave as they stood waving back in front of the check-in door. Jon wasn't sure, but he thought he saw a faint smile come across Hal's face again as the Honda drove off down the road, starting the course towards home.

FORTY-ONE

On the Road Again

The Honda raced against the setting sun as the car sped through what remained of the Pennsylvania Turnpike. Jon pushed the pedal to its limit until he had to slow down, dodging the destruction left and right. Nothing Jon hadn't seen before. The carnage was all he knew now. Death and carnage. It was more of a background piece, something that would be present no matter where he ran, forever lingering around him in a sinister aura.

More phone calls led to more voice mail machines. His mind ran wild as he thought back to the Mirchs. Emily. Everyone back at White Haven. His family. *If I make it back home, would there be anything left? Am I just wasting my time?* one side of his mental voice said, until another would chime in, *NO! You can't think that. You have to keep going. Can't slow down now. Can't turn back. Keep moving! Be a MAN!*

THIRTY-SIX MILES REMAINING. ESTIMATED ARRIVAL TIME: 7:01 PM

Jon was exhausted despite his little nap. His body ached. He rubbed the bandages on his forehead and thought about the comfort of that guest room bed with the floral sheets.

Maybe I should've stayed with them.

NO!

It could've been my last chance at survival.

You keep moving. You wanna give up now? Ruin all the progress you've made so far?

It might already be too late!

You don't know anything, you have no idea of what you'll find until you get there!

Where are they? Are they alive?

I can't answer that, you have to find out for yourself.

What do I do?

Do your best.

Alright.

Keep going.

I will.

The psychological fighting with himself wasn't helping. All he wanted were answers. The not knowing of his family's safety pained him deeply, but it was what it was. He had to keep going. Keep driving. Keep surviving.

FORTY-TWO

Detour

Trees and shrubbery whizzed by. The sun was setting beyond and soon farmlands and rural hills would be beyond the barriers on both sides of the pike. Classical music, still the only active radio station, played from the Honda's dashboard, leading Jon into a late daydream of what's to come. Deep in thought about his family and lost friends, he seemed not to notice that he was approaching familiar territory.

The sign for Camp Valley made Jon's heart roll over itself as his father's voice mail message played again in his mind. He'd listened to it enough times to have it memorized and, if ever held at gunpoint, could recite the message verbatim.

Son, this is your father. I know we're calling you late, but your mother and I are going over to your grandparent's house. Gram's been acting up, must be sick. Pappy called said she'd been feeling ill and called worried so we're just going to swing by to check on them, maybe bring them back to the house for the night. Just wanted to let you know. We will keep you posted. Call us when you get the chance, okay? I'll call you in the morning. Buh-bye.

There wasn't a choice. Jon knew the roads were deadly after dark, hell, the entire world was. His grandparents' house would be safe, right? Maybe his parents were there all along, too afraid to leave the house with grandma and grandpa because of the maniacs.

But they didn't pick up their cell phones.

Stop it!

Jon turned the Honda into the exit lane as the sun's head lowered into the horizon. Soon, the orange glow became a solid black.

***

White houses were on either side of the road between fields of green. An occasional brick house, too. Telephone lines ran along the roads. Jon drove the Honda through the quiet town. Although he was coming from the opposite direction that his family usually took, he knew that Slick Willy's Wings would be just up ahead as the road sloped down passed the fields and the Camp Valley General Store.

There was farmland that stretched out to the mountain that hid half of the sun as it made its descent. Smells of the barnyard lifestyle stuck in Jon's nose. Familiar. Nostalgic, even if it was stinky. A few hundred feet away he could see cows. A farmer stood at the edge of the fence post looking over at Jon's Honda as it whizzed by. The farmer's face looked as if he'd never seen an automobile before.

Jon drove on.

To his right was the general store that sent waves of more nostalgia through him. The white sign with black text read: CAMP VALLEY GENERAL STORE beside signs of the major credit cards it accepted. HERSHEY'S ICE CREAM SOLD HERE next to that. A yellow newspaper dispenser read PUBLIC OPINION on its side. A cage of Blue Rhino propane sat empty nearby. The building itself was old but repainted white. It was a lot rustier and run down back when Jon was younger. The place must've been there since Jon's father was a child. Maybe longer.

Grandpa Barnes would take Jon and his cousins up to the store every time they came to visit. You could say it was another family tradition to walk up the side of the road on a warm summer evening to visit Mr. Fannett, who sold all sorts of candies and treats. The Fannetts operated the store from generation to generation and they lived above the store.

Jon wondered if Mr. Fannett was still alive. Mrs. Fannett, too. They had been old even when Jon was only six, but they always remembered Jon and his cousins. Everyone remembered everyone at Camp Valley. The area was large only because of the fields of farmland. The population itself wasn't much and there wasn't anyone that Jon could remember that his grandfather didn't know or recognize growing up. It was a close community. Everyone knew everyone. You couldn't hide. Especially not if you were attending the local Presbyterian church which Jon was driving by now.

CAMP VALLEY PRESBYTERIAN CHURCH.

WELCOME.

WORSHIP GOD SUNDAYS 9:45.

A typical rural church. Brick laid foundation with a white steeple. Jon had only gone there on special occasions. Christmas. Grandma's birthday. Mother's Day. Father's Day. Although, his grandma would have liked him to go every Sunday. Jon wasn't interested. He never liked getting up early. He also didn't enjoy sitting in a sweaty building for an hour, having to sing songs and drink warm grape juice.

Up ahead, just as he remembered and just as Mark had described it before falling victim to the mysterious maniac epidemic, Slick Willy's Wings stood in the fading light with its red and blue race car. The vehicle wasn't an official Nascar car or anything like that, just a car painted in two colors with a big number seven written in yellow on the hood. It sat parked, propped up just as it always had with the seven facing down toward the entrance.

In the parking lot were several cars and motorcycles. Bodies. Red-stained bodies. The lights were off inside the restaurant, which meant they were eating in the dark, eating each other, or all taking a nice snooze beneath the walls of memorabilia you'd find at any other sports bar and grill. Take Applebee's or Chili's, slap a painted race car on top, and you'd get Slick Willy's Wings: home of the town drunks because there wasn't any other place to go.

Jon kept his speed at over forty miles an hour. *Not much longer now* he thought as the road began to bend around more trees and shrubbery. Farmland returned soon after and Jon knew he would arrive in a few moments at his destination. *Please be there. Please, somebody, be there.* But as he approached the turn into the driveway, his faith began to dwindle.

There was no sign of his mom or dad's car in the driveway. The garage was its own separate structure and the door of it was closed. It disappointed Jon, but he was glad they at least got to his grandparents' place and got them back home or at least somewhere safe. He didn't want to get his hopes up seeing his dad's Ford Explorer and then rushing in to find them dead or gone mad.

The aged, white-painted wood that stacked two stories high with tiny, darkened windows was none other than Grandma and Grandpa Barnes' home. It had the front porch that *creaked* with every footstep and rocking of a chair. The gigantic, crooked tree that stood in the long front yard had been there since the beginning of time. Jon's grandparents' farmhouse looked as it always had, except for the chickens and the cows they got rid of not long before they became grandparents. Jon hadn't been alive yet to see it, but the thought of having access to barnyard animals right in the backyard seemed cool. A lot of things seemed cool when you were a kid.

As a child, Jon was afraid of his grandparents' house. He still was, but back then he was more afraid of the imaginary ghoulies than he was of what he now feared was behind that screen door. When you're a kid it's easy to get spooked by the stories your grandfather tells you. Like the one about the ghosts that Jon's grandpa would see at night, or the stories his cousins Bobby and Marie would make up about the house having a monster that lived in the basement. Jon learned as he got older that monsters and ghosts didn't exist.

Except for now. After what he had endured up to this point, Jon would believe anything.

Every time Jon came to visit his grandparents, he would remember those times when he would play with his cousins during family get-togethers. It was a shame that as everyone got older, the family events seemed to dwindle as everyone had things to do and places to be. In those earlier days, times were simpler, and fun came with ease. Running around the yard. Coming up with silly games. Climbing up that giant tree, even though his grandmother hated when they did that. She was terrified of someone getting hurt. Of course, any time Jon and his cousins played together, someone would start crying over one thing or another. Most of the time it was Bobby, the youngest of the cousins.

Jon wondered where his cousins were at now. He wondered if they were still alive.

It all seemed a lifetime ago as Jon stared at that farmhouse from behind the wheel of the Honda. But there was no time to reminisce on the innocence of youth. The sky was almost dark, and the psychos would be on the prowl any second.

It was time to head inside.

Jon strapped on his backpack from the trunk and pulled out the beach bag filled with canned food. The cool evening's air brought more waves of nostalgia as the leaves on the giant tree *shook*. He'd made it this far and Jon felt that it would be ok to die here. To have his final resting place where some of his fondest memories were made was a fine way to go.

The steps *creaked* with every movement and as Jon got closer to the front screen door, his stomach clenched harder and the nostalgic feelings soon were swept away. Splatters of what looked like blood, he wasn't sure in the dying light, blotted the top of the wooden steps, leading to the door.

The screen door was ajar, but Jon rang the old doorbell to the house even though he knew in his heart that his grandma wouldn't be coming to let him in. *Is that a grandchild I see? Oh, it is! Little Jonny! Come on in, look how tall and handsome you're getting!* she would say, on cue, through the screen every time Jon came to visit.

A faint sound of the bell rang through the crack of the door. Then, it was quiet until another slight breeze blew. Long, silver wind chimes *chinged* and *clanged* on the one end of the porch. Another sound that took Jon back to those summer evenings he spent here. However, the anticipation of horror was too much to keep Jon in those memories for long.

After a moment, he opened the front door and walked into the darkness.

FORTY-THREE

Grandma and Grandpa's House

At first, Jon didn't speak. He was shaken by the darkness and the silence of the house. All he could hear was the sound of his heart beating in his ears and the *ticking* of the large analog clock that hung above the living room couch.

The light switch was useless. No electricity, but he knew his way around the place. Still, it was eerie. A nightmarish version of a warm and welcoming home. For all he knew, there could be new guests lurking around the corner. Lunatics. The thought made him nervous and, for a moment, he thought about running back to the car and grabbing the Glock. Instead, he took off his backpack and laid it on the floor beside the beach bag, not wanting to waste another moment.

"Hello?" Jon muttered and coughed. "Hello? Mom? Dad?" He knew they weren't here. Why would they be if the house looked like this? "Grandma? Grandpa?" His head scanned from the living room to the dining room. Nothing but blackness. All the curtains were drawn, which covered any of the last natural light.

"Is anyone here? It's Jon! Little Jon! Little Jonny! Hello?" Jon looked down and saw the bloodstains that came from outside. Or, came from *inside* and went *outside*. It made his chest hurt on top of his stomach which sloshed the peaches and chicken inside.

The blood trail was all it took for him to turn around and run back toward the Honda to fetch his new Glock from the passenger seat. The trunk *popped* open and he *unzipped* the backpack filled with ammo. Black boxes with gold text read MAGTECH. They filled the bag against the seams.

What the hell do I do? Jon's hands began to shake as he didn't have a clue on how to load the damn thing. *Christ, it's loaded, isn't it?* He remembered Rusty mentioned to be careful as he walked from the guestroom.

Make sure you handle that thing with care, alright? It's gotta loaded, full clip. Only point when yer lookin' to kill. Take it from me. Jon *had* taken it from him.

Jon entered the house again, closed the screen door, and locked it. Then, he turned toward the living room. The *ticking* noise continued to fill the room of old furniture and cheap paintings of rural scenery. There were end tables with lamps and a glass dish of M&Ms. Jon headed toward the staircase that came down right in the middle of it all.

"Grandma? Grandpa?" he said, looking up the steps into a dark hallway. It was pitch-black as there was only one window in the hall, at the very end. He thought about opening all the curtains in the house until the thought of the maniacs seeing him through a window came to him.

"Hello?"

No response.

Jon went over to the dining room where an oval table with a glass surface stood with candlesticks on it. Pictures of family stared at him from a shelf just beyond it. Faces and places frozen in time. There weren't going to be any new additions to the frames anytime soon. He kept moving into the kitchen.

Jon rummaged around until he found a flashlight in a drawer by the refrigerator. Hoping to save battery power on his iPhone, he *clicked* on a fading orange light that was just enough for Jon to see the bloodstains on the white kitchen floor. They led to the basement door that had a bloodied brass knob. *The basement door...oh, Jesus...* The sight of the red trail and painted knob made Jon feel like a little boy again, a helpless child. Pure fear was pumping through his veins as he stared at the portal that would transport him to innocent fright.

"No, not the basement. Please!" he would shout to his cousins after he lost a game of rock, paper, scissors, or when they'd dare him to go down. Marie was older, so she'd always push him around and force him through the door. Bobby was too young and too small to intervene, he'd just laugh and clap his hands.

"Lights off! Lights off!" they'd shout. "Don't let the ghosties get you!" The door would *SLAM* shut as Jon tumbled down the basement steps and onto the dark, cold cement floor.

You know what you have to do, the voice said in Jon's head as his hand shook the light beam on the door. He had the Glock aimed down toward the kitchen's tiles.

You have to go down there.

I don't know if. . .

Move yourself. Open that door and walk down the steps. Follow the blood. Follow it, Jon.

Ok.

Jon's feet began to move toward the bloodied spots that led to the basement door. He had the faint flashlight in one hand. Gun in the other. Heavy breathes came from the depths of his throat, almost hyperventilating him. The closer he got, the harder it was for him to breathe. It was as if he was drowning in a darkened pool, losing air by the second.

Jon grabbed the dishtowel from the edge of the sink and used it to cover his hand as he opened the basement door. It *creaked* its haunting creak as Jon shined his light down the green-painted steps into the cellar. Blood spots were on every other step until they hit the cement floor and trailed off around the right of the stairs. His eyes squinted, trying to adjust to the even greater darkness. Pitch-black. The light helped but it seemed to be fading even more now as the batteries weren't strong enough to penetrate such an abyss. God knew how long the flashlight had been sitting in the drawer without a battery change.

"Is anyone down here?" Jon asked with fear in his voice. "I have a gun! No sense trying to hide!" He held the Glock forward with the wrist holding the flashlight crossing on top of it. He had seen this move in both movies and video games of SWAT members infiltrating an area.

Bump. Bump.

Jon froze after almost losing his balance. The SWAT stance disappeared. He was only on the second step down. His hand leveraged on the wall with the flashlight. The other gripped the handle of the Glock. The flashlight's beam aimed back down at the bottom of the steps after Jon caught his balance again, but nothing stirred down there. He couldn't tell if the sound came from above or below him. His mouth was wide open, ready to say another word, but he was paralyzed from the startling noise.

"He-he-hello?" But it was too soft. A whisper. Jon crept down the steps again.

Bump.

Jon stopped. A weak voice entered the air. It sounded muffled but coherent enough coming from beneath him. "Help me! Please, won't someone help me!"

A jolt went through Jon's spine.

"Who's there?" he asked, louder now. The beam of light jumped back and forth, waiting, begging, for someone to appear.

"Oh, please help me! The door is stuck! Oh Lord, please help me!" the muffled voice cried.

Jon's heart leaped as the voice registered as his grandmother's. A faint and old voice, somewhere in the basement below. *Move.* He hurried down the basement steps as the wooden stairs *squeaked* and *creaked* as he descended.

"Grandma? Is that you? Where are you?" Jon asked with the flashlight bouncing off the wooden shelves of canned food and glass jars. Torn open cases of water bottles sat below. Boxes and cobwebs cluttered every corner. A wheelbarrow turned upside down lay lonesome.

Bump. Bump. "Please, lord. Please!" the old voice shouted.

Jon turned and shined his light on the wooden door that led to the washer and dryer room. The blood spots were beneath a chair propped up against the handle. There were bloody handprints on the legs of the chair. It bumped again and the chair stood, moving less than an inch from the old, brown wood and metal lock.

"I'm coming, hold on!" Jon shouted as he ran to the door, kicking the chair out of the way. He placed the Glock in the back of his pants and pulled the metal lock. The door opened and Jon shined his flashlight to reveal a short, old woman standing in the dark, looking up at him. Her grey hair was stained dark-red and one of her large glass lenses was shattered on her right eye.

"Grandma, are you alright? What happened to you?" he asked, moving in closer and feeling disgusted that someone would treat an elderly woman like this. The left shoulder of her shirt was stained in red as well. She was thin, a kind of thin not healthy for a woman her age.

"Why did you lock me in the cellar?" she asked, now with the spotlight on her. She started walking up to Jon.

An eyebrow raised on Jon. "I didn't lock you down here, grandma. I just got here, I came looking for you. You don't know how happy I am that I found you, but we gotta get you cleaned up. Your head is bleeding, grandma we should get you upstairs." He went to hug her, but she resisted. "Grandma?" He attempted to touch her shaking hands but when he made contact, she swatted his hands away.

A waft of toilet smell bellowed from the doorway. It smelled like a public bathroom that hadn't seen a janitor in a while. Urine. Stale urine.

"You LOCKED me in the cellar!" Grandma's eyebrows curled behind her broken oval glasses with an angered look that Jon had only seen once in his entire life. Back when he and his cousins snuck into their grandparents' room and looked in grandma's expensive jewelry box, she screamed at the children in a voice they had never thought she was capable of. Grandma Barnes was livid that day, but now that all seemed like a good mood compared to the current state of grandma's behavior. "You LOCKED me in the cellar and now you have to be punished you UNGRATEFUL BASTARD!" She never swore like that before.

"Oh no," Jon said under his breath, realizing that she was no longer the sweet and loving grandmother that he spent countless summer days with. She was now one of them. Whatever *they* were, they got to her and took over. "Grandma, please. Just calm down, it's me, Jon. Little Jonny, remember?"

But it was of no use as grandma swung her shaking hands at Jon's head. He blocked it with the flashlight, but she swung again and her long, chewed nails sliced into his skin, causing him to lose his grip on the plastic torch. It fell to the floor and the light went out as the bulb shattered on the cement. Now, Jon stood face to face with his crazed grandmother in complete blackness.

"Gram-" Another claw from his grandmother grazed Jon's head and he jerked backward, blinking and stumbling.

"You will pay, young man. At the hands of God, you WILL pay!" she shrieked in an unholy voice that sounded nothing like her. "God doesn't take kindly to those who treat his followers like this. Locking up an old lady in her basement. What's gotten into you?"

"Grandma, where's grandpa? Where's mom and dad?" Jon shouted at her as he pulled his phone out from his pocket, turning on the camera's flashlight. The Glock was still snug above his butt. The phone shined one hundred times brighter as it lit up grandma's horrific face. She swung again.

The phone fell hard to the cement and the basement went black again. Jon's fingers felt around the cold, hard floor until he felt the iPhone. As he grabbed it and shined it back up, his grandmother was closer now, scowling at him with her religious exclamations.

"The wicked go down to the realm of the dead, all the nations that forget God!" she howled.

"Stop it!" Jon said as he scooted backward with every closer step she took toward him.

"They will be punished with everlasting destruction and shut out from the presence of the Lord and from the glory of his might!"

Bible verses? Are these Bible verses? If they were, they weren't the ones that his grandma shared with him over the years. Not exactly a message to instill in a young, developing boy.

"They will throw them into the BLAZING FURNACE, where there will be weeping and GNASHING OF TEETH!" she shouted as she bent down to grab Jon's legs. He kicked her away with a weak thrust, reluctant to cause any harm to her.

"Gram, that's enough! Stop! What are you doing?" Jon said as she began to stomp down on his feet. First, she got his knee, then the bottom of his foot. Somehow, it hurt. This time, Jon pushed her off a little harder and scrambled himself up to his feet.

"Depart from me, you who are CURSED, into the eternal FIRE prepared for the DEVIL and his ANGELS!"

Jon maneuvered himself back to the stairs and began to climb the steps backward almost reaching the top, keeping the light on his grandmother. His hand hovered behind him above the Glock's handle. *Please don't make me do this. Lord, God, Jesus, please!* Her arms flailed and whipped at Jon as she quoted what sounded like the book of Revelations. Jon wasn't sure. This wasn't a time for Bible study.

"Didn't I teach you, Little Jonny? Don't you remember what God does to naughty, sinning young men?" Just as Jon was over halfway upstairs, she bolted at him, causing him to trip backward, onto his back. The edge of one of the wooden steps connected with the middle of his spine. The Glock tumbled and, by the grace of God, didn't fire. Jon hadn't the faintest idea if the safety was on or not. Either way, no bullets flew.

"Agh!" he shouted as his back arched. The phone's light danced around the ceiling, flashing the image of his grandmother starting down on him with her old, crooked hands as they wrapped like vines around his neck. Jon squirmed and rocked his body back and forth as the cold grip of his grandmother tightened around him, squeezing the soul out of him. He could feel his butt graze the side of the trigger.

Both scared and surprised by his grandma's strength, Jon dropped his phone and pressed his hands hard on her chest. Although more powerful than ever, his grandma's weight remained the same as Jon shoved her off with ease.

"No! Ah! God, please! YOU LITTLE-" she shouted as she flew backwards from the staircase. *CLAP*. Her old and possessed body fell to the bottom of the basement floor. Jon grabbed his throat, taking harsh gasps. He picked up the phone from the step and shined it down on his grandma who lay still on the ground.

"Grandma?" he said, coughing. His back ached. "Grandma, are you ok?" But her body didn't move an inch.

With the adrenaline pumping full-time, Jon got up and ran down the stairs. "Grandma, can you hear me?" He propped the phone's light on one of the shelves behind him. Grandma's mouth hung open and her tired eyes drooped behind her broken lenses. "Oh Grandma, I'm so sorry!" No breathing. No pulse. Jon's eyes began to water. He gave her a little shake, but it was of no use. She had passed as soon as her bony body collided with unmovable cement.

There was wetness on the back of her head as fresh blood began to ooze. "Grandma, please!" But no one could hear him. He wiped his eyes with the back of his blood-covered hand.

Jon looked away and grabbed his phone.

The pain in his heart rocked him and almost sent him collapsing to the floor. The basement walls swirled and turned in every which way. *My God. My God. What have I done?* Vomit rose deep in his throat. Sweats. Harsh, sweats. Jon felt like passing out. Dying. Killing himself by taking the Glock and putting it under his chin and blowing his own grandmother-murdering brains out right here and now. He could end the nightmare once and for all.

Jon couldn't catch his breath. *Wait, just wait. Breathe. Breathe. Calm down. Calm down.* His brain felt like it was whipping against his skull, trying to get out by repeating every thought. *Relax. Relax. You had no choice. You had no choice. She would've killed you. She would've...*

"She would've killed me," Jon said aloud, between gasps. "She would've killed me, and she would've killed them." He turned at his grandmother and closed his eyes. "They put you down here because you were going to kill them! You're sick!" Tears let loose once more, and he pulled himself up from the dirty floor.

In the washer room that smelled sour, he found a big blue blanket with stars and planets on it. Not far from it, he saw stains on the cement where the scent reeked. *How long had she been down here? She must have had to use the bathroom.* It made him sick. A foul way to live in the darkness, trapped behind a door.

He brought back the blanket over to where his grandma lay lifeless and placed it over her body. It was the right thing to do. It was the *only* thing to do. Tears filled his already soaked eyes as he placed his terrified hand over his covered grandma, saying a silent prayer in his mind. If his grandma couldn't get into heaven, he didn't know who could. She had been God's number one fan and now she was about to get a front-row seat to his afterlife concert.

God and the afterlife had been something Jon struggled with in his recent years. He'd question the Bible and what it stood for. Never arrogantly, he was just curious about the old book and wondered if it was possible for there to *be* a God, a supreme creator of heaven and earth. Even *if* there was a heaven, would Jon be allowed in after what he'd done to his own grandmother? Hell couldn't be much worse than what has now become of the living world.

FORTY-FOUR

One Last Sleepover

Jon took the beach bag and backpack up to the guestroom. The place where he'd spend summer nights with his cousins, staying up late and being too loud.

Two beds. One by the door and the other in the corner. Trying to jump from one to the other was a classic game played every time the children shared the room. Grandma and Grandpa Barnes were never pleased with that.

He popped in two Tylenol capsules for his back and the last of the lingering head pain that hid behind his bandages. He drank them down with a cup of water from the bathroom sink. Then, he cleaned his glasses and replaced the Band-Aids and gauze on his head for good measure. He looked at himself, staring into his eyes, down into his soul.

What had he done tonight? Unspeakable things.

His facial hair was darker now in its patchy lines. His eyes were dark as they hung above the light of his phone. It looked like death had not only overcome his grandmother but Jon himself. There were black shadows where his father's eyes once were. He had a filthy face. What had become of Jon now? Who was he?

Jon walked from the bathroom and crossed the hall to his grandparents' bedroom.

With his light still beaming from his iPhone, Jon guided his way through the room. The bedsheets had a hint of blood. There were spots on the pillows. *What happened here?* It was clear there was a struggle. The blanket was off the bed and lay in a pile on the foot of the bed.

The end table on one side of the bed had Grandma's sleeping eye mask and a half-empty bottle of water. Beside it, was her Bible. Behind that was a tissue box with red-stained pieces pulled from its top. Jon didn't want to look any longer. He had seen enough here. No more blood. He was sick of it. Sick of it all.

He walked over to the mirrored dresser where various colognes and perfumes stood by rows of rings, necklaces, and bracelets in a glass tray. Grandma had yelled at Jon and his two cousins that one fateful day they checked them out without her permission. Now, Jon had all of them to himself with no worry of being yelled at ever again. It pained him. He would take another yelling if it meant his grandma would be alive for just another moment. *Maybe I could've helped her. Maybe there was something more I could've done down there. I. . .*

Jon picked up a ring from the tray. A silver band with a cluster diamond. He put it back and plucked another. It was an antique brass ring with a blue jewel inside. A sapphire looking gem. He wasn't sure if it was authentic or not. Either way, he liked how it shined beneath the phone's white light. He tried to place it on his ring finger. Too small. The ring's cutting was too tiny to fit on anything other than Jon's pinky. He pulled it free and pocketed it, something to remember his grandmother by.

Jon left the room and pulled the door shut behind him, closing the scene in darkness. He entered the hallway again and made his way toward the staircase. At the top, his light made a little spotlight into the dark below. He walked down and *creaked* every other step beneath the carpet. His hand touched the sapphire ring.

Stillness. Quietness. That was until Jon's light found its way to the corner of the living room where a vintage record player stood on black legs between the couch and a Laz-E-Boy recliner. Sounds of John Denver and Kenny Rogers began to play in Jon's head as he moved closer toward it. Guitar strings picked in the distant. *Almost heaven, West Virginia.* Jon could hear it now. *Blue ridge mountain, Shenandoah River.* The orange and white paint on the record player had faded over the years but was otherwise in great condition. *Life is old there, older than the trees. Younger than the mountains, blowing like a breeze.*

Jon lifted the lid to the record player and was astounded to see vinyl spinning. JOHN DENVER'S GREATEST HITS. SIDE A the record read. It was as if Jon put it there in his mind. A memory placed back by sound. There was a *rippling fuzz* sound as the record spun. *Country roads, take me home to the place I belong. . .* Jon stood still for a moment, held captive by the music playing from a stationary record in a house void of electricity. *West Virginia, mountain mama. . .*

He was there. He was in a memory. Nineteen ninety whatever. One summer day. Jon turned to his right and saw Grandpa Barnes sitting in his cushioned recliner, smiling and singing along, *take me home, country roads,* with a wooden toothpick sticking out between his teeth. His knee was bouncing up and down, up and down. Jon turned around and saw himself as a young boy sitting cross-legged with his cousins Marie and Bobby, clapping along. Jon smiled as tears budded once more. The face of his yesteryear stared back at him. A baby-faced, brown-haired boy with glasses that made him look like Harry Potter, slapping his hands together to the tune from an era he'd never known. Jon's lips quivered the words with them. *All my memories gather round her.* Sunlight streamed through the screen door behind him and his cousins. The day was bright, and summer was here to stay.

If only. . . if only it were here to stay. . .

Stay. Please, stay, Jon thought, but his mind's memory juice was spent. The memory went just as fast as it came. The record player stopped. The sunlight faded, and the living room darkened back into the haunting abyss it was just a moment ago. His younger self and cousins vanished. Jon turned back around to see the Laz-E-Boy empty. The lid to the record player was still propped up but no record lay in the spindle. The needle was tucked away in its station. Empty. It was all empty now.

What else? There has to be more. There have to be more memories.

Jon swung around and cut through the kitchen and approached the back door that led out onto the redwood deck. The warm night air returned. Chimes *chinged* back here, too. He was alone, staring out into the vast grass field that turned into the rows of corn stock which grew beyond. The sky was dark, and clouds were meddling around the stars and the moon. He could smell farmland. Wet grass. Warm, moist ground and hot summer memories.

Jon touched the ring in his pocket and shut his eyes.

When he opened them, he saw his father and him jumping through a sprinkler beneath a clear, blue sky. His father was lifting him up through the streams of water, a gargantuan smile beneath his brown walrus stache. Little Jon was even smaller than the record player's memory. He was a toddler, laughing and kicking his legs. He wore a blue and green bathing suit that looked to have the characters from the show *Rugrats* on them.

It flashed away. The memory was only a split second. A blink.

Lightning bolted down from the skies beyond and blackness returned yet again. Jon stood, trying to get back any image he had of that memory that had been as quick as the lightning itself. He let out a sigh and smelled the air. The bushes *whistled* in the stirring wind.

With his fingers wrapped around the ring, Jon beckoned the memory back. Even if it was just for one more second of time, he'd take it. *Just one more time, give me something.* Nothing. The wind blew, and the chimes *clanged* beside him. The little cushioned, wired chairs out on the deck looked comfortable, but Jon knew he couldn't stay outside. He had to return indoors and retire to bed. He needed his energy to press on to his final destination.

***

The cans of peaches and corn lay on the foot of the bed in the open beach bag. Jon should've been starving, but his hunger disappeared as his body already feasted on an all you can eat buffet of remorse. The memories were sweet, but the poison berry of his grandmother's passing was a bitter, more overpowering taste.

His heart raced. It hadn't stopped since the basement. Still, he was tired now. As he set his alarm on his phone to wake him up at the crack of dawn, he tried to push away the thoughts of his grandmother. Impossible. She was dead and Jon killed her, whether intentionally or not. It would haunt him for the rest of his life, however long that might be.

I didn't want to. I didn't mean to.

You had no choice, it was self-defense. She was going to kill you.

The thought brought back more tears, which streamed down both sides of his face and onto the pillow. He squeezed his eyes shut and begged for sleep.

Who put grandma in the washer room?

He'd do anything to get a few hours of relief. He needed rest to make his final trek back to his home in Springsdale. The end of the line.

Did she hurt grandpa? Mom? Dad?

Jon was convinced that if his parents weren't there, they weren't anywhere else but lost in the madness. But he had to know for sure. He couldn't give up just yet, no matter how hard it was to keep going. He needed answers despite his dread.

What is the cause of all of this?

The thoughts piled up enough to bring a heaviness to his eyes, the eyes that have seen horrors a young man should never have to witness. He pulled out the ring and felt it again, running his fingers along the edges of where brass met sapphire. His lids fell over his eyes. No memories came, but slumber did.

As the sleep gave its mercy to Jon, his mind drifted away to a dreamless sleep while the sound of raindrops began falling on the roof.

FORTY-FIVE

Early to Rise

Before Jon left his grandparents' house for the final time, he took his grandmother's Bible from her end table and placed it down on the blue blanket. THE HOLY BIBLE it read in gold text over a brown leather face. It was a giant book that contained all kinds of highlighting and notes scribbled in the margins. It was her personal Bible that she received when she was a little girl. The pages were all browned and some even crumpled and ripped, but it stood the test of time as it lay on top of its rightful owner.

"Goodbye, grandma," Jon said as he placed the book on top of her corpse. He wanted to cry, but he had run out of tears. The basement of this old house would be the resting place of his grandmother. All the memories would be put to rest with her on that rainy May morning. "I love you."

The steps *creaked* as Jon climbed back up to the kitchen. He turned and closed the door as if it were the shutting of a coffin, forever entombing Grandma Barnes in the dark.

A soft greyness spilled into the house through the windows. The sun was a bulb of light behind a curtain of clouds. Rain *pittered* and *pattered*. Jon thought it was appropriate as he stood for a moment. Peaceful. The best way to have the house feel despite what had happened. The madness was done here. The rain would wash it away. Even though the scars would never leave Jon's soul, it was time to move on.

Jon put on his backpack and picked up the beach bag of food and headed outside. Glock in hand. One last *squeak* of the door sounded behind him as he walked out into the wet, grey morning. He took a final look at the giant tree in the yard and felt content that he'd had great memories here. That was enough for him.

The Honda's trunk was filled with his bags. The passenger seat held the handgun. Jon started the engine, making the car *roar* to life as droplets fell onto the windshield. His phone was plugged into the car's USB port, ready to take him back to his house, back into the madness and, hopefully, back to his parents.

Grandma Barnes' ring rested in his front pocket, holding the memories of his family.

FORTY-SIX

Home

After miles of traveling of what seemed like an eternity, farmlands and rural roads soon gave way to small-town suburbia. Springsdale, Pennsylvania. The place Jon called home. *Take me home. . . country road. . . If only that memory lasted a little longer.* The Honda drove through familiar scenery of the adjacent neighborhoods and Jon even got a passing look at his old high school where the parking lot looked cluttered. No use going there. School was out at Hillcrest forever. The blue and white knight on the entrance sign would guard the bodies of the students.

Jon saw nothing he wasn't used to seeing by now. A car on the side of the road. Smashed bodies. Clutters of debris. Strangers that went by. What else was new? The only thing that frightened him and brought him to a feeling of unease was the quietness of all the suburban homes that lined the back roads that he took off the Simpsonville exit.

It was so morbid, Jon thought, that these lonely buildings were filled with the bodies of families that once were mothers, fathers, children, and pets. All were most likely dead, maybe even mangled to death by the hands of each other. Those that remained living were destined to move-on if they could muster the mental strength to do so and endure what remained of the cruel new world.

There was a sense of anxiety as Jon got closer to the turn, the turn that would bring him to the entrance of his neighborhood cul-de-sac. Franklin Court. His hands trembled as they wrapped around the wheel. The shakiness could've been from the thought of seeing his parents again, or the thought of finding them dead, or the thought of not finding them at all. It could also be that Jon hadn't eaten much more than some chips and a half can of peaches. Some lukewarm tap water from Mr. Mirch's plastic thermos also sloshed around his stomach. Perhaps it was a combination of all those things. Either way, the closer he got, the more he shook like a leaf.

Keep going. This is it. This is it. He kept repeating sentences in his mind. *Here we go. Here we go. This is it. This is it.*

FRANKLIN COURT it read with white lettering on a grey stone-made sign. Jon's eyes widened. His heart hammered against his tired chest. The moment was finally here.

***

"Mom! Dad!" Jon shouted as if his parents were there to greet him. He flung himself out of the Honda and up the concrete pathway to the door, passing some tulips and daffodils that his mom planted beneath the curtain-drawn window that looked into the living room.

Locked. Jon forgot to get his keys from his backpack. *Damn it!* He rushed back to the Honda and popped the trunk open, hands festering with every zipper and compartment as he hunted for his house keys. There was too much excitement to keep a steady hand or heart.

He ripped the keys out of the backpack's smallest compartment in the front and dashed back to the front door of his house with zero interest in taking the Glock. "I'm coming! Mom! Dad!"

A mahogany door with vertical windows on either side showed nothing but darkness as it reflected the morning's glooming light.

The rain was steady.

The key penetrated the lock and Jon turned it so fast, that he could have snapped it in an instant.

"Hello! It's Jon! It's your son!" he cried out but found no response as he stood on the shoe-wiping welcome mat. There were normally New Balances and hiking boots in the plastic tray on the floor beside him, but Jon saw no shoes today. His parents must've gone out. "Mom? Dad?"

No need to flip the light switch. It was second nature to Jon now. This new world was dark. Besides, Jon was so anxious to see his family again that even if the light switch *did* work, he wouldn't give a single shit about it.

Jon began darting around the house like a weasel. *The kitchen. The kitchen.* "MOM!" he shouted as he raced through the living room. He almost banged his leg on the edge of the glass coffee table and tripped over it.

The room was filled with photographs of his entire family atop the fireplace mantel, on the walls, and above the brown piano that had once belonged to Mrs. Barnes' father from Pittsburgh.

No one was in the kitchen. A couple of L.L Bean and Good Housekeeping magazines lay on the dining table. Newspapers scattered the island. A cold mug of coffee sat on the edge of the counter by the mini TV.

"DAD! Where are you?" Jon asked as he left the kitchen, shooting back through the living room, and over to the basement door by the upstairs steps. He swung it open.

An abyss stared up at Jon as he peered down in the blackness. "Is anyone down there?" The silence answered that for him. Still, Jon thought maybe his parents and grandpa retreated to the basement to protect themselves. Perhaps in the storage closet.

At this point, Jon would be happy just to see that his family was still alive. He'd take psycho parents and a demented grandfather over nothing at all. He just wanted someone.

The stairs in Jon's house weren't bare wood, but nice carpeted steps that led to a furnished basement. In the day, you could see the lovely brown, L-shaped couch in front of the enormous flat-screen that hung on the wall. A billiard table was nearby. Now, it was all shrouded in black. Darkness was now the eternal guest. This basement had zero light penetrating it, only the faint grey of the outside through the living room curtains showed the top few steps of the stairs.

No sign of his mom, dad, or grandpa. He checked the rear storage closet but found nothing. Jon wasn't giving up though. He glided up the steps and shut the basement door behind him before running up to the second floor, into the dark hallway. Rushing to the far end, Jon entered the master bedroom. "DAD? MOM? HELLO?"

Deep seeded fear and hopelessness began to grow in his soul.

They scrambled getting out of bed after grandpa called, Jon thought, looking at the thrown bed sheets. It was a scene that read urgency, much like at his grandparent's house, minus the blood. *Thank God.* His mother's fur slippers were on the floor by her side of the bed.

Jon turned back into the hall and popped into every room, finding no one in the bathroom, his bedroom, or the guest room. He sprinted down the steps and back into the kitchen where he caught a glance of the backyard through the window above the sink.

The fenced-in backyard was green with wet grass. A metal shed lay in the rear corner, its sides streaked with rust. The key to its door was found in the last drawer on the counter. Ignoring the fact that if the key was still placed in the drawer, then his family must not of went out there, Jon grabbed it without thought. He couldn't leave any stone left unturned.

He pulled the glass sliding door open from behind the head of the dining table. The rain was picking up as it splashed onto his hair and face. The lenses of his glasses were covered in raindrops. His shoes suctioned and *slapped* on the puddled ground as he ran through the mud, toward the storage shed.

Knock knock knock on the shed the door. Jon's family could've retreated inside for all he knew, and he didn't want to scare them before entering. "Guys, it's Jon. I'm ok, I'm coming in!" He was talking to no one. The key went into the gold padlock and *clicked* open the silver metal above it.

Inside, Jon smelled the familiar and overwhelming fumes of gasoline. The light from outside was enough to see plastic red tanks of it. Sheers, shovels, a weed whacker, and various landscaping tools hung from the sides on metal hangers. Bags of mulch and grass feed were piled on top of each other. A badminton net was wrapped up in the corner. Beside it, mounted on the wall on two black hangers above a workbench, was the Remington 700.

Jon grabbed it by the stock. Touching it flooded memories back into his mind for a moment like the lightning that took away the memory before. This time, it transported him to a different time and place entirely.

Jon and his father were sitting in the cold wilderness. He could feel the snow falling around him. Then, without a second to soak in the memory, he flashed back to the shed. For a moment, he thought could see the cold breath flowing from his mouth. But he didn't have time to enjoy it. The memories are nice. Bittersweet. The real world, however, still had bitter truths to find. He left the wintery memories alone for now.

He pulled a clear tub from beneath the bench that contained little green and yellow square cardboard boxes. REMINGTON RIFLE CARTRIDGES it read. Ammo. Jon slipped one full set into his back pocket before leaving the shed, back into the rain. Little did Jon know, he would be shooting that hunting rifle again not long from now. Forget the Glock and the massive amounts of ammo Rusty provided, the Remington would be the last gun Jon would ever pull the trigger on.

Running back inside, Jon had one last place to look. Beside the dining table, he unlocked and opened the door to the garage. He brought out his phone and turned on the flashlight to show one car. The blue Chevy. Dad's black Ford was missing. *Fuck!* was all Jon could think and say. *FUCK!* The fucks turned to heavy breaths. Panic. His chest burned, and his stomach churned as the realization that he was alone came crashing down on him like a tidal wave, an unstoppable tsunami ten times as hard-hitting as the feeling in his grandparents' cellar.

He threw his phone into the dark garage. It made a *snapping* sound as the casing crashed to the oil-stained cement. The light whipped around before settling, facing upwards to the rafters where spiders spun webs.

They're dead! They're gone! Oh, God! They're gone! Oh, God!

Jon's breath paused as his tears let loose. His bottom lip quivered from both despair and anger, anger at being too late. A lump in his throat choked him. Dizziness fell over him. He fumbled back into the kitchen and began to wobble as his feet began to carry him like unstable stilts to the front door, stumbling him back into the morning outside.

The silent houses all around the cul-de-sac didn't move or make a peep to Jon's screams for his parents. They sat staring like statues. Franklin Court was empty, except for one disheveled young man whose yelling was making him even more disoriented. All around him the world spun like a whirlpool, sucking him in and drowning him deep into the heartbreaking end to his journey.

Images flashed in Jon's head. White Haven College. Emily. The Mirchs. Grandma. His parents. Memories. Their brightness blinded him until he dropped the rifle and collapsed on the grass of his front yard.

The green grass was wet from the rain that was now picking up to its full descent from the skies. His face, glasses and all, smacked against the moistness with a hard *THUD*. *Alone. I'm all alone.*

"NO!" Jon banged his fists on the ground, grass staining his hands. Wet dirt flung on his palms. *POUND. POUND.* Tears streamed down his red, hot face. All by himself, Jon wept as he lay in the yard.

How many days had it been since it all started? Jon didn't know, and now he didn't care. It was all over. He was too late. His friends, grandparents, and now his parents were gone. All gone. Nothing more than memories now. Ghosts. Why couldn't Jon do anything? Why couldn't he have saved them? Perhaps it was destiny. A brutal fate set in stone.

Why? Why did this all happen? How? There were a thousand questions but only one that could be answered: what would become of Jon?

FORTY-SEVEN

A Rude Awakening

Flashes of light came and went. Jon's dizzy head bobbed as he floated across the cul-de-sac. Someone or something was carrying him, but he had no strength to lift his head up to see what. He thought he heard voices. A woman's, then a man's. He couldn't understand what they were saying.

The cul-de-sac flashed before Jon's eyes. Here then gone as the voices faded in and out.

The world became black.

***

When Jon woke up, he wasn't floating or met face to face with the wet grass and dirt from which he made his bed. Instead, the sight of tan carpet beneath white lights lingered below his wobbling, tired head.

Electricity?

At first, he thought he was in a dream, some subconscious journey back into his basement when times were better. But as he blinked and focused his eyes, Jon found that it was the real, waking world.

It wasn't until he looked up and tried to cover his eyes from the blinding white light that he realized his hands were taped together around the back of the chair he woke up sitting in. His legs were also taped around the chair's legs.

What the hell? Where am I? Jon thought as his movements against the tight tape brought his focus in. It felt like duct tape. He could feel the hairs rip from the skin on his arms as he maneuvered himself.

The room he was in displayed other white lights that sat atop tripods. They each faced a wall, each appearing to have pinned up pieces of paper with black-typed text on them. Jon couldn't tell what they read as the harsh brightness forced his eyes into a squint. It was easier to look down at the carpet instead.

There was no sound other than the faint noise of rain.

The carpet. Jon looked back up at the walls, trying to make out the shape of the room. *Familiar.* He thought for a moment and attempted to hop the seat up and down as the tape gripped his wrists and ankles.

The chair *creaked* as his body thrust upwards in the spotlight. The chair's legs began to shift and lift from the carpeted craters as the wood inched to the right. His glasses bounced off and on his nose. Jon turned his head as far as he could to see stairs behind him, which were identical to the stairs in his basement. Same location and all. The pieces of this place were coming together in Jon's mind. *I'm still in the neighborhood.* It couldn't be his own basement, but he was in a Franklin Court basement, nonetheless. Jon knew this because he used to go over to his friend Dylan's house at the front of the neighborhood. His house had a similar layout.

He jumped the chair again, trying to turn around to face the steps. Wiggling and lashing around inside the prisoned seat, Jon jerked the wooden chair too much. He fell sideways with his head only centimeters from the wall. *Thud.*

"Shit!" he cried out. Now he was screwed. His hands twisted. His feet shook, but the tape held strong, wrapped tightly around him as his shoulder dug into the carpeted floor. The white light lit up half of his face. More of a prisoner than ever, Jon lay with his heart rate rising.

Whose house could I be in? There was no one else outside. . .

Then, a noise. A *thud.* It sounded like it came from the opposite side of the room where the storage closet would be.

"He's awake!" a girl's voice shouted from behind Jon's fallen body.

"Alright, alright. Keep it down, okay?" a man's voice said in reply.

Stepping in front of the white light, two figures walked in front of Jon. Shadows were looking down at him. Jon's eyes could make out a tall man and a girl who was less than half the height of the man. She was holding a crossbow or bow and arrow of some sort.

They both knelt and picked Jon up, chair and all. He let out a groan as his body tilted up and back into the spotlight of the white LED.

"Jon, right?" the man asked in a deep voice.

Jon gave a weak nod in reply.

"We're Dominic and Rae Cooper. We live across the street from you. Do you remember us? You and I went to Hillcrest together. My sister was a sophomore when we were seniors. Do you remember?" the man, who must've been Dominic, asked.

Jon didn't have the energy to compose a thought or a memory. "Where are my parents?" was all he could muster.

The two shadows looked at one another and then back at Jon.

"We don't know where your parents are. I'm so sorry," the girl, Rae, said. She spoke like she didn't want to disappoint Jon.

"Jon, can you tell us what happened to you? Have you drank any bottled water recently?" Dominic asked.

Jon shook his head as he stared at the carpet, completely and utterly disinterested in revisiting his experiences. Not another second could be spent going through the story again, especially not with these mysterious former high school classmates. He didn't have a clue when he'd last drank bottled water. *Who cares?* "I just want to know where my parents are. If you don't know, just kill me." He said it like he meant it, which he did.

"Jesus Christ, we're not going to kill you! We're glad you're not sick, we need you alive! There's a lot we need to tell you. I'm sure everything's been a living hell for you like it's been for us, but I think you just need some time to rest and let us help you the best we can," Dominic said. He sounded genuine. "But we need to know, is there anyone in your house that drank bottled water? Anything like that? Are you able to remember?"

Jon shook his head again as anger showed itself in his mind. *What the hell is this guy on?* He let out a sigh. His head was a drum, and his mouth was dry. All this talk about bottled water wasn't helping his thirst.

"I need some water," Jon said. "Hand me one of those bottles of water, please. Untie me and give me some water."

"No, no, no! Rae, can you get a glass for him, please? And bring down the scissors," Dominic said.

"Sure, I'll be right back," Rae said with her soft, feminine voice.

Why not a bottle? They're right fucking there! What the hell is going on? But Jon was too weak to say it out loud. Talking took too much energy now and he couldn't spend it on his frustration.

Rae handed the crossbow to Dominic and left from beneath the spotlight. Jon could see her hair bouncing on the back of her neck.

Her scent was sweet as she passed by. Fruity and pretty. Something girly.

"We have to be careful with what we drink now, Jon," Dominic said, still in the shadows with his weapon aimed down. "It blows my mind how people like us have made it this far without sipping the tainted shit."

Jon's swallow felt like walls of sand scratching the sides of his throat. He didn't respond to Dominic as he was still confused and angry.

Rae came down the steps behind him after a few seconds. Glass of water in one hand, pair of scissors in the other. Her feminine scent emanated as she passed by Jon. Strong sweetness. She handed the scissors to Dominic who placed the crossbow on the floor.

"We're sorry we tied you up like this Jon, we just had to make sure you were ok. I'm going to cut you lose, alright? Can I trust you?" Dominic asked as he got down on his knees. His facial features were more visible now as Jon could see his dark, buzzed hair that connected to a black beard. A young face behind the scruff. He didn't recognize him right away.

"You can trust me, I'm not gonna touch you," Jon replied.

Dominic *snipped* off the wrist tape. It *peeled* off Jon's skin, pulling brown hairs off his arms. Then, his legs were cut free. Jon rubbed his wrists and took the glass of water from Rae. Sink water. Nice. It flushed the desert from his gullet. Nothing was better than wetting his whistle.

"He seems to be normal. No aggression," Rae said.

"Guess we hit the lottery with Jon," Dominic said, now standing up.

"Thank you." Jon took another hardy sip from the glass.

"We should head upstairs to the kitchen. It would be better up there, so we can tell you what we know," Dominic said. "Rae, could you please?"

Rae nodded and walked over to the other light in the basement that shined onto the wall of printed papers. When she entered the spotlight, Jon could see her beautiful dark-brown hair that draped over a white and black striped shirt. Jean shorts. Smooth legs. She grabbed some papers off the wall and bent over to pick up cardboard boxes. She turned back toward them. Rae looked clean and unharmed. Beautiful. Brown-eyed and beautiful, but Jon had no energy left to get swooned by a woman. He could see her attractiveness but had zero motivation to go beyond that.

"Let's go," Dominic said, turning off the light. He did the same with a spotlight above Jon. Now, all three of them were in darkness. "Are you good to walk?"

"Should be," Jon said. He got up from the chair. His legs were weak, but he managed to straighten himself out. He followed Dominic and Rae up the steps as he held his glass of water.

FORTY-EIGHT

Answers

The rain was steady.

Dominic and Rae's forest green and white camouflage-painted crossbow sat loaded on the kitchen island next to Mr. Barnes' Remington.

With a depressed tone, Jon explained his journey from the last few days at White Haven College to finding his way back to his lonesome home. He left out the details of the Mirchs and his grandma, not wanting to re-open the scars that were yet to start healing. He couldn't face all of that anymore. No parents. No friends. No one. There wasn't an ounce of energy left in his tale.

"I think you may feel a little better after we tell you what we know. It may not satisfy you after all you've been through, but it will be enough to give you an idea of what caused this," Dominic said.

Grey light streamed in through the windows and onto the piles of articles and printouts. Jon, Dominic, and Rae sat at the dining room table above bold and black headlines that were scattered everywhere. CNN. New York Times. FOX News. They all put their biases aside and seemed to have the same message.

IS THERE SOMETHING IN YOUR WATER? STICK TO TAP, NEW STUDIES FIND.

BOTTLED WATER NOT AS CLEAN AND FILTERED AS YOU'D THINK.

Jon's eyes gazed upon the headlines as they went from mainstream sources to mysterious sites with more sensational titles. Uncensorednews.com. Uncutnews.com. FreedomNewsFighters.org. There were even sites based outside of America. Jon wondered how they even got their information.

ENGINEER AT MAJOR WATER COMPANY EXPOSES HAZARDOUS PARASITE IN SPRING WATER.

DEADLY PARASITE FOUND IN CALIFORNIA SPRINGS.

WATER COVER-UP IS COSTING LIVES, YOU COULD BE NEXT.

MAJOR WATER BRANDS ARE KILLING PEOPLE AND NO ONE IS DOING ANYTHING ABOUT IT.

"Have you heard of anything like this before, Jon? Do these articles ring any bells for you? Maybe you saw something on the news before all of this went down?" Dominic asked, pulling up different articles.

In the light, Dominic looked more familiar to Jon. He wore a plain undershirt stained with his sweat. Below, he had on jeans with brown hiking boots.

With the buzzed hair and beard, Dominic didn't look the same from high school. As far as Jon could remember, Dominic was the lanky dude who took AP Bio or Chemistry classes with him. *Mr. Schlansky's class?* Perhaps they had a lab assignment or two together. They weren't close, but Jon remembered he was a pleasant classmate. He never started or wanted any trouble. Kept to himself most of the time.

VIDEO DETAILS HORRIFIC WATER PARASITE AND WHAT IT'S CAPABLE OF.

CEOS REFUSE TO STEP DOWN AMID BOTTLING CONTROVERSY.

MAINSTREAM MEDIA BOUGHT OUT TO NOT COVER BOTTLING METHODS OF MAJOR CORPORATIONS.

WATER BUG COULD REACH GLOBAL PROPORTIONS, NO WORKABLE CURES IN SIGHT.

"I can't say that I have. I'm not really one to watch the news all that much. All I saw was the rioting in New York and the plane crash in Los Angeles," Jon said.

"Oh, there were more plane crashes than the one in Los Angeles, believe me," Dominic said, rubbing his head, overwhelmed. "I don't think you even know the half of what's going on. We've got a real mess on our hands."

Jon took a reluctant sip from the glass. The headlines struck him and caused his thoughts to pick up speed again like an old motor with a fresh tank of gas. He fetched a Ritz cracker from a box and popped it in his mouth.

"I had to print out everything I could find online. When the power got knocked out, I was burning some videos onto a DVD. All we have now are the printouts from across the internet. Everything has to be saved and archived for the future. Do you understand?" Dominic was serious.

Jon nodded. "How were those lights powered in the basement? Batteries?"

"Exactly. Gigantic D-cell batteries," Dominic replied. "We've got enough to last us for a little while as long as we use the lights sparingly."

"Why did you shine it on me?" Jon asked.

"I'll get to that in a minute," Dominic replied.

Jon took a slow sip. *Christ.* "Tell me what's happened."

Dominic let out a breath. A sigh. He shuffled through the articles that Rae helped organize.

You could tell they were siblings. They had the same eyes. Dark and striking, almost black. Rae's hair was a tad browner than Dominic's locks. Jon couldn't remember much of her when she was a freshman in high school. He might not have met her before.

Together, the siblings piled the pieces of news to form a chronological series of events.

"Alright, let me see where I should begin. There's a lot to cover." Dominic held a pile of papers and slapped the edge of them on the dining table, straightening them out.

"I don't plan on going anywhere," Jon said, swishing the water around in his dirty, unwashed mouth. "Take all the time in the world. I've got no family to see or places to be."

Neither Dominic nor Rae said a word in response. Their faces painted the picture of understanding. It was as if they were saying, *sorry, we're in the same boat.*

Maybe they lost their family too, Jon thought. *At least they have each other. I have nothing left.* Jon's eyes watered, but he quick blinked the tears back into their ducts.

"So, we're not exactly sure *when* this all started. The sickness that is. There's no patient zero or anything like that that we're aware of," Dominic began. "As far as it's been reported, sometime earlier in April is the period we're working with."

"Ok," Jon said.

"Are you familiar with how water is taken from springs and bottled?"

"Somewhat, I guess."

"Well, are you aware that most of the water we drink out of plastic bottles comes from California?" Dominic pushed over a picture of the state itself beneath the headline **DROUGHT RIDDEN CALIFORNIA CONTINUES TO BE STRIPPED OF NATURAL SPRINGS.** The map of California was colored with different shades of red. A key above labeled the shades as different levels of drought. Pink: moderate drought. Lighter red: Severe drought. Red: Extreme drought.

Jon shook his head.

Dominic's finger lay on the extreme drought shading of the central coast. "Right here is where most of the major beverage companies get their groundwater. They use California groundwater for their products. As you can see, the region is crippled by drought. Extreme drought."

"Right." Jon was intrigued.

"Of course, the people of California were pissed, protesting and whatnot. But nothing could be done. No matter how many people camped out and wrote letters, these companies wouldn't stop. They have contracts. Big, multi-million-dollar contracts that allow them to drill where they want, when they want, and gather as much water as they're capable of. Problem is, as they gather up all the groundwater, the drought forces them to dig deeper and in other, untouched places. You understand?" Dominic asked.

"Yes," Jon replied.

"So, what we have," Dominic slid out another article from the stack, "are companies taking their machines and sticking them in places where they don't belong." Yellow dozers and pallets of pipe were pictured beneath the headline **WORKERS CONTINUE TO DRILL DROUGHT-RIDDEN SPRINGS DESPITE PUBLIC OUTCRY**. Men in neon vests were pictured working on placing water sourcing machines into a forest stream.

"To make matters worse," Dominic continued, "these guys didn't even examine the land. No preparation, no surveying, nothing. They just took the pipes and went to work. So, they're pumping and pumping this water from the ground without the slightest idea of what could be beneath the stream."

Jon's eyebrow rose. *Lying beneath the stream?* He stopped taking sips from his glass of water and placed it on the dining table, trying not to show his anxiety.

"If it wasn't for one of the engineers that worked at the filtering plant for one of the beverage companies, none of this information would've gotten out," Dominic said, pulling out the **DEADLY PARASITE FOUND IN CALIFORNIA SPRINGS** article. Below, was a photograph of microscopic organisms. White things on a black background. Pod-shaped creatures with multiple antennas. They looked sort of like pufferfish to Jon. Spiky. Odd.

"It seemed that Mr. Leon Freedman was the only person in the whole operation concerned about what was going through the filtering system. What he found was this organism failing to be flushed out from the machines. Both before and after, this thing was present in the water," Dominic said.

"Did he tell anyone? I mean, what is it exactly?" Jon asked.

"Oh, he told everyone he could at the plant. He wasn't sure what it was at first, there was no name for it. He just knew it wasn't normal. Definitely not something he'd seen before. Usually, the water would go through osmosis or deionization to rid contaminants. This was something new and it seemed the higher-ups didn't care or, if they did know about it, chose to ignore it. It didn't help the fact that Mr. Freedman found this out *after* large quantities of water had been packaged and shipped out." Dominic sifted through more articles as Jon was absorbing what he'd learned so far.

The water. . . did I. . . I must've. . .

"Freedman was convinced something was up, so he took matters into his own hands. He began running some tests with the water, seeing how the organisms reacted to certain pressures, treatments, and temperatures outside of the usual filtering process. All on company time might I add."

"What did he find?"

"Well, the higher-ups weren't too pleased with what he was doing. Word was getting around about some mysterious organism floating in the water and that Leon was using company time and equipment to decipher it. People were getting worried, complaining. Not that Leon wasn't complaining enough about the damn parasite himself. They let him go as soon as they caught him in the act. He couldn't finish running all his trials, so he snuck out as much raw H20 from the stream as he could and began running tests at his home. On rats."

"The classic method," Jon said, but still the fear rose.

"That's right, the classic method. He was determined to get answers. What he found was that these rats would either be knocked out into a vegetative state or straight up killed by drinking this mysterious parasite water. It baffled him, but also caused him to make phone calls, pleading with not only his company but the other big players in the game since they were all taking water from the same source. No one seemed interested and a few even hung up, thinking he was a prank caller." Dominic was flipping articles all around. It was obvious he had gone over these materials several times.

"Jesus," Jon said under his breath. Rae shook her head in disbelief at the ignorance of big business.

"It wasn't until one night he heard the rats squeaking and running around in circles in their cages. Clawing and gnawing to get out. The ones he thought were dead were now more alive than ever. Same for the vegetables. He couldn't believe what he was seeing. Crazed live rats. Some even going at each other. Rats biting rats," Dominic said, showing a gruesome photograph of the test subjects. The rats were bloodied and chewed-up.

Jon scratched his head. *Did I drink it? My parents. Are they...?*

"But get this," Dominic said. He flipped another page. "When he flicked on the lights above the cages, the rats began to slow down. After a few minutes, they completely stopped moving and reverted to vegetables again. They were breathing. They were alive. It was the light that seemed to knock them down. So, to test it, he shut off all the lights again and low and behold, the rats started running in a frenzy just like they did before. The fighting with one another revved back up."

The students at the quad. The two men fighting outside of the library that chased Emily and me.

"That's why you had me in the light, right? To see how I'd react?" Jon asked.

"Yes, that's our only way to see if you're crazy or not," Dominic replied. "As silly as that sounds..."

Rae moved her hair away from her eyes.

"So, cut to a few weeks later. We started getting reports around the West Coast of the flu, right? Only it's not the flu we're all familiar with. No stuffy nose or headaches or throwing up. We have people starting to collapse. Outright falling over, falling into a deep sleep. Almost like mini comas," Dominic said.

Deep sleep. Comas. Mark. Kevin. Images flashed in Jon's mind of the college library. *The broken vending machine.*

"But the media was calling it the flu. The 'New Flu.' The 'West Coast Flu.' The latest flu trend if you will. That's what they sold it as. Nothing to see here but some out of the blue illness that they pushed as being airborne. You got it through coughing or sneezing onto one another. The problem was they were making shit up," Dominic said. "They were being bought out to say all this instead of reporting the violent outbursts of the victims."

"Slow down a sec," Jon interjected, "you're saying that at this point the bottling companies knew what it was? That they were the ones causing the sickness?"

"They had to have known something was up. Leon sent letters, emails, videos, photographs, everything. The CEOs didn't want to acknowledge it. Thought they'd run their water well dry with this kind of PR. They must've spent millions on all the mainstream outlets. CNN. Fox. MSNBC. You name it. However, the one place they couldn't stop him was YouTube and underground news sites.

"He'd upload a video detailing everything he'd discovered with his experiments. It'd get taken down and he would have to re-upload it. Every graphic detail. Everything of what it did as far as he could tell with the rats. Luckily, it picked up steam and went viral just as the 'New Flu' was hitting the East Coast in great numbers. People would download the video for themselves, share it on Facebook and Twitter. It made the rounds, but the damage had already been done and more was yet to come. The people weren't rallying around the videos enough to really do anything at that point."

Mom. Dad. Was there water in the house? When did I last drink it? Why am I not sick? Grandma had bottled water in her basement, did she drink it? Her end table. She must have. . .

"So, what is it then? What is the parasite and how does it cause this sleep, this frenzy? What's the science of it?" Jon asked, almost shouting. He'd listened long enough. He wanted the answer, craved it.

"I'll show you," Dominic said in a cold tone. He stood up from the piles of reports and grabbed a black Maglite flashlight from the counter, next to a box of paint masks. Dominic handed one to Jon and put one on himself, *snapping* it around his nose and mouth. He looked like a surgeon.

Rae began to cry.

FORTY-NINE

The Woman in the Basement

Dominic led Jon back into the dark basement with the Maglite. The beam illuminated the prisoner seat where the cut tape still stuck open around the legs. They walked past tripods of switched-off LEDs and saw what Jon once could not see. Boxes were thrown around. Papers. A torn-up, red leather couch with stuffing peeking from the rips. Plastic bottle caps littered the carpet next to piles of empty water bottles. A treadmill next to a TV that dangled halfway off its mount on the wall beside a Pittsburgh Steelers poster.

Blood. There's always blood.

The two of them approached the far end of the basement where the white wood storage door stood with a splatter of blood and, somehow, a clean handle. A circular push lock was engaged on the top of it. Same as the one in Jon's basement.

Beside it, another turned off LED light on a tripod stood with its bulb facing the wall.

Dominic's beam wobbled as he aimed it at the door. His voice crept from his mouth in sobbing breaths.

"Jon, what I'm about to show you is very hard for me and I ask you to listen to everything I say." Dominic took deep breaths like he was having a panic attack behind the mask. He spoke in a whisper. "Stand behind me, I'm going to unlock the door and when we get inside, I'm going to switch on that light and pull it inside. Don't make any sudden movements. We have to do this very carefully, alright?"

"Ok," Jon said in a whisper. He remembered the faint *thud* he heard from beyond the wall. Part of him felt sick with the thought of finding his family back there. His mother and father held prisoner like Jon was, only this time they were mad with the water parasite if that truly was the case. His mind flashed back to finding his grandmother in her basement.

Jon hoped he wouldn't hurl inside his paint mask.

"Take this," Dominic said and handed Jon the Maglite. He grabbed the LED light by the neck of the stand and switched on the bright light against the pale wall. "If the smell is too much for you, just tell me. Rae and I did our best to clean up, but still, pace yourself."

With his other hand, Dominic *clicked* out the lock in the handle, using the fingernail of his thumb. Then, his thumb came down on the grip before he jerked the storage door wide and moved the floodlight inside. The LED blasted through the darkness. Jon saw the concrete room light up in front of Dominic. Beyond him, a woman sat on the unfurnished floor, staring at them with duct tape covering her mouth. She rose as the light struck her face.

The same smell that came from the washer room at Jon's grandparents' house was finding its way into his olfactory glands. This time it was worse. Not only were there scents of urine, but excrement. Shit. A stale, harsh fume. The worst gas station, roadside, public bathroom you'd ever find yourself in was right here in the Cooper's basement.

The woman rushed toward them in a jerking hop. Jon could see her wrists and ankles were bound with the silver tape as well. *Infected, she's infected. Why didn't Dominic bring his crossbow?* The light from Maglite was lost in the brightness as it shook in Jon's hands.

"Step back, Jon!" Dominic shouted and lunged forward into the bound woman. Wrestling her to the ground, he held her beneath the spotlight as she jerked and jived. "Shut the door!" Groans beneath her taped mouth tried to escape its sticky trap. She tried to squirm away from the light, but Dominic dragged her back into the ring. He wrangled her like he was a crocodile hunter.

Jon shut the door and noticed that the inside handle was covered with more of the duct tape. *This shit is everywhere, huh?* It covered the lock with so many layers of tape that Jon didn't know what to do, so he left it shut without a secure *click* of any lock. He turned back, panicking.

With more time beneath the squint-inducing light, the woman began to lessen her lashing out. She became weaker. Tired. Dominic was handling her with more ease as her eyes blinked slower and slower. *Just like Kevin by the ambulance,* Jon thought as the woman's fight finished beneath a soaked Dominic. *The rats.*

"Jon, come here. I need you to just hold her arms down. She won't be any trouble for you," Dominic said, wiping his forehead with the back of a hand. His shirt was drenched in sweat. "Don't worry about the flashlight."

Jon put down the Maglite and ventured into the spotlight of the LED lamp. He knelt on the storage room floor, above a frizzy-haired woman who was bound by rolls of tape and blood. Her mascara streaked her cheeks beneath sleepy eyes. Thankfully, it wasn't Jon's mom. Unfortunately, it was someone else's.

As Jon got closer to her, she opened her eyes as wide as they could be. Dark brown, almost black eyes stared into Jon's soul as if she was shocked awake by his presence. It forced him back a step.

"It's ok," Dominic said, out of breath. "She's gonna be out cold in a second."

Jon grabbed her wrists. The tape was sticky with blood. Dominic gripped her ankles as she let out her final movements before her eyelids came down and slumber took over. The jerking subsided.

"See this? Just like Leon Freedman found with his rats and all the people that collapsed with the flu, they had a reaction to sunlight, any light," Dominic said, panting. He wiped another bead of sweat from his worn face. "Whatever you do, don't take off your mask unless you want to puke all over yourself. We tried to clean her up the best we could but-"

"Dominic, is this your mom?" Jon asked, already aware of what the answer would be. Behind the filth, he could see the resemblance to Rae. She looked like any other upper-middle-class mom donning a pink sweatsuit, except now it looked ripped and torn as if she had a rough morning jog.

Dominic nodded. He spoke with a depressed sound. "It is. We've been keeping her down here for the past few days, keeping her alive, trying to maybe reverse the effects of the parasite. So far nothing has worked. We've tried to force-feed her Tylenol and Benadryl. We tried giving her *more* water, both tainted and untainted. Nothing has worked. When the power shut down, Leon's work went with it. We have no clue if he's working on a cure or is even still breathing at this point."

Mrs. Cooper's chest rose and fell beneath the floodlight's shine, just as if she was a rat or a student from White Haven College. Dominic reached over to her face and peeled off the dirty duct tape from his mother's mouth, trying not to rip the skin from her lips. Her mouth slung open as her sleep continued in persistent deep breaths that came close to snores.

"The bug has been labeled as the 'Aggressive Nocturnal Parasite.' You drink the tainted shit and the parasite gets into your blood-stream. Before you know it, in the next few minutes, it's swimming upstream, all the way to your amygdala. Then the sun goes down and all hell breaks loose," Dominic said with his eyes locked on his mother's.

Jon had learned all about the amygdala throughout his college courses. The limbic system. Fight or flight. The brain is a powerful organ not to be tampered with, especially not with something as in-vasive as a water parasite.

"So, it overrides her body? The parasite controls her adrenaline levels?" Jon asked. It was starting to come together in his mind.

"Right, it emotionally hijacks her brain. That's why when you find she's awake, she's screaming, lashing out, biting, throwing a fit. She has no regard for what she says or does anymore. She has no recol-lection of it either. All she has is pure, unhinged rage coursing through her veins. Every time."

"But why does it only occur in darkness? What is the light doing to make her fall asleep like that?"

Dominic let out a breath through his mask as he looked up into the blinding light. He couldn't look for more than a few seconds before turning back to his mom. "I'm not sure. Some people said it may have to do with the depth of where the parasite was found in the stream. It's only active at night or, at least, when it perceives night. Like an owl, it's nocturnal."

Jon and Dominic fell silent for a moment. The only sound was Mrs. Cooper's breathing.

"I want you to grab the flashlight," Dominic said. "I'm gonna show you what happens."

Jon was shocked at the request. "Maybe we shouldn't. I've seen plenty and I-"

"I think you should see how it all works. The more you see, the more you'll know how to deal with it. Ok?" Dominic sounded like he was in pain.

Jon looked down at Dominic's mother, then back up at him and said, "Alright. Only if you're sure."

"I am. Don't worry, we won't let her do any damage. I've done this before. If anything happens, we just drag her back into the light."

Jon got up from the cement floor and moved behind the LED, picking up the Maglite which was still clicked on. He was sweating behind the mask as his mouth felt moist.

"Whenever you're ready," Dominic said with his grip on his mother's wrists. "Turn off the light and keep the flashlight pointed down. When she starts to wake up, you can shine it on her. It won't be enough to put her back asleep, but just enough so we can see what the hell we're doing."

Wanting to get it over with, Jon switched off the big LED. The only light left was the mini spotlight of the Maglite that aimed down on Jon's shoes.

"Alright, get ready. A few moments are all it takes. Come over here with the flashlight and get ready to grab her feet for me," Dominic said.

Jon's heart wasn't ready. Perhaps he should've braced himself before switching off the sleep-inducing light. He began to panic, unsure if this was such a good idea. With his luck, this would be the time that Dominic's mother takes her son out with a bite to his neck.

No, no. Please. God, no. More flashbacks of White Haven College struck Jon. He saw Mark grabbing onto his ankle. Jon had to shake the memory away.

"Mmmm. Hhhhhhhmmmm," Mrs. Cooper groaned in the dark. Jon began to aim up the light to her face when Dominic stopped him.

"Wait just a few more seconds until she comes to," Dominic said.

"Sorry."

"Mmmmm. Hmmmmmm. Huh? Huh? Hello?" she said with a mouth as dry as sand.

"Mom, can you hear me?" Dominic asked.

"Huhhh hmmm, what? Who's there? Dom? Dominic? Is that you?" she said as her voice was starting to sound more clear in the echoes of the room.

"Jon, go ahead with the light. Grab her ankles."

The beam shined on her once attractive face. Now, it was ravaged by the parasite's control. Her eyes danced. Open. Close. Open. Close.

"Where are we, Dominic? Why are we in the dark? Who's shining that goddamn light in my face!? Turn that off!" she already spoke with a tinge of anger coming up from her throat.

"Mom, you've had an accident."

"An accident? Get the fuck off of me! Why are my hands tied? Did your bastard father put you up to this?! My legs too?! You perv!" she said, even louder now.

"Mom, just relax! We're not gonna hurt you, just take some deep breaths. Ok?" Dominic pleaded, but he was no match for his mother's rage that was building up with every spoken word.

"Who's grabbing my FUCKING legs! FUCK YOU! GET THE FUCK OFF ME!" she shouted and kicked with such force that it caused Jon to drop the Maglite. Both of his hands gripped her ankles, forcing the heels of the running sneakers into the cement. They squirmed.

"Shit! I'm sorry! She kicked me hard!" Jon cried as Mrs. Cooper wiggled like a prisoned snake.

Dominic had both hands around his mother's bound wrists as she shouted out, "OFF! GET OFF! I'M GONNA KILL YOU AND YOUR FUCKING LITTLE FRIEND! OFF! YOU GOOD FOR NOTHING-"

Mrs. Cooper's teeth almost bit down into her son's hand. Dominic was quick enough to feel the sharpness before she clenched down. There was a noise of top teeth hitting bottom. *Tick.*

"Jon! Can you flick on the LED and grab her legs again? She's biting at me! I don't think we can keep her down much longer!" Dominic shouted down at him.

"I'M GONNA BITE YOUR LITTLE HEAD OFF!" she shouted as she lunged her head forward with another bite. A snarl. Jon could see the black figure of her pouncing upwards against the figure of Dominic. The two shadows tangled together.

"Now, Jon! Now! I can only hold her for a little more! She's fucking crazy!" Dominic shouted in a pure panic. He regretted ever wanting to show Jon what happens to his mother in the dark.

Jon jumped up and nearly knocked the entire LED stand over with his shoe. Panic gloved his hands. He grabbed the stock and felt for the switch, *snapped* it on, and the harsh light filled the room once again, exposing the mother and son's violent tussle.

Mrs. Cooper's face raged and scowled like the maniacs Jon had seen before. It was terrifying, but Jon knew if he didn't step back into the arena and grab hold of her feet, she may just follow through with her threat of biting her son's little head off.

She didn't make it easy for him. Her legs wiggled and whipped, making it hard for Jon to get a grip. Once he got in closer and stepped back into the brightness, Mrs. Cooper's movements stopped in mid-jerk as her eyes met Jon's again.

"Oh, well, if it isn't the little Jonny boy from across the street!" she shouted out in a sinister voice. "I haven't seen you since you were a tiny little shit running around the neighborhood! Why don't you get your FUCKING hands off me!"

A frightened eyebrow rose on Jon's face as he held her ankles with a loosened grip.

"Mom, you're gonna be going to sleep again. Ok? Just calm down. Shhh," Dominic said, seeming to ignore his mother's sudden interest in Jon.

"Where's your daddy and mommy, huh?" she asked as Jon tightened his grip now.

"Do you. . . do you know where they are?" Jon felt weird asking this psychotic woman anything.

"Jon, don't worry about it. She's not right in the head," Dominic said.

"Hey!" she said as she twisted. "Come to think of it, I *did* see your mommy the other day! I bet you'd like to see your mommy again wouldn't you, Jonny? Yeah! I bet you miss your mommy, don't you? You son of a bitch! And how about your daddy? Do you miss him?" she shouted. Tucking her legs in, she shot them outwards. Jon's grip tightened more.

"Jon, don't listen to this. It's just the parasite making her talk like this," Dominic said.

"Hey! I tell you what, you bastard, you untie me from my FUCK-ING son's twisted little game, and I'll show. . ." She began to feel the light's rays. ". . .show. . . you. . . tell you. . . where your mommy and daddy. . ."

"What? Where are they? Did you see my parents? Where are they!?" Jon began to shout at the tired, evil woman. He could feel Mrs. Cooper's legs turning into dead weight. Sleeping weight rather.

"Ooooo mhmmmmm. I saw them. . . you little. . . FUCK off me!" she mumbled and gave one last tired jerk.

Jon squeezed her ankles. "Did you see my parents? Tell me! Tell me where they are!"

"Jon, stop! She's making shit up! It's not real!" Dominic cried.

"Untie me. . . I'll tell you, they're... shit... mhmmmmm. . . hmmmm. . . untie. . . now," she groaned again before her head slumped back against the cement with a *thud* of her skull. The parasite's control ceased beneath the light just as it did moments ago.

"Jesus Christ, Jon. I'm so sorry. I didn't think it would get that bad. It seems like she's getting worse," Dominic said above his sleeping mother.

"Did she see my parents? Did she see them before she was infected?" Jon asked, unaware of the situation that just took place. He was angry now.

"I don't know."

In a surprising fit of starving and tired madness, Jon grabbed Dominic by the collar of his shirt. "You tell me right now! Are my parents dead? Did your mom kill my parents?" If you walked in on the two of them, you'd think Jon was a parasite-ridden freak himself.

"Jon! Get off me, man!" Dominic pleaded. "I don't know!"

Jon began whipping Dominic around, just as he did to his mother moments ago. He wanted more answers.

"Please, Jon! I don't know! Get off me!"

"Let's put her back in the dark. Turn off the light!"

"Jon, there's nothing we can do! She's mental! She's mad!" Dominic began to sob. "Please! We can't keep doing this to her. Please! I'm sorry about your parents. If I knew where they were, I'd tell you. Believe me, I would. But we can't do this. We have to stay healthy, stay alive!"

Jon let go of Dominic and stood up from the floor. About ready to take matters into his own hands, the voice in his head stopped him from extinguishing the light. *Wait, just wait. Don't do anything stupid.*

Dominic adjusted the collar of his shirt and said, "My mom was up early a few days ago for her morning run. She usually runs around the neighborhood and then outside of it, up the road and back. Maybe she saw your mom or dad then. I don't know!"

A few days ago? When was that? Jon hadn't the slightest idea what day of the week it was. Everything blurred together. *How many days has it been? Fuck!* Jon's back remained facing Dominic. Dominic was still on the ground by his mom, who was still away on a parasitic siesta. Jon felt for her and knew that his outburst was a mistake. It would get him nowhere.

"Rae screamed from the kitchen that morning and when I ran down to see what had happened, my mom was already out. She drank a bottle of water, of course. She'd been running all morning," Dominic said.

"You couldn't have known," Jon said, softer now behind his wet paint mask. Still, he didn't turn to face him. He was too embarrassed after clutching Dominic's neck.

"Oh, but I did. I did. I had already been following the story for the past week or so. It scared me pretty good, so I got my sister on board with it. My mom wasn't having anything about it. Called it 'fake news' and a bunch of 'mumbo jumbo.' Even after I showed her the articles and the news footage she refused to listen. The data didn't matter to her."

"What about your dad?"

"Don't have one. He walked out before I was old enough to form memories."

"I'm sorry. I didn't know…"

"Don't be. Didn't know the guy. Nothing to be sorry about, Jon."

Jon felt sadness for Dominic. Even though his mother still breathed, she was nothing more than a furious entity. Having to see her like this and having to handle her like she was a wild animal must be a true, living hell.

Still, her words itched at Jon's mind and took him away from the present moment. They replaced the feeling of despair with a curiosity that couldn't be ignored. An angry curiosity.

I'll show you…

"You know, it's interesting," Dominic said, "she doesn't eat or drink anything. I've brought down food for her and she didn't seem to care one bit for it. Won't even drink any water, tainted or untainted. I can tell she's lost weight. I'd imagine if we don't kill her, or she doesn't somehow kill herself, she'll eventually wither away."

"Wonder how long that would take. My grandma was pretty frail but mustered up enough strength to choke me. This parasite may just be keeping them alive enough to keep fighting." Jon thought back to his horrific encounter in Camp Valley.

"Oh man," Dominic said, exhausted by it all. He blew tired air from his mouth. "Well, let's head back upstairs. There's nothing more for us to do down here at the moment. I say we get some rest."

Rest? There was no time for rest.

I'll tell. . .

"I'm sorry I couldn't lock the door when we came in, you put duct tape all over it," Jon said.

"Yeah, sorry. Since we trap her in here, we have to cover the inside lock. Initially, she was feeling the walls until she came to the door and must've let herself out. That's why the basement looks like shit. She was a bull in a china shop out there. We lock it outside and then clog the lock with duct tape so she can't tear it with her nails. We're lucky we got enough wrapped around it so we can still control the turn lock on the outside, it all works through the knob itself."

I'll show. . .

"I see," Jon said. His mind was pumping with the thought of waking Mrs. Cooper back up.

"Yep. Thank God we got a shit-ton of the stuff, too." Dominic pointed over his shoulder to one of the metal shelves on the side of the room. A gigantic donut of duct tape sat on the edge of one of the levels.

Untie me. . .

Back Upstairs

"She sleeps when we sleep," Dominic said as he and Jon walked back up the basement steps. The Maglite lit the way to the gray kitchen. "Besides, if she's constantly awake and flipping out, she might just break out and we can't have that. We'll go as long as we have batteries and when we run out, we'll get some more. I told Rae we'd eventually have to break into the neighbors' houses or raid Walmart."

The two of them *snapped* off their masks and threw them in the trash bin by the island where Jon's rifle lay on the marble table next to Dominic's hunting bow and leather arrow bag. On the dining table, the half drank glass of tap water sat by the Ritz crackers. Jon was unsure if he should be drinking water at all anymore.

"So, the tap water is untainted as far as you know?" Jon asked.

"Yep. Crazy to think that purified water turned out to be the one that would cause a worldwide epidemic. For years, I've read that tap water was filled with fluoride and chemicals to rot your mind. That's why these articles interested me so much," Dominic replied. "I guess if we lived in California we may have issues with the tap."

Jon grabbed his rifle and walked into the dim living room where photographs of the Coopers sat on end tables beside fabric couches. He stood, looking out the window across the asphalt. His house, 524 Franklin Court, stood silently. No new cars in the driveway. No one to be seen. It remained just as it was when he arrived not long before. His hand found his front pocket and ran his fingers atop the brass ring.

"I think you should stay with us, Jon," Dominic said behind him, still in the kitchen. He was slinging the leather bag of arrows over his shoulder. "I mean, you're free to go back to your place, but it would be better if the three of us stayed close. If something happens to my mom…"

I bet you miss your mommy. I'll tell you… The words played back in his mind. *I'll show…I'll tell. . .*

". . . if she breaks out," Dominic said, his voice fading back into focus. "We'll keep a lookout for your folks. In the meantime, you can bring some of your clothes and whatnot over. The guestroom is untouched. Clean sheets. We've got food that will last us for a little while if we eat little by little."

Show... tell...

"Ok," Jon said, still staring out at his empty, lonely house. It looked like a reflection of himself. "You think that parasite is contagious?"

"I don't think it is. Nothing points to that," Dominic said. "I think it's strictly from the water. Now, of course, there could be a way perhaps if you mix an infected person's blood with yours, maybe. I don't know if that's ever been tested. I wouldn't risk it."

Jon nodded. "I've gotten blood on me from the parasite people, but it didn't get into any cuts or anything. Not that I'm aware of."

"Hmm." Dominic rubbed his beard.

Jon sighed and said, "I'll stay. Let me grab some things and I'll be back in a few minutes."

"Alright. You want me to go with you?"

"No, I'll be fine. It'll only be a few minutes," Jon said, holding up the Remington.

"Call out if anything happens, I'll be here. Do you need my phone number?"

Jon almost said yes, but once he grabbed for his phone, he realized that he had thrown it into the garage, making it crash on the hard floor.

"Don't have a phone," Jon said as he opened the front door of the Coopers' house and stepped back into the rainy morning.

FIFTY-ONE

Not a Wink

Jon returned to the Coopers' place with an old Nike gym bag and the Rehoboth Beach bag. Dominic greeted him at the door with a finger over his lips.

"Rae's asleep upstairs. We can't make too much noise, okay? Come on in," Dominic said, holding the door open for Jon. He eased it closed behind him. "Feel free to take these articles upstairs if you wanna read more. I know I could only explain so much. I'm still trying to understand myself."

Jon picked up one of the articles with a headline that read: **WHY THE NEW WATER PARASITES ARE NO LAUGHING MATTER**. He wasn't actually going to read it.

The two of them walked up the carpeted steps to the upstairs hallway. Two doors on the left. One on the right. Down the hall, the master bedroom lingered. A bathroom sat between. The hall looked like the one in Jon's house, except this one was painted a dark brown and had photos of the Cooper clan hanging along the walls.

"This is the guest room," Dominic whispered. He led Jon into the room on the right. On the opposite side of the cul-de-sac, this would be Jon's bedroom, but here it was designed for guests with plain sheets that were as grey as the sky outside.

"Thanks," Jon whispered back as he lay his bags on the bed. Dominic shut the door behind them as they stood in a cream-colored bedroom that looked out over the neighborhood. Black curtains, which didn't match the colors of the room, were on either side of the window.

Dominic's whisper was louder now as he said, "We sleep during the daytime now. It takes some getting used to, and Rae and I aren't fully adapted to it yet, but it's what has to be done." He walked by the window and dark curtains. Pulling them closed, they blacked out the room except for the lines of light peeking around the fabric.

Dominic continued. "I gave you my blackout curtains. I figured you'd need more time to adjust to the schedule. I'm pretty much there myself. I can almost fall asleep as the sun comes up now. Same with Rae."

"Thanks," Jon said. His mind was elsewhere.

The light re-entered the room as Dominic pulled back the curtains. "We have little battery-operated alarm clocks, although you yelled so loud outside we didn't need it today." He sniffed a laugh. Jon was silent. "There's one on the end table there, I set it for seven-thirty. That'll give you almost an hour before the sun goes all the way down. That will at least allow you to get your bearings straight for the night. It's not gonna be easy, but the trick is to make yourself super tired at night until your body can't take it. My mom helped with that."

"What do we do when we wake up?" Jon asked.

Untie me and I'll...

"Well, we basically keep a lookout, try some things on mom and see if we can get anywhere with a remedy."

"Have you seen anyone come through the neighborhood at night?" Jon was still holding the rifle by its stock.

"Only once." Dominic was peering out through the rain-stained window. "I believe it was the Hannigans next door. Their daughter, Molly, was good friends with Rae. Does the name sound familiar to you? Molly Hannigan?"

"Yeah, I think so. The Hannigans. I've seen them out and about before." Just like with the Coopers, Jon hadn't spent much time with his neighbors other than Dylan, and that was years ago. Maybe a block party BBQ once or twice. Perhaps he saw them at the community yard sales.

"It was the night after my mom collapsed, infected. Rae and I were just done getting mom settled downstairs when we saw lights beaming through the living room windows. I wasn't sure what was said but it appeared Mr. Hannigan got out and started yelling up at the house. Bitch this and cunt that. You know how they talk."

"That I do."

"All of a sudden, Mr. Hannigan starts punching at the front door. I mean, full-on winding up and letting it rip on the wood. I guess he was locked out? I don't know. I think they were having marriage trouble and the missus changed the lock or something. Somehow, though, he gets in. Then the screams came."

"Oh no." *I'll show...*

"I had to cover Rae's mouth. I didn't want him to hear her and come get us next. She ran and called 911 and they said they were sending the police, but before she even hung up the phone, Mr. Hannigan came back out of the door, covered in blood. All over his shirt and tie. He gets back in the SUV like nothing ever happened. He drives off and we never see him again.

"The following morning, Rae and I go over to the house. Rae wanted to go in after the dad left but I said absolutely not, we're gonna stay inside until the morning. Well, then the morning came. I promised Rae I'd take her over to check on Molly and…well…we found her beaten to death."

Jon blew air from his mouth. *Untie me. . .I'll show…I'll tell.* The thoughts wouldn't let up, not even to let Jon become emotionally invested in Dominic's story. The death of innocent families and friends were getting stale now. Old news. Say something to Jon that he didn't already know.

"And that's pretty much how it all started in terms of getting to bed during the day," Dominic said. "We were so exhausted between our mom and seeing Rae's best friend and mother taken from this world that we both collapsed. We woke up before sundown, holding onto each other. It's sick, Jon. Really sick… Rae and Molly were about to graduate and head off to college. Now it's all over." Dominic wiped his forehead as he shook it and turned back to Jon who was still looking past Dominic, staring at his house.

Untie me and I'll show you…

"I'll let you get some rest, Jon. I'm sure you're tired of it all. We need our energy to face another day. If there even *is* another day. But we have to try. I'll die before giving up. I'll die before I let my mother die, you know?" Dominic stood and stared at Jon for a moment.

Jon nodded. *I'm sure you're tired of it all.* Dominic was fucking right he was. But even though he felt as tired as he ever did in his entire life, Jon was awake. Wide awake with no interest in rest or sleep.

I'll tell you. . .

"Bathroom is down the hall on the left before my mom's room. All the water's cold. Don't be looking for a nice, hot bath. Also, take this." Dominic pulled a mini orange flashlight from his pocket. He threw it on the bed by Jon's belongings. "So, you can see where you're pissing. If you need anything else, I'm across the hall. Rae is in the first room. Best not to wake her, so try to be as quiet as possible."

"Ok, thanks a lot," Jon said as Dominic let himself out. "I appreciate all this. Really."

Dominic nodded. "Have a good night, or day should I say. I'll see you in the evening." Dominic's head disappeared from the side of the door as it closed shut.

Now, Jon stood alone in the guestroom. He walked over to the window and scanned across the houses around the cul-de-sac until he stopped at his house. Again, he stared as the words of Mrs. Cooper played relentlessly in his head like a broken record. A vinyl record playing an ominous song against his skull, drilling the words deeper and deeper.

I bet you'd like to know where your mommy and daddy...

I'll tell you...

Untie me...

I'll show you...

Her eyes of rage had subsided for a moment when she locked eyes with Jon. Why? Did she know? Did she truly know where Jon's parents were? Could she show him if he let her free?

The pit of his empty stomach growled and moaned. He was weak with days of poor nutrition, lack of rest, and physical and emotional turmoil. There was no denying that he was at the end of his rope. But as he stood, staring toward the house in which he was raised, his mind was scheming. Planning.

The hunger he felt was no longer for food.

Off in the distance, beyond 524 Franklin Court, a *rumble* of thunder rolled through the sky.

FIFTY-TWO

The Storm Approaches

Rae slept beneath her puffy white comforter. Her dark, curly hair lay askew on the pillow as she breathed. Dreaming. She was beautiful. Naturally pretty. The most gorgeous thing Jon had ever seen as he stood above her in her bedroom, giving a thirty-yard stare into her closed eyes, making sure she was asleep.

Flowers were everywhere. On her sheets. Paintings of them on the walls in pink frames. A little glass rose sat on her dresser by her selection of perfumes and fragrances labeled from Victoria Secret. Sweet scents and floral imagery surrounded the room. There were photos of her and her mother at the beach. She and Dominic standing in the front yard with painted faces. Rae a cat and Dominic a mouse. A picture of her and Molly at what looked like homecoming or prom, donning ruby and sapphire dresses and corsages on their wrists. They were laughing.

She was a girly girl. An innocent girly girl it seemed. Jon would've liked to have known her better. He would have liked to have known a lot of girls better. He wondered where his old girlfriends were just then and if they were still alive.

Rae didn't stir in her bed despite being eyed long enough to bring her out of a slumber, just as Rusty did to Jon not all that long ago. *Peaceful, deep dreams,* Jon thought.

His filthy and tired appearance contrasted Rae's room. Although it was dark, he looked as if he was a parasite in her comfortable abode. His eyes were wide, psychotic. Jon looked out of his element, like a puppet being controlled by someone else.

Jon hadn't even tried to sleep. His mind wouldn't let him. All he could think about was his plan. His last stand.

He stepped away from the side of the bed and walked past piles of thrown clothes on the carpet. LIVE. LAUGH. LOVE. was decaled on the wall by the door in black cursive. Memories of Melissa's dorm room fled by. *Girls aren't that much different from one another, are they?*

Back out in the darkened hallway, Jon crossed over toward the guestroom where Dominic's crossbow and arrow satchel lay on the bed beside the hunting rifle. He stole it from Dominic's room as he watched his eyes, checking to see if they were sound asleep before Jon went through with his plan.

The only noise in the house was the rain against the roof and the occasional thunder that crept closer and louder with every *boom*.

Gotta get this over with quick, Jon thought. *If you're gonna do it, you gotta do it now.* He pulled out a Swiss Army knife from his Nike bag and placed it in his left pocket. Grandpa Barnes had given it to him many years back and its age showed through the scratched red paint and spots of dirt stains on the blades.

Meow.

Jon snatched up the rifle off the bed, spun and aimed the barrel of the Remington at nothing but air. Beneath him, a small, black and grey-furred cat stood on all fours, staring up at him. *Jesus Christ!* Jon wanted to shout. *A cat, ugh.*

Meow. Softer now.

"Get out, scram," Jon whispered. "Go away. Shoo!"

Meow was all the cat could reply as it showed its tiny, pointed teeth. Its whiskers waved. Yellow eyes that looked like snake eyes locked on Jon as if the cat had caught him in the act, which it did. Jon was preparing to do something behind the Cooper kids' back and the cat saw it all.

Using the barrel of the rifle, Jon attempted to shoo the cat out of the room. It only made the *meows* louder.

"Go, go! Get out!"

MEOW.

Alright, fuck this. Jon didn't want to touch the cat with his hands. It could trigger a reaction. Itchy eyes. Bumps on his wrists. There was no time for any of it. He also didn't want his cover to be blown by a stupid cat. All this way. All this suffering, and a cat would be the one thing that stopped him from getting the real answer to his question?

Where are my parents?

I'll tell you. . .

I'll show you. . .

Untie me. . .

He waited a moment, listening carefully for Dominic or Rae. Nothing. The cat hadn't won yet.

Jon kept his eyes on the feline as his body turned to place the bag of arrows over his shoulder. *Don't move. Don't make a peep you little son of a bitch.* He grabbed the crossbow in one hand, the Remington in the other. It was loaded. The cat was lucky it wasn't at eye level when Jon turned around to its almost mission-sabotaging *meow.*

Here we go, this is it. Jon headed out of the guest room, armed to the teeth. He passed the two bedrooms, placing his head against each of the doors. No noises were detected inside other than breathing and the faint sound of a low snore from Dominic's room. The rain against the house was an excellent relaxant, but the thunder would soon drown it out and wake them from their sleep. If they got up, God knows what would happen if they saw what Jon was going to do.

Jon moved with stealth down the steps. His Vans left imprints on the carpet. With the weight of the weapons, he was thankful he wasn't trotting down wooden stairs with a loud *banging.* The jig might've been up then.

Glancing in the kitchen, Jon saw the papers still on the dining table. The glass of water. Crackers. Nothing changed. No one else was down here. The clock above the couch in the living room *ticked.* Its hands showed it was almost 1:00 P.M. Dominic set the alarms for 7:30, which would give Jon plenty of time as long he did this the right way. He grabbed another paint mask from the pack, *snapped* it over his mouth, and turned toward the door on the side of the staircase. The basement.

Behind him, the cat followed without meowing.

Jon opened the door to the basement, careful not to make it *squeak.* He stared down into the black abyss and began his descent into the darkness. The cat remained on the top of the steps, watching the strange young man fade away. Its tail curled.

Once Jon reached the bottom, he put the weapons on the floor. He fetched the orange flashlight that Dominic gave him from his right pocket where it bulged the denim. *Clicking* on the rubbery button, the light produced a weak beam. It would have to do.

Jon grabbed the chair that once bound him and started back up the steps with the flashlight aimed upwards. He held the wooden seat to his chest.

244 · OLIVER C. SENECA

"Get lost!" Jon whispered to the cat. "Shoo!"

The cat remained with its golden eyes judging Jon.

On the top landing of the basement steps, Jon lowered the chair down and closed the door, propping the chair against it from the inside. The cat's gaze broke as the white wood shut. The cheap shine from the flashlight was all that remained. Jon picked up the chair and firmly placed its back against the knob. He pulled the door to test its leverage. Much like the five-dollar light, it was good enough. It would buy him some time if Dominic and Rae woke-up while Jon did his deed.

I'll tell you if you untie me. . . I'll show you. . .

Her eyes.

The orange light struggled to penetrate the blackness of the basement as Jon approached the storage room that contained Mrs. Cooper. His last resort. White light came from the bottom crack of the door where the carpet becomes cement, which meant the batteries in the LED light were doing their job, keeping her asleep and the parasite's power at bay.

He had hidden the crossbow and arrow bag behind the TV. His goal was to keep it tucked away from Dominic or Rae in case they intervened. They'd try to kill him if they found him. And if he hid the weapon in the room with the mother, who knows if she could find it and shoot it without hesitation.

Now, he held the light and his father's loaded Remington.

Jon placed his palm on the knob of the storage door. There was no racing of the heart. No swirling thoughts. He was still, a feeling that Jon hadn't felt in a long, long time. He was drained both physically and mentally, but somehow stood without buckling and breathed without gasping. Maybe he had nothing to lose. Perhaps it was because he had a plan. Either way, it wasn't Jon as everyone knew him.

He *clicked* out the lock with his nail, turned the knob, and walked inside.

FIFTY-THREE

The Storm Arrives

Jon shut the door behind him, mindful of the tape over the lock on the handle. He realized Dominic could easily open the lock as he was the one who demonstrated the trick of getting in, but he would have to keep faith that his duct-taped chair would hold long enough at the landing's door.

Mrs. Cooper lay on the cement floor, curled and dead-looking just as Dominic had left her after their wrestling match. She was a poor creature, confined to bloody tape that wrapped around her middle-aged body. The smells remained. Shitty, stinky, and sour.

Jon knelt beside her and put down the rifle by her feet. He grabbed the giant roll of duct tape from one of the metal shelves on the side of the room. He pulled on the roll of tape, tearing away a long strip, using his teeth to cut it. Then, he wrapped the fresh piece around Mrs. Cooper's old ankle bind. Another piece. *Rip.* Another around the wrist restraints. He was careful not to pull the tape too fast. Any noise could wake up her children.

All that was left was the chewed tape that covered her lips. Jon was gentle with peeling it off. He found either blood or red lipstick painted on the sticky side. No way to know as her lips were chapped and cracked, raw from the bites. Jon wasn't sure how many times this tape was pulled off and stuck back on when Dominic and Rae were trying to reason with her. Now, it was Jon's turn to reason. He placed a new piece of tape on Mrs. Cooper's lips.

Would he take her life if he didn't get the answers he was looking for? He hoped it wouldn't come to that, but Jon didn't ruminate. His mind was clear for now.

Jon stood up and walked behind the LED lamp to the switch. The orange flashlight was in his hand. Soon, it would be the only light left. He felt the plastic lever on the back of the lamp and *clicked* it off. Darkness. Jon only had a few moments before the demon woman awoke. He shined the flashlight on her face as she began to stir.

Jon moved down to the cement floor and placed his hand around the center of the Remington, pulling it closer to his side, preparing himself. Then, he placed his hand on her chest. She was wearing a thin golden necklace that must've popped out from beneath her sweatsuit.

Mrs. Cooper's eyes began to flutter. Jon moved in closer and made his hold on her body firmer as her chest became more alive. Awake. The breaths became shorter.

"Uhhhh. . . hmmmmm. . .," Mrs. Cooper moaned under the fresh sticky tape. "Hmmmmmm. . . hhheeeeeee?"

The beam from the orange flashlight made her head move side to side as if Jon was holding something stinky in her face. He removed the tape, trying not to pull too quick to piss her off right away. He kept his hand on the edge of the piece in case she spoke too loudly.

"Hmmmhmmmmm. . .uhhhh. . .hello?" Mrs. Cooper said with her eyes still closed. The light annoyed her.

"Mrs. Cooper, can you hear me?" Jon asked, careful not to speak too loudly himself.

"Uhhhhh. . . hello? Who's there? Dominic? Rae?"

"Mrs. Cooper, it's Jon Barnes."

"Who? Don Harms? Where's Rae? Dominic?"

"No, Jon Barnes. Jonathon Barnes from across the street. Do you remember?"

"Why do you have your hands on my chest? Tryin' to grab my tits?" Her volume rose. Jon was quick to place the tape back over her mouth. He held his hand down as the residue set back onto her lips.

"No!" he said, not in a shout, but in a harsh whisper. "Mrs. Cooper, my name is Jonathan Barnes. If you calm down, I will let you speak, do you understand? If you make too much noise, I'm not gonna let you talk. Got it? I just want to ask you some questions." Jon was starting to feel emotion again. Anger. It was a slow burn, but he could feel madness budding inside his stomach already.

"Hmmm. . .hmmmmm. . .hmmmmm," she said. Her eyes were opening now. They were as black as they were before. Maybe even blacker, somehow. She hadn't frozen as she did before when she first laid eyes on Jon.

"Do you hear me? Do you understand me? Can you be quiet for me? Shake your head yes if you understand," Jon commanded.

Mrs. Cooper's head just squirmed in its uncomfortable motions. No clear yes or no answer.

"Hmmmm. . .hmmmmm…uhhhhhh."

Jon pulled the tape back halfway and Mrs. Cooper tried to bite him. He covered the mouth and pushed down on her neck with quick reflex. He wanted to shout at her.

"Mrs. Cooper, listen to me. I'm gonna let you go. Do you understand? I will cut you free from all this tape if you just listen." He was rocking her head to and fro as he spoke down at her twisted face. "I'm Jonathan Barnes. You said you know where my parents are?"

No coherent response came from the woman.

"Do you want to be let free? Do you want to see your family again?" Jon asked.

Funny. Jon was asking this poor woman if she wanted to see her family again, but it was Jon who wanted that. So much so, that he was attempting to level with a full-blown psycho. It made no sense to reason with her, but Jon was persistent. *He* wanted to see his family again and he'd do anything to get it.

"Hmmmm! Hmmmmm!" Mrs. Cooper's eyebrows were curled. She was already mad. The parasite was alive and well in her brain, controlling her anger to make her like a rabid dog. It was as if she became hostile faster than before, waking up early for a morning snack. Her body began to rock.

Jon tried the tape again. Her bite returned. Teeth *clacked* teeth. He replied by *slamming* her head down hard into the cement ground, unaware at his own strength. He didn't want to kill her, but the madness was growing inside of him as the bud of impatience grew into a stem.

Mrs. Cooper seemed slightly dazed by the *thud*. Her eyes fluttered for a moment until her bearings returned with more rage. She began to rock more back and forth, back and forth. The parasite was not pleased.

"Mrs. Cooper!" Jon said, louder now. He was getting close to losing his cool. "Mrs. Cooper, I want you to listen to me! Where are my parents?" He removed the tape. Why he thought he would get an answer instead of a vicious snarl and bite was anyone's guess.

He slammed the tape back down with a *slap*. Her head hit the ground again, this time not as hard. Another flutter. More anger. Jon moved up and placed his knee in the middle of her chest. She flailed. Leaning behind him, he picked up the rifle and presented it to Mrs.

Cooper. The orange flashlight's shine was only strong enough to show the barrel in front of her face.

"See this?" Jon said. Now, he sounded like he was infected with the parasite. A mad man. "This is a loaded rifle. High fucking caliber rounds. How would you like it if I shoved it right in your mouth and fired?" He was unaware that he was speaking at regular volume now.

Mrs. Cooper showed no interest in the threat, only more squirming and flailing. "Hmmm! Ermmm! Hmmmm!"

"Alright. Not a fan of the Remington, I see." Jon threw the rifle to his side and straddled on Mrs. Cooper's chest like he was riding a horse. "How about this?" Jon slipped out the Swiss Army knife from his pocket and presented that beneath the faint beam. The light made it look black. He peeled out one of the blades with his thumb. "Something a little slower, hmm? I can either cut this tape off or cut out your fucking throat." Jon spoke behind gritted teeth. He was twisted. He hadn't consumed the water, aka the tainted shit, but he behaved as if the parasite had him in its clutches. "How about it? Now, where are my parents? Where are they, you fucking bitch!?"

He RIPPED the tape off in a lip-shredding tear. Blood flung from around her mouth and into the dark. A shout began to follow, but Jon placed his hand down over the wounded mouth, covering himself in hot blood. "Eerrrghhhh! Ahhhhhh!" Mrs. Cooper squirmed, eyes going almost white as they traveled up into her head.

"WHERE. ARE. MY. PARENTS!?" Jon shouted over her snarled screams. He was gone. Mad. Totally sabotaging himself and not caring who heard him anymore.

"WHERE ARE THEY? TELL ME!" He rose the Swiss knife high into the blackness, ready to strike into her jugular, ready to cut where it counts and end it all right here, even without the answer.

Mrs. Cooper bit Jon's hand with an audible *crunch*. All of her teeth turned red.

"Fuck!" Jon shouted as he flung himself back. The orange light glided through the air until it landed with its beam facing away from them, toward the metal shelves that held bags of ice melt.

Now, Jon and Mrs. Cooper sat as shadows. One without lips and one with teeth marks dripping blood from his hand. Both were furious and bleeding.

With a chunk of his hand turned into a slice of pizza, Jon scrambled and kicked his feet away from the squirming worm that was

Mrs. Cooper. All he could see was the entity kicking and inching her way toward him. Blood spilled onto his pants.

He dropped the knife and grabbed his hand that was drenched both in his and Mrs. Cooper's blood. The pain felt as if the teeth were still lodged into his skin. His right hand, the dominant hand, was shaking in pain as his other one attempted to squeeze the holes shut.

"You little son of a bitch!" Mrs. Cooper shouted at him through the dark. "You little fucking pervert!" She made spitting noises. She was hacking up blood and phlegm. Something wet landed on Jon's left forearm. "Come here! Come over here! Agh! Agh! I'm gonna tear you limb from limb!" she choked.

Jon's mind bounced as the voice sounded closer.

What have I done? What do I do?

The light. Turn on the light.

He stood up and approached the LED, the savior of the situation, and *clicked* on the switch behind it. Mrs. Cooper wiggled her body far enough outside of the spotlight so that her head wasn't exposed. However, once the light was shining, her body reacted as if the parasite sensed an oncoming sleep.

Jon couldn't see her face, which may have been for the best. Only the top of her battered head hung below the edge of the shadow. He grabbed the stock of the light and attempted to aim the beam down into her eyes, those vicious, vicious eyes. Before he could execute the tilt, she lunged at Jon with her bound ankles, scooting herself with impressive speed and distance.

Bloodied teeth beneath torn-off lips sunk into one of Jon's shoes. There was a first time for everything and now Jon had just experienced a full-grown woman trying to bite his foot off.

Mrs. Cooper didn't penetrate her fangs through the shoe, but it was enough of a chomp and shock that it sent Jon sideways with the LED lamp. On his way down, the lamp's light flashed across the walls and metal shelving. Boxes and large plastic containers covered in dust whipped by for a moment before Jon caught a glimpse of Mrs. Cooper's body on the floor. She stared as Jon tumbled.

It was only for a second. A flash of time. But what Jon saw was the most horrific looking victim of the parasite he'd ever seen in the past few days. Sickening. It was the starved woman with a torn-open mouth. She looked like some fucked up clown with a bright red face.

Blood oozed and dribbled down her chin before it puddled on the floor. Repulsive. And Jon was responsible for it.

No, I'm sorry he thought. I didn't mean to.

CRASH. CRACK.

Stillness. Darkness.

The little orange flashlight got its time to shine as the only source of light yet again. Jon lay on the cement floor in a splash of blood that once belonged in the back of Mrs. Cooper's head. He stained the shoulder on his shirt and the wetness bled through. The smell of metallic scents made him feel as though he was back at White Haven College. It was the same smell that came from the countless bodies that spread in the grass between the dorm buildings. Soon, he'd be just like them if he didn't get up.

Silence filled the darkness for a moment until Jon could hear laughter, ghoulish, mushy laughter. Choking.

"Something a little slower. Something a little slower," Mrs. Cooper said. "I like something a little slower."

Jon, surprised and intrigued by her tone of voice, got up from the ground. It was too dark to see. Mrs. Cooper seemed to have put herself up against the wall with her face touching the cement. She was moving, inching at something. Jon couldn't see.

The rifle. The flashlight.

He was quick to grab both of them, although he had to hold the flashlight with his bitten hand. The rifle was too heavy on it. He aimed the low beam on the back of her beaten head, which faced away from him. It looked as if she was eating something.

Jon inched closer and spoke to her. Softer now. No more yelling, although who knew if Dominic and Rae were currently kicking-in the basement door and sending the chair down the steps in a tumble.

"Mrs... Mrs. Cooper. I'm gonna ask you one last time," Jon said.

Mrs. Cooper kept at whatever she was doing. *Eating? Licking?* Then, she spoke with a driveling sound. "Slower heheheh shlower. You dung sonofabish bashtard unnghh. Dead. Dead. Dead."

Jon crept closer to her and raised the Remington with his left hand. It shook beneath the weight of the heavy wood and metal barrel. "Please. I just want to know where my parents are. My name is Jonathan Barnes. You said if I let you go, you'd tell me where my mom and dad are. Remember? From earlier today? You said-"

"Your parentsh are dead and sho are you!" Mrs. Cooper turned and lunged at Jon before he could get a straight shot out. A bullet *POPPED* from the rifle and blew a hole in one of the cement blocks of the wall. Her hands were free from the tape. One of them gripped Jon's Swiss Army knife as she moved forward.

The tip of the pocketknife shot straight for Jon, but before it could take his eye out, he swung his chomped hand at the woman. The orange flashlight *conked* the side of her head and she stumbled for a moment, long enough for Jon to juke around her and head for the door.

A *BOOM* of thunder filled the dark basement as Jon thrust the door open. The storm outside raged enough to spill its rumble down the stairs.

After the punch with the plastic orange light, the beam's power seemed to be depleted. Jon could see someone running down the steps with a bright white light. They ran past the upturned chair with duct tape on the legs. It appeared to be Dominic coming down to save the day and fix the catastrophic mess that Jon unleashed upon the Coopers.

The beam made Jon squint as it was at least a thousand times more powerful than the orange piece of shit he had. He was about to spin and use the old fingernail trick to lock Mrs. Cooper back in the smelly prison where she belonged until he felt a sudden sharp sting on his back-right shoulder.

Deeper and deeper the sting penetrated him until Jon fell face first onto the carpeted floor. His glasses cracked under his weight. The blade retracted from his skin and muscle with a slimy sound. He fell onto the rifle. The metal rod bruised his chest. Blood flowed from the carving, mixing with the wet stain of blood that wasn't his.

"Ahhh!" Jon shouted. "Agghh!"

He spun his body around as he reached for the wound. Pain shot through him like lightning bolts, making him wince and convulse. Dominic's mother was above him, about to strike again and finish it all until a *POP POP POP* sound blasted Jon's eardrum. Wetness rained down onto Jon's face and body. Ringing noises filled his ears and his eyeballs stung.

The figure of Mrs. Cooper fell backward and back into the storage room. Dominic's bright light was examining her until it struck Jon's face, not helping the pain. He couldn't see. He was convinced that there were bits of glass in his eyes. Jon blinked. It stung. There were words in the air, some even from Jon, but all he heard was the *ringing*.

Dominic put the Maglite down to examine Jon. A black pistol was in his hand, resting on his leg. He placed the Maglite on the floor, and once the light was propped and the powerful beam lit up the back of the basement, Jon saw it wasn't Dominic after all, not even Rae.

It was somebody else.

FIFTY-FOUR

The Storm Continues

The sound of thunder brought Dominic out of his dream. He was back in high school, about to take a test he didn't study for. An anxiety dream. Dominic was used to those even though in the waking world he had been a straight-A student. Science and math were his specialties.

Dominic could never figure out if he was naturally intelligent or heavily driven to be successful to get back at his absent father. Although he had never met the man, there was always a thought deep in the back of his mind to prove himself to his father. To show him. Whoever *he* was.

Dominic also wanted to pay his mother back for all of the raising and lessons she had to do on her own. The mysterious Mr. Cooper had sent child support payments, that you could at least give him credit for. This allowed Mrs. Cooper to stay at her nursing job without having to work multiple jobs like the other single mothers she knew. Still, Dominic wanted to be a world-renowned scientist. A doctor even. Something bigger and badder than your average career. That way, he could put his mom in a house twice as big.

Rae, on the other hand, seemed to manifest her repressed feelings against her disinterested father in another way. Instead of studying hard and having goals and dreams to work toward, she spent her time partying with her girlfriends and getting together with guys who had no ambition. Or, in other words, she often found herself in trouble.

There were many late-night lies. Rae would be one place when she said she was at another while associating with people who may or may not be behaving within the law. Underage drinking. Smoking weed. Trouble. Plain old trouble. A classic case of a rebellious young girl without a positive father figure in her life, hanging out with her peers that came from similar origins.

Dominic had tried to be that positive force for his little sister, but what else could he have said to her that his mother hadn't already yelled and screamed about? *What were you thinking? You could've been killed! Give me your phone! You've lost your car privileges! You're grounded for the next three months! Where are you going?*

The question then arises: who's the positive father figure for Dominic? Well, he'd probably go on and on about his heroes, the closest thing to fatherly figures. Neil DeGrasse Tyson. Stephen Hawking. Carl Sagan. Those were the guys that Dominic looked up to and followed. He collected each of their books and DVDs. He even had a poster on his wall of Neil Tyson in red and blue colors, like the classic Hope picture of Obama. But instead of hope, it read SCIENCE.

Science. . . if only we knew how to stop the parasite, Dominic thought to himself as the rain fell harder against his bedroom window. He had slept for a few hours.

Mom, how much longer can I do this to you? To us?

Waking thoughts began to take away from Dominic's sleepiness. Obsession of the parasite flooded his mind when it wasn't turned off in slumber. Sleep was the only escape. Now, with the thunder rolling closer, he wasn't sure if he'd be able to drift back away into anxious dreams of high school days.

POP. POP. POP.

Dominic's body jerked upright. Rae screamed from the other side of the wall.

"Rae? Are you alright?" Dominic shouted. He stood by the edge of his bed in boxers and a white undershirt.

"No! What the fuck was that?" she shouted back through the wall.

"Are you hurt?"

"I'm fine! It sounded like it came from downstairs," Rae said, sounding like she was jumping into some pants. "We gotta get down to mom."

Dominic yanked up a pair of jeans that were crumpled by the bedpost. His eyes darted from left to right, searching for the cross-bow and arrow bag. *I left them by the dresser,* he thought. The bow and arrows weren't there, nor were they in the closet, by his desk, or anywhere. *Where the fuck are they?*

There was no time.

The siblings scrambled outside in the hallway. The rain was plummeting down, and more sounds of thunder struck from above.

"Do you have the bow?" Dominic asked. His eyes were wide. All of his tiredness had evaporated.

"No, I thought you had it!" Rae replied. Her hair was a sleepy mess and her knee showed through the tear of her yoga pants. She put them on too fast.

"Shit!" Dominic turned and *knocked* on the guest room door as Rae began descending the stairs with panicked steps.

"Rae, just wait a second!" Dominic said, getting no answer from the guestroom door. "Jon! Are you ok? Did you hear that noise? We're going downstairs to check on our mom!" Still nothing. He opened the door and found the bed sheets made and untouched. No Jon.

"Jon! Ah, shit!" Dominic searched for his weapon to no avail. "Rae! Wait a second!" No sign of the Remington rifle either.

Rae was at the bottom of the stairs now, not waiting a second. She turned and headed toward the basement door. Jamie, the family's grey Tabby cat, sat on top of the couch by the living room window, watching with her golden eyes. Her tail curled.

Dominic came clambering down the steps. He turned and grabbed Rae on her shoulders, pulling her back from the basement doorknob which she was about to turn.

"Rae, stop! Let me go first! Stay behind me, please!" Dominic said.

She tried to step forward from her brother's grip, determined to get down into the cellar.

"Did Jon shoot mom?" she asked as if she already knew. "Did he?!"

"I don't know!" Dominic shouted, pulling his sister back again. "But we can't just run down there, we don't know what the hell is going on!" Dominic shouted so loudly, that it broke his voice. It was as if he was going through puberty all over again.

"Ok, ok," Rae said, sounding like tears were about to win her over. She stopped pulling.

The anxiety was killing them.

"Fuck, we need a flashlight! Go grab the one from the pantry," Dominic said.

Rae swiped her mess of a hairdo away from her face and sprinted into the kitchen. She opened the wooden pantry door. HOME

SWEET HOME was written on a wooden placard that hung with little pieces of rope on the door.

Rae sprinted back out of the kitchen, holding a circular, red flashlight. On the side was a black switch that, depending on how far up or down you pushed it, changed the size of the bulb's spotlight.

"Come on!" Dominic said and waved her over. He took the light from her shaking hands. Her nails were bitten and chewed down. The remaining polish was chipped.

Dominic twisted the knob and the entire basement door flew off its hinges, *BANGING* on the steps as it tumbled down into the dark in cartwheels. Rae screamed as Dominic jutted back, almost tripping them both backward. Both of them gained their balance and moved down the stairs again. The light's glow jutted back and forth from the walls to the steps. The chair that bounded Jon lay upside down on the carpet as the light whipped by. Soon, another light's rays met theirs. Dominic steadied the beam, causing both lights to become perpendicular to one another.

Jon, I pray to God you didn't do what I think you did... Dominic didn't want to see what he feared his eyes would show him. He knew it would be too much, especially for Rae.

When the two of them reached the bottom, they saw a figure shining a powerful light back at them from the back of the basement.

"JON!" Dominic screamed at the outline of a man. The fear of being unarmed crept up his spine. A bullet could fly through the darkness and take them both out, but the thought of his mother shot dead before finding a cure made him want to fight instead of flight. "JON! WHAT HAPPENED!?"

"TURN OFF YER LIGHT!" the figure shouted back.

Dominic's adrenaline was pumping so quickly through his veins that he didn't realize the voice sounded nothing like Jon's.

"PUT DOWN YER BEAM NOW OR I'LL SHOOT YOU! PUT IT DOWN! SHOW YER FACE!"

"WHAT DID YOU DO TO OUR MOM YOU BASTARD!?" Rae screeched with fresh tears already flowing. "WHAT DID YOU DO!?"

With Rae's cries traveling across the basement, the figure put down his light first. Dominic's beam now put the man in the spotlight. A tall, thin man with a shaved head wearing a white wife-beater shirt dotted with blood, stood still at the opposite end of the

Cooper's basement. He wore navy slacks that looked to be both too wide and too short for his legs. In his left hand was a Maglite and in his right was a black pistol.

Dominic and Rae stood shocked and speechless as their light introduced Rusty Mirch.

FIFTY-FIVE

The Storm Rages

Jon blinked hard and jerked his head. His stinging lids came with visions of white noise. Snow flew across the darkness. He couldn't seem to get focused and the wounds on his shoulder and hand weren't giving him any help with the situation. Rusty's face surprised Jon, although he had no energy to show it now. The plan to get answers from Mrs. Cooper went horribly wrong and now Jon believed it was all going to end right here in the foggy dark, bleeding out on the floor of his neighbors' basement with no answer to where his family was. He failed the mission. Game over.

A hand touched Jon's chest. His munched hand was held, making it feel like it was stuck in a campfire. The light flickered through the white noise and made the stings return to his retinas. Rusty was speaking words that couldn't be understood. If it even *was* Rusty. Jon recognized the face for a moment as it flashed in a daze, but it could've been his mind playing tricks on him right as it was about to turn off for good.

Jon's mouth moved but no words escaped. Rusty got up, disappearing into the white noise. Only a shadow of him remained standing in the dark. He looked to be facing away at something else. Suddenly, he was lit up by a brightness. *A tractor-trailer, watch out,* Jon thought. He was thinking he was back on the turnpike with Emily and the tollbooth worker. But the light didn't approach or get brighter, only stayed. It shined on what Jon could now confirm was, in fact, Rusty Mirch, decked out in his father's garb. Fuzziness danced around. The snow of the white noise painted the dark walls.

Rusty spoke as he shined his light at whatever he was facing. Jon's ears still *rang* and he wondered how Rusty could speak, let alone think to himself, after firing a gun in such close quarters. *A ghost, Rusty's a ghost. Soon I will be too.* Rusty's lips continued to move through the haze until he brought down his beam. Noises. Words. Spoken words came from behind Jon it seemed. They floated through the dizzy world and Rusty spoke back with Jon not understanding a damn thing.

***

Dominic hadn't seen his mother yet, but Rae did as she pushed her brother's flashlight to the left, exposing what was left of her mother. Jon's body lay just before her mother's. She screamed and covered her eyes until her screams of woes turned into screams of rage. Rae bolted toward Rusty. Dominic tried to grab her arm but couldn't make contact.

"You KILLED her! You fucking BASTARD!" Rae shrieked as she dug her balled-up fists into Rusty's chest, pounding against his heart, hoping to punch it out and clutch it in her palm. "Why would you do this to us? WHY? How could you?" she bawled. She sounded like she was going to hyperventilate.

Rusty put his arms around her as she beat him, embracing her as she fought like a wild animal. "C'mon baby-"

Dominic pulled her away with a coursing rage of his own. "Don't you lay a finger on her! Rae get the hell away from him!"

There was a punch to a face. Grabbing. Smacking and pulling. Running.

Then lightning struck.

***

There was a quick flash. Another *POP* crashed over the basement and the *ringing* returned with a higher pitch that made Jon's bee sting eyes cry. He felt blood spill from his ears.

His vision had reduced the white noise snow to a blur. Between his poor vision and the aftermath of what happened, he could only make out Rusty and another dark figure that stood before him. *Dominic, it must be Dominic. Unless there are other special guests.* It looked like they were holding each other by the elbows as if they were two long lost friends finding each other after many years away. *It's so great to see you!* Jon imagined one was saying to the other. That was, until the dark figure fell to its knees, then to its ass and back.

The bandage on Jon's head had been ripped off from the fall to the floor. No blood seeped from the old wound. It was scabbed now. Not that it mattered. His back was cut deep.

A few feet beside his body, the figure of what appeared to be Dominic lie slumped on the carpet. The flashlight Dominic brought down was still lit and faced his jeans.

Jon propped himself up on his elbows, causing the pocketknife wound to ache. Blood spilled from it. Jon tried to reach over his shoulder with his left hand to feel for the puncture, but it was just below his reach. He sat up further and reached, bending his bitten hand. He felt the wetness of the raw flesh exposed, clinging to the back of the shirt. It hurt like hell.

"Jon," a faint voice said, penetrating the *ringing* noise. It was almost a whisper. Jon knew it was from Dominic beside him. It had to be.

Moving in a drunken-like crawl, Jon picked up the light from the floor. It was round and fat. He shined it on Dominic's shirt as he remained on all fours. A red hole was leaking in the center of Dominic's chest. Streaks fell on either side of his torso. His head was turned to the side, facing to where Jon crawled over from.

"Dominic, is that you? Are you ok?" Jon asked. Of course, Dominic wasn't ok, but there was an interference inside Jon's rational thinking. You could ask Jon if two plus two equaled four and he wouldn't be able to tell you right away.

"Jon," Dominic repeated. "I need you to get my sister. I need you to get Rae. He's going to take her away."

Thunder filled the room again, sending Jon into a slight convulsion of more pain. Dominic remained on the carpet, bleeding. His chest rose and fell with a delay.

"He's got a gun," Dominic croaked. A cough brought red up from his throat. "You have to get her, Jon. Please."

Jon blinked long, heavy blinks at him. They were both bleeding. Dying. Dominic was going first it seemed. But Jon didn't want him to pass just yet. He wanted to confess, explain to Dominic that it was *he* who stole the crossbow from his room. It was *he* who came downstairs in the basement with a plan to find his parents through interrogating their mother, even if it meant further torture. Jon didn't expect to have Rusty in the mix and have him shoot Mrs. Cooper in the head, but he still felt the need to apologize for that too.

"Please, you gotta stop Rusty," Dominic gurgled, drowning into himself.

Why was Rusty here anyways? For the girl? Mr. Mirch had mentioned something about a girl and to not bring up any females while Rusty was around. *Sensitive like his father,* Mr. Mirch had said, but Jon was spinning from his head injury. If only it was just his head. Now, his hand and shoulder wept red tears. Jon hadn't had these many continuous accidents since he tried his hand at sports. No pun intended.

"Dominic, I'm so sorry. This was all my fault," Jon said over the blurred body. "I came down here while you and Rae were asleep. I couldn't get what your mom said out of my head. I know you told me not to listen to what she said about my parents, but I couldn't stop believing that she knew. If it wasn't for me, she would probably still be alive behind the door. I unlocked it and woke her up. I'm sorry."

For a moment, Jon thought Dominic would rise and strangle Jon for what he had just said and finish him off with never-ending punches to his head. Instead, there was nothing. No response, not even a sound from Dominic. He just lay blurrily beside Jon with what looked like a big, red plant growing from his heart. Silence. There was only heavy rain. More thunder.

"Dominic?" Jon prodded his knee and gave it a little shake. "Stay awake! Don't fall asleep! I'm sorry, Dominic! I'm sorry! Dominic, this is all my fault! Dominic, don't fall asleep!" He began to cry hot, stinging tears.

Please, you have to stop Rusty. Those were the last things he had said. *Please. He's going to take her away.* The words played again, loud enough in Jon's mind to drown out the thunder and rain. The Coopers sure had a way of making sentences stick in Jon's mind. *He's going to take her away.* They echoed in the basement.

"Ok, ok, ok," Jon said, starting to get up. He was on his knees and began to bring himself up to a kneel. His body protested. *Snap.* The face mask came off and Jon took deep breaths. *Here we go.* He placed a hand on the floor to keep himself from falling over. *Here we go. C'mon.*

Jon got up from the kneeling position and stood straight up as the room began to spin in blurred lines. Dark swirls teetered his flashlight as if he was standing on a boat lost on the ocean.

***

"Get the fuck out of here!" Rae screamed at her bedroom door. She had locked it in hopes of keeping Rusty out.

The drawers on her mirrored dresser were torn and thrown about. Makeup was scattered on her carpet. Lipsticks and eyeliners spilled next to the mounds of clothes. Rae sat in the corner of her bed against the wall, clutching a pair of crazy scissors she had found in the drawers. Her eyes were red and swollen. Her hair was a mess, along with her face. She screamed as Rusty *banged* and *knocked* again.

"Baby girl, you gotta let me in!" Rusty said in an unsettlingly casual tone. He sounded unphased from his recent murders. He wanted Rae and only Rae. He didn't care who he had to kill to get to her now, even if it was her own mother and brother. "C'mon, sweetheart, let's talk about this!"

Rae shook in a mixture of fear, anger, and heartbreak. All the trouble she had gotten herself into throughout the years have been leading up to this point. That's what she thought to herself as she yelled her cries across her room. "LEAVE! LEAVE!" Were all the nights sneaking around with boys like Rusty worth it? She would have to say no. But she was young and naive. Rebellious. She had no idea it would come to this.

"Oh, now c'mon sweet thang, you know I ain't leavin' without you. Yer all I got left and I'm all you got left."

"NO!"

"C'mooon. Open up, sweetie. Baby."

Rae clutched the crazy scissors tight. They were plastic children's scissors that cut curvy lines in paper. They were of no real use in this situation, but it was all she had.

"Raeby baby!"

"Don't call me that! You MONSTER!"

"Raeby, yer bro is hurt real bad downstairs." Rusty was speaking in a baby voice now. "I'm afraid he might die unless his little nurse sissy wissy doesn't come and patch 'em up."

"You killed him, you FUCKING PSYCHO! You killed them both! GET OUT!"

Dominic had done his best to take care of Rae and she knew she could always count on him, even after all those countless times she screamed and fought with him over her lies and trickery. He had to be a father figure. A position they both knew was too much for him. Still, he had tried. She was sorry she didn't listen to him enough.

Maybe she wouldn't be curled up like a feral cat right now. Maybe her mother would still be alive. Maybe Rusty wouldn't be knocking on her door, speaking in twisted voices, trying to lure her out. Maybe Dominic would still be here to take care of her.

"Hey! I don't wanna hurt you, you know that. Don't you know that baby girl? Don't you know I always loved you and you only? And you love me, right?"

Rae stopped replying to his taunts. Her throat felt burnt to a crisp.

"I know you do. Remember that night? Remember what we did that night after the football game, baby? Sweet thang? You and I, alone. Together in the back of my truck. Remember that Raeby baby? We put the bed down. . ."

Rae was sick to her stomach but there would be nothing to throw up. She hadn't eaten. She hadn't drank. All she had was an empty helplessness in the pit of her stomach. The pit of her soul.

"That's right. Boy, was that a late night, huh? You and me doing thangs that you couldn't tell your momma about. That's right. Dirty thangs. Sexy thangs. You remember that, baby?"

How could Rae forget? You'd think a girl with her natural beauty would hold out for someone with more class, like a gentleman who at least had an ounce of ambition in his life. Someone that she could bring home to mom one day. A guy who would make her mom laugh until her mom would blush and have a crush on him herself. Instead, she chose to take a shortcut and hookup with a backwoods hillbilly, low-life scumbag like Rusty fucking Mirch.

She had been drunk, of course, they all were. Alcohol made any situation more comfortable. Especially between the opposite sexes.

"Why don't you let me in, and we can recreate that night, how-sabout it? If you come back with me, we can make it like the first time every time. Repopulate the Earth, whaddya think? Someone's gotta do it!"

Rae had lost her virginity to Rusty. An act that would forever bring waves of regret and disgust in her mind. It made her heart cringe.

"Raeby baby girl!"

Hillcrest versus Huntington was the matchup. Molly Hannigan, Rae's bestie since first grade, was there as she always. She and some other girls from school brought vodka and the group of them drank with the guys from the hick school behind the bleachers. Rusty wouldn't have been someone that Rae would've given a second glance to, but once she had an unknown and illegal amount of Russian water in her, his striking eyes became that much sexier. Sexier than ever before. Oh yes, she had known Rusty. Previous football games brought the two opposite towns together and allowed the students to mingle.

"OPEN IT UP!" he screamed now. The sweet-talking games came to an end. "I'M NOT KIDDIN' NOW!"

A couple of the other girls started flirting with the backwoods boys. Soon flirting turned to touching. Touching turned to kissing. Plans formed to leave the game early for a little match up of their own. The group of them had to move elsewhere before being caught in the act. Molly was starting to lock lips with a boy named Chris, who came with Rusty. They rode together in Rusty's rusted red Ford pickup. How appropriate.

"I MEAN IT!"

"Why don't you guys take the rest of this," Molly had said, handing over the last of the Smirnoff. Only the bottom of the bottle remained. Rusty took it out of her hands and she gave him a wink and he winked back. Behind them, the crowd broke into a cheer as the Hillcrest Knights scored a touchdown in overtime, winning the game.

"Have fun." Molly smiled before turning with Chris, leading him somewhere beyond the fence of the football field. Her blonde hair waved and danced as the two of them faded away. Now, it was only Rae and Rusty, standing together in the victorious evening.

"BACK AWAY FROM THE DOOR BABY, I DON'T WANNA HURT YOU!" Rusty drew his gun.

Both Rae and Rusty were as drunk as skunks, waddling out of the field grounds. They laughed as they bumped and stumbled into one another across the parking lot, quick to compose themselves as soon as they saw an adult or fellow classmate. She put the hood of her zip-up jacket over her head. Rusty hadn't even tried to hide the bottle.

"You gotta get rid of that, there are cops here!" Rae said, covering her mouth to muffle a laugh. Rusty drained what remained and chucked the bottle into the grass by the asphalt.

"Hop on in, purty lady," Rusty said in an intoxicated, exaggerated hillbilly accent.

"Thanks, partner." Rae smiled, tipping an invisible cowboy hat on her head.

Rusty jumped in the driver's side and they drove out of the Hillcrest High School parking lot. They went up the road to a quiet place beyond the trees.

POP. The doorknob to Rae's bedroom shot to the floor in an instant. She screamed an aching scream that rubbed her throat raw.

Rusty shouldn't have been driving that night, or any night during high school for that matter. He drank more than he attended class. But tonight, under the spell of teenage fever and liquid comfort, nothing mattered, not even to Rae. They couldn't help but touch and feel one another as Rusty drove with one hand up the hill and around the bend until they found a spot on a gravel road that pulled off behind the trees. Between the leaves, you could see the lights of the dog food factories that shined orange orbs across the autumn air.

Touching and feeling turned to deep, long kisses. Hot anticipation. Clothes were pulled and tugged on. Breasts felt. First Rae's jacket came off. Beneath was a white spaghetti strap with a black and pink Victoria's Secret bra. She grabbed his zipper and squeezed what grew. Rae had done this before, but never what came after. The main event.

The clutch got in the way of the heat between them.

"Let's go to the back," Rusty said between sloppy kisses.

Rae pulled back for a moment. Her shirt was off and only her pushup remained. "Are you sure? What if someone sees us?"

"No one will, hardly anybody comes up this way at night."

Rae laughed and gave him a playful slap. "Oh, you've done this before, huh?" Her mouth was wet from kisses and hot from the vodka. "You're not even from around here, fella."

Rusty chuckled. "I'll shut the lights off. Promise nobody will see us, baby girl. If someone does, I'll just say I was gettin' a tick off you." He winked.

She laughed a loud, drunken laugh. She slapped him again. "You're too fucking funny."

Another kiss.

The two of them climbed out of the pickup and walked around to the bed of the truck which Rusty pulled down with a *clank*.

"Shhh!" Rae said with a finger over her lips. She grabbed Rusty close to her. He picked her up and carried her onto the back bed.

Inside the metal toolbox by the window, he pulled out a navy-blue blanket that unfolded and covered the entire bed of the truck.

"Romantic," Rae giggled.

They lay in the smelly blanket and grabbed and touched some more. Kissing sloppily, she unzipped his jeans and he lifted his brown T-shirt that read HUNTINGTON HAWKS in faded white letters over his head. Then went his underwear. Then, her underwear. Bra and panties. Both of them were now naked and hot between the heat of the moment, breathing heavy and kissing warm kisses and licking lips. Faces. Necks. Places. It was all happening so fast.

Rae whispered something in his ear and Rusty could only make out one word: condom. He came prepared and slipped down to his bunched-up jeans around his ankles. A square, silver-wrapped package with a ring shape bulging from it peeled from his pocket between his thumb and index finger. DUREX was printed on it. He kicked his jeans away to the end of the bed, almost knocking them off to fall to the gravel.

"Right here," he whispered back to her and they continued sucking faces. Grabbing. Touching. Feeling. Rae helped him put it on. Their hearts raced in sync. She climbed on top of him and as the autumn breeze blew through the cool night's air, Rusty was inside of her. The orange orbs twinkled in the twilight with the stars above. She gasped.

"Here I am baby girl!" Rusty shouted with a sinister smile. He aimed the barrel of the Glock down to the floor. His finger was still on the trigger. "Now, why you wanna treat me like this?"

Rae gasped, only this time it wasn't from pleasure. Rae was terrified. She sliced her scissors at the air. "Go away! Back away! Now!"

Rusty nearly fell on the floor laughing. A hardy laugh bellowed from his belly. "Is that what you had planned for me? All this time I thought you were just waiting for me to break in and thwack me hard with a baseball bat or somethin', and I get a pair of fuckin' scissors? Kindergarten scissors?"

Rae's *snips* remained daggering the space in front of her as the twisted ex-lover approached.

Who would've thought the redneck would've kept his feelings after all this time?

Rae woke up after the sunset gleamed over the horizon, passing over the city and the factories beyond the trees. She was sitting in the passenger seat of the pickup, wrapped in the blanket from Rusty's toolbox. The truck reeked of sweat and a mixture of various alcohols, although she only remembered having the vodka. Rusty snored in the driver seat as Rae lay awake. Her head thumped. Hangovers weren't something new to her, but this one was the worst she ever had. For many reasons.

The sounds of his deep snores and hungover dreams disgusted Rae in a way that made her ask herself the question that many people have asked themselves since the dawn of men and women relations: *what did I do last night?* The answer: Sex. Dirty, drunk, virginity-taking sex.

She wanted to cry over what she had done, waking up in some hick's pickup truck, naked and wrapped in his smelly, semen-stained blanket. *A whore. I'm a fucking whore-slut* she thought to herself. Rae stopped her tears from letting loose. She didn't want to be that girl that cried after a drunken one-night stand. That would give her the label of the crazy woman who would drive men away with her emotional baggage that she couldn't carry. Although, if you'd ask her today, she would say she was crazy for even *considering* sleeping with this dirtbag.

Rae scrambled to put on her clothes and found her phone in the back pocket of her jeans. Her brother had called a million times. Her mother a billion. It was going to lead to a grounding, no doubt. Months. Years. Maybe even the rest of her life.

"Goodbye, Raeby baby," Rusty had said, watching her walk toward her house. He was riding high, looking at that beautiful piece of ass he scored. Those jeans never looked better. "Call me, you got my number, right?"

Rae turned and gave a half-hearted smile. She waved, and he waved back as he rode off in his rusty wagon. Rusty's rusty wagon, the place that would forever live in Rae's mind as the spot she became a woman. She approached her front door which opened before she even stepped on the concrete walkway. Mrs. Cooper was standing in her robe, arms crossed. Dominic stood just behind her with a stern face.

They told her that they called the police and that she lost her phone and going-out privileges. All rightfully deserved. She had been a bad, bad girl. In more ways than one. And now, with the man who had given her her first night of making love, the man who took the life of his mother and brother, the man who never stopped loving Rae, was back to take her away, back to the life of trouble and hell that she wished she never gotten involved.

"Come here!" Rusty shouted with a psychotic look taking over his striking eyes.

Rae could scream no more.

***

Spinning. Spinning. Dizzy. Spinning. Sickness.

I'm gonna faint, Jon thought as he grabbed at the air, hoping to find something to lean on. *I'm gonna faint and never wake up.*

His bitten hand found the edge of the leather couch. The contact was painful but necessary. Jon was about to go down. He took heavy breaths, but the sickness would not subside as the odors emanated from the storage room. That piss and shit smell. Awful. Jon regretted taking off the paint mask. There was no time to search for it now, it was hard enough fetching the Remington. He held the grip in his good hand.

His shoulder still bled with no signs of clotting.

Ok, ok, ok. Here we go. We gotta go. Up, Jon. Up and out. This can't get any worse, can it?

With a deep breath, Jon stood up from the couch and felt nausea renew itself in the pit of his stomach. His injuries begged him to fall, to keel over and let every fluid from inside of him let loose.

Please, you have to stop Rusty.

I know, I know. But how am I gonna shoot like this?

Blackness surrounded him. The light of the flashlight only inched him closer to the stairs. He leaned again on the opposite end of the couch and gagged. Thunder *BLARED* and lightning flashed, sending its light down the stairs for a half-second. It beckoned him up to the horrors above. His knees buckled as if he was walking on stilts about to snap.

I'm coming. Rae. I'm so sorry.

***

The scissors had been a total failure. Rusty had no problem slapping them out of Rae's hands, even though she had clutched them as hard as a mother holding onto her baby for dear life. Now they sat on a pile of socks.

Rusty's hands were soaked in sweat as he smothered Rae's face against the wall. He squeezed and squished her cheeks. The squeezing wasn't harsh, but the contact sent chills through Rae's body as she wept and tried to pry her head away. They were both on their knees on Rae's bed. His body pinned hers hard.

"It's so good to see you," Rusty said with bad breath.

Rae closed her eyes, trying to push Rusty away with her mind but only found his sharp eyes staring back into hers when she looked again. Her hands were behind her back, against the wall. He was an inch away from her face. An odor all too familiar bellowed with his words. It was hot and harsh on his tongue. Could be vodka. Maybe whiskey. Perhaps both. He tried to kiss her lips, but she sucked her own into her mouth, under her teeth. She made a *hmmm hmmm* noise into his fingers as she flinched away.

"Rae, baby girl, it's been such a rough time for me. You remember my grandpa? Member how I told you 'bout him?"

Rae was in no mood for conversation.

"I guess you never got the pleasure. Not even my grammy or my old man got to see yer pretty face. I guess we never got serious, you and I. I wish we did. Oh, I sure wish we did." He felt her black, wavy hair and ran his fingers through a curly strand. Rae shuttered.

"Either way, they're all dead. You'll never get a chance to meet them now. Nope. First, my grammy died from stroke. Then, the demons got my dad and last night they killed my granpappy. He was all I had left back home in Huntington and they killed him. All he was tryin' to do was level with those freaks. He had too much of a heart, my pappy. God rest his soul. It cost him his life and now I'm alone." His eyes appeared to water, but Rae gave no ounce of sympathy. She looked away with swollen-shut eyes as Rusty continued his fascination with her hair.

"Except, I guess I'm not really alone anymore, am I? I got you now." A tiny crack came from Rusty's voice. "We got each other." His fingers went over to her lips. He leaned his own lips in again into rejection. He pulled back, eyebrows curled like a sad puppy. "Won't you forgive me? Won't you give me another chance?"

Rae shook her head between his palms.

"Why not? Is it cuz what I did to yer mom? Yer older brother? I know, I know. I'm sorry, baby."

Rae began to sob even though she thought she had cried her tear ducts dry. She sucked in air through trembling lips. Her throat felt heavy and mushy.

"Shhh. Shhhhh," Rusty said and put his head beside hers against the wall. He whispered in her ear. "I had no choice, baby girl. She would've killed you eventually. It was just a matter of time. What else could you have done? Yer brother on the other hand, well, he attacked me. It was only self-defense."

Those words struck Rae in her gut, reigniting the fire of rage she had felt in the basement moments ago. It shot through her chest and sent flaming anger up her throat. Her arms flung out from behind her back, shot upwards, and pushed into Rusty's chest, sending him off the side of her bed with unexpected strength.

Rusty's face read bewilderment and his head almost banged against the leg of the mirrored dresser's chair. *Thud.* The Glock, which Rusty had holstered before climbing on the fluffy bed to pin Rae, bounced from the leather pouch and stopped short of where the scissors landed.

Rae leaped from the comforter with her hands extended out to snatch the gun. Her hands met steel. Then, Rusty's hands met hers.

"Get off of it!" Rusty shouted and yanked on her wrists. She wasn't letting up.

The two of them performed a tug of war with the weapon. Its barrel faced the closet door where pretty dresses, shirts, and pants hung. Various colors formed a rainbow collection of apparel in contrast to the littered floor of unwashed clothes.

Rusty pulled a mighty pull and Rae went right along with it, falling on top of him. They jerked and jived as Rae was now atop Rusty, just as she was on that night that she climbed in the bed of the truck. Disgusting. Only this time, she had a mission that was miles more important than getting her cherry popped.

She rose her hand and landed a slap across Rusty's right cheek. His grip on the Glock loosened, but what Rae thought would result in the gun slipping from his hands, resulted in the family murderer socking her right in the face. Knuckle to eye. Her head bounced back like a punching bag and her hands slipped from the steel. She grabbed her left eye, waiting for a white ball on a red and pink string to fall between her fingers.

***

Jon was proud that he made it to the steps without vomiting. He had tripped over both the duct-taped chair and the surprising location of the upstairs door. Somehow, the damn thing was kicked-in and sent flying off its hinges.

Still, he had a long way to go. The steps were going to be a bigger challenge than he thought. The dizziness hadn't stopped, and when the waves of nausea hit, they hit rough. Good thing he had a free hand. He had ditched the flashlight once he could see the streaming light from the storming sky outside. Now, he used the Remington as a crutch. He leveraged himself up the stairs, placing his other hand on the wall.

The storm grew louder as he climbed with the speed of a snail.

***

Thunder *ROARED* overhead. The room shook. The dark house trembled.

"Fuckin' bitch! Yer just like yer brother. Up to no good. Lookin' for trouble," Rusty said as he holstered his Glock. This time, he made sure to *snap* down the buckle behind the handle so that little back and forth wouldn't play out again. "Baby girl, I don't want to hurt you. You know that. It hurts me more than it hurts you, believe me!"

Rae's eye was still intact, and the pain was only now coming into feeling as the shock of the blow was so out of left field. She hadn't expected him to do that. But why not? He had killed her last two living family members without hesitation. All Rae could do now was wait for the final blow or shot. Whichever Rusty chose, he would get his way. A black eye was nothing.

"Let's go. It's time to get outta this hell house," Rusty said. "I'm gonna take care of you. Back in Huntington, you and I are gonna start life anew. We're gonna forgive one another for what we've done here today, alright? God will forgive, he always does."

Rae cried out.

"No more pain. Just love. You and I, together. We're gonna ride this out. C'mon! If yer good, I'll letcha use my gun. Hell, we got a ton back at the house. You and me gonna be like Bonnie and Clyde, baby." Rusty hunkered down and grabbed Rae's arms. "Up we go, c'mon! Let's take a ride in the Rustymobile!"

***

Jon had just made it to the top of the basement steps when he heard something that wasn't thunder. Boots. Loud shoes. *Clambering* came from above. He could hear it through the ceiling. Voices. No, just one voice. A man's voice. Rusty. Slapping. Someone hitting the wall with their hand. A picture fell and glass *shattered*. Jon covered his head, unaware that he wasn't near the commotion. Not yet. He swayed on the step and dropped to his knees, peeking his head up and around where the door had been.

The morning gloom sent a blurry image of the living room into Jon's eyes. A dark smudge sat on top of the couch. It was Jamie, the cat that had only good intentions. She sat like a statue with her eyes aimed at something that Jon couldn't see but could hear coming down from the stairs in a struggle.

What do you see? What do you see you little bastard?

His heart raced, pumping blood both inside and outside of his body. Too much had seeped through the shirt. His face was as pale as a ghost. To say Jon was lightheaded was an understatement. Time was ticking. Life was ticking.

Jon pulled out the Remington from beside his legs on the steps below, positioned himself diagonally, and brought the rifle out and onto the carpet. Under the barrel, Jon placed his left forearm to prop the shot. He waited for the noisy tornado that was Rusty to come down and take the bullet. The sights were aimed between the front door and the side of the stairs. All he had to do was time it, look in the scope and pull. If Rae was dead, the least he could do was avenge her death.

A faint *meow* came from across the room.

Try not to hit the cat. He figured it was ok if he did anyway. *Collateral damage.*

After a flash of lightning and a *rumbling roar* of thunder that trembled the whole house, a tall figure with the blurred features of Rusty Mirch revealed itself from the staircase. Jon had almost gasped and choked on air when his finger came mere micro-inches from pulling the steel lever back. Rusty had Rae wrapped in his arms. A bullet could've as easily struck her as it would him.

"C'mon!" Rusty shouted. The *ringing* had subsided again, and Jon was all ears. "It'll all be better if you just relax. Just relax!" He jerked her body left, yanked it right. Her arms flailed and clutched at nothing. She squirmed.

With the trigger left unpulled on Jon's rifle, Rusty walked through the living room and threw open the front door, bringing in the sound of the storm. Heavy bullets of rain *clapped* on concrete. Thunder. The blur of them leaving the residence without noticing the bleeding gunman on the carpet.

Jon's heart couldn't rest. He pulled his legs from the basement steps and began to crawl on the carpet. First, he moved as if he were paralyzed from the waist down, dragging his legs as if they were two logs of skin dangling from his behind. He looked like a handicapped person thrown from their wheelchair. Then, after he heard Rae scream, he found his feet. He moved up to all fours.

The cat provided no input as Jon approached the front door.

Rusty shouted at the girl. "C'mon, let's go! Don't fight me or I'll make it two black eyes! You hear me? Get in!"

Jon was now outside of the house, on the concrete path that led to the driveway. He pressed forward and dropped onto the spongy grass that covered his front in muddy browns and greens to go with the red on his back. He felt the razor rain send daggers into his shoulder wound. His head and body trembled as if he were having a seizure.

Ba-ding. Whizz. Ba-dong. Grass flew up in Jon's face. Mud and water splashed around him in big gooey gobs that weren't from the sky, but from the bullets of Rusty's Glock. Jon had been seen by the hillbilly bastard. Rusty saw him crawling like a cripple across the Cooper's front lawn with his father's hunting rifle, shaking with spasms.

"Jon!" Rae screamed, but her voice was overtaken by the thunder and the *whizzing* bullets. "Jon!"

"For fuck's sake!" Rusty cursed.

You have to get her, Jon. Please.

He's going to take her away.

Jon pulled up the Remington again and used the same method he had used a second ago with his forearm as the tripod beneath the barrel. Rain dropped and spilled across the rifle, trickling wetness to the trigger. He slid up further, getting his eye, if you could even it call it that anymore, to the scope. Droplets splattered the sights and Jon used his good hand to turn the dial to bring some focus to the blurs.

Whizz. Ba-ding. Ba-dong.

"Jon!" Rae shrieked.

Jon's eyes came into focus. Clear, they were clear. Only instead of the two smudges coming into the form of Rae and Rusty, a deer stood in the crosshair of the scope.

FIFTY-SIX

The Storm Passes

The buck wasn't standing in the cul-de-sac. Instead, it stood frozen in the cold November morning as flakes fell around him. Staring. Jon could see the breath steam from its nose and mouth. He blinked. Again, and again. Blinking. The deer remained. Jon retreated his head back from the scope and his eyes told the story of years past. He couldn't control his movements. He could only watch as a spectator inside himself.

"Go on, son. Pull," Big Jon whispered in Jon's ear.

He couldn't hear his father as the thumping of his heart pounded in his ears. There were no thoughts, just a twenty-one-year-old trapped inside of a twelve-year-old version of himself and a young buck staring at one another, eyes locked. Motionless. Both were statues sitting in the freezing November morning.

"If you're gonna do it, you gotta do it now," Big Jon said.

Jon pulled the trigger.

A thunderous *BANG* sliced the silence of the snow. The buck's head snapped back, and a flutter of fur popped with a flash of red. It swung around before collapsing to the ground. All of this happened in slow motion. Jon's heart seemed to stop at the sight of it. Big Jon put a hand on his back and patted. His father's words faded in.

"Son! You did it! You got him, son!"

"I did. . . I uhh...I did, didn't I? Holy shit."

Big Jon laughed a hearty laugh that sent cold breaths out beneath his snowflake-littered mustache. "You did, you most certainly did! Holy shit is right!"

Jon couldn't believe it. The anticipation. The buildup. It was all worth it. To pull the trigger and send the bullet flying in an accurate headshot for the first time out was a feeling he would never experience again. His father was just as excited as he was.

"C'mon, let's go take a look!" Big Jon got up from his post and adjusted his camo hat. Inside of his hunting pack, he pulled out a digital camera. A black lens horned the front of it. He flipped off the circular cover on the front and it dangled on a string.

The two of them stood and ventured out into the snow-covered field where the dead buck lay on the edge. Leaves *crunched* under their boots that left imprints on nature's white blanket. Jon still couldn't believe what he had done. The closer they approached, the higher his heart rate went.

"Wow Jon, you damn near knocked his eye out! That's just above the lid there!" Big Jon proudly proclaimed. His camouflage gloves examined the downed creature, showing his son the hole in which his .308 bullet formed with speed and precision that was as smooth as butter. "I'm proud of you son, very proud." He patted his son's shoulder again and got up from the slumped deer. "Go ahead, grab his antler there. I wanna get a shot of this. My son's first buck!"

Big Jon crouched a few feet away in the snow and brought the camera to his eye. Jon grabbed the one lone antler of the buck and held the head up. The tongue hung from the side of the deer's dead mouth. The Remington was in Jon's other hand, standing with its barrel facing the sky. He felt just like his father from that Polaroid photograph and his grandpa from the even more ancient, black and white one. They had shot and killed bucks when they were Jon's age, both getting their picture taken afterward. It was this photograph that marked the beginning of manhood.

Now, it was Jon's time to leave his boyhood behind and become a young man. He smiled at his dad with his rifle and trophy, not only smiling at his newfound maturity but also at the feeling that he and his father had done something together. They accomplished something in which they both shared an equal, genuine fascination and enjoyment. The connection was there. Jon, at that moment, before the camera snapped a moment in time, felt like there was no difference between him and his father. He was his father, and his father was him. They were the same that day.

"Alright, just like that son. Lookin' good! Ready? One, two, three…"

With the click of a button, the camera flashed a bright white light that shined over the field of snow. It filled Jon's wide eyes with a blinding ray that took him from the early winter morning, back to the soaked late spring.

FIFTY-SEVEN

The Storm Ends

"Jon!" Rae was in Jon's ear. She shook him awake from the memory. He wished she hadn't. "Jon! Speak to me! Please don't die, please don't go!" She was weeping and pulling up on the back of Jon's bloodied shirt. The rain had soaked in with the blood and made his entire top a drenched, red mess.

The water puddled and streamed to the edges of the asphalt circle and dumped into the sewer drains.

There were no more daggers from the sky and the thunder had trailed off to a low *crumble* toward the north. Jon, somehow, was in the middle of the cul-de-sac, lying next to Rusty, who had gone the way of the buck. A .308 caliber bullet struck him just above the eye. A bloody hole went from Rusty's forehead to the back of his hillbilly buzzcut. Jon almost laughed at the sight of his revenge. *First, you hit me with your rifle. Then, I shoot you with mine.* He rubbed his scab. It had split back open from the fall on the asphalt. It was dripping with wet blood.

"Jon, you're alive! You did it!" Rae exclaimed. She helped turn Jon's body over and held him.

"I. . . I am. . . I guess I am, aren't I? Are you ok?" he asked.

He could feel her nod her head as she hugged him close. Jon held her too. They were both drenched. They rocked for a moment in each other's arms, tired from the fight that seemed to last lifetimes.

"I'm sorry, Rae," Jon cried. He swallowed lumps. "I'm so sorry. Your mother. . . Dominic. . . "

She cried too. She couldn't speak, only feel, only hold. Jon's shoulder wept, too. His hand felt cool. The two of them sat in the middle of the cul-de-sac, slumped in the aftermath of chaos. They saw sights and heard sounds that no man or woman should ever have to endure.

Rae pulled her head back from the embrace. Her hair was a pitch-black mop. Her left eye was swollen. Still, her beauty remained as if she fell from heaven. "Let's go. We need to get you inside and cover your wounds."

"My h-house," Jon stuttered. "Let's go to my house. We can't go back in there…your house…it's…"

Rae nodded. Jon didn't have to utter another word. She understood. It would do no good for her heart and mind to see what remained in her house. She would, at some point, return to see the aftermath. But not right now. She needed to get somewhere safe with Jon.

"Can you move at all?" she asked.

"I think so, just a little bit."

"C'mon, we'll go slow."

"How about fast?"

They began to rise from the asphalt. Rusty's body lay motionless with his new piercing above his brow. His mouth was locked open as if he just had walked into his surprise birthday party. Neither of them gave another glance to him as Rae brought Jon up to his feet. He put his arm around her neck, which was red with scratches from Rusty's torturous hands.

Together, they limped and stumbled across the street to 524 Franklin Court.

FIFTY-EIGHT

Memories

"In the pantry, on the wall," Jon had answered to Rae when she asked if he had a first aid kit. His voice was weak, and he lay with his wet back on the living room couch, shivering. Mrs. Barnes wouldn't yell at him for having his soaking body stain the sofa because Mrs. Barnes, as well as the rest of the Barnes gang, were gone. Dead? No one could answer that. The last person who might have seen them, Mrs. Cooper, was now taken out of the game with three bullet holes to the head. Jon accepted that he could only see his folks alive in his memories.

Jon was white as paper. Like a ghost, you could see through him. He hadn't thought about how much blood he'd lost or how much time had passed since he got a nice little jab in his back. His mind was as clear as his eyes were when he was injected into that memory. No obsessing over every little thing. No constant questioning.

Things were strangely calm, and it was nice to be out of his head for once. The only thoughts that remained were of Rae.

It was just her and him now, two people who have had their lives ripped and torn to pieces by a microscopic parasite. Bottled water of all things. Corporate greed was to blame. If only the word had gotten out sooner or someone had paid closer attention to the operations.

It didn't matter, it was just Jon and Rae in the world now. She would come out and take care of him, using the basic nursing skills her mother taught her over the years. Good thing she had listened every now and again.

Jon would tell her what happened in the basement. She would cry and Jon would be there to hold her, and she would be there to hold him. Together, they would have to learn to forgive, but not to forget. They couldn't forget the memories they had before this all went down. That's all they had left to hold on to. Memories.

Jon put his good hand in his pocket and felt the sapphire ring still intact. He rubbed it, remembering the room it came from, the house it came from. His grandmother who owned it. His grandfather who loved her. His cousins. His parents. They all loved each other and always will no matter where they were now.

In the pantry, Rae was fumbling with the first aid kit that was bolted to the wall. She decided to just rip the damn thing out.

Inside the big white box with a red cross in the middle, packets of bandages and ointments *rattled* around. She yanked the four screws out, popping dust from the holes in the paint.

The living room spun. Jon smiled. *To die in the living room, very ironic.* The walls seemed to breathe as the ceiling descended toward Jon then ascended back up. He was ready to go if it truly was his time to leave this earth. He hoped when he passed that he would show up in that memory of him and his father again, back in the brisk November air. Big Jon and he would drive home in the Ford and talk and laugh about the day. How the deer looked. How Jon's aim deemed him a buck-shooting prodigy. They would pull up in the driveway and run inside to tell mom what had happened and show her the picture. She would grab her chest and say, "Oh my goodness. I can't believe you did that! My goodness! Jon, what did you teach your son to do?" They would all laugh and have leftover Thanksgiving food. Turkey and sweet potatoes. He could smell it now. Corn and stuffing, although Jon hated stuffing. But still, they would all be together. A family.

Jon's eyelids began to close. They would open, flutter for a moment, then close again. His heart beat with a slow *thump* that struggled with every pump.

Rae rushed back out into the living room and stood above Jon, unwrapping and uncapping various things. She was alarmed at his sickly appearance. Jon just smiled, hearing the noises fading in and out around him. Rae said something, but he didn't know what. Her hands moved frantically. Jon grinned as he caught what glimpses he could of her. *What a woman,* he thought. He closed his eyes again and the words and sounds came and went.

Between the waking world and the sleeping memories, Jon might not have been aware of the sound of tires pulling into the driveway. He only smiled and nodded at Rae and her angelic voice. However, the sound that he *did* hear made his eyes shoot wide open. It was a sound that was so familiar, that it made Jon's heart rate skyrocket to the moon.

It was the sound of keys *jingling* and *jangling* outside the front door.

ACKNOWLEDGMENTS

First and foremost, I'd like to give a big thanks to Lawrence Knorr, Chris Fenwick, and everyone at Sunbury Press who not only gave me the opportunity to have my first novel published but gave me priceless knowledge on editing and the process of completing a book. You've made my dream a reality.

Thanks to my older brother, Rich, who introduced me to Stephen King novels and changed my life forever. He was also the first person to read this book and give me feedback on it.

Thanks to my mother and father for always supporting me. I've worked with my father since high school and he's always allowed me the freedom to pursue my passions. He also helped me review and polish this book before it was published.

Thanks to my friend, Brandon Ulp, for taking my very first headshot. You're a talented dude.

I'd also like to thank my grandparents, sister-in-law, and niece for their undying love and support during this project.

Finally, I'd like to thank you, the reader. I appreciate each and every one of you for taking the time to read my work. I hope you've enjoyed it because there are a lot more stories to come.

ABOUT THE AUTHOR

Photo by Brandon Ulp

Oliver C. Seneca was born and raised in the suburbs of Harrisburg, Pennsylvania. His first foray into storytelling came in high school when he was accepted to the Capital Area School for the Arts where he focused on filmmaking. Oliver became passionate about writing after reading The Long Walk by Stephen King. Oliver is a graduate of The Pennsylvania State University and, in addition to writing, he works in his family's law practice.

www.olivercseneca.com
https://www.facebook.com/olivercseneca/
https://www.instagram.com/olivercseneca/
https://www.twitter.com/olivercseneca

Made in the USA
Lexington, KY
19 November 2019

57265518R00175